I0764883

Praise for P.D. Singer's work:

This story is extraordinary, with characters that are immensely complex and pacing that is so fast I felt as if I were riding a wave that kept on building. I admired the author's ingenuity, audacity and skill in writing a story based on the money markets that evolved into an exciting adventure and love story. *The Rare Event* absolutely blew me away and changed my perception of the world of hedge funds.

Jessewave, Reviews by Jessewave, *The Rare Event*

The bottom line is that I couldn't put this book down. I devoured it in a single sitting.

Lisa, The Novel Approach, *The Rare Event*

The mountains, the town, and the people they meet are vividly drawn and very much a part of city-boy Jake's new experiences, and the firefighting that Kurt and Jake occasionally have to do leaps off the page.

Cryselle, Reading Reality, *Fire on the Mountain*

If you are looking for a book about two men who are perhaps both a bit naive and yet love each other very much; a book where the romance is balanced with exciting action sequences, with humourous situations and with tense and thrilling scenes; then this book is for you. Highly recommended with a grade of 'Excellent'.

Jenre, Well-Read, *Snow on the Mountain*

… I really enjoyed Blood on the Mountain. Read it for a cracking plot, and a wonderful couple that deserves their Happy Ever After.

Pippa, Mrs. Condit and Friends, *Blood on the Mountain*

Overall, this book was simply delightful. The mix of quiet moments and tense action scenes made this a real page turner…

Jenre, Reviews by Jessewave, *Blood on the Mountain*

Also by P.D. Singer

Novels

The Rare Event

Fire on the Mountain

Snow on the Mountain

Fall Down the Mountain

Blood on the Mountain

Return to the Mountain

Novellas

Donal *agus* Jimmy

Shorts

Cross the Mountain

Prep Work

O'Carolan's Seduction

On Call: Afternoon

On Call: Dancing

On Call: Crossroads

Training Cats

On Call: Omnibus

Slip/Slide/Snow (in the Out in Colorado anthology)

SPOKES

P.D. SINGER

ROCKY RIDGE BOOKS

Warning: this book contains adult language and themes, including graphic descriptions of sexual acts that some may find offensive. It is intended for mature readers only, of legal age to possess such material in their area.

This book is a work of fiction. All characters, companies, events, and locations are either products of the author's imagination, are used fictitiously, or are mentioned as historical fact. Any resemblance to actual persons, living or dead, places, or events is entirely coincidental.

Cover art by L.C. Chase and P. D. Singer

Edited by Eden Winters

ISBN-13 978-1-62622-006-5

Published by:

Rocky Ridge Books
PO Box 6922
Broomfield, CO 80021
www.RockyRidgeBooks.com

Great thanks are due to the team who helped me to the finish line:

To Eden Winters, Angela Bendetti, Amelia C. Gormley, Jo Niedermeyer, and TD O'Malley, for constant encouragement, advice, and the occasional shove forward.

To Zahra Owens, for language and cycling help, and Elisa Rolle, who kept Luca from sounding illiterate in his native tongue.

And to Bruce, whose great love of cycling got the whole project started.

In Memoriam:

Wouter Weylandt

September 27, 1984 - May 9, 2011

Caddero sulla strada inseguendo un sogno de Gloria. Che raggiunsero nella luce del sacraficio delle loro giovani esistenze.

Glossary

Many of these terms are French, which I used because of the greater familiarity of the *Tour de France* for US readers, but there are equivalent Italian terms.

Breakaway/break: one or more riders escaping from the front of peloton, usually as the result of a sudden acceleration.

Commissaire: a race official with the authority to impose penalties on the riders for infractions of the rules.

Directeur sportif: the on-the-road manager of a bike team.

DNF: Did not finish

DNS: Did not start

Domestique: literally, servant, but in racing parlance, the riders who support the GC by chasing down breakaways, collecting water from the team car, yielding equipment, and otherwise putting their GC into a position to win. A super-domestique or lieutenant stays with the GC during critical times, and may win stages or other honors.

Draft: to ride in the aerodynamic slipstream of another rider at great energy savings.

Fuga bidone: a break that gets too far ahead of the peloton to be caught.

GC: General Classification. The ranking of the accumulated time or placements, whichever basis the race uses to determine its winner. The GC of the team is the rider considered most able to achieve the best ranking, and the other riders support him to achieve this at the cost of their own individual placements.

Gruppetto: the stragglers following the peloton, trying to make the time cutoff to stay in the race.

Hors catégorie: "Beyond category." An extremely difficult climb. Climbing routes are graded by steepness, length, and the distance already covered when the route reaches the climb. Category 1 climbs are next most difficult, followed by categories 2, 3, 4, and 5.

KoM: King of the Mountains, a title gained by accumulating points by being one of the first riders to summit the defined climbs in a race or stage. The KoM is awarded a prize jersey, usually red or polka dot, and in a stage race may wear it on the next stage. In Italian: Gran Premio della Montagna.

Lanterne rouge: the red lantern, as in the lamp on the back of the train. The last rider in the race or stage.

Moto: a motorcycle, generally with a cameraman riding on the back, with a driver skilled enough to weave through the unprotected cyclists.

Musette: a feed bag with a long handle that can be collected on the fly.

Palmarès: a cyclist's list of accomplishments, including wins, stage wins, KoM, and intermediate sprints.

Peloton: the main group of cyclists riding in a bunch.

Soigneur: a staff member who takes care of the riders, a combination valet, masseur, and racing support. One soigneur may take care of two to six riders.

Stage: a race may be run in segments on consecutive days.

Time limit: in order to remain in the race, a racer must finish a stage within a certain percentage of the winner's time. The percentage varies with the specifics of the stage.

Time trial: a race by an individual or team against the clock. Riders start at intervals.

1.HC, 2.1, 2.2, etc. Race classifications. The first number indicates the number of stages (1 is a one day race, 2 has two or more, up to twenty-one) and the second number indicates the quality of the teams expected to ride in the race. A 2.2 stage race may have mix of a few pro teams and more continental and regional teams, whereas a 2.HC, such as the Giro d'Italia, will have pro teams and a few other teams invited because of their strength.

SPOKES

P.D. SINGER

CHAPTER 1

THE BIG SILVER sedan blew past close enough to touch, and he damned near did. Christopher Nye shook his fist at the receding vehicle, once he'd wrestled his bike under control.

"Stupid gas-burner!" Stu Fallon made his point with a one-fingered salute. "There's a whole other lane they could have used—why'd they have to nearly run us down?"

"Most people around here give bikes enough room." Christopher shot a wary glance behind lest some other three thousand pound weapon guided by a moron was sneaking up on him. "There's enough cyclists on the road, you'd think they'd all understand."

"I'd like them to get sucked into a slipstream and then ask if they had enough room," Stu grumbled, but he'd already gotten to speed again, and Christopher wouldn't waste the breath to help him complain. At least this bright, crisp January day didn't have the additional hazard of snow, which made it perfect for a brisk run out to the wide spot on the road that was Hygiene, Colorado. Still a couple of puddles at the side of the road, though.

Bright jerseys and spandex leggings dotted the roads in and around Boulder. Fewer than in June, a rainbow of cyclists hugged the roads' shoulders, even in winter. Christopher and Stu would have less traffic to worry about once they reached the north edge of town. Then they wouldn't be run off the road every mile or so.

Close to thirty miles of gentle rolls and near flat called to him. Christopher had just tightened his chain and adjusted the derailleurs, his leggings were comfortably worn in and the chamois lining greased heavily; nothing on man or bike would chafe. He had layers he could peel down if the breeze dropped, but the mid-fifties temps probably wouldn't persuade him to remove the arm warmers he'd put on with a short-sleeved jersey. With a last tweak to his helmet and sunglasses, Christopher followed Stu up the road.

"Checking out my butt again?" Stu called, once they made the turn onto Jay Road.

"It isn't any more attractive than it was last time. How you can ride so many miles and still have such a scrawny ass is beyond me." Christopher sped up and around Stu, who dropped back to trail in Christopher's wake. They'd take turns fighting the air, letting the other draft. It wasn't the same degree of relief as riding in the midst of a peloton would be, but even one rider to create a slipstream made a huge difference in how hard they had to work.

Christopher didn't like thinking about the peloton, that massed group of cyclists riding only inches apart. His last race had gone smash when he'd been hemmed in on all sides. Someone had thrown an elbow at a rider in front, sending a ripple of motion sideways until someone hadn't reacted fast enough or accurately enough. Wheel caught wheel then, handlebars caught hips, and twenty cyclists had gone down in a tangle of metal and rubber. Christopher had gotten off lightly for meeting the road and someone else's bike, leaving some skin on the pavement and taking a cleat mark on his chest, but he'd shied from riding with a lot of people since. The pros and the group I/II riders could probably have stayed upright and possibly even disciplined the elbow-thrower, but the group IV riders like Christopher didn't have those skills yet. And if he couldn't make himself get back into the peloton, he never would.

But the season was young—he didn't have to apply for his racing license again for another month or two. Training was enough, even with the inadequate scenery perched on Stu's saddle. He had zero interest in that particular ass anyway. Stu was a friend, straight, and the best matched riding partner Christopher had. Thinking boner-inducing thoughts while trying to maintain tempo for two hours was only going to interfere with getting fit after a month of holiday indulgence and weather-enforced idleness.

They'd swapped off the lead again after they'd reached the true country roads, letting Christopher look around more than at the road ahead. Enough breeze came off the hills to their west that he and Stu both zipped their jackets to the throat. Cottonwoods along the creek beds made brown lace against the fiercely blue sky, and last year's grasses at the side of the road whispered drily at their passage. He felt good, swinging along at seventy rpm in a gear that wasn't his tallest, but that would be for later in the season. For now, maintaining his pace without challenging his anaerobic threshold was the goal. That, and enjoying himself.

The road grew narrower, the Ute Highway being on the same scrawny side as Stu's behind, but the reservoir to their right sparkled in the sun. One pickup truck had gone around them since they'd made the last turn.

"Coming up on the left!"

The yell was upon them almost as soon as the riders were—a pack of fast-moving cyclists zipped by, a blur of turquoise and black.

"Let's catch them and draft!" Stu's enthusiasm had to be twice his speed, which picked up substantially.

"Fat chance." Christopher accelerated too, even though the other riders were pulling away without looking like they were working for it.

"Are those the Garmin-Sharp guys?"

"Nah, they wear blue with black and white trim." Christopher had cheered the Boulder-based pro team in the *Tour de France* and every other race he'd been able to see.

"Wow." Stu dropped back to their previous pace. "They passed us like nothing and that one guy is sitting up to take his jacket off." The team hadn't stopped, but one of the backs now sported unbroken turquoise instead of a black V.

Wow, indeed. The bike handling and speed that had just blown by on what had to be an easy training ride made Christopher feel like he'd barely graduated from a tricycle. Those riders could have cut their racing teeth as juniors, with decent equipment and some support from their family. Or town, if any of them were Belgian—Belgian riders grew up on bone-rattling cobblestone streets where every passer-by could assess their form. Maybe some of them were from Italy, where small boys dreamed of growing up to be the next Fausto Coppi or Gianni Bugno. Or France, where a three week stage race was practically a national holiday and a stage winner never had to buy his own drinks again. A few might be Americans, but they didn't learn to race on a discount store bike with five unusable gears.

He'd started years too late to dream of belonging to the elite, but he could expect to get from Boulder to Hygiene and back in under an hour and a half. Christopher pulled back into the present, adjusting his grip and his expectations.

Once home, Christopher opened a new document on his laptop, thinking back to the dozen riders who'd sped past him.

Antano-Clark may have just arrived in Boulder, but they're already blowing the locals off the roads. Looking for the advantages of living and training at altitude, this newly formed team hopes to make stars out of such workhorses as Luca Biondi, formerly of Duclos-Wurth, who finished a surprise sixth in last year's Paris-Nice stage race, and Rolf Knecht, from Kastibank…

He finished the article, built mostly from press releases, some scuttlebutt, and what he'd seen that day. Should he save it for Stu to proofread? Maybe not this time—he could do without the shit Stu would give him on the subject. His editor could find the stray commas for once. Emailing it to *CycloWorld*, Christopher considered that his other great dream, seeing his byline in print, had been a lot more achievable and even built upon his cycling. His parents never chided him about his expensive journalism degree turning into tiny articles and an evil day job in a shop: he'd get there. Maybe he should start carrying the Nikon currently gathering dust on the bookshelf.

Picking out faces to attach to names simply hadn't been possible today. Christopher couldn't know if he'd seen sprinters or climbers, *domestiques* or the general classification stars. The pictures from last May's *CycloWorld* weren't helping him figure it out, but he stopped on a Duclos-Wurth profile article, just to try. Damn but Luca Biondi had a nice ass.

CHAPTER 2

Journalism wasn't going to replace the evil day job any time soon, but the email from the bank announced a pleasant addition to Christopher's coffers. He was getting enough small news items and product reviews off to a couple of cycling magazines that he could allow himself to dream of a day where he didn't need to discuss the merits of a thirty-eight toothed chainring versus a thirty-nine toothed chainring with a rider who would never get out of the lowest gears on a mild incline.

Working at the bike shop offered some compensation, though. Members of the pro teams came in just often enough to recognize him, trade some bit of information or insight for the personal service, and keep those small payments coming. The Garmin-Sharp boys came by infrequently; they had endorsement deals or sponsorships for almost everything a cyclist could need. UPS drivers probably got hernias delivering boxes of hardware and clothing to their team headquarters, but the new team wasn't quite so completely supplied. The Antano-Clark riders were in and out of the bike shop on 9th Street and Pearl a few times a week. Twenty-five cyclists who needed one or two things at a time made for a pretty consistent black and turquoise parade.

Three men bypassed the wavy steel rack in front of the shop. Wheeling the bikes inside rather than risking the tools of their trade to the hopeful but inadequate security of a chain lock made perfect sense to Christopher—he wouldn't tempt passers-by with bikes each worth more than any five things he had for sale. Maybe three—a road bike that weighed less than fifteen pounds even with the saddle was the only thing in stock that even came close to costing as much as the custom-made monsters squeaking across the cement floor.

"Anything I can help you find, gentlemen?" Christopher ambled over to the accessory rack that occupied the attention of two cyclists, who balanced their bikes against their hips while they removed their helmets. The third had gone to the rear where the mechanic worked.

"Do you have Cham-Paste?" The taller of the two ran his hand through sweaty blond locks. His personal rain spattered Christopher.

Wiping his face gave Christopher a moment to restrain his temper. Anyone who dripped on him had better kiss him first. "No, but we have almost every other kind." Fifteen brands of lubricant to prevent chafing against the liners found in all good bike shorts, and this guy asked for the one the shop didn't stock.

"You are disgusting again, Rolf." The Italian lilt in his companion's voice would have taken the sting out of the comment for Christopher, but Rolf shot him such a look that Christopher wondered what the term for "stink-eye" would be in Flemish or whatever Rolf's first language was.

The other cyclist kept his sweat to himself, wiping his forehead with his hat, which was a strange chili pepper-patterned contrast to the team colors. It probably didn't matter, since it was concealed under his helmet most of the time. His medium brown ringlets had been squashed close to his scalp but stood out in exuberant profusion where they hadn't been restrained. His sunglasses dangled from their cord over his chest, not interfering with the rebuke in the cyclist's blue eyes. "The rest of us use the chamois butter without complaint."

"But of course you do." Perhaps Flemish had a term for "uber-stink-eye," because Rolf could certainly do it.

Christopher took note, wondering at the attitude he displayed to his team mate. Christopher didn't have to be introduced to Luca Biondi to know who he was—that face had smiled, grimaced, and exulted from the pages of a dozen issues of *CycloWorld*, and was currently whipping across the big screen TV that played a canned selection of race clips and ads for bike-related merchandise. Also knowing that, on paper at least, Biondi was the strongest rider Antano-Clark had, this was probably the team captain on the receiving end of the disrespect. His estimation of Antano-Clark's chances in the *Tour de France* dropped two notches.

"As will you." Biondi's face did not change. "You will use what we can get."

"I'll have someone ship a case from home." Rolf slammed the tube of chamois lubricant he'd been examining back on shelf hard enough to knock the others over. "It is the best."

"May I quote you on that?" Christopher thought he should have a useable tidbit to make up for having to set the display up again. The "best" product often had the biggest advertising budget that month, but still, Rolf Knecht's opinion might make good print.

"No!" Rolf snatched up a different brand to examine the list of ingredients and squirt a small amount into his hand, rubbing his fingers together. He'd chosen a particularly greasy sort. Christopher had tried it but felt like he was going to slide right off his bike. Rolf grimaced at his now-shiny hand.

"You are most fussy about what you rub on your butt." Biondi picked up a tube of sunscreen.

"Unlike you!" Rolf spat out a word Christopher didn't recognize.

Biondi did, and perhaps it was best Christopher couldn't understand or even identify the language he snarled back. The short, bitter exchange resulted in Rolf's whirling to the door with his bicycle, leaping on once he reached the sidewalk. The rack of lip balms he knocked over on his way out rang and rattled for a few seconds after the rider disappeared from view.

"Rolf is on edge today; I ask forgiveness for him." Biondi's apology added to the shock Christopher was quite certain was making him look stupid. "I'll fix this." He set a tube upright, smacking it into place. He stared at the shelf, not glancing at Christopher.

"Uh, you don't have to…" Catching a tube that rolled to the edge of the shelf when Biondi picked another up, Christopher set it on its wide cap, his hand brushing the cyclist's. The brief contact went straight to his groin, though perhaps his stupid-face kept it from showing. Not that Biondi was looking. What the hell had Rolf said? Something obscene about a product every serious cyclist used?

"My teammate made the mess." Biondi knelt to collect creams from the littered floor.

The fallen rack allowed Christopher a strategic retreat. Cursing his reaction under his breath, he righted the stand and collected the handfuls of tubes on display cards. By the time he had the balms hanging neatly again, Biondi was waiting quietly at the register, his bicycle at his side like a well-trained Great Dane. Scurrying over, Christopher focused on the bright teeth showing against the rider's lightly tanned face—he'd recovered something of his earlier mood, but the strain hadn't left his eyes. Lycra cycling leggings, or possibly cycling shorts with separate leg warmers—Christopher dared not look closely enough to decipher which Biondi was wearing—didn't leave a lot to the imagination, although the pliable chamois liners did soften the outlines of the wearer's package. Something he had no business looking at.

"Thanks." He unfolded the bills Biondi offered. "You didn't have to do that."

"I did. I don't want you to remember Antano-Clark riders for bad things only." He tucked the sunscreen into one of the elasticized pockets on the back of his jersey. "My name is Luca Biondi, and I hope my team will be welcome here another day." Extending his hand for the change, he smiled like he meant it, holding Christopher's eyes with his light blue gaze.

"You will. Uh, they will. I'm Christopher Nye." *Smooth, real smooth. Try not to come across as star-struck or hopelessly horny, will ya?* Brushing his fingertips across Luca's palm while counting out quarters and dimes probably spoiled any hope of appearing suave. Luca didn't seem to mind. "I could try to get some Cham-Paste for Rolf."

"That's kind, Christopher, but it's not the Cham-Paste Rolf truly wants." The smile flickered, then returned. "I will be back another day, to be sure of a welcome." Luca wheeled his bicycle out of the shop, swinging one whipcord leg over and joining the west-bound traffic on Pearl Street. Christopher followed with his eyes, the floor to ceiling windows letting him enjoy every flex and twist.

Luca Biondi was welcome to anything he liked.

The third team rider lurked in the back, where Christopher found him thumbing through a magazine, swinging his helmet by one strap. He looked up from the pages, eyes wide.

"Can I help you find something?"

"No, no, nothing, thank you." The rider craned his neck to see over the racks. "Have they both left?"

"Yeah. They seemed a little annoyed with each other." Understatement seemed like the best way to information.

A muscle jumped in the rider's jaw. "You could say that. I don't want to get caught in the middle. No matter who's riding GC, I just do my job."

The domestiques in the team fetched, carried, fought the wind, yielded their whole bicycles or one wheel if needed. The "servants" had their moments as climbers or sprinters if they had the strength, but the general classification riders were the ones who stood on the podium to accept the accolades due the winner. The rest of the team existed primarily to make it possible for the GC to succeed. "Isn't Antano-Clark in enough races to make two or three GCs necessary?" His journalist's ears waved frantically enough to create a small draft. *Mustn't scare the source.*

"We are, but when Luca was announced as GC for Paris-Roubaix, Rolf thought sure he'd get the *Giro d'Italia*."

"And he didn't?" If Rolf was riding the big Italian stage race at all, he'd be some kind of super-domestique.

"He's not doing Paris-Roubaix, and he'll be riding the *Giro*, but as Luca's lieutenant."

Rolf had just been cut out of the two highest-prestige races of the early season. "Maybe he'll be GC for the *Tour de France*?" Rolf would want his conditioning to peak for late June instead of May for the *Tour.* Christopher held his breath—none of this had been in the cycling news so far.

"We don't know, but I wish the *directeur sportif* would make up his mind, because Rolf's going to crack if he doesn't know soon." The rider spoke softly, glancing around as if he expected Rolf to pop around the corner. "There'll be hell to pay if Luca gets that too, even if he's twice the rider on time trials."

His lips tightened and he stared at the magazine, though he now held it with a serious tilt.

"How's Luca looking for the early season races?" That was a much safer topic; Christopher would stop pushing a man who looked like he'd already said too much.

The rider looked up with a sunny visage. "Good." Slapping the magazine back on the rack, he zipped his jersey back up. "Training at altitude sucked at first, it sucked for all of us, but it's like he's part Sherpa. Climbs like he could ride that bike up Everest."

"Whoa, that's some endorsement." The *Giro* had several stages in the Alps and the Dolomites. The classic races in Belgium had *hellingen,* the low but brutally steep Ardennes hills, rather than mountains to go with its *pavè* flats and climbs. Christopher grinned back. "How about sprints?"

"He's so going to kick ass at sea level." The rider clapped his helmet back on, wheeling his bike toward the door, with a detour at the register for his magazine. "Luca is looking damned good."

Christopher watched the rider leave, but it was Luca's broad smile and black lycra-clad legs he saw in his mind's eye. Yeah, Luca Biondi was looking damned good.

CHAPTER 3

STU BEGGED OFF riding, pleading the need for a rest day. Knowing Stu, he'd probably overdone the twelve-ounce curls the night before. Christopher could choose his route to suit himself, so a moderate pace on a long climb sounded good—it was a very mild day for February.

He'd gained altitude steadily riding up Lefthand Canyon and in a mile or two he'd start the serious climb toward Ward, a small town about three thousand feet higher than Boulder. He wondered what category of climb the entire twelve miles to the top would be considered.

"Coming up on the left!" was becoming a familiar refrain. Twice in the last two weeks he'd been overtaken by the team. A clump of riders went around him two at a time—and yes, Biondi was in the pack. *Will he recognize me?* Christopher had no illusion of being easily identifiable in what was nearly a uniform worn by hundreds of cyclists today—a black, white, and red jersey, black Lycra leggings, helmet, and sunglasses.

Once around him, the riders slowed their sprint, reforming into a peloton. All Christopher saw was ten of the most toned hind ends on the planet, attached to steel-muscled legs, drawing away from him. One rider dropped back, and it didn't matter if he was dressed the same as the rest of the team and hiding behind high tech shades, Christopher could pick out the slender, wiry physique of his favorite GC rider.

"Join us!" Luca surely didn't ask every random cyclist that. Before Christopher could make his mouth say "yes," Biondi was giving him a shove toward the pack. Coming off his bike became a real possibility, because Luca had one hand on Christopher's rear end and had increased his pace. Without intending to, Christopher pedaled faster, but he couldn't accelerate fast enough to keep that hand from getting *really* smashed against his ass.

He'd seen dozens of races where spectators, mechanics, or coaches had physically flung a rider back on the route, pushing until he was going so fast the pusher was left behind at last. Even a helping hand from the team car was possible, depending on what had happened. A coach or *soigneur* could bring a rider back to speed, giving momentum with a friendly boost through an open window. And there weren't a lot of places to grab on without spilling the cyclist across the pavement. A rider who got bent out of shape when someone touched his butt would have to work seven times as hard if he had to slow or stop for any reason.

Knowing the theory and having a helping hand shoving him toward the other riders were two very different things. That hand belonged to a man Christopher spent a large and growing amount of his waking hours dreaming about, and there wasn't one damned thing he could do besides say "Thanks," and pedal harder.

They caught up with the peloton quickly, giving Christopher another split to his attention. He had two very important things to focus on, the hand on his body and the wheels that suddenly closed in by his bike. Only the prospect of wiping out half the team let him concentrate on his bike-handling—Luca was barely six inches off his handlebars, and the rest of the riders were closer yet to one another. No wonder one stray dog or spectator could dump fifty riders into a multi-colored pile-up.

Or one rider. *Please don't let me be the one who splatters the team.* He'd have to stay with the peloton of his own ability, but they were such experts that they could probably recover from any foolish move he might make. *I'm at the back—they'll ride right past me.* His shifted until he pedaled only a few rpms faster than Luca, who looked like he'd go as far as Salt Lake City today before tiring.

Luca pushed him, and now dragged him closer. "Gear up!" he shouted, and somehow that last inch eased Christopher into the slipstream of the group. The wind went away—the resistance he fought against disappeared. Gearing up didn't seem like a burden now; he could drop tempo, maintain speed, and keep up with riders who could and had left him in the dirt.

The downside was Luca's hand disappearing too.

Not that Christopher expected a public groping for the next several miles, but it was Luca's hand, the hand he'd been dreaming about, on one of the spots he'd been dreaming it. Now gone. Rattling over a patch of rough asphalt brought Christopher's attention back to the road.

"Fun, yes?" Luca could speak easily at this pace, Christopher was both pleased to see and chagrined not to match. He settled for nodding and smiling, hoping that Luca could see his efforts were going into keeping up rather than speech. "The peloton breaks the wind; we work the domestique*s* like dogs to save our strength for the final run to the top."

"We can't keep him, Luca," another rider warned. "He can't take a spell at the front."

Oh, God, no. Christopher was working harder than anyone else already, even drafting on the other riders. If he had to take a turn in the front echelon, neither his strength nor his bike-handling could keep him there more than twenty seconds.

"He can stay with us for now, Laurent." To Christopher, he added. "Today we all lead for a time, but Rolf and I will sprint for a mountain finish. Exciting."

Good practice for the big races. Rolf looked good up ahead. Didn't look better than Luca. Nobody looked better than Luca. Would love to see the sprint. Too bad he'd probably be miles behind when it happened.

Even his thoughts were gasping for breath at this pace. Luca never stopped talking to his teammates. "Does this road remind you of the switchbacks of the *Col du Galibier* or the hills above Lake Como?" he asked one, and they chatted about asphalt quality in France for a while. "How would the Motorola team do at two thousand meters?" he asked another, and they had a good laugh over training at altitudes other teams reached only in airplanes.

Luca kept Christopher in the conversation, turning to catch the nods and shakes that were his only contributions. He needed every molecule of oxygen for his burning legs. Fatigue poisons were building up faster than he could clear them. He couldn't even suggest a local road that would feel like the cobblestones of northern France or Belgium.

The peloton shifted around them; Luca had to move forward in some prearranged rotation, leaving Christopher at the back. The view was fine, still, although Christopher's vision was beginning to go a little gray at the edges. The other riders didn't try to talk to him, but no one seemed overtly unfriendly. Not even Rolf.

They still had six miles of climbing to go when the fluidity of the peloton brought Rolf to the rear. "You're keeping up well," he remarked. "Do you ride this route often?"

"Yes," was a gasp more than a word. "Not at this pace," was an admission he didn't like making, but it was better than looking like a liar, since he was so clearly struggling. He'd been pedaling squares for a while now. The riders around him moved as easily as when they'd caught up to him. Standing up on the pedals would give him some extra power, but he'd wobble, maybe clip Rolf's bike. None of the other riders were standing on their pedals—neither would he.

"We're going to descend, then come up again. Even so, it won't be as challenging as the *Alp d'Huez*." Rolf sat straight up, riding no hands and taking a drink of water from the bottle that had been clipped to his frame.

Of course not. This was just the road to Ward, Colorado, not the most brutal mountain stage of the *Tour de France*. Tomorrow the smug bastard would probably want to ride to the top of Mount Evans, just so he could sneer at entire teams for never riding at fourteen thousand feet.

"If we did the Super-Jamestown route it would be nearly comparable, but the road has snow." As if he'd suddenly noticed Christopher's struggles, Rolf asked, "Can you get to the middle of the peloton?"

Since Christopher was down to wondering just how many more revolutions he could force from his screaming legs, he shook his head. If he'd been in the middle from the beginning, he could have enjoyed half the wind resistance that the leaders battled. Or brought the entire group to the pavement.

"You lack confidence in your skills?"

Christopher wasn't going to turn his head to see the expression that went with that assessment. The tone of voice was enough.

"You do look very tired."

Thanks, asshole. Exhausted was about the size of it. Luca should be dropping back again shortly; Christopher hoped to have a few more yards with him, just to prove that he'd made it this far.

"Ah." Rolf twitched his handlebars one sharp right-and-left. It might have been rough pavement or a stone, or it might have been the movement of one particular rider through the peloton. Christopher would wonder about it later—he had just enough mind left to respond. Badly. Rolf barely veered toward Christopher's front wheel, but it was enough to panic him. Over-responding, he leaned an inch too far to the right. The air took him like a fist.

He didn't stop moving forward, though the other riders surged away from him as if he'd stopped. Every bit of effort he'd expended in the slipstream wasn't enough to keep him going at their pace without the shelter of their draft. The climbing would begin for real once they rounded the big curve, and there would be no keeping up with the team at all once they reached the ten percent grade.

He should stop—Christopher passed his lactate threshold a long time ago and was running his anaerobic tanks dry. Going on would be torture for no good reason. He pulled off the road, too tired to look for a dry spot. Just a spot with no snow. The bike clanked when it dropped. He dropped beside it. Missed the sharp rock. Sitting was too hard. Ground cold on his back. Oh well. Breath might come back. Eventually. Legs numb.

He closed his eyes—gray edges around everything. The roaring in his ears subsided gradually. His pulse came down from 200, letting his heart stop thrashing in his chest like a trapped rabbit. When he opened his eyes again, it was to a full visual field of brilliant Colorado blue with a worried man in an orange and green jersey surveying the damage.

"You okay? Should I call 911?" The rider held up his cell phone as if it needed only the final digit to call the paramedics.

"I didn't crash—I'm okay." Okay was a relative thing, but Christopher sat up, knowing that to stay on the cold ground for long would stiffen his muscles.

"What happened?" The stranger offered a hand, pulling Christopher to his feet. "Did you get run off the road?"

"Sort of. I was riding with some of the Antano-Clark guys," he clarified. "Ran out of gas."

"You made it this far with them?" The cyclist looked uphill—they were about four hundred yards below the big curve known as the Turn of Events. The grade above the curve varied from eight to twelve percent. It was two thousand feet of altitude and twelve miles down to the city. "Pretty good."

Put that way, Christopher had earned the compliment. He fumbled his water bottle out of its rack on the bike. He hadn't been able to drink on the way up—that might have given him the capacity to go another mile or two with the team. Which would have let him drop out on the steep section and look like a weenie instead of a rider who lost the draft. He wasn't sure what would have looked worse, failing a *hors catégorie* climb or just losing the group. Had Rolf dumped him on purpose? He couldn't tell.

"Do you need an energy gel?" his rescuer wanted to know.

"Have some, thanks." The pouches on the back of his jersey yielded two packets of a high-carb, electrolyte-laden goo that tasted like chemical fruit and had the consistency of semen. Christopher sucked the packets flat, chasing them with the rest of the water. Feeling in his legs was returning, not a good thing.

"You aren't going to try the ascent, are you?" The rider stared at Christopher's thigh, where a muscle jumped uncontrollably.

Christopher shook his head. "Need more water, and I'll get home about six times faster than I'd get to the general store." A constant stream of cyclists through Ward had convinced the storekeeper to stock sports drinks, energy bars and gels, and sugary treats. Another two miles of near vertical made those goodies as inaccessible as moon rocks.

The whirr of bicycles jerked their attention from Christopher's quivery knees to the road, where turquoise and black riders strung out like beads on a chain, whipping around the big curve and downhill. Crouched low over their handlebars to hide from the wind, they spun by one at a time.

"They've got to be hitting forty-five." Another rider whizzed past, pedaling slowly. At this speed, pedaling was more to keep his muscles warm than to add velocity.

"At least. Nobody's riding the brakes." Christopher looked for Luca, not able to pick him out. He could have been the first one by.

"You kept up with that?" The rider gawked at another pair of Antano-Clark riders whipping by.

"Not on the downhill—I keep thinking I'll hit a rock and smear myself." Thirty miles an hour with one hand on the rear brake lever was fast enough for Christopher, and still more than fast enough to risk missing a curve.

"Hear you on that. Are you going to be okay to get down?" The cyclist helped Christopher pick up his bike, then threw one leg over his own ride.

"Gravity does it from here." And a good thing, too, because getting one shaky leg over the cross-bar was plenty of work as it was. "Thanks."

"Hope I don't find you in the same position on my way down."

"I'll let you call 911 if you do." Any cyclist who passed him on the descent could just sail on down—today. Competition had to take a back seat to survival. "You're more likely to see those guys coming back up."

"Back…" The cyclist shook his head. "Huh. Take care." He stood on his pedals to get the bicycle going again. Christopher would have helped if his own ability to move wasn't so limited.

Gingerly pedaling across the lanes to the far shoulder, he steered downhill, being extra cautious in his fatigued state. The gels and water had brought him back far enough that he could manage and even enjoy the ride. He was halfway back to town when the turquoise and black pack passed him again, going the other way.

Christopher hoped Luca would whup Rolf a second time.

A SHOWER, a nap, and a meal left Christopher feeling vaguely humanoid once more, though every bone in his limbs had turned to lead. Might as well get some mileage out of today's ordeal. He'd decided to write an article for CycloW-orld on the advantages of drafting. The joy of looking at the round, muscled ass of the rider in front was one benefit he didn't plan to mention, and at least Luca had been ahead of him before his vision had started to go. He'd gotten about 400 words onto his laptop when his cell phone rang.

"Luca Biondi here. Christopher Nye, please."

What! Christopher nearly dropped the phone, his fingers going nerveless when the sense of the words penetrated. How…? Why…?

"Speaking," he said, through lips gone suddenly dry.

"*Ciao,* Christopher." His name had never sounded so sexy; Luca's light Italian accent turned it to some kind of music. "I call to see if you're okay after the ride."

No, okay was not the first thought that sprang to mind. "Hit by a truck", "pounded by hammers", or "face first into the wall" were all more accurate than "okay." "I'll live."

"You should live well. Did you eat something?"

"I had a turkey sandwich." Slapping meat on bread was the extent of his ability to forage once he'd gotten home. "And I drank lots of water, some sports drink." The "wha?" circled endlessly through his brain—he hoped he'd said the next sensible thing.

"*Bene.* That helps, the protein and the carb, the liquid." Luca's voice dropped a note. "How high was your heart rate?"

"I'm not sure. Maybe a hundred and eighty?" He shaved his previous estimate. If Luca's had gone above 120 before the final ascent to Ward, Christopher would have been very surprised.

"Too high! Christopher, you let us push you too much! How long?" Any flirting tone Christopher thought he'd detected vanished.

"Half an hour?" he guessed.

"Too long! You are a brave rider; don't be a foolish rider!"

Since Christopher might have less than seven molecules of glycogen left in his muscles, it was too late to avoid being foolish.

"Next time you come on the flats with us." Luca was suggesting a next time? "What of tomorrow?" he now wanted to know.

Lie in bed, turning slowly to stone. "I hadn't planned yet."

"Do slow, gentle recovery ride," Luca pronounced. "It chases lactate from your muscles. Tomorrow and the day after. I do the same for tomorrow."

"Okay." Getting back on his enemy the bicycle didn't sound like a good idea at all. He could agree and then stay in bed until the last possible moment before work.

"Half hour, slow pace. No hills. Where is good place?"

"Out and back to Niwot." Christopher figured Luca either knew the route or had maps.

"*Bene.* I meet you at 28th Street and Iris. Eight o'clock." Now Luca sounded pleased with himself.

"Eight?" Oh, damn, he actually could make that. The lure of seeing Luca fought with the knowledge that he didn't really have to be out of bed until nine to get to work on time. "Luca, I don't think your recovery ride is quite the same as my recovery ride. The team will grind my ass into the road."

"No, they won't." A throaty chuckle came across the miles to tickle Christopher's ear. "Tomorrow is you and I alone, no team. You set the pace, I promise not to grind ass."

If that wasn't the most double edged promise Christopher had ever heard. "You and me? Uh, why?"

"I see your face on the descent, I worry. I push you—I have to make you well again."

"Um, thanks." A sense of honor and obligation was all well and good, but Christopher had hoped for something more.

"And I push you to the peloton today, because I see you in the store, I like you."

That might only mean in a friendly sort of way. Christopher tried not to read too much into it; it could be the combination of that sexy accent and tiredness.

But it didn't matter. He could find out tomorrow if there was anything more to it than riding, and even if not, he'd had Luca Biondi's hand on his ass once.

CHAPTER 4

CHRISTOPHER COULD manage a half hour recovery ride, even with the distance to the rendezvous point. Stripping off his underwear, he mused that he wouldn't be stirring for anyone but Luca. To be invited on a private ride by the sexiest thing on a bike would get him to do far worse than drag himself out of bed an hour and a half earlier than he'd planned. If he could figure out what that something worse might be.

Standing in the shower spray that had to be considered therapeutic more than hygienic, he let himself remember Luca's steely glutes flexing with every thrust of his carbon fiber thighs, all encased in spandex tight as skin. Riders to his right and left—he moved smoothly between them, pedaling in such smooth circles that the power never fed the bike unevenly. Even on the incline, his bike didn't rock with the effort. Beautiful.

Luca's slender, whipcord body would be beautiful too. Every rope of muscle outlined, long, strong, rippling with his movements. Did Luca leave the hair on his legs over the winter? Every picture Christopher had found of him, on line and in the magazines, showed his legs shaved. Whether for aerodynamics or to make treating injuries easier, his shaven skin was damned hot. Funny, this might be the only mystery those skin-tight leggings concealed.

Because every flex and motion showed so clearly. Now, in the safety of a non-moving bathroom, Christopher could think of what he'd watched. His cock rose, lifting under the spray, and he slid his hand down, bringing the slippery bubbles. Rising and falling with the rhythm of Luca's peddling, Christopher's hand helped him remember the fluid action of Luca's legs, the way they bent and straightened. The way they straddled his bicycle. Christopher envied the saddle—the support it gave that rounded ass, the slender point of the seat poking between Luca's thighs, rubbing the flat plane behind his balls, slick with chamois cream, touching him all the way up the mountain and back…

Christopher's cock throbbed in his hand, the waves of orgasm pulsing from deep within, rolling outward with every spurt of come. Shaky with the explosion, he leaned against the wet tile while the water beat lightly on him.

He had to get this out of his system now, because he was going to spend at least part of the next hour watching the same sight he'd just imagined. Swabbing himself with the towel, he decided that today was a good day to wear a jockstrap under his leggings.

THE WAITING rider in black, white, and yellow had Luca's springy brown curls peeking out from under his helmet, and a big grin that said he didn't need a turquoise jersey to identify his riding companion. Christopher pulled up beside Luca, still amazed that they were really going riding together.

"Ready? I follow you to get your pace. You keep your heart rate under one-twenty, okay? We take it easy today. Out, back, flat, slow. Better for your muscles than sitting." Luca waved Christopher to make the turn up Iris.

Leading was easier on his libido, which reminded Christopher that it had more than enough time to recover. He concentrated on maintaining his pace without flinching every time traffic whizzed past, which on this road and at this hour, was constantly. His sense of timing, verified by the bicycle computer mounted on his handlebars, said he was doing about eighty rpm, and his gear was low enough not to offer much resistance. He hoped Luca wasn't bored to tears behind him. Too much to hope that Luca was watching his butt with the same interest Christopher would try not to display when they swapped positions.

They'd reached the turnoff to 63rd Street when Luca spoke. "Christopher, what is your heart rate?"

"Um…" Christopher poked the computer to clock mode and rested his fingertips on the base of his throat, counting. "About ninety. I think." He might have missed a few beats or miscounted the fifteen seconds in his rush to answer the question.

"But you aren't sure?"

"No, but it's still under 120, what's the problem?" Christopher thought he'd been doing very well to keep the confounding factor riding behind him from raising his pulse.

"It's good to be sure. If it was high as 120 now while we go slow, I would worry. You didn't wear your heart rate monitor?"

"I don't have a heart rate monitor. I sell them, I can't afford them." The cheap cycling computer was the best he could afford right now, and it didn't have that function.

"Pull over."

Christopher turned right, into a parking lot that had a few cars scattered about and some big cottonwood trees to one side. He stopped at a picnic table under the trees. "Okay, why?" They leaned their bikes against the table.

"My heart rate today isn't so important—I pace you, I'm good. Your heart rate we need to know." Luca reached up under his jacket and jersey, fumbling with both hands to produce a sensor on a black elastic strap. "Pull up your jersey."

Startled, Christopher reached for the hem edge, hesitating a moment, but Luca's "lift, lift" flip of fingers had him exposing his belly and chest. Luca wrapped the strap around Christopher's chest just below the nipple line, coming close enough for Christopher to smell his hair. Close enough to kiss. Luca unclipped a monitor from his own handlebars to pop onto Christopher's bike. He poked a button. Nothing happened.

Nothing happened to the monitor, that is. Christopher was glad he'd put on the jockstrap and hoped it was enough.

"There isn't enough contact gel." Luca licked his fingers, sticking the damp digits under the monitor. Christopher forced himself to move neither closer nor farther away. Luca poked the monitor again, but nothing happened. One corner of his mouth pulled back. "Hold still."

He pulled the sensor down from its resting spot just below Christopher's nipple, bent, and licked. Popping the sensor on the damp spot before Christopher could twist away produced a series of beeps. Upright and frowning, Luca poked the monitor to silence, and again, to get the quick beeping.

OMG, Luca had just licked him! *Licked… Right there… A little higher and… Or a little lower… Or not here at all, in the middle of a parking lot, idiot.* He didn't mean a thing by it, except to get a good contact. And now the damned machine was betraying Christopher's interpretation. The display flashed 105, then 106.

"It was working before." Luca quieted the device.

"It's working now." If the monitor had an infrared detector, Christopher's burning face would light that up too. He pulled his jersey down over his stomach, wishing it covered him to approximately the knee. Maybe he should put his hand over the traitor display, now flashing 110.

"It is? Oh, it is." Luca smiled broadly, exposing very white teeth with a slight gap between the front two. His eyes, hidden behind the wrap-around sunglasses, could have been looking at Christopher's flaming face or at his groin, and the happy note in his acknowledgement was the only thing keeping Christopher from wishing himself swallowed by the earth. "Good!"

So Christopher didn't have to worry about his desire offending Luca. It wasn't the same as being sure of a welcome. He swung his leg over his bike, ready to ride away, not ready to ask for more. And not sure how he was going to pedal with this boner he'd just popped.

"We have no margin to your maximum right now, Christopher." Luca didn't reach for his bike. "If you wish to ride, I should look at your pedaling. I think you work harder than necessary."

Christopher knew perfectly well he worked harder than necessary; what he didn't know was how to fix it. Following directions out of books was a poor substitute for direct coaching, and the people who coached the best around Boulder either worked for one of the pro teams or cost three hundred bucks a session.

"What do you want me to do?" He surveyed the parking lot, which they had mostly to themselves. Luca couldn't have found a better diversion to take his mind off things he couldn't pursue here and now.

"Ride in a big circle around me, moderate pace. Do nothing different than usual." Luca marched out into the parking lot, his gait clunky because of his fixed-sole cycling shoes with their pedal clips on the bottom. Again he flipped his hand, "around, around." Christopher complied, rolling counterclockwise. He made three circuits around his new coach before Luca called out to switch direction. Another three laps, and then Luca called him to halt.

"We use big machines with sensors to determine this for the team." Luca sounded apologetic. "I think I know where problem is, but the leggings…"

"I'm not taking them off." His heart rate had calmed down as he rode, but shot up again by thirty beats a minute with the suggestion.

"No, no… That's not…" Luca either choked or snorted. "I ride beside you, feel how your muscles contract. Some part of rotation gets not enough energy. If you permit me to touch you."

If he permitted Luca to touch him… The real wonder was that he hadn't already begged Luca to touch him. And that Luca asked so formally, after what he'd done already, seemed strange, but then Christopher realized he'd put himself outside the circle of pro riders by reacting. He *knew* coaches, fans, and other riders pushed one another, but had never experienced it until yesterday. He *knew* riders had to be of easy modesty with their form-fitting clothing, close quarters, and the occasional need to line up at the side of the road for a group whiz during a long race. He knew all that, and yet, a little slurp to improve the performance of some equipment had him reacting like a nervous virgin.

Or like a man who was afraid to reach for what he wanted. Which was only too true. So if all he was going to get right now in the middle of a parking lot off a moderately busy street was some world class coaching, he'd take it. "It's fine. Do what you need to."

Describing a large loop around the parking lot with one finger, Luca showed Christopher what he wanted. "I ride beside you, feel how your legs work, okay?"

Christopher nodded. *Coaching, this was coaching...* He set off, and in a moment Luca was beside him, his legs working in tandem in such a perfect way that Christopher despaired of duplicating such effortless motion. Then Luca gripped one of Christopher's legs, his fingers lying atop the thigh, his thumb dropped downward. Torn between worrying about the desire his freshly engorging woody was betraying and worrying about what amateurism his leg was betraying, Christopher almost forgot to pedal. *Focus!* he reminded himself. *Ride!*

They made a lazy curve at the corner of the parking lot, Luca on the outside. He shifted his grip closer to Christopher's knee, which was a bit of relief. Christopher stared straight ahead—he'd probably run into one of the few parked cars if he glanced aside. Around again, and now Luca cupped Christopher's thigh from below, the gesture too reminiscent of what he'd do as a lover, with Christopher on his back, legs parted...

Scraping a pedal against one of the concrete parking chocks brought his attention firmly back to the here and now. Hitting that differently could have put them both on the ground. If he landed on Luca, he wanted it to be on purpose, naked, and with no protruding bicycle bits as inadvertent sex toys.

He could only hope Luca's powers of concentration were well developed and centered on quadriceps and biceps femoris, and not on the glans penis that was doing battle with the jockstrap. Awkward didn't begin to cover this—he was uncomfortable and could do nothing about it without making things worse. *Just pedal, idiot!*

Luca didn't react to the scrape, either by swerving or retrieving his hand, but after another half-circuit that put them back at the picnic table, he called a halt. "You're mashing," he informed Christopher, who thought he'd been behaving himself pretty well for a guy who was getting groped.

"And that's bad?" he guessed.

"Could be better. Lance Armstrong mashed too, and still became pro. But—" Luca lifted his chin in what could have been reminiscence, but could have been a really good look at the chaos in Christopher's revealing leggings. Damn the dark glasses for hiding Luca's eyes! "When he stopped mashing, he started winning.

"Your stroke has power from three o'clock to six o'clock in the circle. Very little from twelve o'clock to three o'clock, you miss needed part of cycle." Luca had unclipped both feet from his pedals to stand astride the bike; now he pedaled one leg in the air to demonstrate. "From twelve to three you need more quad." He patted the top of his thigh. "And from five to eight o'clock you need the scraping."

That term had popped up more than once in Christopher's reading but he still didn't know how to translate it to movement. "How?

"Like getting mud off shoes." Luca's quick foot drag gave sudden illumination to words Christopher had read without understanding. "Adds power to upper part of circle too. You try."

One circuit of the parking lot made a believer out of Christopher, though trying to keep both legs synched with extra flex and scrape felt like the training wheels had just come off. "Again!" Luca urged, and the movements started to make sense. "Again! Is better!" Christopher's simple bike computer agreed—he was getting another two mph over his usual with this gear and rpm. The discovery fixed his other problem as well.

"That's going to take some practice," Christopher admitted when he returned to Luca.

"It does. We work on it every winter, hours on the rollers and the diagnostic machine. Have to break old muscle habits. But—" Luca reached over to give Christopher's thigh a light slap. "—makes big difference, gets higher wattage."

"Sure does." Christopher thought of showing Stu what Luca had just shared. "Can I quote you on this?"

Luca nodded, his spring curls dancing lightly. "Yes. You practice it on way home."

On his way home—! A quick glance at his watch showed Luca was absolutely right. They'd spent all the time he had in this parking lot. "Yeah, I better go." Though he'd much rather practice his new skill with Luca ahead or behind him on the road.

"Don't be late for work." Luca swung aboard his own bike.

"Right. Hey!" His crusty look was probably diluted to uselessness behind his own dark glasses."How do you know? And how did you get my number, anyway?"

"Very helpful boss at shop." That grin was pure cat-got-the-cream. "Happy to know Antano-Clark riders get great service." Luca clipped one shoe into the pedal.

If Christopher were late and explained why, Brendan would probably look the other way. Still best not to press it. "Okay. And thanks. You're headed back?"

"Not yet. I ride an easy hour, then home and pack. Team goes to Snow Mountain Ranch for high altitude training. Roads are clear, no snow forecast. Go for three days."

That would give them another three thousand feet of elevation, even on the relative flats from Winter Park to Granby. Christopher had to admire the training that would give them the sort of boost others had to resort to banned drugs to get. Altitude or EPO? When riders could prove they were at ski-resort altitudes to explain their performance, no one should ask them for blood samples twice. "Great. Wear a lot of sunscreen, the snow will focus the sun on you and you'll fry." Christopher recalled what Luca had bought at the store.

"I will. I need another tube when I return. Maybe..." Luca paused. "We ride again after?"

Again! Hell yes! But— "Your teammates may not be happy with that." Having no illusions about his performance or his luck on catching Luca on recovery ride days, Christopher also didn't want a charity ride. Luca would ride with him and then go train for real.

"Then maybe... we go to dinner without team?" Why did Luca look braced for a "no"?

Maybe because the shock kept words stuck in Christopher's throat. "Yeah. Sure," he finally managed to stammer out. "Love to."

"I call you." Luca pushed off from a standing start, gaining speed across the parking lot in a way that could have almost been fleeing.

On his way back to town, Christopher thought half about his pedaling and half about the promised evening with Luca. Their first date. It was a date, right? Luca did have people to hang out with if that's all he wanted, didn't he? As Christopher surged down the road with his new technique, he had to correct himself. Dinner would be their second date.

CHAPTER 5

"DID YOU eat the batteries or the whole damned rabbit?" Stu draped over his handlebars, head bowed and chest heaving. The bike looked like the only thing keeping him from toppling over. They rested on the shoulder of Highway 93, where Christopher couldn't decide which view was prettier: Coal Creek Peak or Stu gasping for air. Christopher wasn't even breathing hard.

"Fricasseed with a side of carrots." The last three days of riding had been spent practicing Luca's instructions; Christopher had made endless back and forth passes on a relatively flat and very deserted country road east of town. Concentrating on technique left him without a brain cell to spare on traffic, so he'd made sure there was none to be wary of. Starting slowly, as his second recommended day of recovery riding, he'd picked up speed almost without realizing it. The additional power he could give the bike made his first choice of gear too easy—in order to keep the rpms down, he had to gear up. And up. After three days on the flats, Christopher could turn over the same rpms in a substantially higher gear, with a corresponding increase in speed.

Out on the road today, he'd still needed to adjust technique constantly to make sure he hadn't reverted to his old patterns. No wonder Luca said they spent hours practicing.

"Seriously, what did you do, pop some steroids?" Stu looked like he might stand up straight again any minute.

"Nothing that easy for you to duplicate. I got some coaching. Still working on being consistent. Here's what he told me…" Christopher explained; the satisfaction of whupping Stu once was sufficient.

"Obviously it works." Stu was back in the upright and interested position. "So the effort to your leg changes so the power to the pedal doesn't, okay… This makes more sense than what we were reading. You should write this up for one of your articles. Your coach would probably love to have his name in *CycloWorld*."

"He did say it was okay to quote him." Christopher had asked; Luca had agreed.

"Who?"

"You have to buy a copy of *CycloWorld* to find out." Christopher smiled, enigmatically, he hoped, and crossed over to the other side of the highway—the junction with Highway 72 had a light. Stu shouldn't have more "out" when he'd only have trouble with the "back." "This is a good turnaround."

Stu followed; so did his questions. "I'll just find out when I proofread for you!"

Gearing up by one sprocket gave Christopher an easy spin but made Stu quit asking. He hadn't decided how much to mention—if his ride with Luca was a date, Stu wasn't entitled to know. But riding technique wasn't anything personal, it wasn't like telling the world that Luca had asked him out. And Luca had given him permission.

He led the way back to Boulder, letting his friend draft as compensation for tiring him. Then Stu got another rest break—Christopher pulled over when his cell phone rang.

Luca's voice floated through, warm and inviting. "*Ciao*, Christopher."

Entirely too aware of Stu parked behind him, Christopher tried to keep his pleasure from hijacking his voice completely. "Heya, Luca. How are the mountains?"

"Cold. Very little oxygen here—every blood cell has to work thrice. We leave for Boulder soon."

Imagining that Luca had called before getting into the team van, he tried to estimate their arrival. Two hours, maybe. Enough time to finish the ride and clean up, plus some. "But good training?"

"Yes, I tell you about it at dinner, okay?"

"Sure. Did you have a place in mind?"

The answer was almost lost in the *whoosh* of a passing VW Bug. "—Italian place on Pearl Street, close to bike shop, okay? Casual."

That only narrowed it down slightly; Christopher could think of three eateries that matched that description. "Fine. It probably won't taste like your mother's cooking."

Luca laughed. "Nothing tastes like my mother's cooking. I pick you up at seven, okay?"

"Great. See you then." Christopher gave his street address and directions, only stumbling over a couple of words. Luca, framed in his front door, ready to come in… The time was going to crawl along.

"Hot date?" Stu snapped him out of his reverie.

"None of your business." Clipping back into his pedals, Christopher wished that Stu didn't take such a lively interest in his social life.

"Aaaaand… you aren't discussing who coached you, and it's 'Heya, Luca,' all husky, aaaaaand—"

Christopher took off, interrupting the unwelcome perceptions from behind, but Stu found enough energy to stay on his tail and continue snooping. "And Luca Biondi lives in Boulder now!" Stu shouted, making himself heard even over the wind and a pick-up truck passing. "You have a date with Luca Biondi, don't you!"

Christopher shifted, going three gears higher than he'd been riding four days ago, and left Stu in the dust. Luca hadn't said one single thing about being out.

FINALLY CONVINCED he'd shaved closely enough to remove whiskers that hadn't planned to grow until sometime next week, Christopher managed to dress himself in a freshly pressed blue button-down shirt, black jeans with a sharp crease, and hang the tie back in the closet. Even with the knot pulled down to his breastbone like he'd seen in a magazine, this was still Boulder; a tie wasn't casual. He glared at the clock for not fast forwarding to seven. It gave him enough time to brush his teeth again. He'd already cleaned the kitchen, remade the futon so that its linens looked like upholstery, locking that untrustworthy furniture into couch position, and vacuumed all four hundred square feet of the basement apartment in the old divided house on College Hill. Luca might come in later.

Three sharp raps on his garden level door at two minutes to seven made him jump. Luca, with a tentative grin, stood in the stairwell, a bike at his side. Christopher only noticed that after he'd stumbled through a greeting and tried to shut the door behind them.

"Oh." He looked at Luca's ride. "A mountain bike?"

"My 'go around town' bike."

That made sense; Luca wouldn't leave his racing machine outside the grocery store. Christopher went back for his own worn-out Trek road bike, which hadn't run more than errands since he'd bought his pride and joy, freshly rinsed from the day's ride with Stu. Adjusting his expectations and wearing a heavier jacket, Christopher followed Luca down the hill toward Pearl Street, pulling up at a brick-fronted restaurant a block from the bike store.

"It is a nice night for a ride," he commented, securing his bike to Luca's and the railing around the outdoor eating area at the restaurant, empty now.

"No car," Luca replied, following a server to a table for two in the corner. "No need."

His springy brown curls, lightly tousled from the ride, framed his face and tried to brush his shoulders. Christopher had never seen Luca when he wasn't kitted up or mussed from his helmet, and the view was niiiiice. How long would one of those curls stretch? Would Luca laugh or be irritated if he let it bounce back, maybe after a kiss... "I suppose not, but isn't it tricky to do the grocery shopping?"

"Why would it? That's what everyone did at home. With baskets or backpack, easy." Luca hadn't picked up his menu yet, his eyes locked on Christopher.

Under that intent gaze, Christopher wondered if that one unruly lock of hair was standing up like a dark brunet exclamation point at the back of his head again. He resisted the impulse to smooth it down. "Where is home?"

With a sigh, Luca picked up the menu. "Where the team is. I grew up in little town in the Veneto. You wouldn't know name, but about fifty kilometers from Venice, at foot of hills."

There was a map on the menu; Christopher offered his to Luca. "Show me?"

Tracing a semicircle on the eastern side where the "boot" of Italy flared out at the top, Luca told him, "The Veneto is region, has states. Venice, here on the coast. Po Valley is flat from sea to here, then hills, growing to mountains."

"The Dolomites?" Christopher hazarded, not wanting to sound provincial. He'd looked up Luca's *palmarès*, his racing record, not his home town.

"Yes, and Alps. Region reaches up to touch Austria. My town is here." "Here" could have been one of several—the map was small compared to Luca's fingertip. A waiter stood by, absorbing the geography.

Christopher hadn't even looked at the menu. "Dishes to share," he read, but Luca was there ahead of him.

"May I order for us?" he asked, and at Christopher's nod, made several choices. "We get more if we're still hungry after these."

The plates appeared in a whirl of words Christopher barely registered: *gnocchi di zucca, carpacchio, tortelloni.* "Looks like belly-buttons, no?" Luca popped a folded pasta into his mouth.

Pull up your shirt, we'll compare. Damn, don't let the suaveness slip.

Polenta di funghi. A bite of that put a smile on Christopher's face and sheer bliss on Luca's. "I am true *mangiapolenta,* Christopher. Northern Italian."

"So it tastes like home?" Christopher wanted another mouthful of the polenta. Did Luca? The morsel on his fork wavered—he could offer it to his companion.... Too soon. Too intimate. He savored the bite for Luca, rolling it over his tongue with *mmm...* rumbling in his throat.

"Almost like home." Another forkful disappeared between Luca's lips—Christopher never thought he could be jealous of a mushroom.

"What do they do in your town?" He'd eaten the edge of hunger away, and could talk again, though each bite needed to be savored.

"Bicycles!" At Christopher's double-take, he laughed, sun-crinkles showing at the corners of his blue eyes. "The entire Veneto is crazy for bicycles. Racing. Touring. Lots of tourists."

"Sounds good." He must have grown up with what became his profession. "Your family, too?"

"My father is butcher, his father and many fathers before him. Our town has bicycle camps; close to the mountains, can ride to plains or hills all in one day, teach people to ride like pros. Or dream they ride like pros. My mother made breakfast for one of the camps, twenty hungry Americans, Belgians, French. I cleared plates."

"But you didn't ride with them?" So close to paradise!

Luca finished his bite of *carpacchio,* a slice of buffalo slick with olive oil and a caper on top. "I rode. That was my pay, and part of my mother's, for me to ride with foreigners, learn from coach who won stages of *Tour de France* and *Vuelta de España*. Won other races, too, had great *palmarès.* Learned much."

"Enough to ride with the Italian junior national team." That was an early note on a long list.

"You check my p*almarès*?" Luca paused with a forkful of gnocchi halfway to his lips.

"I checked everyone on Antano-Clark." Christopher found the last tortelloni. 'Best Young Rider' in three major races had also grabbed Christopher's attention; what Luca had done with the white jerseys that came with that particular honor? "But I remember the details of yours. So, this camp—people came from all over to learn to ride?"

"All teenagers—we rode during morning, lecture in afternoon, sometimes watch clips from races, learn what was good, what was bad, naps for hot time of day. Worked on technique after sleep." It looked like some good memories—Luca smiled into the one glass of a light Chianti he was stretching out through dinner. Not part of anybody's training diet, but he'd ordered it anyway. Part of his culture—Fausto Coppi would have had three, he'd said, and Jacques Anquetil might have finished the bottle.

"A lot of different nationalities—is that how you learned English?" Christopher wondered.

"Also school, a bit, but yes."

Feeling stupid and terribly mono-lingual even after three years of Spanish classes, he still had to ask. "How many languages do you speak?"

Luca silently ticked them off, considering. "Four well, two a little. French and German, have to talk with teammates. Enough Flemish to insult Belgian riders. Important to insult them so they understand. A little Spanish, talk with Columbiano riders, they understand enough Italian. Many riders speak some English."

Maybe Flemish was what Luca had used on Rolf in the shop, but Christopher wouldn't ask. "Sounds like a great way to grow up." Idyllic, and he could have had that, had he only known to ask for it. His parents had always accommodated his interests, but he'd come to cycling late, and they thought that at twenty-six, he could pay for his own indulgences. "And in the evenings?"

Luca looked up from the dessert list. "Free time. Healthy teenage boys, courting pretty girls in nearby towns." He bent again to the page, though surely he knew what was in tiramisu.

"Did—" Christopher would ask it. "Did anyone court the butcher's son?"

The flickering candle on their table and the intimate lighting made Christopher doubt what he saw, but Luca's soft answer of "Yes," went with the flush on his cheeks.

"I'm sorry. I shouldn't have asked." In the countryside of Christopher's mind, two lithe young riders pedaled to a remote barn with a cozy hayloft, or found privacy among grapevines with green clusters of unripe fruit hanging down. "I didn't mention our evening to anyone, but my buddy figured it out."

Luca put the dessert menu down with the air of a man who'd never taste anything sweet again. "Thank you. Christopher, I—I do not want the closet, but—" No wonder he'd fled after making the invitation; Luca had to be terrified of his own boldness. "But where I grow up, it is not right to be—to want—but I do. At home I could greet you or any man with kisses on cheeks, right, left, hello. No meaning but friendship. But for anything more, no. Here, people look funny if men kiss men's cheeks, but for more, no one cares. One big reason I came to American-based team."

Running his hands through his hair like that in his agitation was not keeping any doors shut. "Some people do, but not so many. Especially around here; no one gets in your face about it."

"If I stayed here, no problem. But races are in Europe, where *paparazzi* stalk cyclists and top riders live in homes behind tall walls. What I do will not stay on one side of ocean only. So I live, not in closet, but like—" The handwaving didn't quite translate. For the first time, Christopher heard Luca grope for a word. "Like—*frate.* Religious man. No hair." He set his hands atop his head, pulling his hair tight to his scalp.

"A monk?"

"*Sì*, a monk." His hands came down to lift the wineglass to his mouth, and the remaining puddle of red disappeared in two gulps.

"Would it really be so bad for people to know?" Christopher could speak discreetly.

A shadowed V appeared between Luca's formerly straight brows. "For world, maybe not. For home, very bad. One bad crash, or scandal with team, and I'm back in the Veneto with big knife and side of beef, trying to sell *bistecca* to people who do care."

Put that way, Luca did have a big point, but— "Did you ever actually want to be a butcher?" Christopher had never had the slightest desire to follow his father's footsteps in the business world.

"No, but it's what Biondis in our town do." Luca looked genuinely puzzled about the choice.

"Except for the one who got on a bike and rode away very fast." Christopher wouldn't push, but he did want Luca to see the bigger picture. "You can choose about riding back."

"I plan to ride up and down France, Belgium, and Italy for many years. And even so—" Luca peered into his wineglass as if mystified by its emptiness. "My family shouldn't find out from newspaper."

"That would be awful."

They skipped dessert after all, but there might be something sweeter than gelato once they got home. The evening was cold enough that they'd have the bike path along the creek to themselves if Luca wasn't quite ready to head back to Christopher's place. *Paparazzi* didn't lurk around Boulder much; if anyone jumped out of the bushes by the creek, they'd probably want wallets, not pictures. Christopher hadn't reckoned with Luca looking down.

"A brick street!" he exclaimed. "Not good as cobblestones, but almost! You didn't say you worked by brick street!"

"Uh, Luca, this is a pedestrian mall, there's usually hundreds of people; we can't just sail back and forth in the middle of downtown…" Christopher found himself talking to empty air.

Suddenly Luca was back, having whipped around a raised garden in the middle of the mall. "No good to practice on mountain bike—need skinny tires. Trade!" Luca put one hand on Christopher's handlebars.

"We'll get in trouble, Luca."

"Look, late, no people, no one cares. No one here to care, just you and me." He shook the handlebars gently. *Get off. Now.*

"So now I'm your domestique." Christopher yielded his old road bike. A few people walked the mall, diners leaving restaurants like themselves mostly. Luca wouldn't squash any—he could navigate through the throngs that crowded the bike races without coming to grief.

"If you ride with me. Else you are *soigneur*." He was gone again.

He was probably to the end of the four block brick mall before Christopher got the gears sorted out and moving on the mountain bike. It wouldn't be so bad to play soigneur*:* they acted as valets, medics, masseurs, spare sets of hands in general, and rode in the team cars during races. He'd give Luca a massage at first opportunity, for sure. Once he brought the man to a halt.

If he could bring the man to a halt. Maybe he shouldn't expect more than a kiss or two from his skittish companion. Christopher eyed the cross street nervously for traffic and shot across it as fast as he could on a bike built for ruggedness rather than speed. He wondered how many times Luca would lap him before calming down enough to consider a kiss. A man used to living like a monk might need a lot of laps.

Luca shot past, laughter trailing in his wake. "American cobblestones too smooth!"

"Too new!" Christopher shouted at his back, pedaling without hope of catching up.

A shrill tweet pierced the night—the very sound Christopher had been dreading. Luca was on the way back when one of Boulder's finest, patrolling on a bicycle himself, blew his whistle repeatedly until Luca stopped. Christopher hurried from the other direction in time to catch the end of the tooting and the beginning of the harangue. Luca looked stunned at first, but his face grew stormy. His deep breath signaled disaster.

"He's terribly sorry, officer," Christopher inserted before Luca could uncork invective in five languages or worse, in the one the officer was sure to understand. "He's on a pro team, the brick looks like cobblestones, he needs to practice, it looked safe with no people, he's from Italy where they do this all the time…." Gabbling out the apology with one eye on Luca to beg him for silence, Christopher thought he'd hit a good note and repeated it. "One of our pro teams."

"So you're one of the Garmin-Sharp guys?" The officer glowered but his voice said "intrigued." "Thought you knew better than this."

"Antano-Clark," Christopher and Luca said in unison, and before Luca could explain, Christopher took over. "They're new; they haven't been in Colorado very long, sir." A second's pause, then Christopher repeated, "He's from Italy." Luca stayed blessedly silent.

"I'll give you a break this time then. Consider yourself warned. This is a pedestrian mall…" The cop admonished them a bit longer. "Are you understanding any of this? Is he…?"

"I. Speak. English." Luca clipped each word, all lilt gone from his voice.

"I'll make sure he does, sir."

"Okay then." The officer turned to Luca. "Save it for the *Tour de France.* And win it." He waved them down the cross street.

Glad to escape, Christopher led Luca back toward his home in silence. They brought the bikes inside and had them propped against the wall before Luca exploded.

"*Poliziotto ignorante! Idiota,* he did not know who I am! Any village in Dolomites everyone would know all riders by face, speak to them by name! Be glad for wanting to ride there! This one with his tweet tweet, win the *Tour de France* but don't ride here! Tweet!" Punctuating his wrath with a blow to the air, Luca didn't even seem to see Christopher. "Antano-Clark trains to peak for the *Giro d'Italia*! 'Win the Tour!' he says, like that's only bicycle race in world!"

"It's the only bicycle race in his world, Luca. Like for people who don't know horse racing, it's all Kentucky Derby, or all car racing is the Indy 500." Daring to come a few steps closer when Luca stopped striking out at the world, Christopher had to point out a few contradictions. "You liked Boulder because people didn't know your face and follow your every move. At least he knew that much and let us off a couple of hundred dollar fines for riding on the mall."

"That much?" Maybe Luca's confusion was partly from not knowing what the Indy 500 was.

"Yeah, I said we'd get in trouble. Look, Luca, *I* know the *Giro* and the *Vuelta* are just as important as the *Tour*, and I know that Paris-Roubaix is a huge race, and that the Flèche Wallonne is a Classic. And that you won a white jersey there three years ago and what a great honor that is." Luca would win no more "Best Young Rider" awards; he was twenty-eight now, two years too old to qualify.

Christopher slipped Luca's coat from his shoulders, playing the soigneur. "And I also know, Luca," he said, discarding their jackets and coming to stand close, his voice gone low. "If you were standing there wearing it, I'd still want to take it off and kiss you."

CHAPTER 6

"TAKE IT OFF…?" Luca repeated, his anger transformed into something less frightening, at least for Christopher. Last time he'd seen that expression, there'd been a real deer in the headlights.

"We could leave it on at first, if you wanted." Spooking Luca out the door looked like a real possibility. Trying to control the urgent spike of lust at the thought of Luca wearing nothing but a white prize jersey, Christopher held out his hands but didn't come closer.

"I want…" But Luca's eyes flicked to the open drapes in the wall behind the paisley-covered futon, now folded to a couch.

Doubting the proximity of any determined photographer with a long lens, Christopher drew the drapes, heavy enough to keep out the morning sun—or curious evening passers-by. He flicked the table lamp on and doused the overhead light, asking, "Better?"

"*Molto bene.*" Luca took one hesitant step closer.

Christopher could settle his hands on Luca's waist now, their faces near enough for their breaths to mingle. Luca was about two inches shorter than Christopher's own 5'11"—not reaching down to meet his lips might just kill Christopher before Luca decided about that first kiss.

Nearly thrumming with tension, Luca tipped back, inviting Christopher's mouth, pausing before a final decision. Hands on shoulders, he could bring Christopher closer or thrust him away, and a long wide-eyed stare made Christopher fear he'd be pushed back. But Luca lifted his face that small fraction that said Christopher could lean just far enough to brush his lips across Luca's, slowly, once, twice. "I won't do anything you don't want."

Suddenly Luca lunged against him, as if that one assurance was enough to break all the barriers and strip the *frate* of his hair shirt. He knocked Christopher backwards onto the futon; he had the presence of mind enough to splay his legs rather than knee Luca. Quickly mouth to mouth again, Luca parted his lips, demanding that Christopher do the same, and he was only too glad to comply. With Luca's lithe upper body crushed to his chest, his tentative embrace became a total enwrapping. Christopher gripped a fistful of soft brown spirals, not to pull but to feel the softness crush against his palm. It was the only soft thing about Luca—slender, wiry, and erect, pushing against Christopher, grinding their erections against one another.

Clothes were an imposition, but to push Luca away, even for the seconds it would take to strip him, was unthinkable. Not with his tongue in Christopher's mouth, his arms like cables around Christopher's neck and waist. When Luca was ready to move on, Christopher would help, but this need, this overwhelming need in Luca's every movement had to be answered. And if he was so damned hard it hurt, and trapped in a bad position inside his shorts, he still wouldn't push Luca away even for a moment, because he was terrified Luca wouldn't come back. Too erratic, insistent but tense, the man was a coiled spring who would shoot across the room if moved.

Luca drove against him, silently thrusting with all the strength that had propelled his bike more than a thousand miles this season alone. Trying to match him without passing him, Christopher lifted his hips to the driving rhythm, closing his eyes under the assault of Luca's tongue, wet and insistent, knowing Luca's heart was beating every bit as fast as his own. With his hand flat to Luca's back, Christopher could feel its reggae beat knocking against ribs.

This couldn't last, not with the way Luca rubbed his cock against Christopher's, each stroke gradually shifting him to a better lie. Damn but he wished he could get their jeans out of the way.

Luca froze, all but his thudding heart and his pulsing cock—Christopher froze with him, his own climax not yet urgent enough to keep him moving. The smallest groan escaped Luca at last, a whimper almost. He slid down to his knees, bringing his head to rest on Christopher's chest.

Silently he begged Luca not to leave him like this—Luca had to know, just from his heartbeat, that Christopher hadn't come yet. He tightened his grip in Luca's hair, just for an instant. *Let go, you promised not to push. But please…*

Luca tipped his face up, meeting Christopher's eyes. Damn but the man was beautiful, his face the classic shape found on statues two thousand years old, the ringlets falling behind his ears where Christopher stroked them, his mouth so close to Christopher's crotch that he couldn't help thrusting slightly against Luca's chest. That brought the fear back into Luca's blue eyes—Christopher stilled, cursing himself for an idiot. A wound up, horny, wanting-to-come idiot, who might end up with his own hand yet if he moved again. "Sorry," he whispered.

"You need," Luca whispered back. "I touch you." But he didn't move, nor did his eyes lose their wariness.

"With your hand." Christopher found a few words that would give him release and take that look off Luca's face. "Your hand will be wonderful." He drew Luca up to sit on the futon, one arm around him, one hand to hold Luca's. Nuzzling into Luca's curls, he found himself begging, "But please, soon."

His shirt had come untucked in all the rubbing; Luca reached under the flapping tails to grasp Christopher's cock through the denim. Tentatively he rubbed, growing bolder when Christopher did nothing more than moan softly. It was good, but not enough—Christopher tried not to thrust into Luca's palm.

"Be still."

Obeying, feeling hands fumbling at his zipper, Christopher tried to be patient. Luca couldn't possibly be completely inexperienced, not after his blushes at the table, but a jumpier partner was unimaginable. Making no sudden moves, Christopher lifted his hips enough to let Luca slide his clothing down. Not very far—the elastic on his underwear stretched across the base of his cock.

Luca must have made up his mind. he snuggled into Christopher's side, his strong fingers wrapped around Christopher's cock in the same grip he used for hours on the roads, pulling and sliding the skin over the shaft. "Not enough" was rapidly becoming "plenty". Christopher buried his face into Luca's hair, the scent of his scalp better than any perfume. Gasping warm mouthfuls of the intoxicant, Christopher wanted to push Luca over, climb on top and thrust until warm fountains pulsed between them. He stayed where he was, letting Luca decide how much and how hard. "Soon" became "now:" Christopher could say only, "Luca!" before the explosion took him, the warm fluid spurting from him in the waves of pleasure.

He sat gasping with Luca's hand around his slowly softening cock, catching his breath. Wetness reached his skin; his come had to have been dripping down over Luca's hand. Poor guy must be getting kind of sticky in there, too. "Let's clean up."

With a small snort of laughter and the other hand cupped to catch the splats, Luca followed Christopher to the tiny bathroom. He rinsed off under the tap Christopher opened for him, and then peeled down, rinsing the soggy underwear without an apparent care. The jeans had a small wet spot when he'd taken them off, and a large soaked spot when he finished. Luca made a face and started to pull his wet clothing back on, his discomfort suddenly returning. Christopher dragged his eyes away, but Luca's ass really was everything he'd been dreaming of.

"Wear something of mine." Christopher found a pair of basketball shorts on the back of the bathroom door.

Cleaning up, Luca had had the ease of a man used to casual nudity with the team, but that hadn't lasted. He dragged the shorts over his butt without untying the drawstring. "Thank you." He stayed facing the mirror, head bowed, where Christopher could see but only dimly understand the thoughts chasing across his face. "You must think I am…" He circled a finger toward his face. "Crazy."

"No, Luca. I don't." Well, he had, but there was only one other thing that made sense, and it was a lot more likely. Turning Luca to face him, Christopher stroked the backs of his fingers against Luca's cheek, the most intimate but unthreatening thing he could think of. "I think someone's hurt you very badly."

Luca nodded, leaning into the hand Christopher turned to cup a cheek. "Maybe one day I tell you. Trust… hard to do. To be boyfriends? I only know from movies, since… Never do, only sometimes, find someone for ten minutes, fifteen minutes. No names, no trust. No dinners."

"Sounds lonely." Sounded hellish. "Luca, whatever he did, I don't want to do. Even if you decide not to go out with me again, or if we don't last beyond when the team goes back to Europe for the racing season." Gathering Luca into his arms as if he could protect the man from his past, Christopher murmured, "I don't ever want that look on your face because of me. On anyone's face, because of me."

"I think I am right that you are good man," Luca mumbled into Christopher's neck. "And maybe, can coach me on boyfriends?"

"We've been doing pretty good so far," Christopher mumbled back. "Boyfriends talk to each other and help each other. It's not just kissing and sex."

"I talk all night, you listen. And kissing and sex, maybe not so good this first time."

"So tomorrow night we'll do it again and it will be my turn to talk." Christopher would take Luca out, though the small check from the magazine wouldn't stretch to anything as lavish as what they'd shared tonight. "And this first time isn't over yet, unless you have to leave." He squirmed a kiss through the curls onto Luca's forehead. "It was good, just… frantic. Excited and fast," he clarified, just in case Luca didn't know the word. "We can keep going, only slower." He led Luca back to the futon. "Just kiss me, real slow."

He opened his arms; Luca stepped within the embrace and demonstrated why he was a coach's dream, letting Christopher set the pace. With the first rush of desire slaked, he could brush his tongue gently across Luca's lips, feel Luca match him. The soft nibbles and caresses they'd been in too much of a rush for earlier were all they did now. The slight tang of the wine on Luca's breath didn't worry Christopher; it had to be wearing off and he was still willing, eager. His hands traveled softly up and down Christopher's back, his fingers pressing the hollows of spine and his palms the ridges of muscle.

Exploring Luca in return, Christopher stroked the light but strong layers covering Luca's back and shoulders, wishing he dared slide a hand under the elastic waistband. That would be daring too much, but he did slip downward to cup one steely glute, his fingers curving around the delicious swell of Luca's ass. Risking a soft squeeze, or two or three, he pulled Luca more tightly against his chest, until Luca sagged, bearing Christopher down to the couch-shaped futon.

The treacherous were-furniture now decided its own personal full moon had arrived. The untrustworthy latch gave way. A screech and a thump later, Christopher and Luca sprawled on what was now a mattress. Christopher fully expected Luca to leap to his feet.

"Sorry. I'll put it back up." His heart pounding an extra twenty beats per minute for fear Luca would panic, Christopher tried to wiggle upright, but Luca didn't let go.

"I wished for bed. By magic bed is here." Far from fleeing, Luca twisted them until he lay atop Christopher, their feet dangling over the edge, and started nibbling at Christopher's neck.

Oh, Lord, Luca was hard again, hard as Christopher, and his lips and tongue found Christopher's mouth again. So what if it felt like advancing the humping; Christopher scooted them higher onto the futon. Offering his neck more completely, Christopher let those full lips find the ridges of muscle that had to connect directly with his erection. He thrust back against Luca's insistent hips.

"Can I touch your skin?" he dared ask, his hands catching crinkles of cotton against Luca's back.

For answer, Luca sat up, straddling Christopher's groin, to strip his shirt away. With great deliberation, he unfastened Christopher's buttons, sweeping the edges of shirt to each side, to run his hands over the exposed skin. Long strokes and tiny flicks at his partner's nipples couldn't have been any party of Luca's hasty, trustless encounters. Christopher wanted to feel their explorations as if he were Luca's first real lover, and pushed thoughts of barns and grapevines away. He concentrated on running his hands up and down Luca's sides, learning the scars and finding the small patches of hair at his nipples and breastbone. When at last Luca lay against him, the heat of his skin was a gift.

"We could be naked." Luca made the suggestion at last; Christopher would have come in his clothing before pushing Luca to strip, and could only murmur his assent into the curls that tickled his nose.

Rising to stand over Christopher, Luca dragged the shorts down and paused a moment, nude, glorious, his erection jutting away from his body and bathed in the weak light of the tiny lamp. The shadows traced upward, painting the ridges of Luca's abs with darkness. His face caught only traces of light, but that had to be a smile.

"You're beautiful," Christopher breathed, afraid to reach out, just as he wouldn't touch a classical figure in a museum. But this figure breathed and gazed down on him, so he lifted a hand to Luca's leg, smooth as the marble he resembled. "Amazingly, fucking beautiful."

"I am skinny cyclist who chooses blind lover." Luca dropped to his knees, his hands at Christopher's fly. Shedding his clothing seemed to take his inhibitions, too; Luca patted *up, up* on Christopher's hips to pull his jeans away.

"I see you just fine. You're perfect and I like looking at you." So what if Luca's upper body was thin; every pound of muscle there was so much dead weight to haul up a *hors catégorie* climb. Christopher was guiltily aware that he lifted weights as much for showy musculature as for the endurance he needed, but Luca seemed happy, from the way his hands traveled up and down Christopher's body, dancing lightly over every part, including his hard and leaking cock.

If Luca needed all night to decide what he was willing to do, he could have it, but he bent to lick at Christopher's tip, first with a tiny, tentative flick, growing into a full-circled swipe and then engulfing him in an excruciatingly slow descent. Silence wasn't possible for this; soft moans trickled from Christopher's throat and only seemed to urge Luca on.

Two could play at patting the other into position. Christopher coaxed Luca over him; that sweetly curved cock and heavy balls bobbed over his face. Luca didn't miss a beat when Christopher started to nuzzle and explore, finding the soft prickle of clipped hairs at Luca's groin, and the shaved smoothness of his inner thighs. At last he could get a double handful of that round, tight ass.

Lost in the warm musk and multitude of textures on one end and the wet heat of Luca's mouth and hands at the other, Christopher groped for a better hold on Luca's butt.

Luca jerked his head up. "Not in!" He clutched the base of Christopher's cock too tightly, and relaxed only when Christopher agreed.

"Not in, I understand." He didn't, not really, but he'd promised not to do anything Luca didn't want. Early days yet, they had fallen into bed without really talking; he'd find out more once words were back on the agenda. Moving one hand to Luca's cock and the other to caress his back, Christopher eased them back into what they'd been doing. Luca went back to stroking slowly, his lips to Christopher's sack, maybe in case he needed to yell again. He wouldn't. Christopher was going to stick to the things he'd already established were okay; he could do a lot with hands and mouth.

So could Luca. He sucked Christopher back in, swirling his tongue along the shaft, the ring of his fingers pushing a climax ever nearer.

"Almost there," Christopher gasped—he needed to let Luca pull away in time if he didn't want a mouthful. Guess he didn't, but warm lips against

Christopher's balls more than made up for the sudden chill. Fire rolled through him, the heat splashing his belly with every pulse of his cock in Luca's firm grip, and he cried out against the granite thigh beside his head.

"Turn around," Christopher mumbled when speech was again possible. "Let me suck you."

That beautiful cock had been out of sucking range, curved toward Luca's stomach. Christopher couldn't have slid it into his mouth without a severe backward bend, but now Luca knelt over him, leaning on the futon's armrest. Concentrating solely on his mouthful, Christopher closed his eyes, feeling the slide of skin as he slid his lips over Luca's shaft, tasting the warm musk of his earlier exertions. Luca helped, thrusting with surprising control and did not pull away from Christopher's hand on his haunch.

Control didn't last—Christopher guided the wild thrusts safely, flicking madly against Luca's cock and finally swallowing hard to match his gasps. Luca stayed long moments after his final spasms before he slithered backward out of Christopher's grasp, falling as much as lying down into the crook of his arm. Christopher killed the light with his free hand. They didn't need to see for the last kisses of the night.

Luca awoke once in the night, half sitting with a yelp of surprise.

"It's okay, you're with me—Christopher." He didn't want to turn on the light: he'd never get back to sleep, but it wasn't necessary.

"Chris—" Luca calmed down, running a hand over Christopher's face and chest. "—topher. Ah." He wrapped himself against Christopher's back, and sighed again into his dreams.

CHAPTER 7

THE PHONE chirped from Christopher's pocket—*please let it be Luca.* Last night ended too soon—every night ended too soon, it seemed, but in the best way, in a tangle of arms and legs and the sweet exhaustion after sex. No encore this morning, but the insistent nibbling on his ear when Luca tried to rouse him enough to say goodbye was a good memory. For all that Luca still jumped at shadows, he'd never sneaked out while Christopher slept.

No, Luca woke him each morning, and if he brushed kisses across Christopher's eyes to send him back to slumber for another hour, it was only after a few minutes of conversation—*Where do you need to be today?*

Work, writing, riding, none of those answers were as important as "With you." Which didn't mean he could drop bicycle components all over the store in his rush to hear Luca's voice.

And Luca inquired every morning: *We see each other again tonight?* Unless he said, "We ride today, get up," or once, "We ride out Highway 93 tomorrow, okay? Busy tonight, but meet me at market on Broadway and Baseline, 7:30." Funny how he never questioned that Christopher would be where he wanted while wearing spandex and a jersey, but always hesitated over the two of them doing anything in street clothes. Or without any clothing at all.

This morning Luca had offered Christopher a choice of Thai or Nepali—he seemed to be trying to eat his way through every eclectic dining possibility in Boulder, which would take months and cover the whole world. But always with the question mark—*We see each other again tonight?*

Yes, hell yes—did he even have to ask? Christopher shoved a set of handlebars into his armpit, freeing a hand to fumble the phone out of his pocket.

"*Ciao,* Christopher, hey." Luca's voice crossed the miles to caress his ear. And then thump him upside the head. "Change of plans for tonight, sorry."

"What—?" *I don't want to see you, you're too big a risk for me, I can't take chance....* " Every terrifying reason he had yet to hear rattled through his head. What the hell could have happened between this morning's "I see you about eight, we get *ceviche* at Aji, okay?" and now?

"Big meeting at last minute. Very important, this man comes from New York just to see me."

Nearly dropping the phone, Christopher juggled three wheels and the handlebars to the mechanic's bench. Ignoring the mechanic's double take at the noise, he pelted out the back door in search of a quiet spot to hear the rest of this bombshell where no one could see his face. Who would be coming to see Luca that Christopher could actually compete with?

"Um, sounds important." *Sounds like pulling my heart out and stomping it.* He huddled out of the brisk wind behind the dumpster.

"Very." And Luca sounded so happy about it. Damn it. "One of team's sponsors, source of much money. Maybe source of more."

Oh. A sponsor. Well. Christopher sagged against the green bin. Guess if you have the company name written across your chest you talk to the representative. "Then it's good news?"

"Possibly. Could be very, very good news, depends on what we say to each other tonight. I talk with manager and sponsor, maybe until late, certainly past dinner."

Managers and sponsors had to be accommodated, yeah. Christopher pushed his panic back into its "Break heart when needed" box. "I'll miss you, but if you need to be there, I understand."

"Thank you, Christopher. Ah, I may be very full of energy after talks. Need to go for ride to work off energy." Oh man, Luca's voice dropped a good octave. "A ride ending at your place. Okay?"

Bring on the energy if it made Luca growl like that. "Sure." His own voice suddenly had a burr in it.

"Or I might be sad." If Luca's pause was to add unseen theatrics, Christopher wouldn't be the least surprised. "I might need shoulder to cry on."

"I'll dry your eyes," Christopher promised. He'd kiss every tear away and keep on going. "Do you really think you'll be sad?"

"Have big towel ready. But probably we use it for shower in morning." Luca's laughter returned, tinged with hope and excitement, and not sounding too different from his anticipation of travel, races, or getting Christopher's clothes off.

"Okay. I'll see you later tonight." Luca wasn't blowing him off, anything but that. No, he was bringing Christopher his triumph, or his unlikely sorrow, whichever needed to be wallowed in with a lover's help.

"I tell you about it when I get there," Luca promised. "See you at home."

Home? Luca's words filled him with a warmth the cold wind couldn't touch.

At 10:07 Christopher leaped off the futon to answer the fusillade of knocks at the door. Luca tumbled in, wind-whipped and grinning, throwing down his pack and nearly dropping his bike in his rush to pounce on Christopher. Two could play the eager game—Christopher's genuine stumble under Luca's hurtling weight became four extra steps and a collapse on the futon. Pinned under his squirming lover, he gave as good as he got, with probing tongue and thrusting hips.

"You don't seem to be crying," Christopher observed about five minutes later. They'd frotted themselves into climax almost as fast as Luca had come on their first night. Not a bad thing really, some joy in each other and then talk. And then round two would come, more slowly, more thoughtfully, and a lot longer.

"No crying, none at all." Luca seemed content to stay on top, his weight on his elbows and their noses in brushing distance. His curls fell down over their faces, making a private twilight for Christopher to gaze up into Luca's eyes. The sun-crinkles around them creased into delight now. "I make up for no dinner tonight with a week of dinners in France. Or Italy. Or Belgium, or wherever rest days are and you can come."

"Whoa! Italy?" Christopher rolled them over to their sides and sat halfway upright. "What? When?" His jaw could barely come up enough to form the words.

Oh shit. Too much—Luca shrank in a way that should have been history a week ago. "If you want to come."

"Oh, yeah, sure, but, I'm just surprised." He reached to Luca's jaw, cupping the classic features and stroking with his thumb. The tension leaked away; Luca leaned into the caress. "I know you have to go soon. I just didn't know you wanted me to come along on your turf. I didn't think I could—" He had to override Luca's sputtering, no matter what he'd said about secrecy before. "I don't have a lot of money, Luca."

"Oh." Luca's smile put happy creases around his mouth. "Money is little problem. If tonight works out, no problem. Not a done deal yet, I can't say details until all names are on contract, but already we talk about photographers and locations and magazines."

"That's great!" Christopher leaned down to place his congratulations lip to lip. Who were Antano-Clark's sponsors, and what had they been advertising, or not advertising yet? He sifted through the *CycloWorld* ads in his head, discarding every product as unrelated. Who could think of gears or helmets while getting kissed by the sexiest guy to ever straddle a bike?

And Luca wanted Christopher to come to Europe.... And he was right here, right now, and wearing too many clothes. Christopher pulled away again, just long enough to fix that little problem.

"Up, up, Christopher. We ride this morning." The smell of coffee made any further *Zs* impossible, and strong fingers working into Christopher's shoulders made them undesirable. Which was not the same as wanting to get out of bed.

"Huh?" Peeling his eyes open and his mind from the fuzz of sleep, it did occur to him that Luca had ridden his racing bike last night, not the mountain bike. He rolled over to find Luca in leggings and a jersey, not yet zipped over the undershirt. "Okay, give me a minute." He dragged into the bathroom to finish his wakening.

"'ere're 'e 'oing'?" Christopher asked around a mouthful of toothpaste.

"Where did you go yesterday?" Luca asked.

"Up to Ward. Took me about an hour and a half." All the way this time, with chance-met companions to draft on and switch off with, not the combined might of a pro team to drag him up the mountain. They'd maintained a tempo Christopher felt comfortable with, leaving him pleasantly well-worked, if without the joys of Luca's company or the dubious delights of Rolf's. With his new pedaling skills, he'd led enough of the way at a pace that gained some backslaps and attaboys around the water urn at the general store.

"Then let's go out to Lyons and back. About thirty miles. Not too hilly." Luca rinsed his coffee cup and left it upside down in the drainer.

Christopher paused half-in, half-out of his jersey. "Better check your metric conversions; that's closer to forty-five miles."

"Not if we skip Lee Hill. Pretty road but we don't need to ride it."

Lee Hill had thirteen hundred feet of vertical with that ten percent grade at the top. Skipping it after his climb yesterday sounded pretty good, except— "Won't you be bored?"

"No, Christopher." Luca came over to run the zipper closed over Christopher's chest, pressing the tab down and reaching up for a kiss at the same time. "I won't be bored."

"I didn't mean because you'll have my ass to look at." He caught Luca's upper arms, holding him close for a stern look that melted in the heat of that bright smile.

"Your ass is very not-boring, but the ride is fine. I climbed all day yesterday." Luca pressed in, chest to chest. "Let's go, okay? I have another meeting with New York guy today, I want to ride first."

"Okay." Christopher let go. He wouldn't dispute Luca's choice of route—he could get to Lyons and back even after the effort of yesterday, but something was off. "If that's where you want to go."

"That route is good practice for a time trial."

When he put it that way, of course, any question disappeared. All television coverage of cycling included a dozen discussions from the commentators regarding how big stage races were won or lost on time trials.

Christopher couldn't say it wasn't a pretty ride, with the foothills rising to his left, coated in their-green-black pines and junipers with their evergreen smell that mixed with the nearby sage. The occasional house poked through the trees, whiffing of money. The topography of the road had just enough roll to it to require the intermittent shift of gear, and he could bask in Luca's assessment.

"Getting better power now! Not mashing!" came from behind, just before the turnoff to Lefthand Canyon Drive. "Good!"

Oh yeah. Christopher only had to think about his pedaling every two minutes now, instead of every twelve seconds, and his gear choices had gone another notch higher. Maybe they should turn left—he wouldn't mind doing the Ward run again. He stuck his arm out to signal.

"Straight to Lyons, Christopher!"

"But I'm feeling pretty good!"

"Looking good, too, but I want to stop and see something by town."

Poor guy; he probably never got to stop and look at anything. Christopher dropped his arm. "Okay!"

Luca buzzed around him to take the brunt of the wind. Christopher didn't think he was quite through leading, but time trials meant the riders raced alone against the clock, and if they caught up with another rider, or worse, were overtaken, they still couldn't draft. Luca would want the front for endurance training.

They passed the turn, crested a slight rise, and dropped into the gentle valley, fast enough that Christopher hoped not to encounter any loose rocks.

Thirty-nine miles an hour maximum, declared the bicycling computer when Christopher dared to look. They had a gentle uphill again, and the brush at the side of the road was no longer rushing by in a blur. "Whoot!"

The scenery was truly fine along this stretch of road—Luca all bent over his handlebars, his ass flexing just out of touching range. And the red rock among the juniper and sage looked nice too.

Just when Christopher was ready for a water break, Luca pulled into the parking lot for a fieldstone quarry, one of several they'd passed. Their tires crunched against the broken stone paving the lot. Large sheets of red and buff sandstone stood propped against pallets of thin-cut slabs, the dark shapes of primeval creatures writhing in fossilized seabeds.

Christopher tilted his head back to squirt water down his throat, one eye on the skeletal figures, the other on Luca. He, too, slaked his thirst, but no sooner had he racked his bottle than he knelt beside a slab where dozens of ancient fishes had come to rest. Luca ran his fingertips over the skeletons, tracing ribs and backbones.

"Strange, to dry the ocean and lift it so near the sky." He grinned up at Christopher, the strength of his wonder enough to pull Christopher down to his haunches to admire the school of fish. "Like the Alps, with many clams on the peaks."

"This one's different." Christopher picked out the form of something much toothier on the same slab. "A predator."

"Chasing dinner into the sand." Luca spun stories for each of the slabs, though his view of the life and death of some lacy fan-thing was probably more exciting than the creature had been aware of at the time.

Rocking to keep his balance, Christopher was glad of the break. His legs weren't quite as jelly-like as the invertebrate on the slab Luca admired next, but closer than he wanted to admit. He remained standing to check out the rest.

"So much of this rock all over town." Luca straightened in a hurry when the high-pitched scream of a stone saw destroyed the quiet. He waited for a break in the noise, which only lasted a few seconds. "University buildings, houses. I like it. Maybe get a fossil for house." The saw shrieked again.

"Let's go!" Christopher thought every filling in his teeth would vibrate out from the sound. And he was ready to go again, making it to Lyons where they refilled their water bottles at a convenience store and turned around.

He said nothing when they came to the turnoff that would take them up Lee Hill—even the gentle rolls of their current path were just about enough. Yesterday had cost him more than he thought. He did give the road a baleful look—beyond Lee Hill lay the steepness of the Jamestown route, or worse, the near vertical above Jamestown, and if he survived that to reach the Peak to Peak Highway he would end up in Ward again, where he could have the joy of the gradient down into town. But no, not one foot would he go to challenge the cruel hills.

Once they hit the city limits it was straight down Broadway, where every light was another moment to let the lactic acid drain from screaming calves and thighs. Head tipped down, Christopher waited for Luca's movement to tell him when to cross streets and when to wait. Once at his own door, he fumbled at the lock so badly that Luca took the keys away to let them in.

"Drink, Christopher." Luca pressed a bottle of sports drink into his numb hand. "Shower. Sleep a little if you can, and do stretches before work. You'll be okay, and I'll be back later to take care of you. Not very late, New York man has to go back today. I have to run home, clean up and get to meeting." Luca wrapped his arms around Christopher, which felt more like support than caresses. They sat down hard on the futon and Luca stole his helmet.

"You had a long ride too. I should drive you home." And he'd get to his feet, too, if Luca would just let him up. His lower back ached. Couldn't be he was getting old, but he'd hurt more and more after riding these days, and it wasn't anything Luca was doing to him in bed.

"Not so long. I'll be fine. Quick trip home, fresh clothes waiting." Luca kissed him, right next to Christopher's nose where he didn't get in the way of the air: nice.

"But—" Christopher flailed, trying to stand. "Your house is up above NOAA." The National Oceanic and Atmospheric Administration cuddled into the earth about half way up the foothills.

"No problem." Luca dismissed more vertical with another hug. "Twenty minutes to home if I go slow."

Oh Lord, Christopher'd sooner try to climb the wall than ride another hill today. "But—"

"No buts. I'll be fine. So will you, but I'll set your phone to ring in an hour so you get to work. And you sleep, be lively when I come back tonight, okay?" Drawing anxious thumbs across Christopher's eyebrows, Luca leaned in to enforce his command.

"Okay, but—"

"No buts. You take care of yourself here, and I get home and take care of other business. And then come see you later, best part of my day."

Best part—um, okay, but…. "I'm about to fall down and you're going to take another hill at speed."

"Listen, Christopher." Luca took his shoulders in a grip tight enough to demand attention. "You're tired. That's okay. You are fine amateur rider, you go distance and speed most people can't go. You go farther and faster now than two weeks ago, you go farther and faster two weeks from now. But."

Always a but. Christopher wobbled and hated that Luca was all that kept him from swaying like an aspen in the wind.

"You compare to wrong standard. I'm GC for a world class team. I go farther and faster than everybody. Handful of riders in this world go as fast. If they beat me it will be strategy and strong team, not always speed. Yes, I go one more hill now."

"So today was a pity ride." Fuck. Maybe the stupid futon would shape shift again into a small brick with him hidden in the middle. He'd worked hard, just as he feared, trying to match Luca's recovery ride, or half a recovery ride.

"No, today was a very great pleasure. We both went a good pace and saw something that belongs in museums. For sale in the middle of a parking lot. No one from my team ever stopped to look. They laugh when I say 'Let's stop.' That makes you better than all Team Antano-Clark in this important way."

But not faster.

Except—Christopher was the one Luca came to celebrate with, the one he spent free time with, the one he held behind closed doors. Maybe strategy did outweigh speed.

"Okay, I believe you." Christopher leaned forward for a kiss and then toppled backward with an exaggerated *oof.* "Just make sure you go faster than Rolf."

Luca gave him an odd look on his way to the door. "Always."

CHAPTER 8

THEY'D WORN each other out last night, but not enough to sleep, and started talking about what made a top rider—why was Contador a champ, what made Pantani tick. A brilliant rider who'd retired fifteen years earlier came up in the conversation. "What exactly were people getting on Big Mig about, 'not showing the emotions of a champion'?" Christopher wanted to know.

Luca had exploded. "The emotions of a champion! The champion races! Emotions are for private life, not the race! For public, confidence, appreciation for team, humility."

"Humility?" He decided to poke a bit. "Why shouldn't the champion strut a little?"

"Champion did not do everything alone!"

"What about the party-hard guys who win forty stages of the big tours?"

"Image." Luca smiled: had he hung out with the party-hard guy, or was he not a big enough fish in other seasons? "And maybe everyone expects party man to blow up in the mountains. Big racer, not champion, just scares other guys who live quiet and still can't catch party man in sprint. But they finish the stage races, party man doesn't, can't be GC."

"But the party man has a good time and gets the palmarès," Christopher argued. Stage wins counted as well as any other race.

"His team not so happy, they don't have good time, they work hard. True champion should be humble," Luca pronounced with great finality.

"Can I quote you on that?" Christopher indulged a small dream of an article on Luca's opinion, sometime after a notable win. "My headline will be 'Champions need humility'." He added air quotes with bent fingers.

"Okay, you write that," Luca agreed with a voice that sounded far away. "Also luck. Luck is small difference between fast racer who doesn't finish and man on podium. Goodwill of team can make that luck. Team works hard, but makes better luck sometimes. For GC they like."

Christopher couldn't leave this well enough alone, though he'd already heard Luca's philosophy. "And you really think they won't like you if they know you're gay."

"Not taking chance, Christopher!" Luca jumped up from the futon to whirl around the postage-stamp of a living room. "First year as GC, no history. First year as team, no history. Sponsors hard to find, harder with bad results first year. This team must succeed, I must succeed, or I can't stay in US. Other Boulder team has good GCs and many *domestiques*—they have no place for me if I fail with Antano-Clark."

Watching Luca stomp around naked would be a lot more pleasant if they were discussing almost anything else. "There are teams that race strictly in the US." Christopher had written about several of them.

"Big step down, sorry but true. Rising sport in US, but will be years, maybe never, until same scale as what I do now. Even if US team does Tour of California or US Pro Cycling Challenge, still racing the European teams, so same problem.

"Or I go to mountain bikes. Can you see little guy like me chasing the 1.8 meter, 80 kilo guys over the too big, too many rocks and trees hill with bike on shoulder? Chasing from far, far behind. Never catch up. Wrong sport for me, Christopher. Or maybe start running, do triathlons, make living as butcher."

"Okay, okay, just asking, Luca." He rose to catch the whirlwind, and with enough kisses, they subsided into the blankets for a peaceful night.

Christopher's first thought this morning was the same exultation that had wakened him three mornings running. *He wants me to come to Europe. He wants more than these few days.*

A silky brown curl tickled his nose, the same way Luca's invitation tickled his mind. This was becoming his normal wake-up routine; he'd spooned behind Luca for eight of the last ten nights. They stayed in Christopher's microscopic basement apartment because Luca's house in the hills also contained three teammates. Sharing a dwelling made sense when they only expected to live there a part of the year, but it would have been nice to have the option of sleeping on something beside the lumpy futon.

Maybe it was too much, too fast—Luca had all but moved in—but Christopher didn't want to slow down. The warning red X on the calendar kept a small pit of ice in his stomach. All too soon, Luca would crate his bicycles for the flight to Europe. The racing season had begun. Antano-Clark could already boast a win in the early spring one-day races, though the *directeur sportif* hadn't put Luca into any early events, wanting him to spend as many days at altitude as possible. The powerhouse sleeping in his arms would take all that mountain-grown strength to Flanders in little more than a week. Christopher kissed the back of Luca's head softly, both wanting not to disturb him and hoping he'd wake for a sweet interlude to start the day.

This morning Christopher didn't want anything getting in the way of how he felt about Luca. *I could be falling in love. And damn the calendar.*

Nuzzling softly against Luca's neck, he murmured, "Good morning."

"Good morning, yes." Luca turned in his arms, and they rubbed cheeks, the rasping serving for the kisses that they wouldn't morning-breath on each other. "Good start for day, you sell many bicycles, write many words."

He had sold several high-dollar bikes this week, but Christopher had chalked it up to spring coming, not the goofy smile that seemed like a permanent fixture. "That works. My turn to do you?" His hand slipped downward, stroking Luca's side. That was the one thing they hadn't tried. Christopher had been content to let Luca direct traffic and he hadn't hinted at going that direction.

If Christopher'd said, "Let's invite the team in to watch," Luca couldn't have gone rigid any faster.

"Okay, I can play with this morning wood."

The wood in question had taken on a certain resemblance to damp pulp. Luca twisted away.

"It's okay, Luca; if you don't want that, we won't." Caresses against soft skin weren't undoing the damage to the mood. "I thought we just hadn't gotten to that, but if you don't like it, no problem." Dang, it had been days since Luca last threatened to bolt right out the door.

"I like, but…" Slowly he subsided against the futon. "I can't."

Christopher remained quiet. If he left a silence too long, Luca would fill it.

"Eighty kilometers on bicycle today."

"Gotcha." Christopher's own rides lately had been somewhat less than comfortable, even with the ointment in addition to the chamois cream. Still, there seemed to be more to the story. Luca filled the silence in a different way, rolling atop Christopher, making words irrelevant.

RIDING TOGETHER had some obvious drawbacks most days, but Luca was perfectly willing to go the gym with Christopher. With a niggling suspicion that they were going on Luca's "light work-out" days, unsupervised by the coaches, Christopher was still happy to go somewhere that Luca considered "just guys" but that felt like a date.

They certainly set the machines differently. Luca went for light weights, lots of repetitions, while Christopher suspected that his heavier weights, fewer reps routine might draw some criticism if he asked for opinions. Luca hadn't inquired about goals, although he knew Christopher's riding wasn't the only reason he worked out. He enjoyed the results too—every time he gripped Christopher's deltoids or lats in moments of passion made Christopher glad for the time he'd put in on upper body work.

It had taken him only one trip to the gym to see Luca's different emphasis. No one could say Luca wasn't strong—he was, but compared to Christopher's build, his upper body looked thin, and his legs were coated in cables, not sheets of steel.

Tonight Luca came to observe Christopher on the crunch machine. "Going for the washboard look?"

He didn't want to dignify that, since his six-pack would be of six ounce cans, not liter bottles. "Core strengthening."

"Good thought, but wrong exercise." Luca observed. "Front only. Fast track to aching back on the bike."

Well, fuck him now, that's what Christopher had been trying to deal with. That and not depending on Luca as a personal trainer for everything he did. He stopped, and mopped his face with the last dry corner of his towel. "What should I be doing?" Goodbye, abs.

"Something with more back and glutes. Floor exercises help core, and also keep you from crashing when looking over shoulder. I show you." Luca headed to a machine-free section of mats. "Pushup position, try to touch foot to elbow. Look at knee." He demonstrated, getting his foot far closer to his arm than Christopher thought could be done anywhere but on a mattress. "Works back, butt, front. Maintain control, put back down." He uncoiled and repeated a few times. "Switch." His left foot went just as far as his right.

Coming from a world-class rider, this had to be good advice. Also, harder than it looked. Christopher's foot came nowhere near as close, and straightening out nearly toppled him. "Okay." He tried again, feeling pulls and stretches in unaccustomed places in his torso. "Everything's working."

"Exactly. Machines not always best for what you need." Luca watched another attempt on this nameless exercise.

Christopher switched sides and had to splay his arms farther apart to keep from tumbling. A few passers-by watched curiously and went on to their own routines. "So this is the key to staying upright and pain-free."

"Part of it." Luca nodded. "Bands are good. Especially for adductors. You want strength without bulk there. Else bike saddle is very uncomfortable."

"No kidding." Christopher sold a lot of replacement seats to riders overburdened with inner thigh muscles. "Some brands are thinner than others." He lifted his foot again, though it came nowhere near his elbow. Luca had made it look easy, but he was very flexible, something Christopher had already determined privately.

"Pressure points not always the same, have to swap out on different stages. But always with cut-out, distributes pressure better."

"Really." Maybe it was time for an article on a bike component that had a lot more visibility than the glove linings Christopher was still collecting data on. *CycloWorld* had mentioned.... Maybe if he impressed them enough, he'd have a shot at some of the race articles, although Ryder Martin usually covered the American road races. And he had no chance to take any of the European coverage away from Dave Pauwels, who'd written every Classics article for the last three years. Christopher had to start somewhere, and a pro with an opinion was talking to him. "Any you like especially well?" Christopher folded to sitting, fanned by his waving journo's ears.

"Jindo XRR have right width for me. Rolf likes Cassowary HTs." His snort might mean he didn't like Cassowary saddles, or that he didn't like Rolf again today.

"You aren't riding a Jindo, though." Christopher hadn't seen the distinctive metal kanji character Jindo riveted to the back lip.

"Smooth leather, too slippery. K-Aeros have right shape and little holes in leather. I stay on better, even sweaty," Luca explained.

Diverted by the thought of Luca's sweaty butt, Christopher still remembered to ask, "Can I quote you on that?"

"You sell some saddles, okay." Luca was on his feet in one imperceptible move. The man was part lightning bolt. "I go use the glute machine, need some reps."

Maybe he'd sell a lot of saddles. Christopher filed away his tidbits and tried the proto-pretzel core move again. And when they got home, he'd have Luca run naked checks for improvements in his balance and flexibility.

Christopher pulled a couple of cans of chili off his kitchen shelf. "My treat." The cans went into the pockets of the heavy jacket on the arm of the futon. "The sports expo will be fun." That and he could afford the price of entry—donations to a food bank were enough to get in. Luca tended to grab the tab anywhere they went, but Christopher had his pride.

"A theater is dark; we could hold hands." Luca slipped his hand up the curve of Christopher's shoulder. "Let's see a movie."

"True," Christopher admitted, "but we saw a movie the other night, and all we do is look at the screen; we aren't really doing anything together." They hadn't held hands, though their thighs had pressed together for an hour and a half of sheer torment. Christopher's focus hadn't included the screen. "Besides, do you even remember the main character's name?"

"Sports expo is public; people know us," Luca objected. His other hand found its way around Christopher's waist.

"Some of them might recognize you; there might be people who know me, but if we're looking at snowboards and inline skates, we're just a couple of guys doing guy stuff. My friends aren't jerks." Christopher let himself be drawn into the kiss. "Everybody goes."

"So I fear."

"It'll be more fun than sitting in the dark with boners we can't touch." If doing something as neutral as the sports expo was going to be a problem, what was it going to be like if he actually took Luca up on his offer to come to France during the racing season? Were they going to hide in some villa where hounds would eat trespassing photographers?

"We stay here and touch boners?" Thrusting his hips against Christopher let Luca make a pretty persuasive argument. Okay, the hounds might not be such a bad idea.

"And then we go to the sports expo." Christopher backed Luca up the two steps to the futon, whose shape shifting tendencies had been curbed, not by the moon, but by never pushing it to the couch position. Luca fell backward, bringing Christopher down too, for some wild tonguing and slow thrusting. "Wild man," Christopher panted, sliding down until he knelt on the floor between Luca's knees. Without a glance to the draperies, which stayed closed these days, he undid Luca's zipper, releasing the curved, uncut cock that he was becoming so familiar with. Slipping the skin back, he drew his tongue over the head, tasting salt droplets. With Luca's hand in his hair, he set to licking and sucking, enjoying the little gasps and groans. One day he'd get Luca to cut loose and yell, someplace he felt really private. The footsteps from the upstairs neighbor kept Luca quiet, but didn't keep him from climaxing. With his cheek against the soft hairs on Luca's belly, he held his softening prize on his mouth just a moment longer, letting Luca come away from his post-climax high. The sudden raspberry Christopher blew into Luca's navel made him bounce.

"Don't go to sleep on me just yet," Christopher warned.

"Now you?"

"Later. It'll give you time to recover and both of us something to look forward to." He hauled Luca to his feet. "Let's go."

Once he got Luca past the big glass double doors at the arena, the displays stole the last bit of reticence. "Have you ever tried this?" Luca wanted to know, ratcheting the gears on a bit of hardware at a rock climbing booth.

"A little. That's called a friend, and they come in different sizes, for different size cracks." Christopher wouldn't allow himself to snicker about jamming friends into small tight places. "Do you want to try the climbing wall?"

"Maybe something in my contract about not doing such things," Luca murmured, but he got in line anyway. The broad grin while unbuckling the harness after a trip up and down the artificial wall made Christopher wonder what else Luca had missed out on because of his racing.

A boat dealer's display took up the center of the enormous arena's floor. Bright orange kayaks danced across the surface of a pool twenty-five yards across. Squealing children and laughing adults paddled around, occasionally flicking water at each other.

"Do you want to try?" Christopher had learned the basics in a fully aproned kayak—these were open plastic shells, toys really, meant for calm shallows. Anyone who rolled would spill out. In the hip deep water, the worst they would get was wet.

"Looks fun!" Luca peeled off a few dollars and collected a double-ended paddle for each of them.

Once in their orange watercraft, Christopher feathered out into the middle of the pool, intending to scoot to the far end. Luca, meanwhile, was struggling with the laws of physics which made it much easier to go in circles than in lines. His prow swung out; clipped by a passing craft, he got turned the other way.

"Dip the paddle evenly on each side, and undercorrect, because the kayak keeps moving." Christopher paddled backwards, pacing Luca, who threw him a crusty glance before devoting his attentions to arriving at the far side of the pool.

Luca muttered something under his breath when he caught a crab, his paddle barely grazing the surface of the water. The splash soaked a bystander who really should have been expecting such things.

"Didn't quite hear that!" Christopher shot forward, away from Luca's much louder "Smartass!" To the end and back again, to find that Luca had worked out how to do a U-turn and stay in a more or less straight line. Evading a teenager intent on playing bumper-boats with everyone on the water, he swung around behind Luca, and they paddled together for a few strokes before they ran out of pool.

Twenty minutes later they'd exhausted the possibilities of the toy craft on a crowded artificial pond, surrendering their kayaks. "The batting cage is over there, we could try that?" Christopher suggested but was arrested by the sound of his name.

"Hey, Christopher!" came from the line that waited for a turn on the water.

"Hey, Stu!" Christopher thought guiltily that he should have called to set up a ride for the weekend; there was no snow in the forecast. Luca stopped next to him, but with about four inches more personal space than he'd needed most of tonight. "Seen anything here you can't live without?"

"Only my darling." Stu pulled a pretty young woman closer to him, planting a smacker on her temple. "But maybe you can get the shop to cut me a deal on that set of Shimano brakes I've been eyeing?"

"Ugh, I can try." Christopher flinched. "I didn't even want to go by the booth: I spent all day discussing the merits of aluminum versus carbon fiber handlebars. Haven't even looked around until now. Uh, Stu, Liz, this is my friend Luca."

Stu put out his hand. "So you're Christopher's new squeeze?"

Maybe the slang eluded Luca. "Friend, Stu," Christopher hissed.

Luca froze with his hand halfway out. Guess not.

"Friend, right." Stu looked a little too amused. "I'd say any friend of Christopher's is a friend of mine, but I don't want to get *that* friendly." He shrugged and dropped his hand.

"Enough, Stu!" The people passing around them cast sideways glances, though at Christopher's mounting fury, Luca's bulging eyes, or Liz's elbow jabbing into Stu's side he couldn't say.

"See, bad idea, Christopher." Luca practically vibrated in place. "Liz, forgive me." He lifted one hand in a farewell. "Fuck you, Stu." Then he was gone.

"You ass!" Christopher wanted to smack the bewilderment off Stu's face, but instead of lashing out, he turned, craning to find Luca, but he was lost in the crowd, maybe long gone with a head start to wherever he'd go to lick his wounds. Christopher wondered if he'd have to patrol every street in Boulder to find Luca, to apologize, or if he'd go back to the apartment, or worse, to the shared house in the hills that Christopher had never entered.

He barely heard Stu's panicky, "What did I say?" as he left.

LUCA HADN'T gone back to the apartment, and why would he? They hadn't quite gotten to the key stage. Three weeks were still only three weeks, no matter how much of it they'd spent together. Putting his bike on the wall rack in the living room, Christopher wondered wearily if he could coax Luca back sometime before Antano-Clark left for Europe. He tried Luca's cell, going straight to voice mail, and left only the briefest message. "I'm sorry. Call me."

Stu got shunted to voice mail once Christopher saw the number. He was no more prepared to deal with Stu than Luca was prepared to deal with him. Damn it! He'd *told* Stu to treat them just like friends. Trouble was, Stu thought the definition of friendship included snooping into Christopher's sex life. Maybe he should have tried saying, "This is a closet," and slamming Stu's face into the door six or eight times, just to get his attention.

The phone rang again about an hour later, making Christopher's heart jump, then stop.

"Luca, I'm sorry." Get it out before, instead of, hello.

"That was not-asshole friend?"

"I thought so. I was wrong." Christopher waited—what would Luca say?

"We don't see each other tomorrow night."

"You're getting even with me for what he did." He was only too aware that Luca would be leaving for Belgium soon. None of what happened tonight boded well for what would happen if Luca still wanted him to come to Europe. Christopher resigned himself to seeing very little of any foreign country where paparazzi recognized cyclists.

A deep sigh blew into his ear. "No, tomorrow night is dinner for team. I need to be there."

Christopher heard what Luca didn't say. A dinner for the team, the wives, and the girlfriends. "Okay, your dirty secret will find something else to do tomorrow."

"I tell you at beginning what I have to do, and why. I take big chance with you! You say you understand, and then you say this!" Luca exploded.

"It's still true, Luca," Christopher barked back. "It sounds ugly, it is ugly, but it's still true. And I'm sorry for it and I'm sorry you feel it's necessary, but it sucks to be the man you have to hide." He softened his voice, aware he was jeopardizing making his point. "I'm not telling you to do it differently. I'm just telling you what it feels like from this side."

"I make you feel bad; I'm supposed to stop that, right? Be good boyfriend? Do what I can't do?"

"You left without me tonight, and I wasn't the one who caused the problem." *Apologize for that, and I can deal with the rest. Somehow.*

"*Your friend* did."

"I know. And I'm sorry."

"So am I. But you also know three people can keep secret if two are dead."

"I can keep your secret, Luca." Letting go of the handful of hair he'd grabbed out of sheer frustration, Christopher knew he could only promise fully on his own behalf, and Stu had already figured out too much. "I'll talk to Stu. He thinks it's entertaining that I'm gay, that's half the problem. I'll make sure he understands that he screwed up and not to say anything else."

"Thank you." A pause, and then "*Ciao,* Christopher."

Somehow, that sounded permanent.

CHAPTER 9

TRYING NOT to think about Luca having dinner with twenty-five men who weren't him, Christopher typed another few words comparing the padding inside riding gloves. His phone had rung, but one number he didn't recognize and the other was Stu. He hit the ignore key and returned to writing his article, as if someone would really base a purchase on the stats he'd collected. *Cyclo World* was at least pleased with his efforts. They'd like the saddle story even better; he'd include quotes.

Two hours later, he shut the laptop and fell onto the futon. He dragged the comforter over his shoulders, wondering if he'd ever share the lumpy mattress with Luca again.

The morning he awoke to was clear, nippy, and not a day he needed to work. Did he dare call Luca? He paused, his finger poised over the icon he'd ganked off the internet, picturing a triumphant Luca at the finish line in Nice a year earlier. Christopher had seen him look nearly that exultant in bed only a few days ago, and now, it was as if they'd never been together. He took his finger away after a look at the clock. If Luca would talk to him at all, it wouldn't be mid-morning when he'd have ten to twenty-five eavesdroppers around.

Pulling on double leggings and a windproof jacket, Christopher would do the one thing that would let him feel connected to Luca—he'd ride. With a hat under his helmet and toe warmers over his shoes, he'd take to the roads north of town. Maybe he'd see the team.

The whir of his chain kept him company, the wind in his face kept him focused, and the traffic zipping past kept his adrenaline up. A gray SUV passed closely enough to make him wobble in its draft, but the other vehicles gave him wider berth. Traffic would nearly disappear on the lonely roads away from the city; only other cyclists would pass him. He'd been doing more passing than getting passed these days.

Someone on a bike was probably trying to get around him. Christopher could hear the *zzz* of wheels on road, but no one called out, "Coming up on the left." If the guy wanted to draft, he could. For a while. Damned if he was going to pull someone all the way out to Hygiene—if the guy wanted a free ride he could pay for it by leading a while. Stu did. Stu had always been good about trading. And bad about minding his own business. Asshole. Way too interested in Christopher's social life. Accepting but snoopy. Jerk. Maybe calling him "bi-curious" would back him off.

By the time Christopher exercised his anger at Stu and the unknown drafter, who was doing a pretty good job of staying with him, he'd gone miles, up and down a steep but short hill. Time to get off Highway 36 onto a smaller road, a good opportunity for a drink.

"Ever going to talk to me again?" Stu pulled up beside Christopher.

"Didn't know it was you or I'd have gone faster." He could have; his legs weren't burning from the climb.

"I really pissed you off, didn't I?"

"You may have fucked things up with Luca and me, so yeah."

"I was trying to be friendly, Chris." Stu used the opportunity to drink too.

"I didn't tell you about going to dinner the other night because I didn't know if Luca minded you knowing, and it turned out he really, really minds. I think a closet is damned claustrophobic but that's where he is until *he* decides, not until someone like you shouts his business to the world. And he's not talking to me either." The sudden prickle of tears had to be from the foul exhaust of a passing truck, or the wind. No traffic passed, but Christopher didn't move.

"I'm sorry. I didn't even think about that." Stu sounded really contrite.

"I know you didn't. You kiss your girlfriend in public and no one blinks, but he and I can't even stand close together."

"Why not?"

Stu's not an idiot, he's just never had to think about shit like this. "He's not out, Stu. He's scared that getting outed will ruin his racing career, and what if he's right?"

"You're out, and it's no big deal."

"That's because we live in the 'People's Republic of Boulder' where everyone's minds are so open their brains fall out. Maybe most of the other cyclists don't care, but if his team doesn't support him enough, he doesn't win, or if someone on another team objects strenuously, it could be trouble. You know what sort of dirty tricks get played in a peloton." He flashed on the image of an elbow thrown at Luca halfway up the Alp d'Huez, next to a long drop and no guard rail, and his stomach dropped exactly that far.

"Yeah. That's some heavy shit. I'll keep my pie-hole shut."

"Too late now." Christopher stuck his empty water bottle back into its rack. "You can drag me along for a while."

"Sure, sure, now that it's flat." Stu pulled out, heading eastbound.

Must be nice to never have to worry. Christopher didn't live with Luca's kind of fear, not now, anyway. He spent another couple of miles regretting having lashed out at Luca. He'd apologize first chance he got. If he got another chance.

The white-faced black cattle in the field to the right didn't even look up at their passage, though Christopher marveled at the width they were attaining. Another month or two and he'd have calves to watch on this route. The thrum of an engine behind him dragged his attention back to the road—he and Stu both hugged the shoulder more tightly.

The world went kaleidoscope.

Blue below, brown above, white blurring by. Screeching.

Pain.

The world stopped turning—dozens of sharp teeth bit him. Fangs held him upside down, chewing his legs, his back.

Shouting; words he didn't understand. His name. Turquoise and black men rushing, upside down.

His name!

"Luca?"

"We get you, Christopher—don't move!"

Hands on his legs, lifting, making the teeth let go, making the pain dance on skin suddenly wet. Christopher lay flat on the ground, panting through clenched teeth, wondering what the hell happened to him and—

"Stu!" He tried to sit up. Luca pushed him back down and pressed his jacket against Christopher's thigh.

"Teammates looking after him, Christopher. Stay here." Another rider joined them, pushing his jersey against Christopher's calves.

"I have to see!" He struggled to sitting, but strong hands pinned him. Red stained through turquoise fabric. If he bled—then Stu—what? Was he bleeding? Had he broken a bone? Bones? "I have to—"

"Stay, Christopher, stay. You're hurt, you can't help him." Luca pressed harder on his thigh, jamming a sleeve against his bloody hip.

"The ambulance should be here in a few minutes, Luca." Another turquoise and black figure approached. "Rolf and the others caught the car."

Car? Stu? Ambula—? "Wha' happened?" Christopher craned to see. A knot of cyclists moved uneasily on the road ahead of the team car, and much farther down, half a dozen figures on bikes surrounded a white car. Sirens sounded in the far distance, growing closer.

"Car went around peloton, came back to lane too soon. Hit you into fence. Hit Stu. Shh, Christopher, they do what they can for him."

Oh man, if he wasn't moving, they probably thought he had a neck injury, please God, don't let him have a neck injury…Or a back injury… Fucking car, must have been a helluva breakaway to catch it. Rolf caught a fucking car? But, that car had—what had it done? Metal against flesh, steel stronger than bone…. His legs, his back—jelly and matchstick man against speeding iron? He fought again to rise. "Luca… Gotta see Stu…"

He didn't see what signal passed between Luca and the other rider—different hands took over the pressure on his wounds. Luca shuffled on his knees to hold Christopher to his chest, head cradled against the team logo that covered his heart. "No, Christopher, you can do nothing for him, you don't want to see… Please believe me… You don't want to see…" The catch in Luca's voice arrested him, pausing him in his struggle to get to his feet. "You must be okay, stay here…"

The sirens screamed their arrival, going silent but with lights still flashing; the paramedics clattered around, offloading equipment from two ambulances. The cyclists yielded their places to the paramedics, who waved bright lights in his eyes. "Stu, how's Stu?" he demanded.

"The other paramedics have him," was the only reply, followed by inane questions about "how many fingers" and could Christopher wiggle his toes.

"Let go, sir," one told Luca, who didn't yield. "Let go! We have to assess him; he may have broken bones and he needs stitches." Luca did release him, but hovered over them all.

In the end, they strapped Christopher to the backboard, only lifting him to the gurney after slapping Luca away like a mosquito. "No, you can't ride with him, sir; back away. Back away *now.*" A cop, huge in blue, pulled Luca aside.

"Later, Luca," Christopher croaked. "Tell them what happened."

He could see Stu's form on the other gurney, a blanket over him, not moving when he was loaded into to the other ambulance. *Please not a back injury, not Stu, not a man who lives on his bike…* The doors slammed shut; the vehicle swung around into the westbound lane. From inside the ambulance the siren wasn't as loud as he'd imagined. Through the tiny rear windows he could see the other ambulance turn to follow.

No lights. No sirens.

Chapter 10

The emergency room was a blur: hurry up and wait, X-rays, stitches, a blood draw he didn't understand after some garble about "Any reason we should double glove for blood contact, sir?" An interview by a cop who couldn't believe that Christopher had nothing to add to the team's assessment of the collision.

"I was upside down in barb wire. No, I didn't see," he explained wearily for the third time. Shouldn't the tatters of spandex be a clue? And where they'd been cut away to allow the doctors access to his shredded skin?

No one would tell him a thing about Stu. "Where can we reach his parents? Or his other family?" said more than they intended. He had to hear the words—he had to see. He couldn't believe until he'd seen for himself, and even then, Stu was a prankster. He could have set this up.... Yeah, right. But—

"I know, but I'm not telling you until I see him, damn it. I know he's dead," finally bought him a few moments alone with his friend. What was left of Stu lay immobile under a white sheet, his helmet still askew on his head.

"I'm sorry," Christopher whispered. "I'm so sorry." What a half-assed accord they'd come to—had they made up or were they still working on it when the car struck them? They'd fixed their friendship—hadn't they? Still there'd been so much they needed to talk about. Christopher stroked Stu's face. Any other time he'd punch Stu's arm, but now? *Get up, get up, the joke's gone old...* But Stu didn't open his eyes and yell *Gotcha!*

Seventy-two stitches in his legs and back were going to be a bitch, starting with the ride home. The few bucks in his pocket wouldn't pay a cab from Longmont to Boulder, and the bus would be a special brand of hell. His mother wept, fretted, and begged to drive him home, but since she was in California, he'd find another way. "I'm not hurt that bad, Mom," he insisted, not saying a thing about his heart, and refused firmly when she'd planned to fly out and take care of him.

God knew where his bike was—Christopher didn't. Intensely grateful to the woman from Victims' Assistance who drove him home, he fumbled open his door and fell through.

The futon was empty, though he'd dared to hope Luca would spring up to embrace him. But no. He stumbled to lie flat upon it, the tears coming now, for Stu, for all the lost hope, for all the things he'd never learn, never do. A few were for himself, for being torn and tattered. A few more, for not having Luca there to cry on.

The first knocks barely cut through Christopher's fog. but the next set was much louder and demanded attention. Attention he wasn't willing to give.

"Christopher! Please, let me in!" The familiar voice and the frantic pounding prodded Christopher to drag himself upright enough to hobble to the door. He yanked it open to admit the one person he was willing to see right now.

"Christopher, oh, Chris…" Luca vaulted through, white plastic bags dangling from his arms, batting against damaged skin. Christopher clutched him, ignoring the thuds of the bags in his relief that Luca was there. "I came as soon as I could. I'm so sorry."

So sorry. Words that Christopher expected to hear many times, words both true and useless. "Oh, God, Luca, I can't believe…"

"I'm so sorry," Luca repeated, and his shoulders were shaking too. "Poor Stu. And you. Where are you…" He pulled back surveying the ripped jersey that Christopher hadn't the strength to change, the missing leggings replaced by traceries of black stitching over livid gashes, covered by snowy bandages that pretended nothing was wrong. His white socks were stained with blood at the ankles. "Did I hurt you?"

Some. But it didn't matter. Wounds on his back and hip were nothing—he needed to be touched. "Don't worry about it." Hurting meant he was alive. Stu wasn't. Stu was beyond pain. *Stu….*

"Spoken like a cyclist." Luca returned to clutch him, more slowly but no less fervently. "But you will not ride again tomorrow or for many days, you aren't some stupid pro who can't stop to heal."

"No." It might be a lifetime before Christopher got back on a bike. The cost was too great. The days to come would be filled with too much sorrow. He hadn't called Liz yet, or Stu's parents. Luca held him, and that was all that kept him from falling.

"I tried to call." Luca spoke into the side of Christopher's head. "It rang but you didn't answer. I worried."

"I didn't hear anything." With his less damaged arm, he groped into the rear pocket of his jersey. "Great." The phone's glass face was a spiderweb of cracks, and chips protruded. "I need to call…." To call people who would never be the same for what happened today. He was the last person to talk to Stu, to hear his voice. They would have heard the news from the police, but they had to hear firsthand from him. They had to have the opportunity to ask questions, or to hate him for living when Stu didn't.

"Use mine. But not yet. We clean you up first. Feed you." Luca took the ruined unit from his hand. "Makes it possible."

Yeah. Possible. It would never be easy. Christopher let Luca lead him to the bathroom and strip him of his wounded clothing. He sat, head bowed, on the edge of the tub while Luca dabbed and scrubbed, rinsing the washcloth in a swirl of pink. He barely helped Luca dress him in a T-shirt and the same loose shorts that Luca had worn their first night together.

The bags contained savory tidbits from the Italian restaurant, or nothing that wouldn't taste like ashes right now. Christopher drank the broth only because Luca insisted he have something—"You're shocked and need fluids and some food." Any noodle that slid down without chewing got swallowed; the other lumps in the soup were too much to cope with. He pushed the cup away before Luca was ready to let him.

"No more, please." He folded over his lover's shoulder, dry of tears but too worn for anything else. "I—" He had to call others who'd be as devastated as he, and he couldn't even state the need.

"How can I help you?" Luca murmured.

"Dial." He whispered the number and took the buzzing phone from Luca's hand. Holding tight to Luca, Christopher whispered the useless words. "Liz? I'm so sorry…"

Luca brought more tissues while Christopher dug for the Fallons' number, and wiped his cheeks. "How am I going to tell them…?" The words stoppered his throat. "When I can't believe… How can Stu be gone?" But Stu hadn't jumped up spitting ketchup, delighted to have scared the crap out of everyone. Laughing… Stu wouldn't laugh again, he'd never tell anyone's secrets.

"I will be your strength."

Christopher felt Luca's lips at his temple, Luca's arms around his shoulders. With shaking fingers, Christopher dropped a slip of paper into Luca's lap.

Luca stopped before hitting the last digit. "This is hard, but you can do it, Christopher. Bearer of burdens." He touched the last number. "I am here with you."

"Mr. Fallon," Christopher choked out. "I'm so sorry…" He answered questions as well as he could, accepting regrets for his own injuries. He'd gotten off so lightly when Stu… No wonder Mrs. Fallon couldn't bear to talk to him, even though he asked.

"I almost didn't answer," Stu's father told him. "I didn't recognize the caller ID."

That wouldn't have gotten Christopher off the hook, but only made more attempts necessary. "My phone got smashed. I'm using Luca's; he's one of the team that caught the driver."

"Thank him for us." Mr. Fallon sounded a thousand years old. "We'll let you know about the funeral."

Funeral. He hadn't even considered Stu would need… The now-silent phone slipped from his grip, sliding between his legs. "I've never buried a friend."

"I have. It's hard, but we do it." Luca gathered Christopher more closely. "Were you friends again, before…?"

Before the unspeakable happened. "Yeah. We talked. He didn't understand before…." Christopher ran through their conversation. "He said he was sorry. He wasn't trying to drive a wedge between us, or even give you a hard time. He was just being… Stu." And he would never be Stu again. "But he was sorry."

"He must have been a good man or you wouldn't have been his friend." Luca leaned back into a stack of pillows, pulling Christopher down against him. "I'm sorry we didn't become friends too."

"Sometimes he was a jerk, but he was a good guy." The best, most of the time. Until total jerkhood busted out, and it didn't last. Yeah, Stu was a good guy, and now Christopher would have to watch him be lowered into the ground. Only Luca's strong arms around him kept Christopher from shaking right off the bed. He clutched tightly, to warmth, to life, to Luca, who was his one defense against the universe right now.

Luca held him while his teeth chattered from the chill of death that had taken Stu and breathed down Christopher's neck today. That could have been him in the silent ambulance, it could have been both of them, and no one but Luca to tell the world what had happened. The nearness of it swelled in his throat, bursting out with a sob that burned his gullet.

And Stu was gone…

Christopher woke in a wet, snotty mess, worn from weeping and not rested for the sleep that had beaten him over the head. Luca lay under him, exactly as they'd lain down earlier. "You're still here." Had the pain pills fogged Christopher into forgetting the days?

Luca jumped and curled around Christopher. "Yes, still here."

"I thought you had a team dinner tonight." But Luca was still here….

"Yes." But he didn't try to get up; he moved nothing but his thumb against Christopher's arm.

"Shouldn't you be there?"

"This is more important." He leaned his cheek against Christopher's head. "You are more important."

I am? He dared not question it.

Luca did get up, but only to strip off his clothing and lie back on the bed, under the covers this time. He snuggled against Christopher's back, careful not to jostle the stitched places, and wrapped his arm over Christopher's chest.

Christopher clenched his fingers into Luca's. "I'm glad you're here." *I'm glad you're alive.*

"I stay with you." His brush of lips over Christopher's nape suggested Luca wasn't going anywhere.

Luca's breath eventually went even with sleep. Christopher stared into the darkness.

CHAPTER 11

LUCA'S PHONE sang them awake in the morning; Luca spoke in Italian, punctuated with words Christopher understood, like "Broadway" and "Euclid Boulevard". "My soigneur comes with your bicycle. Our mechanics repaired it, Paolo declares it fine."

"Thanks." *I think.* The question of renewing his racing license was well and truly answered. No way was Christopher obligating himself to racing when that meant training alone. If he could push himself back on the roads at all. "The team car collected it after…?"

Luca settled Christopher on his shoulder, cupping the back of his head. "Yes. The police took Stu's. They wanted yours but we convinced them pictures were enough."

"Thanks." Christopher leaned more heavily against Luca. "How do you ride again after something like this?" He couldn't say the words: *after you lose a comrade.*

"Christopher—" Luca's hand made a slow trail through his hair. "We know the sport is dangerous. With everything from road rash to broken bones, injury rate is one hundred percent. We get hurt riding. We know it happens, that something will happen to us. And yet the need to ride stays. Goes away for a while, comes back. Maybe not at pro level. Maybe only for fun, but if fun is long descent at sixty kilometers per hour…" He sighed. "Then might as well stay pro."

"I'm not talking about me." Christopher flattened his hand against Luca's side.

"I know. But no one can say what will happen. Maybe lightning strikes. Maybe get illness. Maybe walk in front of bus. Maybe grow old and never wake up. Lots of maybes. But we name our races for our fallen, we honor them by riding. We honor them by not giving up. When it's right for you to ride again, you will." Luca glanced at his watch. "You will know when. And I want clothes on before Paolo gets here."

Luca slid out of bed with a brushing kiss to Christopher's head. Of course he'd want to be dressed before the arrival of the one representative of the outside world allowed to join them here. Christopher heaved himself to his feet and made up the futon, clicking it to couch position before Luca returned from the bathroom. His crooked smile had to mean *Thank you.*

The knock at the door interrupted their coffee: Luca opened it to reveal a middle-aged man, sun weathered and thin. Was this what old cyclists did? Held bicycles and changes of clothing for the young champions? Accepting the bag and motioning him in, Luca stepped out of the way of the bike Paolo wheeled through the door.

"We are sorry for your friend," Paolo told Christopher. "And for your injuries."

"Let Paolo examine your stitches, Christopher. He does excellent wound care." Luca disappeared into the bathroom with the bag of clothing, while Christopher lay face down on the futon to be tended by the soigneur with his tube of ointment. His hands were gentle, but they weren't Luca's.

"Don't stress the stitches," Paolo pronounced. "Stay off the bike, advice I always give and no one follows." He aimed a sourly affectionate look at Luca, who reappeared in cycling gear and his street shoes.

"There is always stage or race to overshadow good advice." Luca knelt to examine the bicycle. "What did the mechs do?"

"New brakes: a line broke and the handle tore off, and new grip tape. Adjusted the derailleurs: it shifts very smoothly now." Paolo spoke proudly.

"Thank you." Christopher spoke faintly—the team mechanics could do wonders.

"Which brakes?" Luca squeezed the handle experimentally.

Any of the big manufacturers might have sent boxes of components to the team. "From the bike Poldi crashed last week."

That didn't seem like much of an endorsement to Christopher. Luca clarified, "He hit a rock, cracked the fork. We're waiting for a replacement, stealing components while we wait."

"Did Poldi get cracked too?" Cracking the fork took a serious hit, and the wheel would be a goner.

"Road rash and bruises, and he's waiting for us to ride," Paolo said. "With the rest of the team."

That was Luca's cue to stop being a human and turn back into a cycling machine. "Wait for me in the car; I will be a moment only."

Paolo slipped out the door, leaving the two of them alone. Luca held out a hand to heave Christopher to his feet. "I'm sorry to leave, but I'll be back tonight. Sleep as much as you can, eat something. I'll text you when we get back from the ride. We have weights and race tapes today, and I expect to spend some time with the directeur sportif about last night, but I will be here later. If you want company."

Wrapped in his lover's arms, Christopher couldn't imagine not wanting Luca's company. "I'll be waiting."

With a last kiss, Luca broke the embrace and opened the door. Christopher watched him march to the turquoise and black team car with three bicycles on the roof rack. Paolo waited at the wheel.

There'd be some sick-making hours to wait until Luca texted. If he texted. Fear would be Christopher's new companion every time Luca headed out.

FOR THREE days running, Christopher received cheery texts of "Good ride!" or "Crosswinds above Jamestown but fine," and had managed what little sleep he could get in Luca's arms. The "double glove" comment at the ER came clear when an envelope with test results he hadn't requested came. He left it out where Luca could see, and next day found a similar sheet with it. Luca had been tested for everything under the sun, including a few diseases found in the Amazon Basin more than American bedrooms. He'd shrugged it off. "They offer me contract, they expect me to be healthy."

Guess that took care of the condom issue, if they ever actually got frisky again.

The red X on the calendar loomed, marking the day the team headed for Belgium. Christopher spent the days writing or at work, his boss's good will not extending to sick days for anyone not actively bleeding. Christopher had to strong-arm Brendan about funeral policy.

"I'm going." That and a significant look at the newspaper offices directly across the street brought a grudging agreement.

In his one suit, last worn for graduation, and a tie to choke him, Christopher headed to his sad errand. Luca had inquired the details but made no promises. *He has his own bosses to answer to.*

The service would be simple and graveside: Stu's father had asked Christopher to be a pall bearer. *The last thing I can do for Stu.* So different from letting him draft behind on a bike. Now Christopher could only gaze at the large portrait of Stu on the easel, surrounded by flowers, too bright against the still-brown winter grasses. His parents had sent a spray of blooming somethings. The scents mixed with the odor of newly turned earth.

People gathered around the open grave in murmurs and tears. Christopher kissed Mrs. Fallon's cheek and let Mr. Fallon pull him into a rough embrace. Liz's fingers were vices on his arm—he wouldn't be able to feel anything from the elbow down, but she needed the support and the pain would keep him from breaking down.

One last group of mourners appeared from a turquoise and black vehicle at the end of the line of cars. Five men in dark suits approached. Luca, Rolf, three more whose names weren't surfacing, all joined the group. Liz accepted their condolences quietly and with a sharp look at Luca, she retreated to clutch Mrs. Fallon's hand.

"Thank you," Christopher whispered. Luca was here. The others got polite words, even Rolf, who said little and betrayed nothing with his face.

"Christopher." Mr. Fallon's voice came from behind him, and a hand rested on his shoulder. "It's time." Christopher turned to see the hearse pulling up. Stu's last ride. "We need a sixth. Joel couldn't get here."

"I will do it, please," Luca spoke up.

"This is Luca from the team." That offer needed some explanation, but Mr. Fallon was already nodding his thanks.

The journey from the hearse to the gravesite was the longest Christopher had ever taken, his burden the heaviest he'd ever carried. Many hands did not make light work; they only made the task possible. Knowing Luca marched behind him, helping to support Stu, kept Christopher from stumbling. He had to do this, and he couldn't do it alone. But he wasn't alone. They laid the casket on the bier and stepped back into the group.

Christopher could only gaze brokenly on the well-polished casket that would be lowered into the earth. How long Rolf had had his hand slipped into the crook of Christopher's arm he couldn't say, nor how long Luca had been holding his hand. The other three cyclists bunched behind them, their presence warm and close. They made a peloton for him; they sheltered him from the winds of his grief. Christopher clenched his fingers into Luca's and stayed upright.

Those who were close to Stu were invited to speak, once the minister had finished his service. Christopher managed to say his words of remembrance without breaking down, though his throat closed on his final, "Goodbye, Stu. Ride on."

"Would anyone else like to speak?" the minister inquired, and it was barely a surprise that Luca stepped forward.

"We, the Team Antano-Clark, only knew Stu at the very end of his life, but he was one of us all the same. A shrine overlooks Lake Como, *il Santuario della Madonna del Ghisallo*, the shrine of cyclists. There we remember our lost ones. *Caddero sulla strada inseguendo un sogno de Gloria. Che raggiunsero nella luce del sacraficio delle loro giovani esistenze.* We will place his name among cyclists." Luca stepped back. Christopher wove his fingers back into Luca's.

THAT NIGHT in bed, Christopher lay against Luca. "What you said at the funeral today, what did that mean?"

"I said the words on the statue at the chapel at Ghisallo," Luca told him. "It means 'They fell on the road, following a dream of glory. They reached the light in the sacrifice of their young lives.'"

"That hurts to even hear." Christopher turned his face into Luca's shoulder.

They hadn't made love since before the crash, between grieving and Christopher's wounds, which looked more like embroidery and less like carnage now. Luca had been there every night, and even now, he touched with the gentle hands of comfort, not the demands of a lover.

"It helps too," Luca assured him. "There is something larger."

Not really. Dying in a dumb accident didn't have any greater glory to it. Christopher kept that thought to himself, because to say it would doubt Luca's certainty that he was doing something good. "I'm still happier every time you text me after you ride. Then I know you're okay."

"I know. That's why I do it. I don't want you to worry about me."

"How can I help it now?" Christopher propped up on one elbow so he could look into Luca's eyes, nearly black in the dimness.

Luca cupped his cheek. "I can't stop riding."

Whoa. "I'm not asking you to. I wouldn't." Christopher jerked back at the implication. "It means too much to you. But now I'm scared for you in a way I wasn't before." A flash, a split second. A man on a bike one minute, a body in an ambulance the next. Nothing left but a bloody patch on the ground. If he closed his eyes he could see Stu, lying too still on a gurney. And in the next second, Stu wore Luca's face.

"I'm skilled. I'm careful."

Both true, but not enough. Stu'd been careful too—the car's driver had not. "You're careful as you can be, but you can't plan for everything. Didn't one rider have a career-ending crash because he hit a turtle?"

Luca snorted. "Jack still hears about that turtle."

"How do you plan for a turtle?" Or a careless driver? Or a ruthless opponent? Torn between laughing and crying, Christopher sat cross-legged in the dark.

"You don't. You plan what you can plan, avoid surprises if you can, and if you do crash, hope you and the turtle are both okay. Christopher, what happened to Stu was an accident. Not usual." Luca sat up, coming close enough for his breath to whisper across Christopher's cheek. "If all I think is how not to crash, I ride slow, and I crash sometime anyway."

"Yeah. Hundred percent accident rate." Luca lying still and pale, never to send another text, never wanting to try some new, exotic restaurant. *Road rash, think of road rash, that came from pile-ups, part of the hundred percent, and Luca would still be with me.*

"Right. Part of the sport. Christopher, feel." Luca took his hand, guiding Christopher's fingertips over roughened skin. "This was Paris-Roubaix four years ago. And here." Another place where the skin rippled, this time on Luca's shoulder. "Tour of Burgos, six years ago." Moving Christopher's hand to his outer thigh, Luca said, "Some is Tour de France from last year and some is Gent-Wevelgem three years ago. Mostly Gent-Wevelgem, *pavè* eats skin. But Christopher—" He pulled Christopher's fingertips across his lips. "I'm still here."

"Yeah, you are." *Luca is here now, with his warmth, his smile, his solidity.* Christopher turned to find Luca's mouth. They toppled in the dark, Luca going over backwards to bring Christopher on top of him. Their mouths welded together, and Christopher licked his relief at Luca's survival.

Not just alive but lively, and still missing the damaged places, Luca hugged Christopher close, wrapping him tightly with his thighs. More embrace than offer—Christopher wouldn't try to enter. Stiffening rapidly, he thrust instead against Luca's groin, meeting him push for push. No worry, no thinking, just here, now, kissing, feeling touching. High wattage no matter how they used it—Luca ground against Christopher.

Mouth to mouth, heat to heat, desperately seeking… Frotting madly against Luca, Christopher bathed in the vitality that came off Luca in waves, splashing against his fear, dissolving his terror that Luca, too, would be taken by the road. The big vessels in Luca's neck thrummed with life beneath Christopher's tongue.

In their bucking, Christopher slid down Luca's body. His cock poked against Luca's belly and was suddenly free, scraping against Luca's ballsack and under, along his taint. Oh for some lube just then, if Luca would allow him in…

Nope. Even the possibility brought his lover to a halt. Luca froze mid-kiss, mid-thrust. "No, Christopher—"

"No, not if you don't want that, of course not." But damn, damn, damn, damn. Better roll over some other way. Christopher slid down farther, removing even the hint of penetration. Sucking Luca's cock into his mouth, he teased away Luca's budding panic with his tongue. Rigid at first, but relaxing under Christopher's attentions, Luca regained his rhythm.

No question but that Luca was alive—thrusting into Christopher's mouth, his buttocks flexing against Christopher's hand. Squeezing the big muscle wrung whimpers from Luca, so did Christopher's tongue over the velvet shaft in his mouth. So alive—everything burst from Luca at once, a half-choked cry and jets of semen that splashed salty against Christopher's palate.

Oh, God, how he wanted, needed. Groin tight, Christopher hung on to his self-control. To lose himself in Luca's body—but no, he couldn't have that. He'd make it good, treat his lover well—but Luca wasn't ready. Might never be ready, not for years, not until his next job as a *directeur sportif* of some team yet unformed kept him in the team car for every stage of every race.

"Come up here," Luca murmured eventually, and Christopher rose to cover him again. Held tightly in Luca's arms, opening his mouth to Luca's kisses, Christopher worked his arms under Luca's shoulders. Reaching far enough to weave fingers into Luca's curls, Christopher flexed his hips, feeling his balls rub against Luca's sack and half-mast cock. His shaft lay between their bellies, rubbing through the slight ooze of his precum.

Luca twined a leg around Christopher's, his callused foot scooting between Christopher's knees. One leg, not enough to be mistaken for the invitation he hadn't made earlier: he wrapped himself without opening up. Why couldn't Luca trust Christopher to honor his word? Maybe one leg was trust, as much as Luca could give. He held nothing back with the rest of his body. Mouth, hips, clutching so tightly Christopher might have liked a little more breath, he lifted himself against Christopher, meeting him thrust for thrust.

Hot skin, slick with sweat, slipping. Hot breath, gasped against the pulsing column of Luca's neck. His throat bobbed with a desperate swallow—Christopher drew his tongue across the flexing ridge to the big strap muscle standing out against Luca's skin. Flicking and thrumming just as Luca had done to him moments ago, Christopher ground against his lover.

A quick slap and two strong hands clutched his buttocks, pulling Christopher down hard enough that anything between them would have been squeezed out of the dimension. So tight on his buttocks it hurt, but hurting was okay, hurting was alive—the wordless noises Christopher mingled with Luca's panting could only come from a living man—and the semen he shot between their bellies was blood temperature—the heat of a living man. Pleasure when he'd only expected to be numb, cradled when he feared to be alone, alive when he'd come so close to being—not. All in Luca's arms.

CHAPTER 12

CHRISTOPHER FROWNED at the two square pictures lying on top of the paperwork and birth certificate he'd need to take to the post office. Three extra shots at the drugstore had at least given him the chance to open his eyes, quit squinching his mouth, and not lift his shoulders to the point of looking like Quasimodo's brother. His passport would look marginally better than his driver's license.

"Everyone looks like criminal at border crossing." Luca offered cold comfort from behind, his arms wrapped around Christopher's chest. "Pictures are good enough; quit obsessing." He poked at the document Christopher hadn't quite finished filling out. "Sooner you get papers done, sooner I buy you plane ticket."

"I should be buying my own plane ticket." Turning to nuzzle Luca, whose chin rested on his shoulder, Christopher rubbed against a newly shaven cheek. "Do I fly to Paris, or Brussels? Antwerp? And catch a train to where?"

"No room to land big jets near Antwerp, *Americano*. Brussels, yes. Passport office goes on own schedule, so maybe *Firenze*." Luca nibbled back—he and Christopher got their lips around some right angles for sideways kisses. "If they take long time."

"Where's that?" Christopher dropped his pen to wind his fingers through Luca's hair.

"Eh!" For a scolding, that didn't have a lot of juice. "Beautiful city in middle of Italy, full of art. Michelangelo's *David*. Old joke about I tell you to meet me by big clock and you go to marble man with no clothes. 'Where is that?' Hah!"

"Oh. Florence. Right." That might need a connection—he'd have to check.

"Maybe I call this town *Macigno* and expect you to find it on map?" Luca asserted his challenge with fingers dug into Christopher's armpits. Damn but that tickled! He twisted in his chair, trying to evade, but Luca's grip was too firm.

"On an Italian map, sure. You DO that!" Christopher's voice rose an involuntary octave when Luca found a particularly sensitive spot.

"Okay, *Americano.*" Luca left off tickling to hold tight once more. "I teach you languages, one word at a time. *Macigno* means…?"

"Boulder," Christopher could finish that sentence. "Now if I can work it into conversation…."

"Soon. First I teach you verbs. Here is more important sentence. *"Tu sei il mio amore."* Luca buried his face into the crook of Christopher's neck and wouldn't come out for kisses or nibbles.

Rubbing his fingers into Luca's scalp, Christopher puzzled over the words first, and then his understanding. Did Luca really say that? Could he really mean that? Maybe the words weren't quite as cognate as they sounded. Maybe Christopher was hearing what he wanted to hear; maybe he was only translating his hopes. Best to be sure. "What does that mean?" he whispered.

"You translate." Luca squeezed an instant too hard and then jammed the pen into Christopher's left hand. Not that he could write that way, but he could get the message. "Finish your papers. Then we go to bed. I have to be up early."

Damn, that's what Christopher was trying to forget—how early Luca had to be up, and why. "You have your passport and everything? Your plane ticket?" *Your ways to leave and get an ocean away where I can't reach out to you in the night?*

"I have everything, Christopher. What I don't have, Paolo has, and what Paolo and I forget, the team has, or can buy." Luca lifted a hand to caress Christopher's face. "Everything except you, and for that, we need passport. Write."

Oh. Yes. Christopher wrote. And then they went to bed. Later, much later, when Luca's breathing went soft and steady, Christopher murmured, "I love you too."

Luca had arrived on his mountain bike last night, and now he would leave it and Christopher behind. "You keep it for me, okay? Ride if you want." He turned from the bicycle leaning against the wall to hug Christopher at the door.

If his apartment was home to Luca's bike, then surely Luca would come back for it. The racing season loomed long. There might be a lot of mountain biking in Christopher's future. "I will. You come back for it, you hear?" Filtered through Luca's freshly-shampooed curls, Christopher's desperation might not be apparent. *Come back. If you can't come back to me, at least come back safe. But come back to me.*

"I will." Luca's own desperation muffled into Christopher's neck. "I will miss you every day. Call you when I can. Text you after riding."

"No holding back on what really happened, either." Christopher fully expected Luca to gloss over pile-ups and shrug off leaving half his hide on the cobblestones. "Don't make me find out the real story from *CycloWorld* or ESPN. I'll only worry more if I do."

"No holding back," Luca agreed faintly, as if he'd been outflanked already. "But you worry over nothing."

Stu's memory was so fresh as to be knives. In fifty years his death would still not be "nothing." "I hope so."

They'd used their time well this morning—Christopher ached pleasantly from their love-making—but he couldn't hold Luca enough to make up for the weeks, maybe months, before he could get to Europe for days that would be all too brief. Their mouths met, in melding more than kissing, with brushes of lip to lip, tongue to tongue. Luca opened gladly for him, inviting Christopher to enter, to stay.

But time ticked on, and Luca came up for air. "Need to go meet team, Christopher."

Going back to bed sounded better, but Luca had somewhere to be. "Okay." Not really—once they left the apartment, they'd have to maintain the sort of polite distance that meant a closet door stood between them. Christopher grabbed Luca's pack and locked up.

Not inches: paces separated them. Luca must have teleported to the passenger door of Christopher's aged Vibe, his suitcase at his feet.

Christopher drove north on Broadway, past half a dozen cyclists who looked to be on their way to the open roads. Luca stayed silent, his smile wry when Christopher pulled up across the street from the big brick bus terminal. One of RTD's deluxe distance busses was visible in the bay, its cargo doors open to swallow luggage for thirty-five people, maybe more. Cyclists and the ones they'd leave behind milled around—knots of men chattered, some hugged sniffling women, one man knelt to cuddle a child, a baby on his shoulder.

"We all leave someone behind for the season." Luca turned from the preparations back to Christopher. "Or part of it."

"I'm going to the post office now, before work." Getting his passport was the easy part, the ticket somewhat harder. He'd sent in two extra articles to *CycloWorld*, and he had ideas for more. If he swallowed his pride and let Luca pay, he might make a second trip. "I'll come see you. I have to watch you race, and wait for you at the finish line."

"Then I go faster, to get to you." Luca snaked his hand over the console to clasp Christopher's hand where he clutched the gearshift. "*Ciao*, Christopher."

"*Ciao*, Luca." One more kiss was out of the question, and his smile would be nearly as revealing. "Good luck." He turned his hand over to clasp Luca's from below. "Talk to you soon."

"Soon." Luca squeezed hard and let go. He was out of the car in a trice, yanking his suitcase and pack from the back seat. He leaned back through the door, meeting Christopher's eyes. His gaze was a kiss in itself, his eyes soft, his lips parted. "Soon."

"Soon," but Christopher was talking to the empty air—Luca had done his teleporting trick again and was halfway across the street with his luggage, calling greetings to his teammates. Not a backward glance, but he wouldn't, not in front of the team. Backward glances for Luca were to determine who was following, and he'd never topple for the looking. Christopher didn't even touch the buckle of his seatbelt.

Rolf appeared from behind a group, waving a greeting to his team captain. Yeah, Rolf would spend months with Luca, hearing his voice unfiltered by any electronics. Close enough to touch. Maybe sharing hotel rooms—the cyclists and staff doubled up, or tripled or quadrupled in the small hotels filled to bursting with one team, maybe two. If Rolf gave Luca any shit…!

The first words he'd ever heard Rolf say to Luca had been grief that sounded sexual. Was that just Rolf being Rolf, or did he know? And would he use it against Luca? When it was a handful of riders and a clerk in a bicycle store, that was one thing, but out on the racing circuit was another. Luca had no trouble bringing Rolf to heel in the shop, but could he keep Rolf muzzled? A dozen kisses or a thousand were suddenly a small price to pay for Luca's safety.

The bus filled with a legion of wiry, fit men who trooped up the stairs once the cargo bays shut. They'd ride in comfort to the airport, where a plane waited to take them to Brussels. Sixty or more bicycles had been broken down into packable components and crated in pods that would disappear into the maw of a FedEx cargo plane. Luca had waved off parting with his time trial bike and his spare, but had stubbornly clung to his favorite until, he reported, Paolo had wrested control and delivered the machine to the mechs. Christopher had done his small part to get this traveling circus on the road. He'd do his best to keep its star happy. He sat at the wheel, watching the bus door close on his lover, and listened to the deep grumble of the diesel engine when the bus pulled out of the terminal, passing the waving horde of those left behind.

Luca smiled through the glass, his hand raised in a salute that Christopher could only answer in kind, not with the blown kiss that hovered at his lips. Two windows behind, another pale form gestured through the window, his face bitter, his middle finger upthrust. He tracked Christopher, turning his face all through the turn onto Walnut Street, leaving no doubt about his target.

Fucking Rolf.

Chapter 13

Eleven hours in the air, plus security, plus a layover, plus immigration, plus, plus, plus. Adding up far too many hours in his head left Christopher fretting about Luca's travels, but his lover was much safer at 39,000 feet in a Boeing 767 than he was on the streets of Boulder. Left with little to do and far too much time to do it in, Christopher opened his laptop. Might as well get started on earning that ticket to France.

When choosing a saddle for your distance rides, comfort is paramount. A seat that has you standing on your pedals on the flat to just, please, don't touch my butt! *isn't going to do your training a bit of good.*

If he was being totally scrupulous, he'd credit Luca here, but the exact words weren't the same and the context was different. Sort of. Christopher hadn't forgotten why he'd been the only one to bottom since they'd first fallen into bed.

Since no two humans have the exact same configuration of pelvis, thigh, and weight, if the saddle that came with the bike is comfortable, count yourself fortunate. Most of us have to try a few before we find the perfect blend of length, width, and material to rub against our tender parts.

Sounded kind of like buying sex toys. If *CycloWorld* wanted a revision, they'd say so. But they'd liked the slight edginess he'd brought to other articles; he didn't expect any pink editorial balloons here in markup. If they ran any edits past him. His words had been changed before, his first clue coming when he opened the covers of the new issue.

Fitting a saddle properly depends on not only on your personal geometry but your riding habits. A recreational rider will spend more time with full weight resting on the seat than a pro will: those legs aren't just peddling the smoothest, most powerful circles, ~~they're wrapped around your back while you're sucki—~~

Whoops, gotta stop letting private thoughts get into the text. Stu would have had a field day proofreading that. If he'd just walk through the front door, Christopher would even let him read the raw text. One time. Christopher deleted the TMI and started over. Every *CycloWorld* piece would get three additional rounds of proofreading, just in case.

...most powerful circles, they're taking as much as 40% of the rider's weight, even when not actively pedaling.

And his elbows are taking the rest, while his glutes, back, and abdominals are propelling his stiff cock in and out... Christopher set the laptop aside. This article just was not going to get written until he made love with his Luca-memory and could sit up with the ghostly presence of his arm over Christopher's shoulders and his voice whispering details about saddles. *"Cut-outs distribute weight better..."* mingled with the *zzz* of his zipper.

Giving himself over completely to the reasons why weight had to be directed away from the perineum by a saddle but attention completely given to it while in bed, Christopher relived their morning's farewell. The herbal, grassy scent of Luca's shampoo clung to the pillows—Christopher buried his face and conjured his lover.

Would Luca do the same, dream of Christopher and touch himself in solitude? Would he ever get any solitude? Would he ever be alone when he could pick up the phone and whisper his doings across the miles? Would Christopher be somewhere private when Luca called to speak his need?

He'd have to be. He'd just have to be where he could do *this*—could wrap his fingers around his cock and make believe it was Luca's mouth doing all the lovely, filthy things he'd whisper about. Oh my, what he'd murmur back—he'd make Luca take the same desperate, needy grip and listen to *I'm pushing into you, fuck, your hole is so hot* and other things that he might only accept from four thousand miles away. *God, Luca...*

When he could peel one eye open, the clock glared 9:37 and darkness looked in the windows. Luca would still be somewhere over the Atlantic, a few hours from Belgium. Organized chaos waited on the other end—Luca mightn't have a moment to call for hours. A text, maybe. His night would be gone, eaten by the sun; he'd get off the plane into bright morning light and another bus to the starting point of the race scheduled for Saturday.

Maybe Luca could sleep like a cat, anywhere, any time, draped over anything. He'd gotten very, very good at sleeping draped across Christopher. But he'd be jet lagged, exhausted, and needing to be fit and rested for his first race as GC of Team Antano-Clark. If he didn't call, it would be fatigue, or time zones. If Christopher slept through the chime of the phone... Shit, no. He cranked the volume to "obnoxious" and searched the web for an app to display the time in Paris; that should stand in for all of Western Europe.

Luca's life would be eight hours ahead of Christopher's, his day winding down when Christopher's was dawning. Sleep might be a thing of the past on race days—if he could shake another ten dollars a month out of the budget for a streaming service, he could watch Luca race real time. Maybe that would be his energy gel budget redirected—he gave his road bike a sour look. No riding, no sucking down two bucks of goop per ride.

Or else he could write another article.

Too wide a saddle will chafe; too narrow will feel like straddling a 2x2. Most good cycling shops have a device to measure the distance between your ischia (the sit-bones in your tushia), which will rule out a number of choices. Don't take these measurements as aspersions on the width of your butt, which might be quite narrow in the fashion sense, but use them as a guide to comfort. A man as slender as Rolf Knecht of Team Antano-Clark finds his pelvic geometry works well with a saddle as wide as the Cassowary HT, while Antano-Clark GC Luca Biondi plans to flex his muscles perched on the narrower K-Aero.

Consider the padding: too much may migrate between your sit-bones, while just-right might mean no padding at all. Once you've established correct width, you might be surprised how little padding you require for comfort.

Saddles are high-wear components, enduring contact with your sweaty hind end and scuffing, whether on your garage wall or the road once you've come off. Take a good look at the covering, which might be leather, various high tech fabrics, even Kevlar…

Christopher added a table, sorting fifteen saddles by width and price range. *CycloWorld* needed to cough up any special advertising interests so those units could be included in his rah-rah, and then they had one, maybe two pages, depending how many ads they crammed around the text, of real-live, useful editorial. He hit "Send" on the email and glowered again at the clock. One a.m. was the absolute earliest he could hope to hear from Luca, and that only if he texted the moment the pilot gave the "all clear" to turn on electronics after touching down.

He hadn't texted during the layover. It was only six hours since he'd left, really, but Luca had shot off a couple of teasing messages on the bus to the airport this morning. `Tell post office to hurry passport` he'd sent, and when Christopher promised to beg for speed, Luca sent a smiley with `Good. I miss you already.`

But he had a plane full of snoopy teammates to cope with during the layover, whatever customs issues had to be handled on leaving the country, and… Maybe there were a hundred other things that needed to be done on the way to Belgium. Had he and the directeur sportif defined their strategy for the upcoming race? *Yes, they had,* his memory supplied, *but maybe something changed?*

Testing his phone once again, Christopher verified that the ringer would wake him, the upstairs neighbors, and the folks across the street too. He daren't miss Luca's summons, but a yawn creaked his jaw. He and Luca had been up early, entwined together for joyous antics that had enough desperation to undo the three hours of sleep sex that good should have equaled. And Luca wouldn't call for a couple of hours at least.

Christopher snuggled up on Luca's pillow and tried to forget how alone in the bed he was.

THE PHONE screamed him awake around two a.m. with the single shriek of a text. Once Christopher dropped the two feet he'd levitated, he jabbed "read".

On way to middelkerke flight ok some good news!

Tell!

New york man got on plane at layover. We talked more. Signed.

KEWL! What r u endorsing?

Lots, tell you in phone call. Can buy 3 plane tickets ;)

Woohoo! Go champ! Getting such a great endorsement deal wasn't just money, it was validation of his lover in the highest echelons of racing. Had to be worth five minutes per stage just in confidence.

For what they pay must win every race. Got some sleep.

Good. Feeling ok?

Need to stretch, lie flat. Still 20km to town.

Twenty kilometers that wouldn't be a problem on his bike if Luca were rested probably felt longer than the trip over the Atlantic if he had to sit up straight the whole way. Luca *never* complained. **Massage?** From Paolo, not Christopher, damn it, but if it helped, it helped.

Good idea. not so fun as you

:D think of me.

Not with rolf or paolo in room :p

Shit, he was rooming with Rolf. If he gave Luca a hard time, Christopher might have to flap his arms to get to Belgium, but get there he would, and there'd be some ass-kicking.

Christopher paused, thumbs over the keyboard. This was Luca's lieutenant, charged with leading him until it was time for a breakaway, who'd fetch and carry and make sure Luca was in a position to win. And why did the same man who'd flipped him off on the way out of town support him at Stu's funeral?

He hadn't questioned it before in his numbness, and when he'd been able to feel again there'd been better things to think about in Luca's arms. If he didn't ask, he'd never know, and this felt important to know. Why he and the others of the team had come was clear enough; they'd watched Stu die, but that didn't explain Rolf's actions.

At Stu's service (even now he couldn't bring himself to write 'funeral' and he hoped Luca would understand) rolf held my arm. why?

If the answer wasn't so important, Christopher might have fallen back to sleep in the time it took to get Luca's answer.

Because I asked

Why?

Would have been good to just believe that Rolf had that much humanity in him, but every other time they'd been in the same place it went badly.

So I could

Fuck. Luca's closet was even tighter than Christopher imagined. Guess it was good he was finding out now, before he did something that undermined Luca. And those two were sharing a room. Good bye, hope for privacy. Except—

He knows?

This answer, too, was a long time in coming. *Yes*

How much does he care? Would it affect how Rolf rode?

A lot

Oh great. Christopher would have to get the streaming service for sure, to keep an eagle eye on Rolf just as much as to watch his lover. As if the scrutiny from four thousand miles away would keep him in check, right, but still…

Be careful around him, ok?

The phone *queeped* again, almost faster than Luca could have thumb-typed his answer. *I trust him.*

How could he answer that? Could his own sense of paranoia outwork a closeted man's? Besides, trust Rolf for what? To do his job? To not do something that would create problems on or off the road that would land Rolf with the GC position? Rolf's position was higher now than when he'd been on the Kastibank team, but had he gotten over not being chosen as GC? The long pause this time was Christopher's.

Ok.

But it wasn't okay. Not even close.

Short ride today, longer tomorrow, time trial day after to open 3 daagse van west vlaanderen. Sounded like Luca had had enough questioning if he was back to talking racing.

You'll do good.

Will. Air feels thick and wet.

After Luca's months in high, dry Colorado, it was probably like breathing soup. Air will be rocket fuel.

:D will. Here. Ttyl

<3 But Christopher didn't send that. *Ttyl* went instead. At least on the screen of the phone.

Chapter 14

The fee for the streaming live race coverage, with commentary in English, Flemish, and French would come out of the gel budget this week at least. Christopher stepped around the unused bicycles in the living room to stretch out on the futon with his laptop. The streaming service covered a lot of races every day, but he was only interested in Driedaagse van West Vlaanderen. Three days in West Flanders. Okay, he might pick up more words than he expected from the local commentators, but for Luca's first race of the season he wanted to hear exactly what was going on.

For Luca the race began at 1:30 in the afternoon, or whenever his start slot would come up, about three quarters of the way into a field of nearly two hundred, based on times from the previous year. Christopher flicked open the screen at 5:15 a.m., calculated when Luca would likely start, and set his alarm for another hour and a half. That should give him plenty of time to see what the competition was up to.

He came awake again to riders shooting down a start ramp one at a time, dressed in brightly-hued skinsuits and alien-looking helmets, on bicycles that seemed to be part flying saucer. The solid wheels improved aerodynamics, as did the handlebars meant to let the riders hide from the wind, but they still looked like another species, and all, Christopher hoped, evolved to move more slowly than Rider 141.

Keeping an anxious eye on the leader board, Christopher watched a couple of Antano-Clark riders leave the starting gate. Rolf already had a time—he'd gone much earlier and was at least a minute behind the current leader, who wasn't likely to win the race. Barring a surprise, the winner would come from one of the later cyclists to leave the gate; they'd already know what time to beat and would pace themselves.

What had Luca said about Rolf and time trials? "All muscle, no sense of pacing"? This course was short, less than ten kilometers; even the slowest rider out the gate today needed less than fifteen minutes to make the circuit. Luca would need less, perhaps twelve. A great first race, not too long or grueling, and an event he loved. Another rider left the gate, 136, and please, let Luca get some face time—first race for the new general classification star of a new team should be worth getting chased by a cameraman on a motorcycle.

Aim that camera Luca's way! So what if a dozen other riders already cluttered the course, and no, damn it, don't stop to blather about last year's winner or the prospects of the Olympic champion at position 199! Shaking his laptop wouldn't redirect the commentators. Christopher paced from the kitchen to the futon, sloshing the cup of coffee he'd poured half on the counter.

"Luca Biondi, the last rider out for this new team..." brought Christopher nose to screen, the closest he could get to Luca, whose turquoise and black skinsuit covered him like paint. The pointed, aerodynamic helmet with the tinted visor hid his face. Only the mass of curls peeking out from under the tail of the helmet and his bib number differentiated him from the rest of his team, until he rolled down the ramp and began to pedal.

"Biondi spent the winter chasing the Garmin-Sharp team around the mountains—" The commentator supplied a world audience with half-accurate details, which didn't matter nearly as much as "—Biondi's twenty-three seconds ahead of the current leader at the quarter mark."

Twenty-three seconds, that was huge! Plenty of margin to stay ahead of riders faster than the current leader. Luca filled the screen for a few more seconds before the cameras cut to a couple of well-established stars pedaling warm-ups on the rollers. Who cared? They were missing the story of this race, out there setting a mark for the rest to fall short. One of the stars, in lime green and white with blue flashes, did a double take and nudged the man next to him. Who needed sound to know that the rider told his companion, "Biondi"? The hardness crossing their faces meant their own tactics for the course had just been adjusted. Christopher urged Luca on, to sail uncatchably far ahead of the competition before they ever started.

"Luca Biondi's now forty-two seconds ahead of the current leader," the announcer babbled, "with another two kilometers to the finish." The camera came back to pace Luca from the back of a motorcycle, and panned to the rear view of another rider, now only a few yards ahead of Luca. That rider would get some serious guff from his team for getting overtaken; sucked to be him, but he was caught by the best. Christopher urged Luca to the side, lest he draft off the other rider now where it wasn't permitted. The moto dropped back, following the two, giving an unappreciative world a wonderful look at Luca's hind end. "McCormick's struggling, and Biondi's in superior form. Colorado clearly was good to him over the winter."

The Coloradan who'd been as good to Luca as he could possibly be now hunched over the screen, his legs tense with pedaling every rotation with the current leader. Luca pulled ahead of the other rider, followed by the camera, which didn't spare another frame on the man being left behind.

Had he even broken a sweat? He'd looked like he was working harder on the way out to Lyons, though the only fossil he'd stop for now might be a *T. rex* blocking the road, and Christopher would give even odds Luca would just rattle right over ribs and vertebrae, barely slowing down.

The camera followed Luca to the finish line, where he sat upright for the first time since he'd started, releasing his center grip on the handle bars. Grinning at the camera, which followed him to a stop at the team staging area, Luca dropped one eyelid in a wink.

"That's a fabulous lead. Think it will survive the other sixty riders?" The cameraman pushed directly in for an interview before Luca quite had his helmet off.

"Maybe. What was my final time?" Luca finger-fluffed his hair out to its wild, post-ride bounciness. Those curls needed Christopher's hands fisted in them, to bring Luca close for congratulations of the wet, sloppy kind.

"Eleven point one oh seven minutes." Paolo, in his own turquoise and black team clothing, slathered with sponsors' logos though without a racing number, hurried in with information and a water bottle. "Average speed of 51.32 kilometers per hour."

"Thank you." Luca accepted the water and the numbers. "We have to see. Many good time trialists still to ride."

Christopher boggled, trying to do the math. Damn, that was, was… better than thirty miles an hour over the lightly hilly course. He tuned back into Luca's words.

If champions needed humility, Luca was the best of the best, telling the cameraman how he'd trained hard all winter but couldn't assume he'd keep up with his world class competition.

"The world champion time trialist averaged 51.16 kilometers per hour over this same course last year," his interrogator pointed out. "And you're not sure you can keep up?"

"He might go faster this year." Luca took another pull at the water bottle.

The camera cut back to a cyclist in unfortunate orange, whose time at the split was thirty-eight seconds behind the leader. Nope, so far no one was keeping up with Luca, but there were still fifty-odd competitors to come. With every launch down the start ramp, Christopher's stomach clenched more tightly. Would this be the man who'd bump Luca from the top of the leader board?

Time trials took on an excitement they'd never had for Christopher as a spectator. Watching each racer compete against the clock made it hard to see how they paced themselves—it couldn't be an all out assault on time, or they'd exhaust themselves long before the finish. Even in a prologue race such as this, where the distance was miniscule compared to the thirty and forty kilometer time trial stages of the Tour de France, the overeager could hit the wall.

The camera cut back to Luca between other cyclists. He looked ready to do it all over again, only faster this time. The gap between Luca and his closest follower narrowed by a second or two at a time until only three racers remained.

The cyclist in lime green who'd done a double take on camera shot out of the starting gate, followed by so much commentary on his previous seasons' successes. Yeah, yeah, he'd taken the lead on a forty-two kilometer loop that started and ended in Grenoble two years ago, but that was so much *wah-wah-wah* in Christopher's ears. Old Tour de France stages mattered nothing today.

A minute later, the only cyclist in white with rainbow flashes left the gate to the thudding in Christopher's chest. Would the reigning world champion time trialist permit Luca to best him in his specialty? Would the effort cost him too dearly for tomorrow and the next day?

A dizzying sequence of camera shots knotted Christopher's mind—other riders hitting the finish line, plus twenty-eight seconds, plus thirty-two seconds. Lime-green was nineteen seconds back at the split, and the Olympic champ, the last threat, emerged from the start house.

Pumping legs, whirling numbers on half a dozen riders' clock, motos with cameras so thick they got in each other's viewfinders—Christopher's stomach churned acid. Did Luca's? Would his huge lead survive the next seven minutes? Screaming fans pushing out into the road, barely parting for the cyclists—would someone's clothing catch a handlebar? Would a dog get loose? Waving inflaties obscured the finish line. A thousand cowbells clattered. Rider 195 crossed the line, plus twenty-two seconds.

Lime-green shifted gears and hunkered down for his run into the finish. Woe betide the fan who didn't get out of the way now. The numbers chased themselves across the bottom of the screen, labeled with names to conjure with, names that filled the pages of *CycloWorld* and Luca's stories, and stopped—plus eighteen seconds. *Yes!* Rainbow jersey crossed the line—plus nineteen seconds—was that speed or strategy? Who cared? It was plus something to Luca's time. Christopher pressed his knuckles against his teeth, seeing the champ from every angle the motos could find for his last two kilometers, and his time clock still whirring away. *Keep going! Keep going!*

"YES! " Christopher sprang to his knees on the bed, his laptop rocking to the pumping of his fist. "Plus fourteen! YES!" He collapsed to exult more quietly before the upstairs neighbors started pounding the floor. With Luca's pillow between his teeth to muffle his yells, he cried his exultation to the world. "Luca, you did it!"

Other riders were as stunned as he, telling the cameras anything from "Biondi rode very well today," to "Not sure why he needed to exhaust himself on a short prologue: riding in the top ten today was all I needed to do. I'll save the effort for the longer stages," to "Damn! Where did he come from?"

The camera turned to a bouncing, frantic mass of turquoise and black—the team thronged Luca, ruffling his hair, slapping his back. Rolf hung with his arm around Luca's neck, waving and shouting with the others, and Luca himself? His smile was wide as the sky, his arm upraised. For a moment. He touched his knuckles to his lips and threw a kiss to the heavens. Or maybe just high enough to cross the Atlantic and another thousand miles, to land in Christopher's heart.

"You did it," he mumbled into Luca's pillow. "You really did it." He fumbled that message into a text, not sure when Luca would see or how he could respond. **New entry in palmarès, proud of you** Maybe one day he could end his congratulations with <3.

Christopher still had an hour and a half before he needed to be at work. In less than ten minutes he'd rattled out an account of the race, including quotes from the other cyclists: if they didn't want to stand behind those words, they shouldn't say them, but anyone who said a kind word about the winner got a mention. *Cyclo World* wouldn't want an incomplete account of the race, so parts two and three would have to wait until tomorrow and Sunday.

Too full of triumph to sleep again, Christopher dressed for riding. He ran a regretful hand over his road bike; too many memories mixed with sorrow perched on its saddle. Not today. Maybe not tomorrow or next week. No, today he'd park his backside in Luca's place and take some borrowed courage out on the road. He wheeled the visiting mountain bike out the door, heading south and west with enough gears to smash Flagstaff Mountain into speed bumps and his hands in Luca's grips.

He picked his way through the neighborhoods, avoiding the main street, filled as it was with armored monsters guided by fools. Stu whispered in his ear to be careful and patted his shoulders with icy hands. Luca spoke more firmly, the memory of *We honor our fallen by not giving up* mixing with his fear. The morning was still cool, turning the drips of sweat down his back chilly.

Pausing at the corner of 6th and Baseline, he considered turning back. To go on would put him on Flagstaff Road in less than a block, heading up the mountain over endless switchbacks. Not much traffic, more on two wheels like himself than on four. They were no danger to him, and he'd hug the shoulder, stay away from the cars. Luca whispered *You will know when it is time to ride again.*

Christopher shoved his foot into the toe clip. It was time. Telling Stu to hush up if he wanted to come along, he pushed into a steady cadence. *I've ridden this road a dozen times. I've ridden hundreds of miles safely. I can do this.* Still, every car that went around him put a cold cramp in his gut, and only Luca's remembered encouragement kept him pointed uphill. A metallic monster came far too close in its passage. *We met one of those recently,* Stu mentioned. *Shut up, Stu,* Luca responded. *If I let fear rule me, I ride slow.*

Fear couldn't win, not when he'd found the right gear for a steady pace, not when the pines and grasses murmured about the breeze, not when the power in his legs shoved him and this heavy bike up toward the sky. *Just get to the restaurant,* Christopher urged himself, *and take Luca for dinner there if you win the lottery. Just get to the amphitheatre, just get to the summit.* Small goals kept him pedaling. *Feed power evenly around the stroke,* Luca reminded him.

His phone chimed him to the side of the road after about twenty minutes of steady pace. Losing his cadence was a small price for the respite from the dueling voices. His caller went from offering encouragement inside his head to greetings from across the ocean.

"*Ciao,* Christopher."

"Luca! That's all? No 'Wahoo, I won!'?" But Christopher could have drowned in the two words.

"Okay, I did, but short stage of 2.2 race." His grin came right through the phone, belying his calm.

So what if it was a second tier stage race? That only meant more national and regional teams mixed in with all the top level pros. "Yeah, and I know who followed you, so don't give me 'too humble'. They weren't expecting that, I could tell." He propped the mountain bike against a tree and found a handy rock to sit on, a chunk of reddish sandstone that wouldn't dump him onto the asphalt.

"You saw?"

"Yeah. You're worth getting up in the wee hours for." Christopher arranged himself comfortably on his rock, a knee up to support his elbow. "You made it look easy. Everyone else had to work for it, and they couldn't catch you. Not even close. You did good."

"Was easy, this time. Surprised them all, and high-altitude conditioning still very fresh. Three months from now will be more like everyone else except for strengthening from racing."

"Yeah." Red blood cells had a finite life span, one of the things that gave away the EPO-using crowd. "Can I quote you?"

"Yes. Not about tactics for next stage though, but here's what we going to do…" Luca shared state secrets, bringing Christopher's heart to his throat, before turning to other things.

They mumbled words that would have been sweet nothings had they been together and private. News of tiny hotels and bigger races had to do: what Luca hoped for the next day, how a small room with a single bed for himself and another for Rolf made Christopher's basement apartment look palatial. "Are you alone?" came up.

"Yeah, but not exactly private." Damn, had Luca managed to be alone except for his hope? "I'm most of the way up Flagstaff Mountain." Standing, Christopher held his phone lens out to catch his own smiling face framed against the panorama of Boulder and Denver glittering out to the horizon fifteen hundred feet below, filtered through pine branches. "Here's where I am."

"*Bellisimo.*"

It was more than just beautiful; it was a small triumph to lay at Luca's feet. Nothing compared to having bested the top riders at their own game, but it was all Christopher could offer. He snapped a picture of Luca's bike, its seat raised to accommodate his longer legs. "Here's how I got here."

"Oh, Christopher." Luca's accent caressed his name. "You did good."

Chapter 15

Once Christopher fled the bike shop for the day, he dashed home for some video editing. The streaming service would keep today's stage on file indefinitely, but he had to snip out the winning ride and Luca's triumphant salute for his own private collection.

Damn: tomorrow's stage would start so early the birds wouldn't even be thinking of getting up. He set the alarm for 4:30 a.m. and loaded the coffee pot so that one blind swat would produce enough go-brew to get his eyes all the way open. Going to bed early was no problem—today's early start, the exertion of his ride, and remembering everything Luca had teased him with on the phone made him sleepy hours before his usual bedtime. Just because he hadn't been able to find a spot where he and the bicycle could go unseen and still stagger back to the road didn't keep Luca from taking advantage of the one-sided privacy.

"Tell me again where you put your tongue," Luca had mumbled and eventually gasped when Christopher told him that and a great deal more besides. They could talk without being overheard but Christopher wasn't about to risk stray hikers with his shorts down. "I tell you all about my tongue when you have privacy," Luca promised when he could speak English again.

Christopher had privacy now, but Luca should be sound asleep in a Belgian bed, with fucking Rolf stretched out three feet away. Christopher wrapped his hand around his cock and swore to be somewhere he could do it again when Luca called.

The wee hours rolled around, and Christopher would have hit the snooze for anyone else but Luca. Instead, he knuckled the sleep out of his eyes and hunkered down to see four hours of maneuvering, tactics, and sinewy effort.

"Yesterday's surprise time trial winner, Luca Biondi, is cruising in the middle of the peloton, flanked by his teammates, and keeping up easily. There was some concern that he'd burnt himself out in a showy effort in his first race of the season, but he looks like a man out for a casual spin…." As if a measly 9.5 kilometer time trial would seriously sap Luca.

The announcers prattled on, filling the air time and the miles. One hundred seventy-four kilometers, a hundred and eight miles, would give them plenty of time to babble, until the race sorted itself out into a display of strength and challenges. The hazards of the road, the peloton, and of tactics hadn't gone away though—this would be no walk through. He took notes when the leads changed, when the announcers mentioned something he hadn't noticed on his own, when Luca spoke to a teammate or occasionally to the thin air, which meant he was acknowledging instructions from his directeur sportif through his radio helmet.

Half a dozen riders went down navigating a roundabout in an unpronounceable town—Luca and most of Antano-Clark were on the far side, streaming past the circular obstacle unhindered. All six got up and rejoined the race, though one's black and white jersey showed skin and red at the tattered shoulder. *One hundred percent casualties.* At least it wasn't any worse than road rash.

The miles ground on, the motos working back around the peloton to get different views of the parti-colored mass of men. Twenty kilometers to go. The pot of coffee issued a reminder. Luca's promised tactics hadn't materialized yet—a quick trip shouldn't be an issue. Right? He wasn't such a crazed fan that he'd have to take the laptop with him. Was he? No, but fuck, yeah next time he would because here he was, stuck with his dick in his hand and the announcers getting excited and he couldn't make out one word in ten over the sound of his own running water. "Breakaway!" *Faster, faster, faster….*

Skidding back onto the futon, his screen was full of turquoise and black, green with yellow, orange, some brown (who thought up that uniform?), and one black-suited rider with blue flashes who'd jumped into the fray without any teammates to support him. And Luca was in the center of the battle.

"—riders from Antano-Clark, Mondiale, Duclos-Wurth, Euskatel-Euskadi, and an optimist from Team Sky have staged a breakaway from the peloton. With twelve kilometers yet to go, the odds are good that the peloton will reel them in and pass them."

"Unless Biondi has the legs to take it alone, I imagine we'll see him finish somewhere in the center of the pack," opined the talking head, who didn't have any idea what kind of legs Luca had. Of course he could take everyone in the peloton, and everyone in this breakaway, which included— Christopher compared jersey numbers to names, decided most of them were trustworthy, and kept his eye on Rolf.

Okay, he was pedaling like hell, leading out, letting Luca draft like a good domestique should, and glancing at the orange-suited rider next to him who did the same for his own team star.

"There's a three second gap between the breakaway and the peloton," intoned the announcer.

"And it's growing," observed the other.

"Go! Go!" Christopher urged them.

The group did, accelerating to a five second gap and then a seven second gap, even though the peloton surged after them. The leaders of the breakaway group fell back, to be replaced by another of Luca's domestiques and a different rider in brown and white.

"Three kilometers to go, and the peloton is not catching that breakaway!" Not in the first circuit around the Belgian town of Harelbeke, and not in the second.

But Luca—he was biding his time, Christopher knew, conserving his strength over this last small urban stretch, even as he spent it to leave one hundred eighty pursuers in the dirt. He'd been on the road four hours already—if his legs were screaming he didn't show it.

"One kilometer to the finish," said the announcer, and at that moment the tiny pack fell apart. The Antano-Clark rider peeled to one side, letting Luca shoot out as if he had some mystery gear no other cyclist had ever dreamed of. Others pelted after him, leaving the tatters of the group in their wake. The Mondiale rider and the optimist left it too late to make their move. Luca drew ahead in his sprint to the finish.

"Go! Go!" Christopher bellowed. If he'd had a cowbell, he'd have deafened himself with the clatter.

Luca shot under the arch of the finish line, his arm flying into the air with his triumph, his grin wide as the ocean that separated them. "YES!" Christopher shrieked even as he counted *one thousand one, one thou—* "YES!"

Not that Luca needed the few extra seconds to stay in yellow, but he'd opened up enough of a gap that his two closest followers didn't share his time. One second was enough to add to his lead, the overall lead that would have been his anyway if he'd stayed with the peloton, cut by nothing—none of his challengers today had come within twenty seconds in yesterday's time trial. Those who'd been close but too slow yesterday were too slow again, bumped to plus twenty-six seconds, plus twenty-seven. Luca—and Christopher—could breathe easy until tomorrow.

Two stages and another leader's jersey—Christopher twirled around the living room, between the bikes, and into the shower. He had to be to work in twelve minutes and couldn't wait to see Luca on the podium being dressed in yellow for leading overall. He'd watch that part tonight.

Christopher's phone buzzed in his pocket, and nearly hit the floor in his fumbling attempt to see the text *right now.*

Won stage :D no crash.

Great sprint finish! Plan worked! He glanced over each shoulder, wary of the manager questioning why he was poking his phone instead of hanging miracle fiber socks on a display rack.

Have no blood left.

Attacked by FIC vampires. They'd both expected the *Fédération Internationale des Cyclistes* to take an active interest in Luca, and only a joke kept Christopher from being bitter at the implied distrust. Not that plenty of other riders hadn't created grounds for suspicion of any top performer. If the FIC officials thought they'd find banned substances in Luca's blood they could be looking a long time. Maybe they should jab random athletes in Colorado for comparison. Christopher would hold out his own arm if it meant they'd leave Luca alone.

Nice to win stage. Would have had to finish back of pack to lose overall lead.

Better to keep it.

Now have two jerseys, two fuzzy dogs. Share with you :D

What did the racing officials think cyclists did with the plush animals they presented at stage wins? Multiple stage winners like Chris Froome had to do something with half a dozen stuffed lions per race or risk their homes looking like the display at Toys 'R Us. Christopher suddenly wanted a plush dog in the worst way. Dog will sit by pillow.

OK and you wear yellow jersey then I take it off

Oh damn—he couldn't have this conversation, even in the relative invisibility of text, in the middle of the cycle shop. He fumbled the last socks onto their hooks and held the empty carton in front of his groin on the dash to the stock room. He'd hold it in front of his blazing face, too, if he could. Not here L I'm at work

Sorry, you text me when home, I chase everyone away and tell you more about jersey :p

Will be way after midnight for you. Surely Luca wouldn't wake his roommate expressly to throw him out. And surely Luca wouldn't try to speak so softly Rolf would sleep through their interlude. What if Rolf woke but didn't say so? What if he woke and made a stink? Luca said Rolf "cared a lot". Cared how? You need to sleep so you can win again.

When is next day off?

Tomorrow. Christopher glanced at the clock. Luca had called about this time yesterday. **Will be home tomorrow this time so can play with you**

Will ride fast to have third jersey to tell you about. Oh, Christopher wanted to hear that story. *Tell in the best way :p*

This man was going to be the death of him. In the best way. Christopher shifted his erection inside his jeans and picked up the phone again. :D ok .

He'd get a ton of writing done tonight so he'd only have to add in the third stage and final results to the article he'd send off to *CycloWorld.* Easy.

Another morning to rise at oh-dark-thirty. Maybe he could get used to this. Christopher hit the button on the coffee pot and settled in for another four hour stage. One hundred eighty-four kilometers between Luca and victory, between now and jubilation. Or consolation.

No, they'd have plenty to celebrate, two stage wins already in the bag, and if his margin from the nearest competitors was slender, it was much wider for the rest of the field. Who would rise to challenge Luca? And when?

The early breakaway by a regional Belgian team didn't last: they had their moment in the sun in front of the screeching fans in Eernegem and were reeled in by the peloton about half a kilometer outside the town. The motos had some dodging to do, and one ended up in a ditch, its tumbling camera providing a too-vivid memory of Christopher's crash. Although the announcers had a few minutes of chatter about cyclists crashing, they couldn't come close to describing the bowel-clenching reality. A passing moto let them see both driver and cameraman rescuing their equipment. Christopher sighed his relief.

Perhaps to get even, another moto gave a drive-by look at a row of cyclists who had dropped out of the peloton to take a group whiz at the side of the road. The colorful lineup didn't include Luca; good. If he had to take a leak, and he probably would somewhere during this race, the cameras should let him have privacy for it, even if he had a dozen companions all straddling their bikes with their dicks out of their tight shorts. At least it was considered bad form for the other riders to attack while the leaders couldn't respond.

Most of the teams' tactics kept the peloton well grouped aside from the Belgian teams' showboating—one group broke into the lead and a different team formed a chase group through the town of Heuvelland, only to be overtaken again before they hit the feed zone. Luca didn't scurry after them; not his job, although a few Antano-Clark riders led the pursuit of the upstarts.

No, Luca didn't look too concerned, pulling along about a third of the way back in the peloton, though somehow he managed to be in the top fifteen of every intermediate sprint, hoovering up the points. Someone else wanted to be the King of the Mountain worse than Luca did—one of his old Duclos-Wurth teammates was first to crest what passed for a peak on this stage, all 20 meters of elevation. Christopher had wrinkles in his carpet higher than that. if Luca wanted the honor he probably could have taken it, but not when he had his eyes on the larger prize.

Christopher could look over his article so far, with both ears and one eye on the race. The motos whizzed back and forth across the riders, focusing on this

Big Name and that one, the announcers pattering their opinions of strengths and weaknesses. Christopher considered putting his head down for another half hour's sleep, but Luca had to pedal every mile and a nap seemed vaguely disloyal. Even a piece of toast with jelly felt like betrayal when Luca would get some kind of high carb bars and energy drinks.

Soigneurs in their team colors dotted the feed zone, holding out musettes. They'd packed their riders' long-handled bags with bottles and bars, perhaps some fruit, and for the lucky ones, a muffin or a piece of apple cake. Paolo handed off a bag to some rider Christopher didn't know, and the moto buzzed away before Christopher could be sure Luca got fed.

How much did he have to bribe the motorcycle cameraman to keep his lens on just one rider? Five minutes later he got a glimpse of Luca stuffing something red and white into his mouth and tossing a bit of foil aside. His jersey's rear pockets bulged with bottles and what looked like a tiny Coke can. The musette bag was long gone. Someone on the race route had themselves a souvenir.

A thousand people might have fought over it—they lurked at the sides of the road, encroaching into the road to all but touch the riders. Hadn't they seen the kook with the orange Borat suit waving his plastic flamingo on both the other stages?

Time stretched—so did the peloton. Christopher snapped to full attention at the sound of the Olympian's name "—and Luca Biondi are hard on the heels of the leaders, who look to be tiring." The leading squad shuffled, but all that Christopher cared was that a turquoise rider would be in a good spot to start—or end—a sprint finish.

The route led into the town of Ichtegem, whose bright buildings and cobbled roads might be very pretty without a thundering herd of cyclists on top. With them, the pavè was so many saw-teeth waiting to taste skin. The faster Luca went, the sooner he'd be out of danger. At least here metal barricades kept the crowd at bay.

Luca, the Olympian, and another four riders broke from the leading edge of the peloton. They swung around corners with their bicycles too close to horizontal, their speed all that kept them on their tires. Luca stayed on the wheel of a blue-and-white rider, his legs pumping furiously now, his face taut with his effort. The Olympian swung wide around him, cutting Luca's advantage by inch after inch, with less than a kilometer to go.

"Go, Luca, *go*!" All of Christopher's urgings didn't move him past blue and white, nor keep him ahead of the Olympian. The two riders fought it out on either side of Luca, who stayed with them, his wheels dangerously close to theirs. They shot under the finish arch in a clump, veering apart and slowing enough to reach out and clasp each other's hands, holding them high. *No hands on pavè? Luca, please—!* All smiles, they went from competitors to friends, and their clocks registered the same time. Yeah, their wheels overlapped.

"All right!" Christopher hooted, once Luca put his hands back on the grips. His leading time combined with his last two stages still put him comfortably far ahead of the others. If he didn't have credit for all three stages, he'd still won overall. There had to be something left for the others, right? The leader board flashed results as the trail of riders passed the finish line: plus two seconds for the other three breakaway riders, plus more for the others. Rolf sped beneath the arch, his time reading plus thirteen seconds, and another hundred eighty-some cyclists had yet to finish.

"A very strong finish for Antano-Clark, two riders in the top twenty for the stage, five in the top fifty," surprised the announcer but not Christopher—hadn't these guys all pedaled around mile-high and higher roads for the last several months? In fact, what were the rest of those slackers doing?

Christopher made frantic notes—if his article focused too thoroughly on Luca, *CycloWorld* wouldn't accept it—a writer whose biggest credentials so far were equipment comparisons couldn't suddenly produce a rider profile and expect to have it printed before all the current events were out of date. At least, not if he produced it out of the blue. If they asked for it, yeah, maybe. But a balanced race report was news they needed before the next issue. Dave Pauwels usually had the byline, but if he was off covering some other event.... Christopher scribbled faster.

By the time the broom wagon turned up with two riders who hadn't finished the race, Christopher had an article. He'd mentioned all the teams at least once and trimmed Luca's name four times for balance. He'd edit once more for any lingering TMI, but this should give a good overview. All that remained was the podium ceremony.

Christopher settled into the pillows to watch the King of the Mountain accept his red prize jersey: one of the Belgians on a regional team had made his reputation today. The white for the Best Young Rider might have gone to Luca a few years ago, when he rode to support the Duclos-Wurth stars, but today it matched the white of the Argos-Shimano cyclist who'd worked his butt off. Sprinter's green went to another name from the record books—Luca hadn't challenged for the intermediate points sprints, but still managed to show up in the top fifteen.

The three riders who had joined hands after the finish now mounted the podium, and Luca stood to the left of the man who'd beaten him by half a bicycle length, accepting a bundle of flowers and double cheek kisses from podium girls and FIC officials. All three raised their bouquets to the yells and whistles from the crowd. Christopher didn't need the announcers to tell him Luca belonged in this august company—all three would file off stage in a moment, but only Luca would return.

And now he was back, on the high section of the podium, flanked by a couple of attractive young women whose embraces were a formality. He let them dress him in the yellow jersey, marking him the race's winner now. His first race as GC, and he'd brought home all three prizes. He beamed across the miles, waving yet another bundle of flowers over his head. Holding the laptop with both hands was a poor substitute for gripping Luca's arms to bring him in for lip-to-lip congratulations, but, oh, had he earned them. Christopher's heart swelled too big for his chest—his Luca had done it! Come out of the gate with strength, seized his opportunities and now his palmarès. What a rider. What a man. His man.

Christopher had to write faster, he had to get enough words to *CycloWorld* to get him into Luca's arms again. *With a huge grin, a kiss thrown to the world, and perhaps a sniffle, a rising star accepts his accolades…* Luca disappeared from the screen, bumped by prerecorded interviews. He'd be back, with microphones wielded by a half dozen national reporters shoved in his face.

Now to wait.

THE CLOCK ticked off the time too slowly and too quickly—every minute that separated him from Luca still managed to disappear as he polished his prose. *CycloWorld* just had to want this piece. Stu would have found any weaknesses—he never joked about writing. Why couldn't he have shown a little more restraint on Christopher's love-life? Then they would have been somewhere else when that stupid car—

At last his phone rang. "*Ciao,* Christopher." Golden words. Words to dream about.

They ran through race assessments—"I could have taken the stage as well, but better not to brag"—and post race inventory. "I feel good. Paolo just finished massage and thinks I'm taking nap."

"And Rolf?" Please let him be miles away. Christopher plumped up the pillows and leaned back against them.

"Discussing race plans with the directeur sportif. He may be GC for another tour instead of me, not sure. I like riding *Tour de Romandie*, but like idea of Rolf working hard while I have rest days with you before the *Giro* even better."

"Even if I give you rubber legs?" Days of riding, playing, and making love wouldn't really sap Luca's strength—Christopher would insist on plenty of sack time, awake and asleep. Luca had to be strong for the three week stage race in his home country.

"You can try." Luca's voice went deep and husky. "I like when you try."

Christopher went from half-mast to stiffer than carbon-fiber in two heartbeats. "You were going to tell me about your tongue and a yellow jersey."

A deep chuckle drifted across the Atlantic into his ear. "You look good in yellow, sized for me, not for you, so fits you very tight. Shows all your muscles. I start by pulling zipper down few centimeters, show your throat. Use my teeth to pull zipper, easy to kiss you…."

Christopher slid a hand into his shorts. He'd wear yellow for Luca any time.

Chapter 16

Christopher's phone would chime in the early morning. **Back from training ride, all fine** made him breathe more easily, and the phone calls later that sometimes ended in gasping each other's names, and other times had too much of an audience. Christopher listened to racing talk where Luca referred to friends whose palmarès far outstripped his, and all Christopher could do was gawk at Fabian's tactics or how Jens was favoring one hip.

"Can I quote you?" he asked now and then.

"Yes," Luca would say, or rarely, "No."

The 2.1 stage race the following week brought Luca success, if not quite as stunning as his first race. Again glued to his laptop for the early morning broadcasts, Christopher took notes, bit his nails, and learned to pick Luca out of the bunched team just by the set of his shoulders and curve of his back. His wild, curly ponytail disappeared beneath his helmet for time trials for not being aerodynamic, which must have given him a second or two advantage—Luca won the time trial in the Paris-Nice race and made the podium for three of the other seven stages, third overall.

"Had to do better than last year," he said, and spoke instead of his team's overall fourth place finish. "Three minutes and thirty-eight seconds back of leaders. Good sprinters make up for weak mountain stages on the flats, strong climbers get left behind in sprint. Strong rider with poor body position loses minutes in time trials. We have good average."

Rolf's time trial averaged with Luca's wouldn't have made the top third. Christopher's idea of Rolf's correct body position was "Far away from Luca," but Luca's discussion of elbow position, knee angles, and ability to power through the wind with effective pedaling in a tuck position sounded like Rolf would be getting some hands-on practices instead. Bastard.

A one day race a week after the big stage race put Luca on the podium again. It would be a brutal seven days to come: this was Flanders Week.

"Had to slow down a little, Christopher," Luca chided him for growling about the two riders who'd stood above him for the *Prijs Van Vlaanderen* finals results. "Still very good placement. Sponsors happy."

"But you could have won it." Luca's explanations of tactics hadn't convinced Christopher, not one bit.

"What's more important, showing I could win on a hill with cobbles or surprising all other riders on Alps stages of Giro?" The time Luca gave on the climb he'd taken back with a vengeance on the descent, coupled with a crash that put the leaders on the ground, and one in the hospital. Luca had favored his right leg getting back on the bike but had pedaled away, and insisted later that it was only bruises. "I want them to underestimate me."

Oh hell yes. If he had to save it for a race equal in every way to the Tour de France and coming six weeks earlier, then third was marvelous. "That's important," Christopher conceded, and finally asked, "Are you ever going to tell me what you're endorsing?" That detail kept getting lost in more important matters, like whether Rolf was elsewhere and how long that might last.

Luca laughed. "Did photo shoot. Show you." An email chimed for attention, revealing a picture of Luca fastening a Vuelta Asturias helmet under his chin, his curls escaping every which way against the green background that would be replaced by some cycling scene. "Well vented but still aerodynamic. Be good for hot weather. If it works the way they say."

"You don't know?" Christopher could do an article on helmets, no problem.

"Never used it. Wrong colors for team. Can send you one."

The team raced in turquoise and black, which had to be custom made. Why hadn't he figured that out by himself? Luca's picture had him in a white perforated shell and was destined to be printed out as an 8x11 for Christopher's living room wall. "I'll do a test run for you. Maybe write it up."

"Did you ride today?" Luca's voice went soft enough that Christopher heard *Were you feeling okay about riding today?*

Luca's concern for him choked Christopher into admitting, "No. It's not as much fun as it used to be with you or Stu." He had ridden other days, reporting how muddy Niwot was and that the quarry had some new fossils on display.

"Be hard to keep up with me if you don't practice good pedaling, Christopher. When you ship your bike, pack a set of tools with it. Did you get your passport yet?" Luca stuck every reason for Christopher to push himself into three sentences.

"It takes at least six weeks, Luca." No matter how much he longed to be on the other side of the ocean, the government wouldn't hurry for him without some cash.

"You should have let me pay for expedited process." His reproach was mild, but real, and it stung.

"I can't let you pay for everything, Luca. That's not right." His principles would cost them three weeks. Three long weeks, and even while he wished he'd said yes, he'd say no again. "I'll get there."

"Maybe have new endorsement deal coming. Money to spend on you. Buy you ticket for rest days before Giro. Damiano has villa above Lake Como, we could stay there. He's riding Tour de Romandie, won't need it." The lascivious burr in Luca's voice suggested they'd get less rest than the directeur sportif might like.

"You know I want to be with you." Christopher wanted that more than anything right now, and drew fingertips across his neck, echoing the way Luca liked to start. "But…"

"No buts," Luca interrupted him. "I miss you. Tour de Romandie is a month from now, passport should be here for two weeks by then. I want your hands, not only mine. Kiss you, not only talk."

"So do I." Suddenly aching with the need to pin his lover beneath him, Christopher gripped his own shoulder, face down into Luca's pillow. The scent had faded and laundry soap had taken the rest, but memory of Luca's head denting the foam lingered. "I'd love to get my hands in your hair; I'd turn your head to suck on your ear."

"Ye—oh." Fuck, if Luca had gone from zero to sixty in nanoseconds, he came to a halt even faster. "*Ciao,* Rolf. Paolo," came through faintly, as if he'd turned his head and his whole attention. "Talk to you tomorrow, okay?"

"Okay."

No, it wasn't, but he couldn't say anything else. If they were at Damiano's villa, they couldn't be interrupted like this. Christopher opened another document, intending to inform *Cyclo World's* readers which tools they needed to pack with any bike they shipped.

His passport still wasn't here, but another payment from *Cyclo World* was. Enough to get him about a third of the way across the Atlantic. The email with the payment notification contained a note from his contact at the magazine praising Christopher's race analyses. "Dave said good catch on that dustup in the *Prijs,"* Ron wrote. "He also said don't get any illusions: he likes his job."

Not that Christopher had any hope of taking Dave's place, since he didn't speak several languages or know the intricacies of the European rail system, but it was nice to be noticed. He'd watched the video on the crash about a dozen times: until the horror of seeing Luca go down had faded into something manageable, he couldn't see the details of who clipped whom and how the cascade spread. He still couldn't find what had caused the Kastibank rider to slide, although the presence of a turtle was highly unlikely.

Days went by without a long, intimate phone call, though they could share news, racing, and some laughs. Christopher tried not to think about Paolo's hands rubbing Luca's tired body, tried not to think about Rolf being there to hear Luca's random thoughts, and tried not to cling too tightly to a man half a world away because he mourned for his best friend. Luca was Luca, he was wonderful, he was quicksilver, and he wasn't there if they had too big an audience or if Christopher was caught somewhere in public.

Luca completed Gent-Wevelgem, unlike two thirds of the field, who crashed, froze, or otherwise couldn't make it to the finish line, let alone in second place. "Colder than Snow Mountain Ranch, with icy winds. Good we skipped first fifty kilometers and a climb. Brr."

"Brr," Christopher agreed. "I'd warm you up. Take you into a warm shower, hold you tight, add some friction…"

"Can't," Luca warned. "Would have liked another pair of socks." Damn, if Christopher had to hear about a frigid spring classic where riders could see their breaths and rode in echelons of slow mummies for wearing every piece of clothing they had in their suitcases instead of how nice it would be to cuddle under a down comforter, he'd take it.

"I have two articles in this week's *CycloWorld*." Christopher could add his own bit of good news. "An article about saddles and a two hundred word sidebar on the Paris-Nice race. It's like I'm Dave Pauwels' lieutenant."

"Lieutenants can triumph in their specialty. Good!" His grumbled aside made Christopher wonder who had invaded Luca's sanctum—it sounded like a dozen men clamoring for his attention in the background. "Time to go for press conference. I tell Paolo to get copy of *CycloWorld*, I read your words, okay?"

Fresh ice grew in Christopher's stomach—would Luca think he'd been mentioned too often, or too warmly? Not often enough wouldn't be an issue for the champion—he'd be offering most of the credit for today's success to his teammates.

"Okay. Talk to you later." *I love you.*

Later sucked. Later sucked moose balls the size of dinner plates. It should have been great.

Christopher'd spent the evening writing up "What it's like to ride in a cold wind off the North Sea and how to dress for it" based on Luca's descriptions, some interviews on the streaming channel, and his knowledge of what hung on the racks at the store, and popped that off to *CycloWorld*. Then he'd let himself dream of warming Luca under the comforter and had fallen asleep with his nose buried in the memory of brown curls. He'd even taken his own road bike for a quick climb up Flagstaff Mountain and been home in time for Luca's usual rest day call. They should have had plenty of time to discuss all the sexy things they'd had to leave out yesterday.

And then Luca called.

"*Che cazzo é*, Christopher!" he all but screamed. "What the fuck are you doing?"

"What *what* am I doing?" Christopher fell more than sat on the edge of the futon.

"My name is all over *CycloWorld*—why?" The way he sounded, he wasn't just pacing, he was swinging a fist.

"Well, hell, you were in the top three in four stages of a big race, you're going to get mentioned a lot, what did you think?" Humility was one thing, shunning the limelight completely was another.

"Not that, *idiota,* the saddles. Why?" Somehow a lower tone and Italian epithets sounded worse than his initial anger.

"Why what? I quoted you, yeah, but you said it was okay." Trying to squeeze the exact memory out of his suddenly throbbing head, Christopher reached for his copy of the magazine. "You explained about saddles, I fucking well *asked* if I could quote you, and you said, 'Yes, go sell lots of saddles.' So I did and this is going to sell lots of saddles. Why are you cussing at me because of that?"

"I had interesting phone call this morning, Christopher. Phone call from Jindo rep. Not first phone call from Jindo rep, last time he talked endorsement deal. What do you think he talked this time?" came through as a hiss.

"He wanted to know where to send the contract?" Christopher thumbed through to the article with the byline he'd been so proud of earlier. "I don't know. What?"

"He asks why we talk about endorsement when I tell public I ride his biggest competition. What do I tell him, Christopher?"

"A journalist who knows saddles saw your bike?" Christopher offered. "That even has the advantage of being true. And you were riding a K-Aero saddle. Any photographer with a long lens could have taken a picture of it, figured out what it was. You only told me *why* you like K-Aeros."

"No problem for liking, only problem for telling world I like that when I'm paid big money to tell world I like something else." Nope, not a call about where to send paperwork.

"Isn't that going to be a problem anyway, since you like K-Aeros for a feature Jindo doesn't have?" What can of worms had he opened? The logic-fail bait?

"Jindo planned to make new line of saddles with perforations to get around problem. Now saddles are perfect, and they pay me to ride, they give me special saddles and twenty thousand euro to tell everyone about excellent saddles. They give me money so every time moto shows me on TV, Jindo logo is right there. Now, nothing."

"Nothing?" Oh, shit.

"Nothing, Christopher. Nothing at all from Jindo. Not this year, maybe not next year. Or any year. Strange thing too, about racing camp."

"What about racing camp?" And wasn't that years ago? They'd talked about it on their first real date, but surely Luca was well beyond anything but team practices.

"On rest days when near Friuli, I teach young riders. Two hours before lunch, few days, much money. Now offer is half. 'Magazine is eight euro, why pay extra?' they ask."

"Magazine? Like that would substitute for real time with you?" Nothing Christopher had read in three years came close to an hour spent with Luca circling a parking lot. He better not be licking any students at a camp.

"Magazine, with excellent directions for changing pedaling. Has my name all over it. Your name too. How did that happen, Christopher?" Oh the spittle had to be flying all over his hotel room. "I thought that was accident until saddles magazine, but no. Not accident at all, is it?"

"No, it's not an accident, I wrote that, and yeah, I used your name, Luca." Christopher's hand shook so badly he wasn't sure he was speaking into the phone's pickup. "I asked, every time. I always asked if it was okay to quote you. And the times you said no, I didn't mention anything at all, like tactics. If you said yes, I thought you meant yes, it was okay. But I asked, every single time."

"Maybe you asked, but I thought, okay, tell Stu. Or tell—" Luca sputtered over a name he didn't know, because Christopher hadn't developed any close training partners after Stu. "But tell a friend, two friends. Not tell whole world in a magazine!"

Oh, fuck, had he ever really explained? "I asked to quote because I knew I had to have permission. I wasn't hiding anything."

"When did you ever say, 'I quote you in *CycloWorld,* is that okay?' Never, the way I remember!" His voice shook.

"Maybe not in those exact words, but…" He needed those exact words. "I told you I wrote, and for who, and I asked every single time, Luca. I did."

"You asked, but not for whole thing, Christopher. Never. You wrote about gloves, I had nothing to tell about gloves. I talked about riding, helped you be better rider, I thought, share with friend. Never this. Never thinking telling you anything would mean I lose thousands, tens of thousands of euro, this year, maybe every year. Now I'm rider who gives everything away, why should they pay me?"

"I'm sorry, Luca. I thought I was doing this right."

"Why should they trust me to honor endorsements? Why should they have my face on their ads? No reason," Luca mocked. "Wait another month, they get for free. Problem for me though. I don't have next year to do different, they have long memory. Now I have to win everything, no tactics, no surprises. All I have left are appearance fees. I have to be worth more money to ride in their race, because saying, 'I love saddle' is free."

"I'll stop, Luca." What did he still have out at *CycloWorld* that hadn't printed besides race chat? "I'm really sorry; I didn't think this would be a problem."

"You didn't think. You know, but you don't want to think about it." His voice grew low and fierce. "I have ten years more career, if I'm lucky. If not lucky, might have ten days more career. Or ten minutes. I *have* to make money now, while I can, because all goes away fast. Then what do I do? Be directeur sportif? Hundred old riders want each job. Hundred more old riders want that every year. What then? I cut meat in father's shop?"

Christopher doubled over, acid washing through his gut. "You always talk like you're indestructible."

"Hundred percent accident rate, Christopher. I talk confident because I have to be confident to win. And I talk confident because I don't want you to think of me like—Stu. But I know." His voice dropped into gentleness that hurt all the more for being gentle. "I might meet turtle tomorrow."

"Luca, I am so sorry. I didn't realize—" Ten thousand apologies wouldn't get the Jindo rep back on the phone.

"I'm sorry too. I thought biggest problem of boyfriends was getting outed. Not problem, or not problem yet, no one looks at me funny in locker room or sauna. Maybe they don't know, maybe they don't care. Maybe just my fear, except I don't think so. But never did I think boyfriends would make me poor. I take big risk with you, worth being happy, but real risk to reputation was reliability and honesty."

Too stunned to say more than another "I'm sorry," Christopher rocked slowly. "I won't quote you again."

"No, no more quotes. My reputation might recover from one mistake, but not two. I need endorsement money for rest of my life. Mother and father's lives. What happens when father can't cut meat any more? I have to take care of them too. Can't waste opportunities when all could end tomorrow." Luca stopped for a moment, letting Christopher stare into the abyss he'd helped dig. "I took big risk with you, Christopher. Bigger risk than I thought. Now I don't trust you, can't trust you. What else will you only tell me half?"

"I wasn't trying to tell you only half, Luca." The distance between them now was far wider than the Atlantic and half of North America.

"But you did, and it cost me. I'm sorry, Christopher. I was happy with you."

Was. Oh shit, Luca lived in present tense. "I'm happy with you too." *I love you—please don't say whatever you're going to say next, please don't.*

"Goodbye, Christopher."

CHAPTER 17

Another big stage race started only three days after Gent-Wevelgem, but Christopher didn't get up early enough to watch the cyclists sign in and mount up. Two days of phone silence and grieving destroyed Christopher's sleep; when he did finally fall asleep the race was only a few hours in the future. He woke to find Luca contesting for King of the Mountain on the climb at the Berendries. "He's already accumulated twelve points on the hills, Frank. Looks like Biondi's trying to take it all," the announcer said.

"And he might just do it. If he can get around—"

Christopher would push the star with the long career off the road himself to clear the way for Luca.

"The strong winds have taken a toll on all the riders. They averaged forty-five kilometers per hour the first hour, but after the climbs I don't think we'll see that kind of pace once they get back on the flats. It will take better than that to catch this breakaway. The leaders are increasing the gap to the chasers, and the peloton's falling farther behind the chase. That's going to be quite a deficit."

Oh man, Luca was pushing it for all he was worth, nudging ahead of the other rider. Who cared about the stragglers three minutes back? The cameras came back to the leaders who pounded toward the summit. "The Berendries rises sixty-five meters over less than a kilometer, averaging 7.2% and the steepest section is 14%. That's going to be some pull, and it's the second time the riders will see it today." The announcer offered words of doom—even the Super-Jamestown route didn't have anything over a 14% grade. Luca and the others would be going the next thing to straight up.

And then they went down.

"*No!*" Christopher flipped to kneeling before the laptop. "Oh fuck! Luca!" he roared across the miles. "Are you okay?

Maybe not—he and two others skidded across pavè, entwined in each other and their machines. Slowly, too slowly, they unwound from bikes turned scythes. Luca rolled to his knees, rising to unsteady feet. He put his hand down to a rider in white, tugging him to his feet, and they both offered a hand to the third man on the ground. What were they saying to each other? Were they sorting out who would win now, who would try hardest and who would hold back a little to favor an injury or for some other reason? Or were they finding out what vital bits had broken and by whose fault? What language were they speaking?

They untangled their bicycles and swung astride. Luca moved the least slowly of the wounded leaders—was he hurt? Or just shaken? Oh fuck, that was blood staining his legging, and the shoulder of his jersey and everything under it hung in tatters. Red-mottled white skin showed in the gap. The road had taken its ounces of flesh. Spectators materialized around the riders. They shoved Luca into motion before he clipped into his second pedal. Two men pushed, running alongside him, bringing him to speed. The other riders struggled to regain momentum with their own amateur assistants. Luca had a slight lead, bursting away from his helpers. They could almost pace him on foot on this steep section.

"They're back on the road, Biondi leading, but the chase group is less than two minutes behind now, and the peloton may catch them yet on the descent," opined the announcer.

Oh no, they wouldn't. If Luca had pushed so hard on the way up, he'd be lightning on the way down. Nothing short of another crash would stop him. Maybe no one else knew what that set of his jaw meant, and surely no one else had seen him in his crazed rush to the best goal, but Christopher had seen that desperation on Luca's face, and could only urge him on now as he'd done before. *Go, Luca!* warred with *are you okay?* But Luca was okay enough to summit ahead of the others, and then he started down. Christopher couldn't bear to watch. He couldn't bear to look away.

Luca swooped down the narrow road, crosshatched with cobbles laid down in the time of the Romans. He flew through the curves, veering from the inner edge of the road to the outer, keeping his speed with the widest curve. He was some kind of bionic centaur, leaning over his handlebars.

"Biondi's opened a fifteen second lead on his two closest pursuers, and the chase is two minutes back. The peloton missed their chance to reel in this *fuga bidone*; the breakaway has a good two and a half minute lead on the peloton, and the leaders are uncatchable."

"Look at Biondi take those curves."

Must I? Christopher couldn't look away, even though he needed to find something he could safely vomit on. Acid backwashed in his chest. *Don't find a rock. God, let there be no turtles. It's too cold for turtles. Luca, just get down safely.*

He did. Luca sailed away from the foot of the hill, across the flat, and stayed ahead for another ten kilometers into the town of Zottegem. His legs had to be screaming, his vision blurred—even this dynamo had to be feeling close to five hours of heavy exertion now. Christopher's heart thudded with every revolution of Luca's pedals.

"This is a brute force effort—Biondi left his team behind on the other side of the Berendries, and he looks like he intends to go all the way to the finish line alone."

Oh yeah, he did. Luca intends to go everywhere alone now. "Go," Christopher whispered. Luca fought the wind in single combat, never looking behind to see who might be gaining. The moto stayed with him, its relentless lens recording sweat stains growing across his back even in the freezing wind. "Just make it to the finish, okay? You don't have to prove anything."

And then he was across the line, his speed dwindling to a stop on the far side of the logo-bedecked arch. A teammate ran to him, a blanket in his hands to throw around Luca's shoulders and protect him from the elements and rejoice with a hug, a yell, and a grin.

The noise had gone very soft from Christopher's hearing—perhaps it had for Luca as well. The cowbells and waving turquoise inflaties went far away, and Luca's chest heaved against a man who couldn't possibly love him the way Christopher did. "You did it, Luca," Christopher mumbled. "But what did it take from you?"

He couldn't offer congratulations on a win with a cost he'd made so much heavier than it needed to be. Top three in three stages and a kickass mini-time trial to end it would have taken the yellow leader's jersey. Instead, Luca felt the need for this ass-whupping victory that might just whup his own ass out of contention for the next two days.

Christopher found his phone. **How bad was it? R u ok?** It would be an hour at least before Luca would see his phone. And Christopher could only hope to get an answer.

CHRISTOPHER'D GIVEN up hope and gone to work. Luca hadn't responded. He'd meant his goodbye.

The post-race commentary hadn't offered any clue to the depths of Luca's injuries, and his breakneck finish didn't really help. A few years ago, in the Tour de France, Johnny Hoogerland had been hit by a car, finished his stage, and then been pieced back together with fifty stitches. Luca was just as strong, just as determined. More determined.

A man who stood on the podium for the King of the Mountain, for the intermediate sprints, and for the win and the leader's yellow jersey had to be the most determined man in the entire sport. That didn't mean he'd have anything left for the next day. He'd stood on the podium in enough clothes to weather a Rocky Mountain winter, waving a bottle of champagne and a bouquet that was already showing frost-bitten petals. Thank God for Paolo. Someone had to nurse Luca back from the brink.

An entire display of water bottles went down with hollow pops when Christopher's phone chimed. Later, he'd get them later. He ran for the stock room. Half an hour later than usual—had Luca taken time to bandage before calling? *Please no stitches, or shoulder separations, or other hidden injuries...*

Livid scrapes across Luca's pale shoulder filled the tiny screen. A second picture of a familiar, hairless, and abraded knee showed the rest. Okay, damages, not fatal wounds.

`Looks bad, isn't. Am ok. Ride tomorrow, no problem.`

Relief misted Christopher's eyes and made his thumbs clumsy on the tiny keyboard.

`Good. Glad. U did good. U kicked ass today!`

Christopher racked every water bottle neatly, unloaded two pallets of bicycles, and stared at an uneaten sandwich for half an hour without a peep from Luca. Maybe he was asleep?

CHAPTER 18

If Luca was asleep, he napped until the start of the next day's stage, and then came stunningly awake. His performance today was somewhat more restrained—had he and the directeur sportif had a chat about strategy, or was Luca merely exhausted? Or on the other riders' radar as a threat? His every attack got reeled in nearly as fast as he made it, though he made far fewer today. Finishing fifth in the stage still kept him in yellow, though his margin had been whittled to less than a minute.

Still worth a text of congratulations. Christopher hit send, wishing he dared add something more personal. Nothing came back, though Luca's usual call time was still a few hours in the future.

When his phone chimed, Christopher was deep in discussion with a customer, and couldn't reach to his phone. By the time he rang up the bike, a new helmet (the same brand Luca endorsed because Christopher talked it up), and a replacement saddle (a K-Aero because the customer insisted, not the wider Cassowary that he'd have done better with), half an hour had gone by.

But Luca knew his schedule as well as he knew Luca's. He'd be forgiven for the delay.

Went easy today. All good, Christopher read with knots in his gut untying themselves.

U scared all the other riders yesterday. Miss you.

But if Luca missed him too, he wasn't saying.

Christopher's phone didn't chime again until after the end of the next stage, a brutal day of 112km on the roads and a 15km time trial less than an hour after the road race finished. Luca struggled to get around a clump of riders, finishing third on the road race. None of the clump were his biggest GC rivals, who'd taken the opportunity not to start. Slackers. Think they'd miss a day in the cold winds and be rested up for the next big race on Sunday? Like they'd leave Luca in the dirt in three days' time because they wouldn't take him on honestly now? Christopher seethed through the time trial: no one could get in Luca's way in this stage, and no one stood higher than he on the podium. That yellow jersey meant no less because he hadn't trounced every single big name on the road. If anything, it meant more because he'd terrified the competition out of contention.

`:D` waited for when Luca would be able to communicate. Christopher dared send no more.

`Tired and a little stiff, but all fine` Luca wrote back later, and again, silence met Christopher's reply.

Christopher went home to a cold and empty apartment, where no one and nothing waited for him except an email.

"What are you going to have for us on the *Driedaagse de Panne-Koksijde*?" Ron wanted to know. "Biondi kicked some ass, huh?"

Fuck, wasn't like he had anything else to do. Christopher opened a document and began to write.

Luca had a few rest days, which Christopher hoped he'd spend riding lightly and eating frequently. If he didn't top off his glycogen reserves while he could, there'd be a crash and burn of epic proportions come Sunday. Flanders Week sucked it all out of a rider, and Luca had worked harder than his rivals.

No race meant nothing to congratulate. What else could Christopher say? `I'm sorry, I miss you` begged to text itself, but the thought of total silence in return kept his fingers away from the keys.

His phone did chime around eight a.m. *`30 km recovery ride, nothing happened.`*

`Thanks for saying. I worry.` Would this be another message thrown into the void?

If the phone had turned into a frog in his hand, Christopher couldn't have been more startled.

`I know.`

And that was all.

They fell into a pattern: an early text from Luca on a rest day to relay his safety, a hopeful reply from Christopher, and total silence. If he was racing, and he took Paris-Roubaix in a brutal group sprint, there would be a single line to announce the real story afterwards. What the hell did it mean? Did Luca just feel sorry for him having to suffer in ignorance because he might think Luca had met his turtle that day? Or was there more?

`Why do you keep texting when you never answer me?` *Please, please, please, God, is it because he'll forgive me one day?* Or did he just want to turn the knife twenty thousand euro' worth?

`Do you want me to stop?` shook the phone out of his hands.

Neverneverneverneven, just please answer when I text back, so we can talk and I can tell you how sorry I am and we can get past this. I'll support your aged parents myself if you'd just talk to me. `No.`

Luca said nothing more that day, but in the morning he went out and kicked two hundred well-toned asses up and down the Mur de Huy, steepness be damned, and fucking owned the fucking Flèche Wallonne like that classic race had insulted his mother.

Christopher watched the race in two chunks—the cyclists' five hours on the road got interrupted by having to go to work, and then he spent another twenty minutes arguing Brendan into letting him hook his laptop into the big display TV that usually ran a canned cycle of ads. "Come on, it's a Classic, and our local teams have been doing really well. We'll sell a ton of whatever they're wearing." He'd make sure of it.

He and a customer watched the final ascent of the Mur with matching gapes. "Nineteen percent grade. That's one hell of a climb," the man sputtered. "Biondi's motoring."

"Yeah." The strain in Luca's face signaled the alchemy of steel turning to lead: his bared teeth and slitted eyes reminded Christopher of his ride toward Ward in the company of the team. Luca wouldn't fall off, though, he wouldn't lie in the gutter fighting for air, but he'd know the bite of lactic acid chewing his muscles to tatters. He had only a short distance to go, and then he could rest.

"The team rode up to Ward and beyond Jamestown to train." This wasn't news to anyone but the customer: Christopher could say that without pissing anyone off.

"Huh." The Philistine turned his attention back to a rack of helmets: Christopher had to let the rest of the race finish without his rapt attention, though he noticed a clump of turquoise jerseys finishing together about a minute back of Luca. "Any reason not to use the cheapest certified helmet?"

"If it fits, it will work, but you really don't want terminally ugly and you do want good air flow." Pulling a Vuelta Asturias helmet off the shelf, he told himself he had good reason for what he'd say next. "I saw a picture of Luca Biondi wearing one of these." And so would everyone else who read *CycloWorld* and its competition. "It's supposed to be especially well ventilated, and you remember how hot last summer was."

The man shook out the straps and tried it on. "Yeah, I can see that." He turned back to the television screen, where Luca dragged himself across the finish line, his pedaling tempo wildly high and dropping while he fought with gears instead of raising a hand to the screaming crowd. "Biondi wore one of these, huh."

"Yeah." For an hour or so. Christopher rang up the helmet and figured its maiden voyage might be on the road up to Ward. He needed to sell a hell of a lot of helmets to make up for the saddle incident. Everyone in Boulder was going to have a Vuelta helmet.

The text, when it came, was chattier than usual. *Two minor races in next three weeks. Rolf can have Tour de Romandie.*

This was Luca as Christopher knew him. Not a word of complaint, damned little of explanation, and a whole lot of information in between the lines. The last two weeks had been non-stop racing, all at top effort. He had to be bone tired. He hadn't just ridden the plains and the *hellingen* of Belgium and northern France, he'd destroyed them and most everyone who'd come with him, and ended up owning a season's palmarès that would suffice for a career for almost anyone else. And either he was almost saying that he'd be glad to stop, or… there had been an invitation in there once.

My passport came. The money hadn't, or not enough of it, but he had a credit card and a laptop: he could pay back the one by wringing more words out of the other. Dared he hope?

Hours later, Christopher dragged through his front door. The blue pamphlet with its unmarked pages mocked him from the table next to the futon. He threw it into a drawer. The passport wasn't going anywhere, and neither was he.

Fuck that. Okay, he'd screwed up, he'd screwed up big-time, but he was sorry and he deserved at least the chance to promise that it wouldn't happen again, explain that he deserved a second chance. Okay, he'd said that, maybe said it a lot, but he wanted Luca to look him in the eyes and tell him, face to face, that there was nothing he could do to ever make this right between them. And if there was some begging in there, and promises, and atonement, he'd do it all, if Luca would just stick around long enough to hear it. This text-once-and-disappear shit was getting really old.

Not a damned thing he could do about it without being in the same place as Luca. And that wasn't going to happen for months and months, not until the grasses turned brown of the cold and the racing season shifted to warm and more distant places like Australia and Oman. And if Luca raced there….

Fuck it. He needed a plane ticket, and he needed it now. Last week. He needed to redo time and make himself clear on quoting, and see if Luca's face brightened or went stormy when Christopher hove into sight. He needed to fix what he'd broken, he needed not to be whatever that long ago man was, the one who put fear on Luca's face at the thought of getting close. And to do that, he had to talk to Luca. Really talk.

Come on, fingers; do your stuff. Christopher wrenched open the laptop and started a new document. "The Hell in the Hellingen" hit the top of the page in a clatter.

Watching Luca Biondi power up the steepest helling *in Belgium to win the Flèche Wallonne was to watch a man in hell. These Belgian hills have the perfect shape to create agony. A short, shallow lead-in is the only warning that soon the rider will have to push up a near vertical road, and the only thing that hurts more than an 18% grade is a 19% grade, which you find on the* Mur de Huy…

He finished his applied geology for cyclists and hurled it toward *CycloWorld. Take that, Dave Pauwels. I can get off the sidebar without stepping on your toes.*

Chapter 19

"You do love your local teams," Ron wrote about Christopher's coverage of Luca's 2.1 "keep in practice" race. Luca had claimed in an interview to be riding only for the chance to catch up with his old Duclos-Wurth teammates, something the racing world believed every bit as much as they believed all the stars backed out of the Driedaagse de Panne-Koksijde's last stage because of toothache. But Luca hadn't ridden to shame his old teammates or overshadow his new ones—he finished in the top twenty and applauded his sprinter's intermediate points and his climber's new polka-dot jersey.

Yeah, what little coverage that race had gotten was only because Luca had attended, since the bulk of the skilled motos in Europe were chasing Rolf and company up and down Alps in the Tour de Romandie, and most of the rest had packed up for California. The Tour of California wouldn't end before the Giro started, something Christopher had unhappily ascertained before letting himself dream of Luca in the States in one of the few big events. Riding as a hometown favorite in the Giro was a foregone conclusion for Luca, a decision made the moment the racing calendar came out. The best American riders would be noticeably absent from the Giro too. And they'd be riding much wider roads.

Rolf wasn't doing too badly: he'd made top five in two stages, neither of them a time trial, which Christopher dutifully wrote up for *CycloWorld* as well as the other stages where Antano-Clark cyclists collected sprint points or King of the Mountain points but no jersey-bearing triumphs. Wasn't half bad seeing his byline every other week in a publication that ate content like pizza.

He'd like to not be ripping off covers from unsold magazines, but the new editions were out, and the unsold copies dated two weeks or a month ago had to get credited. The covers would go to the distributor, and the rest would get recycled here. At least he already had pristine copies of all the magazines with Luca on the cover. *Velo News*, *Gear Up*, and *Shifting Times* had also covered the big races, and the frequent winner shone from all of them at least once this season.

The defaced magazines hit the bin with sad thumps; pages fluttered on their landings. Luca's face and a white helmet peeked out and disappeared again. Christopher tore another cover, tossed it into the return pile, and stopped. He thumbed through the remaining pages. *Yes!*

He went to find the manager, printed carcass in hand. "Hey, do you mind if I take this?"

One lazy glance toward Christopher's handful, and Brendan said, "I suppose it's okay. One less thing to recycle."

Hah, this was going to be the best recycling ever.

Once home, Christopher took a blade to his prize. He carefully sliced out the masthead, the table of contents, and his neatly formatted article on saddles. With his biggest, blackest marker, he circled the paragraph that mentioned Luca.

"Have you talked to Luca Biondi about why he rides this saddle?" he scrawled. He added his phone and email address near his byline. Ten minutes of Google-fu and he had the name of the K-Aero marketing manager and a corporate address.

He stuck every stamp he owned on the envelope and carefully licked the flap. If he'd been licking Luca, he couldn't have been more precise—if this worked, it would be Luca under his tongue again.

Maybe. Maybe it would just be a happy retirement for *Signor e Signora* Biondi. Maybe the pages would never get past the receptionist. Christopher mailed the envelope anyway.

A dozen cyclists whizzed down the hill the other way. Wusses. Anyone who got to the top of Gold Hill by going up Sunshine Canyon was taking the easy way out. Bet they'd cry on the *hellingen.* So what if they'd already traveled close to twelve miles and gained three thousand or so feet in elevation and wanted to come home fast. Christopher ignored their efforts and wiped sweat out of his eyes. He'd taken the steeper Four Mile Canyon route, and maybe he'd come back the same way, too. High time he got over coming down a high grade.

Back to taking risks, I see, Stu muttered in his ear. Yeah. He was.

Christopher had little company—no one passed him and he passed no one, and the rider up ahead disappeared for minutes at a time around curves. They were halfway up the 10% section when he caught up with the man ahead.

For an old guy, he wasn't doing too bad. Silver hairs twinkled on the back of his neck, and the grin he threw over his shoulder had some deep canyons around it. How he heaved that beer belly up the mountain was a mystery, but he wasn't stopping, and he wasn't waving Christopher around, either, though he stayed close to the shoulder.

Christopher could pace him or go around. Or he could try to go around. Maybe pace until they got to the false flat, and then he could pass. Stupid tactics. The one thing he didn't want to do was crash and burn in front of someone twice his age. He didn't need a reminder that he'd slacked off on his training, or rather, hadn't pushed himself to get out on the bike as frequently as he needed to maintain his pre-crash fitness.

You will know when the time is right to ride again Luca reminded him. Hah, that was more than Luca had texted for the last three weeks. Those were all *rode this, did ok* or *rode that, crashed but ok* Maybe the lack of oxygen was making the Luca in his head more chatty. Well, the right time had to start right now, because Christopher wasn't going to humiliate himself on this climb.

Who was this old guy? Christopher pondered that for another mile, looking at a much-wider-than-Stu's back end. Boulder was full of old athletes who still performed better than most of the world. Of course, last he'd seen, Davis Phinney wasn't packing that kind of gut.

When they reached the false flat, a climb of a mere 3% that felt wonderful after the last mile, Christopher shifted gears and buzzed around his temporary companion, nodding on the pass. The old guy waved him on, waiting a few yards to start his own acceleration. Christopher's phone would have to chime right when his pride wouldn't let him stop. Whether he responded now or in half an hour, Luca wouldn't have a real conversation.

At the top of Gold Hill lay a microscopic town, a last remnant of the gold rush that had populated this entire region. Christopher pedaled in, looking for the only gold he'd strike around here, which was some sports drink at the tiny mercantile. He chugged the cold liquid, feeling the chill coursing down behind his breastbone, and everything was pretty all right with the world.

Until he looked at his phone. *Little crash on training ride. Bruises but ok.*

Luca's definition of "not okay" required body parts strewn over the landscape. Prove it.

He got a picture back about fifteen minutes later, long after the drink was history and the old guy ambled in for his own cool beverage. Clearly the picture had been taken by someone else, because both of Luca's forearms took up the screen, obscuring his chest, and his face had been cut off at the top. A few wet curls straggled across his collarbone. Some bruising, some scrapes, but no casts, stitches, or splints.

Ok, I believe you now. His disbelief had gotten an answer.

That once.

The display in the caller ID window startled Christopher almost as badly as if Luca was calling. He'd never seen the number, but "*CycloWorld*" was clear enough. Had he done something wrong? Violated a copyright or stepped on an established reporter's toes? He managed to answer while heading to the stock room.

"Christopher Nye, hello." He tried to project confidence, but his knees wobbled him onto a pallet of cycling shoes.

"Hey, Christopher, it's Ron Kittel from *CycloWorld.* How are you doing?" Ron always emailed: Christopher had never heard his editor's voice, and didn't know how to assess the combination of strain and good-will in his words.

"Fine. What's up?" If it was bad, Christopher needed to know, *now.* Did they not want any more of his articles and were cutting off the funds he needed to get to Europe? At the rate he was going, he'd make the Vuelta in the fall, or the Tour de France in June if getting back didn't matter.

"A little bad news, a little good news. Maybe. That part depends."

"Depends on what?" Get. To. The. Point.

"On whether you have a passport. Do you?" Was that hope? Fear? Both?

"Sure do." Would he end up in Australia with it? "Am I going somewhere?"

"Possibly. Can you shake loose and be in Italy for the Giro?"

"Maybe: the Giro starts next week." YESYESYESYESYES!!! All practical matters receded to nothingness. Forget rent, forget his job, forget everything else, just give him that plane ticket! "Why so sudden?"

Ron sighed deeply. "That's the bad news. Dave Pauwels was checking out part of the race route ahead of time, and he crashed. Crazy Italian driver knocked him right down an embankment."

Just like Stu… Christopher's blood ran cold. "Is he—"

"He broke his pelvis and a couple of other bones. He's already out of surgery, and he should be okay, but he's not going to be covering the Giro or anything else for a while."

"That's good." Christopher warmed slightly, enough to realize how that sounded. "I lost a friend in a similar accident recently. I'm glad Dave will be okay."

"Sorry about your friend. You're out in Boulder, so… Was that Stuart Fallon?"

How did he know? "Yes, that was Stu. Uh—"

"Amy has a desk full of clippings and police reports. She's doing a story on car/bike accidents. She said there was another cyclist involved in that one."

"That was me."

"If you want to talk to her about it, she'd like the input." Damn, how could Ron just flip from casual sympathy to "ooh, data, shiny" without thinking of the real cost?

"Stu was my best friend. I'd—have to think about it." He'd think so long the magazine that story published in would have its covers ripped off, but he wouldn't say no outright without a plane ticket in hand. "It's still pretty fresh."

"Hmm, there is that. How badly were you hurt?"

"I landed upside down in a barbwire fence and needed seventy-two stitches, but it's just scars now." Bright red scars on his soul, paler scars on his skin.

"Are you riding again? It's essential to covering the Giro. Where you can't go on a train with your bike, you need to go on your bike. Driving over there is hell, parking is worse in race towns, and we can't afford a rental car anyway."

Even if he wasn't riding, with opportunity getting dumped in his lap, he'd be riding. "Not a problem. I just did thirty miles on a mountain route this morning." All the way to Ward, too, if not as fast as Luca and the team.

"Good. So, can you do it?"

Could he do it? Could he get past everything: the lack of preparation, his total ignorance of Italian, his dependence on other racing coverage? Could he do it well enough that anyone at the magazine would still talk to him after Dave was back on his feet?

Could he walk through fire and escape from straightjackets underwater if it meant being close enough to talk to Luca?

Hell, yes. But could he find a hotel room?

"What about travel arrangements? Everything's booked up by now, isn't it?" If he were stopped by stupid practical matters—!

"We'll FedEx you all of Dave's reservations and tickets, and you'll have a *Cyclo World* credit card for your food per diem. Pick up your press packet at the journo booth. It will be in Dave's name but we'll notify them to give it to you. You have a good-quality camera, right?"

Under a heavy layer of dust, yeah. "I do."

That heaving sigh had to be relief for the budget. "Your plane ticket will show up in your email, so just print it out. Did I miss anything?"

The language implant, the universal translator, a native guide.... "What you're paying."

"Think you can live with—" Ron named a number high enough to make Christopher happy to be sitting. It wasn't "get rich" money, but it was "survive while looking for another job after the Giro" money, since he didn't have any illusions about his boss holding his position, nor about keeping this one once Dave could move again. "We'll need tweets during the stage for the web site, written stage by stage accounts, and local color pieces and rider profiles if you can wangle interviews."

Christopher'd get interviews all right. Luca would talk to him if it was official, even if he cut and ran after every personal message. Wouldn't he? "I can do that."

Ron barked a short laugh. "I'm sure you can. By the way, there are more teams in this race than Antano-Clark. Spread the love, okay?"

Not hardly, but Christopher could spread the publicity. "I'll keep it balanced."

"Good. Dave said he thought you could."

That brought Christopher up short. "He did?"

"Yeah. I was going to hire a freelancer on the ground in Italy, but Dave said you loved the sport and would do a good job. Prove him right, okay?"

Not exactly the sport, or not entirely. Almost too stunned to reply, he nodded, only finding words when he realized Ron couldn't hear his head rattling. "I will. Thank you. Thank Dave."

Christopher emerged from the stock room to search for his manager, making three complete circuits around the store and into the back rooms. Italy! On *CycloWorld's* business! Where Luca would be!

"Looking for something?" startled Christopher into noticing Brendan was standing at the register. How many times had he walked right by?

"Uh, yeah." Christopher reached past the blue and white tops and the black ones with sky blue rectangles to grab a turquoise promo jersey off the rack, and made a quick dash for the helmet rack, where he found a white Vuelta Asturias. "Ring these up for me, okay?"

"Why?" Brendan laughed. "Are you going to play dress-up while you're watching the Giro?" He tapped the keys and rang in Christopher's discount. "Or fantasize taking your rightful place on Team Antano-Clark?"

"Actually—" No better time to drop his bombshell. Christopher signed the credit card slip and handed back the pen and paper. "I'm covering the Giro for *CycloWorld*. I leave next week."

"You? *CycloWorld*?" Brendan dropped the pen, letting it clatter at his feet. "When are you coming back? Are you coming back?"

Christopher shrugged. "Don't know. And don't know." *Only if neither* CycloWorld *nor Luca will keep me.*

THE NEXT several days were a whirl of planning, biting nails, and packing. Christopher shoved two sets of Allen wrenches between the foam sheets protecting his disassembled bike and no electrical converters. The huge chunk of blue sidewalk chalk was the fourth item into his bag, but he didn't remember he'd need to plug his laptop and phone into round-pronged outlets until he'd gotten off the bus at the Denver airport.

A chance passage by a kiosk alerted him to his error. While he was shelling out twice the retail value for the converter, his phone summoned him.

On bus to Napoli

Luca could either sweat out Christopher's meaning or text back for clarification, and at this point Christopher didn't care which: he had to navigate the international gates.

See you there

CHAPTER 20

Okay, this wasn't as bad as he feared: Christopher was able to get from the airport to his *pensione* without any mishap. While his cardboard bicycle box had survived the attentions of baggage handlers in two nations, it almost didn't fit into the taxi. The bike rode in the back seat of the tiny cab, and he sat next to the driver. They had a pleasant, handwavy conversation, and Christopher was able to work one of his few words of non-bedroom Italian into the conversation. *Ciao* covered a lot of ground.

Once he'd reassembled his transportation, Christopher shoved a notebook, pen, every map he owned and a few he'd acquired at the airport into his jersey pockets. He'd check out the race route.

Dodging murderous traffic mostly by hiding in the peloton of local riders on their way to work or school or wherever, Christopher managed to get around the first circuit of the route without incident.

What a mess of surfaces! So far, he'd enjoyed the asphalt, cringed on cobbles, and wondered at the huge basalt slabs that made up the coastal road. A storm grate came within an inch, okay, here it was 2.54 centimeters, of putting him on the ground, and manholes provided unexpected deep drops. The unleashed, territorial dog quotient was a lot higher than he was used to. Whatever the word for "dog" was in Italian, it was probably the same as "pain in the ass" or "hazard." They'd better be tied up come race day.

The racers would ride the lightly hilly first circuit four times, but Christopher did one loop and turned his attention to the second loop. If the roads were blocked off for his recon ride, he'd feel a lot safer, but they swarmed with Fiats and Opels, all of them honking madly. Maybe the horn was mounted on a pedal next to, and mistaken for, the brake.

He found the finish line, which looked like the rest of the commercial streets here, but would be packed with screaming fans in two days' time. Where could he watch the race?

Wherever it was, he wanted to be here, in the last kilometer of the race, and he'd need to be here early. Crack of dawn early. But okay.

Pedaling back to his *pensione*, he passed a charcoal and burgundy striped Golf with a roof rack and an open trunk. A forty-ish man unloaded groceries. Christopher nearly went by before opportunity slapped him to a stop. "Hey, Kastibank! Need some help?" Please let the man speak some English.

"I trust you why?" His arms were full and his face suspicious.

"Because you have the key to my bike." Christopher wound his cable lock through the Golf's door handle and his bike frame, and stuck the key between the man's fingers. "I'm just a rookie journalist and I'm trying to get to know people. I write for *CycloWorld*, I'm brand new, and I need all the help I can get." He dug another couple of bags out of the car's open trunk and shut it. "Where are we taking this?"

"Upstairs."

Christopher followed the Kastibank soigneur—he had to be a soigneur—to a postage stamp of a bedroom. The toaster oven and mini-fridge didn't look like they were part of the normal furnishings, the way they stuck out into the very narrow passage between the wall and the bed. "What are you making?"

"My riders like *apfelkuchen* in their musettes," the man told him, and warmed rapidly under Christopher's interest. "I make fresh every night and wrap in foil for them." A cut cake graced the top of the toaster oven. "Here, taste. My test cake."

Nibbling at first and then taking a big bite, Christopher's universally translated *Mmmm* broke down the rest of the barriers, and he had lots of notes and pictures before his new buddy Markus unlocked his bike from the car. "You talk to Sylvain with Lampre, okay? Twenty years in cycling and no journo ever talked with him."

With his pal to make a phone call, Christopher rode three streets over to speak to Sylvain, who had stories, banana bread for his riders' feed bags, and an introduction to Karl with Duclos-Wurth. Karl made muffins with raisins for his riders, and had a smile for his former domestique who was now a star. Karl sent him to Arnaud, who fed him rice cakes made with apricot jam.

Arnaud sent him to Paolo. "He makes his rice cakes with strawberry jam."

Paolo met Christopher on the street and wouldn't bring the conversation into the small hotel. "You haven't made Luca miserable enough? You have to chase him to the place he should triumph?"

"Hello to you too, Paolo. I'm here because I'm covering the race for *CycloWorld*, and I'm doing an article on the tastiest carbs in the feed zone. Arnaud from Mondiale sent me to you, but if your rice cakes are like your attitude…."

Kicking himself for his big mouth on the inside and refusing to back down on the outside, Christopher stared Paolo into submission. "Luca knows where I am and if he wants to talk to me, he'd say so. I showed up to talk to you, but if you don't want to be quoted, okay. I just hope you're not giving him sawdust held together with chain grease."

Paolo swelled all the way to Christopher's chin and stuck his jaw out. "I am *not* giving him sawdust." Grabbing Christopher's arm and towing him up two flights of stairs, Paolo dragged him past all the narrow doors leading into bedrooms. Some of the doors were open, and the sound of men's voices carried. Did Luca lounge in one of those rooms, playing cards or backgammon with his teammates, or did he stand in an ancient cast iron tub shaving his legs for the race? Was he out giving interviews to more established journalists, or donating pre-race blood samples to the FIC officials? Did Christopher dare yell and find out?

No. Wrong approach. Paolo led him to a cramped bedroom all but impassible for the kitchen equipment he'd shoehorned into it. A microwave perched atop a mini-fridge, with a rice cooker for the third layer. The hotel was so old Paolo probably blew a dozen fuses per batch.

Paolo thrust a red and white square at Christopher. "See! Not sawdust."

Well, well. Insulting them until they apologize really does work. Christopher chewed thoughtfully, delaying the moment when he'd have to swallow and let the reasonably tasty morsel join too many companions already jostling in his stomach. White rice and jam was carb city, just what a cyclist with fifty kilometers yet to go needed. A journalist three blocks from his own hotel wouldn't need dinner tonight.

"No, it isn't. It's pretty good." Let Paolo wonder if Arnaud's were better. "Do you use this recipe because a particular rider likes it, or because the team nutritionist advised it?" Just because riders at the pro level needed close to five thousand calories per race day didn't mean all calories were equal to their needs.

"I change recipes, keep them from getting bored with same thing in a long race. Luca likes rice cakes better, Rolf likes brownies, they both like spice cake." Paolo made a good argument that he took the best care of his two charges, with much handwaving and samples. Christopher took notes. "So, you want some more of my sawdust?"

The chocolate brownies were pretty good. Christopher took another square. Had he ridden far enough to earn the calorie deficit required for this? One big loop around Naples wasn't the 130 km the teams would do. "It's pretty good sawdust."

Paolo grinned at him, like the village idiot had just succeeded in counting to three. Christopher decided to risk counting to four. "Any advice on a good place to watch the race?" He'd asked the other soigneurs the same, receiving four different answers, and only two he was confident in being able to find.

"Best place for you—" Paolo led him out of the room and didn't leave his side until they'd reached the sidewalk. "—on a television in Colorado."

Luca's single text later that day didn't refer to Christopher's presence. Did Paolo's protectiveness extend to not even mentioning his visit? Did Luca think Christopher had been joking about getting to Naples? Or would that look too much like a conversation?

Stuck in hotel room, can't go anywhere.

Poor guy. Luca would hate being trapped indoors, especially on such a beautiful day. Even with the traffic. He was probably using his limited floor space to do his pretzel exercises, and worsening his teammates' stir craziness. Maybe he and Rolf were discussing tactics—how the lead-out would go, and could they use another team's tempo setter to do the hard work of breaking the air.

Christopher would give him something to think about besides how being sequestered before the race reduced the possibility of being slipped a banned substance.

Check with Paolo. He has some really good brownies.

Would he check? Would he ask his soigneur why Christopher knew this, or would Paolo deny having treats ready? Had Luca and his pals already finished off the pan? Christopher didn't expect to find out—that would require a second text, which had only happened the once since their big blow-up.

All the same, it was kind of nice to imagine Luca struggling with the need to find out.

Would Paolo deny that Christopher had been in their hotel at all? Somehow Christopher didn't think Paolo's protectiveness would extend to outright lies, at least not to Luca. What he'd say to Christopher, though— Except why lie when he had no trouble at all being blunt?

Opening the Internet window on his smart phone let Christopher bring up coverage of another race that had ended earlier in the day. Good thing he could get the streaming video on his phone, because finding an unsecured router for his laptop was an iffy proposition. He'd want "as it happened" coverage from up and down the course, since he'd only be able to see a short section directly. Thank goodness for the cell phone and Internet coverage in a cosmopolitan city. Some of the other stages would be a lot harder to track.

His questions weren't really answered when his phone chimed again. Christopher shrank the window and grew the text.

How do you know?

Two could play at this game, and time for him to score one. Luca could go ask Paolo and find out more than could fit into a text. Christopher put his phone in his pocket.

CHAPTER 21

THE RACE wouldn't start until 11:00, but taking Arnaud's suggestion of watching the first three loops on the lower route from the steps of the cathedral and then scurrying up to the press area at the finish meant getting there not long after sunrise.

No sense in crowding the riders before the race, Arnaud had advised. "The cyclists will mostly snap at you before the start of this first stage. By Tuesday they settle and will talk to stranger."

Christopher had plenty of being snapped at already just picking up his press pass. If he was going to do this, he'd need a thicker hide, but he'd rather start with friendlier people. The soigneurs wouldn't have their names in print for a week or three, though he'd already emailed the "treats in the musette bag" article. He'd refrained from ranking their cooking, since their spirit of competition might not remain friendly if someone was *rouge lanterne*, the tail end of the treat list.

Shivering slightly, because the cathedral's shadow extended over the steps, Christopher wished for a T-shirt under his turquoise jersey. He'd arrived before the crews putting up barricades to block off the streets. Traffic would be diverted around the race course, but for as short a time as possible. A busy city couldn't stay blocked all day. He bided his time, waiting for the crew.

Once the cops wielding whistles and light batons shooed the last of the traffic off the street, Christopher dashed out to the roadway. Other fans would be adding their favorites' names just as soon as it was safe, but he wanted a big chunk of pavement. Scrawling "Biondi" across the center lanes wasn't as good as a hug and a kiss for moral support, but Luca might see it and be encouraged, and heh, the others might see it and waver. There'd be plenty of "Wiggins," "Spartacus," and "Nibali" on the pavement up and down the course. Christopher took another lane to add "Go" in blue chalk.

The advertising caravan came along a half an hour ahead of the riders. Crazily bedecked vehicles sported inflatable cartoon figures or giant packages of snack foods. A triple-life-size inflatable cyclist rode atop a tiny car, chasing a motorized mineral water bottle. Busy staring at the horses-and-jockeys float advertising a racetrack, Christopher forgot to be wary of the swag being thrown to the crowds. A shower of chocolates bounced off his head and chest, and the spectators around him were faster than he to catch the small cans of Red Bull and T-shirts emblazoned with Fiats. He ate one of the candy missiles he'd captured and shared the other two with the small boy and his father who'd taken up spots on the cathedral steps.

The child plucked at Christopher's turquoise jersey. "*Alè*, Biondi!" he piped, his mouth smeared with the chocolate. "Go Biondi!" The father echoed the child perched on his shoulders.

"*Alè*, Biondi," Christopher agreed with Luca's smallest fan. Was Biondi still going? The earbud feeding him news through the streaming service stopped his heart.

"Seven cyclists down, looks like a manhole cover caught—was it a Cannondale or a Lampre rider? The two went down at the same time and fouled the rest. The peloton has split; half the riders are trapped behind the crash. The fallen are sorting themselves out. Dinesen of Kastibank has his front wheel off. He's at the side of the road, waiting for the team car to come along with a replacement…."

Oh shit, not even one full lap on the first circuit and riders were hitting the dirt. Christopher strained to hear names, but Biondi wasn't in that list. And oh, there he was in brilliant turquoise, flying past the spectators who screamed his name and crowded the roadway against the barricade of Army men in blue and green T-shirts. Not pushing on this first lap, and he'd gained two minutes on half the peloton already.

Oh fuck, this race was made of crashes: thirty men went down when an over-exuberant white mop-dog bounced into the roadway. Once again the needed beating for the owner failed to materialize: if Christopher were dictator, or at least an FIC official, there'd be a ten second bonus for every rider who landed a blow. What was so hard about leashing animals? Every stage race featured at least one loose beast and sometimes enormous bloodshed in its wake.

Luca's lead on the group had grown to two and a half minutes, and he'd taken four of his domestiques with him. They kept him sheltered from the wind and from the crowds that pushed into the street to touch and offer benediction to their idols. "Biondi!" they screamed, and Christopher screamed himself to hoarseness with them. The Olympian at Luca's side got screams too, for his riding and his reputation, but fewer—he wasn't one of their own.

"*Alè*, Biondi!" Christopher high-fived the child and his Papà, and shot off through the crowd. The news that joined him while he pedaled wasn't good.

Five riders had fallen here, another fifteen had gone down there. The announcers blamed everything from uneven roads to the riders having been kept indoors too long, but what mattered most to Christopher was not hearing Luca's name.

Racking his bike and running to the press area with his pass in hand let him make it to the stands before the leaders finished their fourth loop and began the eight smaller circuits that would end the race. A jumbo screen showed the peloton, strung out like peacock beads with a five minute gap from front to back.

"Two minutes behind the leaders," someone commented in English.

"Go, Biondi!" wasn't journalistic impartiality, but then, neither was his jersey. Keeping the cheering inside his own head might just pop his eardrums.

The leaders whipped under the arch for the first of eight passes. Rolf and another Antano-Clark climber contested the hill with the other specialists in the breakaway group. Christopher counted fourteen: huh, there'd be a King of the Mountain point left over for someone two and a half minutes back.

Luca's head was down though his legs pumped smoothly. He looked—tired. No, he couldn't be, even after a brief 9% grade. Not so soon, not when another sixty kilometers separated him from victory. The Olympian on the Sky team sniffed sideways at him. *Don't be so contemptuous, buddy, Luca wiped up the road with you in three big races last month.*

Done with the climb, the group shuffled around. A Garmin rider led tempo, matched with an Antano-Clark rider who hadn't fought for King of the Mountain. The breakaway disappeared around the bend, motos and team cars swarming after them.

In the third short lap the finish stretch became the feed zone. The relatively straight section following the climb was safe enough to risk handing out musettes. Soigneurs in team colors dotted the side of the road, long-handled bags in their outstretched hands.

Antano-Clark, the black and blue clump of Team Sky, and the blue/white/black of Garmin-Sharp and a smattering of other colors moved briskly, though not to extend their lead while the riders chewed their soigneurs' offerings and recovered enough for the next forty kilometers.

The promotional chocolate was a misty memory; Christopher dug an energy bar out of his jersey pocket. Every one of those musettes had energy bars as well as the team treats, but maximal nutrition shoved into one's mouth didn't always feed the soul. Christopher's soul and belly both growled when Markus filled the screen, handing over a feed bag to the first of his Kastibank riders to crest the hill.

"Whoa, but that *apfelkuchen* was good," he muttered.

"There's *apfelkuchen?*" Another journo turned to him, hunger in his eyes. "Where?"

"In the Kastibank musettes." The tip of Christopher's tongue reached out to remember the chunk of fruit that had clung to his lip. "The soigneur gave me a taste yesterday."

"Did he?" The other journo went speculative. "Hmm, they'll be crazy busy until the next rest day…."

Horse-trading time. Was this how the riders did it? With a little false promise here and there, and some real help, often followed by a real drubbing? "His name is Markus, and you might want to wait until before the Tour, because my article's already on line and will hit print next week. Give the readers time to forget." Christopher grinned lopsidedly and offered a hand. "Christopher Nye from *CycloWorld*."

"Bob Rasmussen from *Gear Up*. Good thought." They chatted a bit, each with an eye on the big screen. "They're running a special ferry out to Ischia tomorrow—use the gate marked with pink banners."

Had he just picked up a real tip or some misdirection? "Thanks. Hate to miss a time trial." Hate to miss Luca kicking ass, eighteen teams at a time.

"Pedal, pedal, pedal, pedal. Nothing exciting except the clock." His companion yawned. "Not like a mountain stage."

How'd he get to write for a magazine with eight times *CycloWorld's* subscribers without understanding time trials? "Depends on how you look at it."

Every head in the stands turned when another sunken manhole cover claimed half the peloton, either putting them on the ground in heaps or blocking their passage. The shot from the helicopter camera looked like confetti thrown at the road.

"The leaders have put another twenty to forty seconds between them and the group," intoned Bobke through the earbud. "That's going to be tough to make up. Half the GC contenders are trailing the leaders just from getting caught behind crashes. Have you ever seen so many crashes, Phil?"

"I don't think I've ever seen a Giro stage where so many riders have spent so much time off their bikes." Phil had thirty some years of races to draw on, so Christopher wasn't imagining the carnage.

But he hadn't seen Luca fall yet, though here he and the other leaders came up the grade. They'd dropped two from the group, and the others clustered tightly, fighting for the King of the Mountain points. And oh, Luca looked like hell. He hadn't lost any ground but his balance looked off, and they still had two laps to go.

"Biondi may have exhausted himself in the Cobblestone Classics earlier this spring, Bob," was Christopher's worst fear. Could Luca get through the next sixteen kilometers with the breakaway group? Or would he have to drop back? But he and Rolf were still with the leading riders, only eight of them now on the second to last lap, even though the backwash from the helicopter might blow him off his bike. "Hang in there, Luca!"

Luca hung, and about three kilometers from the finish line, everything about him that looked slow and unwell disappeared. The big screen filled with his grin: Bobke and Phil sputtered their surprise, and a collective gasp went up from the journalists. Probably from all the riders he'd left behind, too—only Rolf followed in the attack. Two turquoise flashes hit the final ascent, their competition chasing furiously but futilely. A gap opened: one second, two, more.

From the screen to life: Luca and Rolf crested the hill unchallenged to speed down the short flat to the finish line. Luca lifted both hands in the air, cutting though the screams and cowbells. Rolf popped a wheelie, whipping under the arch with his front wheel spinning wildly in the sun.

"Antano-Clark goes one-two, and the *maglia rosa,* the leader's pink jersey, goes to Luca Biondi!"

Oh man, if Christopher thought Luca looked fine in white, and even better in yellow, he was going to look magnificent in pink.

The other 198 cyclists, or however many of them persisted to finish, could trickle in as they could: Christopher had to see Luca. He edged out of the stands and followed, though he didn't dare push into the equipment area near the turquoise team bus. He might get a picture or two even if he hadn't a prayer of coming close enough to talk, not with coaches, mechanics, reporters with camera teams and microphones all shoving at Luca. And men in suits—three hard-eyed officials—strode past Christopher.

"Signor Biondi, you will come with us, please. We are beginning the investigation into your use of banned stimulants."

"What use? There was no use!" Luca yelled. "You blacken my name without reason!"

"We'll see about the no reason. Signor, you will come with us." Suited men took Luca's arms.

"Michel Delage!" Luca yelled. "You come!" He refused to move, and the men hesitated to drag him under the glare of a dozen cameras. The directeur sportif pushed past the cameras, only to meet the upraised hand of an official.

"No staff, no coaches. No one on the team, there could be collusion." One of the suits tried to pull Luca's arm: he yanked away.

"Then press. I will come, but with advocate, someone to watch what you do. I will not be accused with no one to see." Furious, Luca stared into the cameras surrounding him. "Member of press, someone who can say what he sees you do to me. You take blood, fine, okay, no problem, you do anything else, someone has to see." He craned to see who surrounded him. "Not you, not you..." With a quick swat to the air, he parted the cameras to see beyond them. "You, hey you! I need witness!" He pointed straight at Christopher. "You, *Cyclo World*!"

Chapter 22

A BOULDER grew in Christopher's throat but he stepped forward into the circle of cameras. "Yes, Mr. Biondi?" Christopher lifted his chin and glared at the FIC officials. "I will be your witness. Ah, signor—" he turned to one of the officials. "What's your name, please? My account has to be accurate."

"Never mind!" He started to leave, pulling Luca. Luca grabbed Christopher's wrist, and they made an odd chain, headed to the building with the red cross and the official logo. Another official escorted Rolf, who recruited his own witness by snagging a reporter's shirt.

Once inside the building, Luca thrust his arm out at the phlebotomist. "Leave me a few drops for tomorrow when you will want the rest."

Christopher pulled his notebook out. "Six vials, two gold-topped, two aqua-topped, two red-topped...." he muttered.

"That matters why?" Luca snarled. He glanced at his blood welling into the second red-topped vial and turned his head away.

"Tells me what they're looking for." Christopher looked up. "The red top means they're looking for ponticlidine."

"I race *pane e acqua*, I don't even know what that is." Shar-Pei wrinkles formed between Luca's brows.

Bread and water. Without performance enhancing drugs, in cycling parlance. And of course Luca did. "It's a fairly new illegal stimulant, and they probably think you shot up with something for that last lap. You perked up an awful lot."

"Of course I did! I was acting!" Luca bent his arm over the cotton ball to stanch the bleeding. "See?" He hadn't had time to remove his helmet before getting frog-marched into this situation: now he pushed the helmet slightly askew, shifted his weight more over one hip, and dropped the opposing shoulder. His face slackened.

"You look drunk," one of the suits blurted.

"I look tired, I look like I can't win, I look like no threat, even if I stay with leaders for 130 kilometers." Luca straightened abruptly, turning back into a very angry man. "That didn't come in a pill."

"A syringe," the phlebotomist said, and shrank. "It's injectable."

"Then you can see for yourselves." Luca yanked off his helmet. "I have no holes in me, except for one you put in." He fluffed his hair madly: nothing fell out. "I conceal nothing, you want to check? Nothing! Not in arms, not in legs, not in anywhere. I did nothing. You check all footage from all motos!"

"You were under a lot of scrutiny," one of the suits drawled. "It would have to be somewhere concealed.

"I conceal nothing!" He jerked the zipper down from his jersey, pulling a few inches out of the fabric. Turquoise dropped to the floor—Luca lifted his arms "You look! You find nothing, because there is nothing, but you look."

One of the suits picked up the jersey and began to examine seams, turning away from the group. The other two officials stepped forward to examine Luca's skin. Hitting them wouldn't solve a thing but—"I still need your names. You, sir, are…?" Christopher demanded what the official had tried to obscure, and got it.

How was Luca standing it? Christopher wasn't the one under investigation, and he still wanted to crawl away into a corner. But Luca needed him to be his advocate, so he swallowed down the fear that threatened to choke him and made his voice even and calm. He insisted on names of all the suits, and the phlebotomist for good measure. "I will have your name, sir, because bad handling of samples has been a problem in the past."

"I don't see anything, but…." conceded one of the officials.

"Oh, you think I stick between toes like addict?" Luca had endured their inspection with only angry glares. Now he bent to pull off shoes and socks. "Nothing, see?" He lifted his leg and spread his toes in the official's face. "Like I could have done anything clipped into pedals, but this is your fantasy, not mine."

"It would have to be well-concealed, and the syringe would still be on him: he hasn't had time to discard anything: his last pit stop was around the eighty kilometer mark, and he didn't show any signs for a good hour after that."

Not much of Luca was concealed now: he wore nothing but his cycling shorts. "Nothing hidden. Look."

He dragged his shorts down, turning them inside out on the way. The beige chamois liner bore stains from all the cream he'd smeared on himself before the race, and Christopher knew exactly how much lubricant Luca liked between himself and the bike. He stifled a smile at the official's grimace when Luca forced him to take the shorts. "Make sure I hide nothing in the chamois, okay? Don't take my word."

"We won't." The official not currently examining sweaty clothing lifted an eyebrow. "It could still be on you."

"Where?" Dressed in nothing but his wrath, Luca raised clawed hands. "You check anywhere you think I hide stuff, okay? I cooperate fully. CycloWorld, you tell everybody I cooperate fully, even with humiliating, slanderous demands that I prove something never happened. I give blood, I hold still, I let officials examine, I demonstrate. And I let officials and press wreck my tactics because now pretending to be tired will fool no one a second time. You make racing harder."

In any other circumstances, Christopher would be all over Luca's naked form, with kisses and caresses, but now he trained hard eyes on the officials. "Gentlemen, you're keeping Signor Biondi standing there. Either finish your examination or admit that your purpose is to humiliate him."

Luca threw Christopher a look full of many things, but "keep the pressure on" was the message he took from it.

"Oh, and let me double check the spelling on your name…."

The official flinched. "He's out of hiding places, unless it's in the folds of his genitals."

"Feel free to look," Luca snapped, and didn't drop his arms. "Or maybe in my crack. Check there too, please, or press can report poor investigation."

"I'm not touching him." The official took one step back. The phlebotomist disappeared with his rack of vials.

"Nor I." The man holding Luca's shorts recoiled. "This was your idea, Friedrich."

"Lift… everything, please." Friedrich's *lift, lift* hand flip reminded Christopher of that long ago day with Luca and the heart monitor.

"No. I do it, you can say I hide something in my hand, I never clear my name." Luca spread his feet for access.

"CycloWorld, what the hell is your name? You do it."

"I'm Fourth Estate, I'm the observer," Christopher snapped. No way would he touch Luca now, as accuser, not lover. "I can't do your dirty work. Now either finish or apologize and let the man dress."

Slowly the official knelt before Luca, and reached gingerly. Luca remained stoic while the man shifted his testicles and slid a finger into the creases where scrotum met groin. "Turn. Bend." The official gulped between the words. "Enough. Nothing concealed."

Luca snatched his shorts away from the official holding them. The man at his feet teleported to the far corner of the exam room before Luca turned the shorts right-side out.

"So, gentlemen, is Signor Biondi's name cleared from all allegations?" Luca couldn't ask for what he needed, but Christopher could demand it for him.

"Unless the A sample comes back positive." The official had recovered some of his aplomb. Christopher would deflate it again.

"Since it can't come back positive for a drug you yourselves admit had no entry route, I suggest you take very, very good care of those vials. And is there some reason you didn't glove up for a physical examination?" Christopher glared over his notebook. Luca helped glare, jerking another few inches of zipper out trying to get covered.

"I, uh, I..." Friedrich spluttered.

"You didn't think to use good procedure, but you'd still try to use the results to discredit a blameless man?"

"You know he's blameless?" Suit Number Three snarled.

"I know what I saw, which was your tech failing to refrigerate blood samples quickly. I watched you examine Signor Biondi and find no punctures, and I know all his samples have come back negative from every race this season. That looks a lot like blameless to me." Might as well grasp the nettle of a missing seven-time winner of the Tour de France. "I believe you're running a vendetta against an extremely successful, clean cyclist because you got fooled so long by another rider."

"He could still be using EPO," argued Suit Two. "And who the hell are you anyway?"

Confidence would only carry him so far until he had to cough up facts. "I'm Christopher Nye, I just started covering European races for *CycloWorld*, and I'm from Boulder, Colorado, in the US. That's where Luca's team trained, and I've been there continuously until earlier this week. You want to argue EPO? I bet my hematocrit is higher than his."

"Do you race? You might be doing EPO too."

"I don't. I let my class IV license from last year lapse." Christopher stared into the man's eyes, willing him to blink first. "Please check. You can have some blood if you want." He held his arm out, veins up.

"Er, no. But we will. Check. You two could be in on this together. Do you know each other? You're wearing Antano-Clark colors." Friedrich pounced, though it wouldn't recover his lost dignity. He was still scrubbing his hands together, as if Luca's skin had transmitted cooties.

In every Biblical sense, too, but that's not for you to know, you officious douche. "And tomorrow I'll wear Garmin-Sharp colors. They're my home town teams. I know most of the Antano-Clark team to talk to, because I worked in a cycling shop. Rolf Knecht prefers Cham-Paste, and Signor Biondi buys SPF 30 sunscreen. It's a terrible conspiracy." Christopher shook his head sadly at the plotting. Humiliation heaped in the right direction might help.

"I still think—"

"Enough, Friedrich." Suit Two glanced toward the door. "We have riders stacked up outside the door for their testing. You've investigated, you've found nothing. There really may be nothing to find. So enough. Wait for the labs."

"Absolutely enough. *CycloWorld* will be looking very deeply into any further harassment toward Signor Biondi. He cooperates fully with all standard investigations, but a repeat of this kind of scene—would not be good." *Lame, oh lame, think of something better.* "You'd be wasting a good ally in the fight to make cycling the drug-free sport you always wished it was if you persist in treating a *paniagua* champion like a felon who just hasn't been caught yet."

Now *that* scored. All three officials clumped together for whispered conference. Christopher didn't try to meet Luca's eyes—the suits cast enough suspicious glances at them already. And yet—would they believe this whole thing had been staged? Luca had pushed: he'd pushed far harder than Christopher had pushed with Paolo, and why?

So he'd only have to fight this battle once.

The suits turned stiffly. Friedrich cleared his throat. "We find…no…." Suit Three elbowed him when he paused too long. "We find no evidence of wrongdoing at this time. Should the blood samples suggest otherwise, we will revisit, but…."

"That is so half-assed." How could they spout that kind of government-type doublespeak? "You owe Signor Biondi an apology. If this is the level of investigations you perform on all cyclists, I'm surprised there hasn't been a greater outcry. And if you only inflict this on Signor Biondi, that needs to be investigated too, since his only crime is to win consistently." Christopher pocketed his notebook and stood straighter. "Well?"

"Signor Biondi—" This was Suit Two. Friedrich must have swallowed a cobblestone: not a word got past. "Thank you for your cooperation. We apologize for the inconvenience, and we beg your understanding. You really did look very different in that last lap."

Luca slumped into his "exhausted stupor" for an instant, then reconstituted into "triumphant winner." "I also apologize: I didn't think my acting was so convincing. Competitors may not have believed it anyway."

Competitors had been fooled into inaction an instant too long, but this wasn't the time to discuss it. "Thank you, gentlemen." Christopher turned to face Luca. "And congratulations, Signor Biondi, on your stage win." That deserved to be noted officially, damn it.

Weak congratulations followed them out the door. A short line of cyclists waited, everyone who'd finished in the top twenty, including slow-on-the-uptake Brad. Several turquoise jerseys dotted the line. Rolf waited to one side.

"Was it bad this time?" he demanded.

"Worse than usual, but I think it might be the last." Luca lifted his eyes to Christopher's. Close enough to kiss, yet still an ocean between them. "Christopher forced them to apologize."

"You?" Rolf snorted. "I suppose you might be good for something after all, *lanterne rouge*. Come on, Luca, you need to comb your hair and change your jersey before the podium ceremonies." He tried pulling Luca away, but Luca wasn't budging.

"Thank you, Christopher. I nearly lost temper."

Nearly? Throwing his clothing at officials wasn't— Oh!

Luca pulled him down just far enough to kiss his cheeks, right, left. "Thank you. I text."

And he was gone. Christopher stood there pretending to be the Dumb American Journo who didn't understand that Italian men could cheek kiss their friends, and he'd stand all day with his hand to his face remembering when Luca's kiss meant more.

LUCA COULDN'T text until after the podium ceremonies, and his message offered little hope. *Thank you. I needed friend in there. Wish to see friend again, but officials already think we plan together.*

I understand Christopher texted back. He did, but he hated it. What should journo friend not mention in article? He wouldn't create a repeat of their previous issues. This is big news.

Ok to say everything.

Ok. But how disloyal it felt to tweet "Race officials admit they had no reason to strip search Giro stage winner Biondi." Painting Luca as the victim today might keep him from excessive scrutiny, and that was Christopher's only consolation. He wrote the follow-up article, fully expecting a tap on his shoulder the next day, demanding a retraction, since they hadn't required Luca to strip with anything more than sly innuendo that couldn't be answered any other way.

However, Christopher could make that look even worse than he already had, and if Luca found himself doing more than giving the required blood samples, he would. The pen was easier to dip in poison than a sword was.

What the hell? His editor was blunt.

I was there, and it was a fucking kangaroo court. They wanted him to be guilty.

Big scoop, wahoo! But don't say anything you can't document.

Watching the team time trials with his new buddy Bob, Christopher basked in the hot sun for the two hours it took to launch all the teams, one colorful bunch every three minutes. Few of the teams fielded all nine riders: nineteen had DNF'd in yesterday's disastrous stage because of injury or equipment failure, and another nine missed the time cut-off and had been withdrawn. "Three Big Names and some strong climbers are out," Christopher commented to Bob. "That will affect today's stage, and all the mountain stages as well."

"So your buddy Luca's chances to win just improved." Bob drew the right conclusion. "How does he look naked?"

"Jayzuz, Bob!" Christopher snorted half his fizzy San Pellegrino water all over the back of a French journalist. Maybe it was a good thing Christopher spoke no French: his *pardon, pardon* at least made the man turn around again. "What the fuck kind of question is that? He was getting grilled about drugs. He looked like an angry naked man." *He looked as good as ever, or he would under better circumstances. Maybe too thin from all the racing.*

"I can't get much of a story out of that, you know. So, what else happened?" Bob prodded for details for the third time. If he brought it up a fourth, Christopher would aim his water-spew.

"Find your own scoop. I'm hearing rumors about Euskatel-Euskadi's sponsorship. Why don't you look into that?" Maybe throwing Bob that bone was more than he should give, but the scent of gossip ought to deflect him.

Team Antano-Clark started last, a position guaranteed by Luca's *maglia rosa*, and also belonging to them by the team's overall top standing. Not only had five of their nine hit the top twenty, but Rolf sported blue—he'd taken King of the Mountain yesterday. No doubt part of their plan, but it was palmarès for him, and he'd pulled hard, he deserved it. Even if he was an ass.

With the solid wall of turquoise broken up with other colors, they looked just fine in their single file paceline, changing leadership every few kilometers to even their efforts. The team they overtook would just have to deal with the razzing.

Team Sky came closest to matching Antano-Clark's time, and their GC, who'd been late to respond yesterday, had a few rueful remarks for the camera at being second. "We were a little slow today, but I think I can make up forty-seven seconds in the next nineteen stages, plus some."

Yeah, well, that was Luca being dressed in pink again, and his team holding bouquets and unidentifiable plush creatures. He'd been characteristically humble—Christopher could have written Luca's speeches for the cameras without ever hearing a word. "Yes, I lead them, but they pull me. This win belongs to the team."

He'd been in and out of the officials' trailer in minutes, emerging with one elbow bent and satisfaction on his face. He'd waved at Christopher on his way back to the bus without making it look like a request for his presence, nor could Christopher push his way into Luca's company, especially with Bob the Barnacle shadowing him.

"What's the matter, no special interviews with the leader?" Bob gibed.

Special interviews, yeah, that was the ticket. `Congrats! Anything to say to the press? ;)`

`Thanks. Press conference at 5. Can't do more.`

No, they couldn't. If it wasn't Bob making Christopher crazy with questions, it was suspicious looks from officials in suits. If he and Luca were alone together at all, there'd be some pointed questions for one or both of them. Shit. He already had a ticket to the press conference. Just like Bob and everyone else.

It didn't get any better in Sorrento, nor could he offer his personal congratulations on Luca's growing pink wardrobe in Matera, Pescara, Saltera, or Firenze. Luca won only one of those stages, but he finished in the top five every time, keeping his total time under everyone else's. Brad flatted out between Sansepolcro and Firenze, costing him more time even with commandeering his domestique's front wheel, and his tune had switched to terse comments about "taking each stage as it comes."

The stages were coming like freight trains now—one more and there'd be a rest day. Restful, hah—they'd spend part of the down time travelling to the start of the next stage. Maybe Luca could sleep on the bus. Christopher didn't expect to nap on the train: the whole concept of train travel was still too new to relax that much, and the floor hummed under his feet.

He parked his bike in the baggage car and found an empty seat for himself and his laptop. He should be writing something, maybe researching performances from last year. They'd be in the mountains, for the first day of more than a week of brutal climbing. Just like home. He closed his eyes, remembering how Luca pulled him up the canyon with the team. How Luca and the other riders looked from beyond, hunched over their handlebars, the thin seats supporting their narrow butts.

If he remembered looking at Luca from behind in too much detail, it could get a bit embarrassing, even with his computer for a figleaf. Maybe he should think about the lead in his legs from the lactic acid buildup and how his vision went gray when he'd left his anaerobic threshold behind twice over.

The race had lost another twenty-two competitors. They'd known what it was like to be dropped, or to fall and stay down while the others left them behind. Maybe he should write a piece on DNF riders. His eyes kept straying to the growing hills around them—the train followed a river bed uphill.

Bob the Barnacle found him. "There's rain forecast for next week in the mountains, maybe even some snow. Think they'll cancel or make everyone ride?"

"Snow in May? Just like home." Christopher brought cold weather gear, not really believing he'd need it, but spring in the Rockies was unpredictable and he didn't expect the Italian Alps to be much different. Did Luca have enough leggings? Did he need more socks? Did Paolo have some magic trunk that produced insulated gloves and wooly hats on demand?

For crying out loud, the man had probably been equipping cyclists since before Christopher learned to read. Yes, Luca would be dressed properly. But Christopher could still offer another pair of high-tech socks. They'd be lucky socks…

"Well?" Bob prodded. "Think they'll cancel the stage?"

Christopher jerked his thoughts away from Luca's feet. "If the roads are impassable, or if it's icy. There's been so many crashes already. Has it ever been this bad?"

"The Giro's always bad; it's the most dangerous of the big tours." Bob loomed over him. "What constitutes a raceable road in this country amazes me."

"And then all the spectators crowd the route. Maybe we should lay them down on the pavement to melt the ice before the cyclists get there. Wouldn't be any crazier than what they do already." The guy in the orange Borat suit would clear a fairly wide patch of asphalt, unless his pink flamingo refused to come out in the snow. Christopher thought he'd seen the man outside of Matera, or it might just have been someone else who liked the style.

Bob laughed. "And leave them there until the leaders arrive. At least they bring out the Army to keep them off the road on the curves. Whatcha working on and where'd ya hear it?"

For crying out loud—did the man do his own research or not? "Checking the race route for tomorrow. Sit down. Have you ever seen a stage on Mont Zoncolan?" He'd pick Bob's brains for a while. He opened a file of pictures he'd downloaded en mass from another racer's website.

"No. It's been several years since they used this stretch. Wonder why?"

Christopher clicked scenes of riders on narrow twisty roads. "Because of this."

Bob choked. "That's bad, even by Giro standards. Shit."

Shit was right—a single lane of asphalt barely wide enough for the two riders abreast tilted toward a nearly sheer drop-off. "No guard rails. And that's a long way down. Fuck."

Bob gulped. "That road's a 9% grade, but it's at least 4% grade across. If that's wet at all, any rider who goes down is going to go all the way down."

"I heard something about nets, and couldn't imagine why they'd need nets or where they'd put them, but this—what the hell's at the top that's worth risking your life coming down?" He could answer that: a pink jersey and glory. But was it worth—this? "These guys are good, the best ever, but taking this descent at any speed is going to get someone killed."

Oh Lord, keep Luca off this road. Even if Christopher had to steal every front wheel from every Antano-Clark bicycle, Luca had to stay off this damned goat-track. The Italian officials considered this safe enough to race? "Where is this? It can't be the entire road." He flicked through more pictures, with spectators on both sides of the asphalt.

"Mont Crostis. And no, most of the route is nice normal hillsides with lots of room, like that." Bob pointed at the screen. "What's the point of sending them up Crostis when no one will be able to see the dangerous section live?"

"People are camping up there, so some of that road has to be slightly less suicidal." And what if something did go wrong? "Can they even get the team cars up there? Or back down?" The route looped on itself; the cars would have to pass ascending riders. "Oh, this is fucked."

Christopher whipped out his phone. `Any comments for the press regarding the Mont Crostis section of tomorrow's stage?"`

Bob poked his nose over, trying to see.

"Quit that! Cultivate your own sources, damn it."

Bob settled back. "Can't blame me for trying."

"Can punch you in the nose for trying. Knock it off." Christopher shoved his phone back into his pocket. Luca might be asleep, or eating, or being circumspect and not answering. Again. How the hell had coming to Luca's rescue, seeing him completely naked, and getting kissed turned into no contact at all? Short of a nod from the podium, Christopher might as well have been back in Boulder, only worse off. Luca hadn't even texted about his riding, and why should he? Christopher was there to see it. Damned officials.

`Very bad road, worse in rain. Joining Berto, Brad, Vincenzo e Damiano to tell worry to race organizers. Meeting in 1 hour, tell u later.`

`K. Be safe.` With five top riders speaking, would the officials listen?

"What did he say?" Bob hadn't stopped trying to see around corners to the screen, but he wasn't leaning.

"That it's a very dangerous road when it's wet." As if Christopher didn't have enough butterflies in his stomach when Luca raced. Most roads weren't actively trying to kill him, but this one looked like it wanted lives.

"Well, duh, we knew that. What else?" Bob elbowed him.

That deserved some payback. "Some of the riders are going to talk to the officials."

"Who? When?" Was Bob actually drooling?

"I could tell you, but then I'd have to make you descend Mont Crostis." Oh, fuck, he didn't want Luca to do that, and now he'd gone and used it as a threat.

"Okay, be that way." Bob slammed back against his seat and tilted it as far as it would go.

"Where are you going to watch the race from?" Anything to change the subject. Or maybe he should just let Bob pretend to sleep.

"I'm taking the press bus from Lienz to the base of Zoncolan. There's a ski lift to the top where the finish is. The trip's about forty minutes and they'll make a couple trips for everyone." Bob opened one eye. "We could watch the race start and then catch the 1:30 bus."

"I might be up earlier." Christopher would be up a *lot* earlier. He needed to ride about 130 kilometers to reach the junction of the Mont Crostis and the Mont Zoncolan roads ahead of the race, rearrange some route signage, and sprinkle the Crostis road with tacks, broken glass, and caltrops. Anything to keep Luca away from that drop-off.

Chapter 23

Officials took riders' worry "under advisement." Means what? Luca texted about two hours later.

It means they're politely ignoring you. Expect to ride Crostis. Vesuvius erupted in Christopher's belly. Maybe pull out of the race?

Maybe finish race and win, not quit?

Oh fuck, he'd gone and flicked Luca's pride. Sorry. That road scares me.

Scares me too. Still plan to win.

Hope you do. *Hope you survive.* Good luck tomorrow. Two category three climbs, two category two climbs, and two *hors catégorie* climbs in 210 km—Luca would need luck on top of all his strength.

Thanks.

Can I talk about meeting?

Yes

Christopher spent the next two hours tweeting and writing, and the hour after that in search of antacids. He returned to an email that made him wish he'd bought a bigger bottle.

Hello, Christopher,

Thanks for bringing this to our attention. Luca Biondi's signed with one of our biggest competitors in the saddle market, which puts him out of our reach.

Sincerely,
Nick Leyburn
Marketing, K-Aero Cycling

What? Luca hadn't said a word about that! Surely if Jindo had come back to the table, he would have said something. He might not want to be all trusting again, but this was the man who texted his ex, just because he knew Ex worried. Did he plan to take the money and let Christopher find out by scanning the ads in a future edition of *CycloWorld*?

No. That was not the Luca Christopher thought he knew.

And wait—he'd taken pictures every day this week. Some horrifically skewed ones, some okay ones, a few where focus was a Ford and not an attribute, and some clear enough to actually use. He downloaded the entire contents of his camera into his laptop and began flipping.

Wrong team, wrong team, wrong rider, wrong rider, right rider but wrong end… He'd caught Luca alone and in profile, tucked over his handlebars, and so tightly that only his face and shoulders made it into the frame. That one was for the wall at home. Christopher kept scanning.

There it was—Luca standing with his bike, seen from the back. His curls covered part of his name on the back of his jersey, but that hardly mattered—riders were a close-cropped bunch, and no one else sported that much hair. Christopher blew the picture up to 400% and zoomed in on the bike seat. That was not a Jindo logo. He cropped the detail and saved it.

Dear Nick,

Did you hear about Luca Biondi's endorsement deal from Luca, or did you hear about it from Jindo? Because I took these pictures in Saltera a couple of days ago.

Sincerely,
Christopher Nye

If that didn't convince K-Aero, then maybe they just didn't have the budget to get the winningest cyclist this season to sing the joys of their products. Fuck. Maybe he should buy Luca one of the new Jindo saddles and get some pictures of that.

A fortuitous meeting with his pal Sylvain gave Christopher some insight on what the riders planned to wear given the forecast, and some directions. He could ride the entire race route to get below the junction with the Zoncolan road, or he could cut off seventy kilometers by going up the valley. He still hadn't located a supply of caltrops, but he'd think of something.

Wandering through the teams' start area, he could hear murmurs in many languages that all mentioned "Mont Crostis." Men he recognized huddled with teammates who had yet to make their fame, and they all glanced up at the sky. Directeurs and soigneurs circulated among them, offering encouragement in words and embraces. One directeur said something to make riders in black with red, aqua and white bars laugh. Christopher recognized him as Johan Bruyneel. Of course this cycling legend would joke about Crostis—he'd actually ridden off a cliff years ago during a Tour de France. He'd bounced down a hundred feet, climbed back up, mounted a new bike, and finished the stage. Was he telling his riders, "If I can do it, so can you?"

The cream of the sport swirled around Christopher, into and out of his viewfinder. Men who stood on podiums around the world and the men who rode to support them, the men who coached, fed, and bandaged all of them. How had he become a part of this? How long could he remain?

He took a hundred pictures: stars and domestiques, climbers who would shine today and sprinters who would finish in the *gruppetto*, stragglers hoping only to stay in the race. Veterans who had ridden a dozen Giros and knew what pain to expect in the coming 210 kilometers, neo-pros in their first major tour. Men who would finish this stage, and some—which ones?—who would not. He recorded them all, the smiling, the grim, the determined.

Antano-Clark riders spoke among themselves, disappearing into the turquoise bus and reappearing. Luca clasped hands with each of them, holding private conversations with Rolf, Laurent, Poldi, the others. Christopher could imagine his words: encouragement, hope, strategy, future success, in whatever language his teammate spoke. Luca turned and saw Christopher, halting his restless preparations long enough for a deep blue glance. Damn it all—he wanted to embrace Luca and whisper luck into his ear, but no. He had to push everything in his heart through one fleeting gaze. *Be strong, Luca; be lucky.*

Fans and journos waved the teams off at noon. Christopher snapped more pictures and cast anxious glances upward—small clouds dappled the sky, but their big, soggy brothers could be on the way. If the race got rained out—oh hell, he'd seen how much it took to actually stop a race in progress. If it didn't require an Ark, the cyclists stayed on the course. But most courses didn't contain Mont Crostis.

"You want to grab some lunch before we catch the bus?" Bob asked, but Christopher wasn't interested.

"I'm going to watch the race from farther down." Christopher had to get going—he had some forty miles to ride and a decent plan to evolve. He'd shoved food and his foul weather gear into the rear pockets of his turquoise jersey, racked his water bottles and studied his maps. He hadn't had a proper ride since he'd left Boulder, and maybe this would clear his mind.

He headed up the green valley a river had carved into the soft stone of the Dolomites. *Pretty country,* Stu commented. *How's traffic?*

"Light," Christopher muttered. "Everybody's watching the race." Until his ghostly naysayer showed up, he'd been enjoying the steady 5% grade, having the road to himself, and the cool breeze.

Nice road, like out to Lyons, Luca whispered. *You and I, we have fun riding this together.*

Christopher hugged the rocky shoulder as a truck filled with goats whiffed past, the first vehicle in twenty minutes. *You pay attention to what you're doing.* The terrible road on Mont Crostis was still hours in Luca's future, but Christopher'd dreamed of Luca and his bike flying gracefully for about three hundred feet to a landing he wouldn't ride away from.

I pay good attention. Nice category three climb coming up.

Any category climb should take all his attention. And would anything divert the Stu in his head? Stu would love this ride: he'd love the idea of pacing the Giro d'Italia, chasing them the back way. But that little voice in his memory had more questions, more salt in his wounds.

Guess you didn't need me to fuck things up with you and Luca; you did fine on your own.

Christopher's grip tightened so much he accidentally geared down too much to pedal, and flailed to shift back, his momentum lost. "I'm trying to fix it. I'm really trying to fix it. Shut up."

But of course Stu never did. *Yup, you're doing great, I can tell. All those romantic dinners with candles, cheap local wine, and food just like his mama's. Not.*

Hell, he didn't need Stu to tell him they hadn't had so much as a proper conversation. "He can't do that during a race. He can't even talk with me—the officials hate us both now. He's responding. He kissed me."

Lot of that Italian hello-kissy in these parts. Doesn't look like it means all that much.

"It's more than I ever got in public back home." And so much less than he'd had in private. "You want to say something useful, think up a way to divert the course."

And with that Stu went silent, because the Stu in his head only had the clues that were in his head, which were still zero.

More miles of really pretty country and gutwrench. Christopher pedaled steadily, trying to keep to the powerful strokes Luca had taught him. He glanced at his faithful, cheap cycling computer, which said he'd ridden farther today than he had in the rest of Italy. No wonder his breath was coming a bit hard. He'd have a few hours before he had to climb Zoncolan, if he had to climb that rock wall. He still hadn't worked out how to do more than watch Luca head into danger.

A green Fiat whizzed past him, sucking him toward the center of the road. Maybe he could stage a wreck with himself as victim and turn the road into a crime scene. Then they'd have to divert the race. With his bike and body strewn artistically across the pavement, he could moan, "I can't feel my legs."

Yeah, if he could find a stretch of road empty enough not to be seen. And the Italian paramedics wouldn't understand what he was saying, and any emergency responders for a bike race would know back precautions.

He needed a better plan: he had two miles to go until he joined the race route, and three hours to scheme. Could he make it rain if he danced just right? The clouds gathering overhead might cooperate.

He reached the fork in the road: north for Crostis, east for Zoncolan. A mob of angry people shouted at officials, baying for blood over the sounds of the bullhorn. Men in green and blue rainsuits linked arms to keep the crowd from running down the speaker. Christopher couldn't understand the words, whether from language or from garble, until it became clear the man was repeating his message in several languages: he finally reached English. The car blocking the road was clear enough.

"The course has been changed. The riders will turn and proceed up Mont Zoncolan. The Crostis road is blocked to traffic and blocked to cyclists. Repeat, the course has changed. By requirement of the FIC, the Mont Crostis portion of the course has been eliminated due to weather."

Eliminated! "Yes!" Luca wouldn't get near that twisted excuse for a road. He had to shout and fist-pump—and if his arm quivered, blame it on forty miles of cycling. "Yes!" So he sounded happier than everyone around him—Luca wouldn't climb—or descend—Mont Crostis.

From the screaming and fist shaking, the Roman spirit that had filled the Coliseum was alive and well, and only the chariots had been updated. Did the crowd really want carnage, or only spectacle? Zoncolan would be spectacle enough for Christopher: he turned uphill and didn't challenge the human fence. The riders' appeal would keep Luca away from danger.

Away from that piece of danger. Plenty still lurked. Christopher climbed until the hill grew steep and the people grew few. He needed to stop by an unmarked section of road.

First to find out what the race was doing. He poked his phone. No signal. Well, well. Guess he was going to be surprised as anyone by what happened. Except the few people here at the fierce curve had radios.

All playing in Italian. Well hell.

He dropped his bike at the shoulder and stepped into the middle of the road with his worn-down blue chalk. "BIONDI," he wrote, using letters two feet tall that threatened to consume the stub before the last *I* was complete.

His task finished, Christopher discovered he had a dozen new friends. "Biondi, *alè*!" they roared and toasted his success and Christopher's good taste in riders with plastic cups of red wine. A young woman filled a cup for him, and then all he could do was wait.

THE ADVERTISING caravan came through, honking and shedding promo like cat fur. Christopher was grateful for the bottle of mineral water a young man threw directly into his hands—one glass of wine midday was more than he was used to. He'd been playing catch with the sons of this extended family, except his end of the game was more like "fetch", and not entirely because of his cycling shoes.

Little he'd heard on the radio made sense, though he could pick out names and a word here and there if it was enough like English or what remained of his Spanish. "*Gran premio montagna*" and Rolf's name sounded together a couple of times; he might keep that blue King of the Mountain jersey another day. Luca's name came up regularly, not that he understood much of what went with it, but if the caravan was here, the cyclists were less than half an hour behind.

And then he could see for himself.

Except he wasn't seeing what he wanted to see most. The leaders rode by, and Luca wasn't among them. No pink jerseys, not until about eight minutes back when the Lampre riders started coming through, and a clump of turquoise jerseys a few minutes later weren't hiding Luca in their midst. Were they? Motos swooped by, and the occasional press car. Team cars with racks of spare bikes and wheels obscured the riders now and then—had Luca gone by in their wake? But his team wouldn't have dropped him back this far—their job was to carry him along until it was time to make his move.

For that matter, he hadn't seen Rolf, though he wasn't looking for a blue jersey, and there were a couple of teams that could have camouflaged him. But Rolf should have been with Luca—a lieutenant shouldn't stray too far from his GC.

A hundred and fifty-some riders toiled past, all that were left. And where was Luca?

The peloton strung out all over the race route—the last rider struggled by more than twenty minutes after the first. He might be rouge lanterne, or he might get dropped for missing the cut-off. Team cars putted by, and then nothing at all.

So that was a mountain stage as seen from the Italian roadside. Christopher had yelled and clapped with his companions, and now they were packing the remains of their picnic. "Biondi?" he asked, afraid he'd get an answer and not understand. The papà's eloquent shrug was clear enough—he hadn't seen their favorite either. Luca had to have been in with the Lampre riders.

Now to get to the top—the leaders had all reached the finish, the last riders would summit soon. If Christopher was going to see Luca at all, he'd better get moving. The road there at the curve was quite steep—he had to stand on his pedals to achieve any forward motion. The papà, the young woman with the wine, and another young man dropped their handfuls and came out to push.

"Dura! Dura!" They yelled encouragement and shoved him up the road. "*Con forza!"* Hands on his back, butt, and bicycle propelled him faster than he could pedal himself, until he finally popped away from his assistants.

"Grazie!" he called, not daring to look back. He cranked, gearing down to rings he almost never used, but then, he'd never ridden a road with a 22% grade, even if it was only for a few meters at a time. The top of the mountain seemed very far away, and parts of the course completely vertical. Luca would be back in Lienz before Christopher ever got to the finish.

Sound from behind made Christopher veer—if cars wanted this road, he wanted to be out of the way. Somehow the tiny vehicles here seemed like more efficient predators than any SUV that ever chased him.

But it wasn't a car, and it wasn't some unknown coming up behind him. Fuck no; it was one of the top sprinters suffering his way up the hill. This rider's face was as red as the print on his jersey, and he looked like a stroke was imminent. Why didn't he just bail? "Party man's" tactics suddenly made a lot more sense.

If he's behind me, the race isn't over. Slowing to let the sprinter by, Christopher called encouragement even while begging the universe to send a sag wagon along before the man's eyeballs actually popped.

But the rider had brought at least part of his troubles on himself with that tall elliptical chainring in front. *Note to self, write about matching equipment to the road. He'd kick some ass with that gearing on the flat.* His mechanics and coaches had to be on crack to let him ride a mountain stage with that setup.

It certainly got him the pity parade—Christopher followed him around another bend into a populated stretch of road. Half a dozen people ran out to push him. Helping hands and strong backs got the sprinter up to a speed about double what he'd managed by himself, or about what Christopher could accelerate to unassisted.

He was prepared for hands on his body for a shove forward, but not for the familiar voice from behind. "Riding the stage today, Christopher?"

If not for the crowd around him, Christopher would have fallen off his bike. "Luca? What happened?"

"Big crash. Fifty riders on top of us." Luca's voice came choppy.

Fifty… Even if he was exaggerating, whatever happened was bad enough to put him more than half an hour behind the leaders. Bad. The team shouldn't have left him. Nor his lieutenant. "Where's Rolf?" Even with their human engine, Christopher didn't have breath for many words.

Nor did Luca, or maybe he was being cagy around their audience. "Team car."

Okay, wouldn't have to hunt him down and hurt him. Someone else would be wearing that blue jersey tomorrow, and Christopher would let the blow to Rolf's pride be pain enough. His KoM credentials would stand forever, as would his Giro DNF.

"I should get off the course." But he couldn't, not with their helpers grunting and hauling them up the hill, calling "*Dura! Con forza!*" and a dozen other things he couldn't understand.

"Ride, Christopher." Luca didn't tell the crowd to let go. "I need lieutenant."

"You need to get off the course." Cyclists couldn't go around commandeering people into the team any more than they could draft off team cars. Well, there was the magic spanner trick to get a pull....

"I need to finish."

Crazy, every last one of them, and Luca craziest of all. No hope of winning, no hope of even making the time cut-off by now, he'd be dropped from the race, so why did he have to kill himself on this fucking mountain? The sprinter had the sense to stop. Maybe his brain had just shut down and stopped talking to his legs: Christopher pulled Luca past the pathetic figure, doubled over his handlebars and sucking in air.

And he'd forced himself to continue to a spot where no one would see.

Christopher was as crazy as the rest now—he pulled, demanding his legs and his gears keep him upright on this horrible, vicious, fucking mountain that was getting climbed just because it was there and they were men. Luca needed to finish. Christopher would make it possible. Luca needed speed. Christopher would make that happen too. Fucking mountain.

The tunnels—relief. Flat. Gear up. Momentum. Fucking concrete legs, pedal. He pushed himself to the limit, not knowing if his vision grayed out from the darkness inside the tunnel or imminent collapse. The buzzing in his ears might have been a moto, or the sound of blood vessels popping.

They burst out of the tunnels into bright sun and deafening noise. Cowbells. Clapping. Screams without meaning. "You go," Christopher mumbled and tried to veer to the side, but the human chain in green and blue rainsuits wouldn't let him through. Couldn't let him through—thousands of people would mob Luca. Crush him. Love him to death.

Just up to the grassy spot, Stu told him. *Stop there. Luca will finish.*

"You did good!" was the last thing Christopher heard before he fell, and he didn't know if the voice was Luca's, or the Luca in his head. Didn't matter: Luca needed all his breath for one last push to the arch just ahead. His turquoise figure disappeared beneath it. Christopher lay down in the grass and wept.

THE PODIUM ceremonies were over before Christopher recovered enough to care. The hordes disappeared down through the tunnels or the back way down a ski lift to a parking lot where team busses and press busses waited. The cleanup crews chattered at him in Italian or German or other languages he couldn't understand, and finally left him alone when he waved them away.

At least town lay downhill.

A goddamned steep, scary, twisty, demented downhill. Ten percent grades that annoyed him on the uphill terrified him going down—hairpin curves at greater than 20% grade that he'd ascended at a crawl he descended soaked in sweat, with one hand gripping the rear brake and the other pumping the front. If he went over the handlebars he'd lie in the road until the cleaners came along. Even with dual braking he went down that fricking mountain way too fast.

When he reached the junction with the Crostis road, Christopher had to spend some time in the bushes with his leggings down. Anyone who got an eyeful shouldn't have been looking. Before he pushed on, he had to take a long look up the mountain he'd just descended. The top was a long way up—if he'd looked at more than the hundred yards ahead of him, he'd never have made it up. He sure as hell wouldn't have survived getting down. And Luca rode that after another 140 kilometers and four climbs.

The rest of the trip went mildly, and fast. What was 5% when he'd just ridden down a wall?

He returned to Lienz to find his hotel swarming with reporters, mikes at the ready, and others brandishing press passes to get at him. "That's him! That's him!"

Somehow using the most pungent phrases Luca had taught him seemed both appropriate and a really bad idea to spread over three continents, maybe four. But—*Che cazzo è?*

"What happened on Zoncolan? Tell us how Biondi ascended!" came in too many voices. Cameras loomed at him.

"Wait, what?" Guess those had been motos.

"Turquoise jersey, no logos, red Specialized Roubaix-Comp road bike, white Vuelta helmet. Has to be you. Tell us about the ascent? Did you know you were riding with Luca Biondi?"

Well, duh. "Someone had to. Rolf Knecht dropped out." No point in denying what however many motorcycle-mounted cameras had caught in glorious detail.

"You didn't know?" One reporter had shouted himself into leadership of the pack and asked this question more quietly.

"Didn't know what?" God, but Christopher was tired and wanted something to eat. He wiped the back of his hand across his face.

"Rolf Knecht is dead."

Chapter 24

What? How? Oh fuck, no. Not— Not even. Please let this be a sick joke. But no, it wasn't: too many solemn faces looked back at him. Christopher stammered, "I didn't know. I don't think Luca knew. He just said he and Rolf were at the bottom of a big pile-up."

Oh fuck—Christopher needed to throw up. Not dead—he couldn't be dead. Rolf was an arrogant little shit but he shouldn't be dead. The bastards never died, just the good guys— And Luca. My Lord, Luca— Did he know? He had to, he and Rolf shared a room, they shared a team, strategies, everything. They wouldn't, they couldn't, keep something that big from Luca, and he'd be— Oh fuck. He had to get over there. *Luca…*

Christopher blew the distance completely off the map in his rush to reach the Antano-Clark hotel, only to find the street in front of it clogged with more press. Four men in blue and green rainsuits guarded the doors as they'd guarded the race route.

How was he going to get past that log jam? Did Luca even want him to get past? Shadowy figures flickered behind the gauzy drapes of the third floor windows. Was that Luca? He became the whirlwind in times of stress, but for this? Christopher stared up.

The drapes parted: a face, too old to be a rider, peered briefly. Christopher's phone buzzed against his back. He all but beat the message off of the screen.

Bob materialized out of the crowd. "Privileged communications again?"

"Shut the fuck up," Christopher snarled. If Bob had a video camera with him, too bad.

You come up I bring you

If Luca came down now, this crowd would eat him alive: the questions would never stop. So—someone who knew Christopher, or how to reach him.

Paolo emerged from between two rainsuited guards and had a brief word with them. Marching through the crowd, maybe over them if they didn't get out of his way fast enough, he parted the thicket of press to find Christopher. "You come." He seized Christopher's wrist and dragged him back to the door. The doors closed behind them, shutting the hubbub out. Someone took his bike and brought it in with them, since Paolo seemed bent on pulling Christopher up stairs, possibly through keyholes.

"He wants you. I don't know why he wants you; you distract him." If Christopher lost his footing on the stairs, Paolo might well tow him along anyway, bouncing his head on every step. "But he won't talk, he won't eat, he says only he needs you. Why you? Stupid American, stupid journo." Paolo's voice was thick. "Stupid man. But he wants you, so I bring you. He wants, I do, but why you?"

They passed solemn men, some talking quietly in clumps, some hovering near their comrades. Christopher couldn't stop to tell them *I'm sorry, so sorry;* the locomotive that was the soigneur didn't stop. He wouldn't shout condolences in passage, but he knew the shadows in their eyes. Paolo jerked him through a doorway.

Luca leaned over a chair, squeezing the back until the cords popped out in his forearms. He rocked back and forth. Christopher wanted to reach out but stopped short. Michel Delage, the directeur sportif, rested his hand on Luca's shoulder, but what comfort could be enough for his pain?

"He was still alive. I wouldn't leave him dead in the road." Luca's hair swayed around his face, hiding it.

"I know, Luca, I know." Michel squeezed his shoulder. "I heard him talk to you."

"He told me to go!" Luca flung himself upright, whirling to pace the four steps of floor space. "He said, 'Go, you didn't ride off a cliff.'"

"I know, Luca." Michel's hand hovered in the air where Luca had jerked away from beneath it. He slowly dropped it. "I was there." A tear track glittered down his cheek.

Poor guy—Rolf must have died under his hands.

Luca stopped short. "Rolf wasn't alone. That was good he wasn't alone." Two steps put him at the directeur's side, reaching up to rest his hands on the man's shoulders. "You kept him from dying alone. I should have been there."

"No, you did what he told you. I yelled at you too. Remember?" Michel drooped. "We didn't think he'd die. Not from a broken collarbone. But… he…" A shudder racked Delage. "The bone was poking out; it looked bad, but not killing. He tried to get up. And then so much blood…." He sobbed once, a long expelled breath that whistled in his throat. Luca held him, his own sorrow wracking his frame.

Christopher stayed silently where Paolo stopped them. Not daring to speak, barely daring to breathe, he stood beside the soigneur, an accidental voyeur to their grief. He couldn't watch; instead, his eyes strayed to the two single beds in the room. One was Luca's. Which one? Because the other had been Rolf's. An open suitcase lay across one, rumpled clothing strewn over the duvet. Rolf's?

"Out," Paolo hissed. "No press."

He wasn't press now, just a friend, but miles gaped between the crushing in his chest and what he could do to share that burden with Luca. Paolo tugged at him, but Christopher didn't follow this time.

Luca looked up. "You're here. Good."

Paolo stopped, pulling back as if Christopher's flesh had burned him. Michel jerked upright, his eyes slitted and his teeth bared.

"Sympathetic member of press," Luca told him. Michel relaxed a fraction but remained tense. "Christopher Nye. Other man on Zoncolan."

"I'm sorry for your loss." Christopher had to find something better than the rote words. "Rolf was a good man." Maybe. Christopher wouldn't vouch from his own experience, but—never speak ill of the dead, and Luca had trusted him, so…good enough.

Luca's lips moved, but his words were nearly silent. "Thank you."

Christopher wanted to spring across the room to envelope Luca in his arms, feeble shelter though he'd be against the grief. Luca didn't move, not one twitch to say he needed that sanctuary. No, not with Michel and Paolo there.

Michel nodded acknowledgement. "He was a good man." Poor guy. He'd lost his rider, who might have been a friend, and his hopes, all in one afternoon. Maybe he had someone to comfort him.

Turning to Luca, he said, "The hearing is in ten minutes: the officials declared the hearing would start at 6:30 in the dining room downstairs. We need both of you there." He turned to include Christopher. "The *commissaires* wish to inquire into the assistance you provided to Luca on the mountain, and planned to proceed whether or not you could be found."

"What?" Christopher gawped back and forth between the directeur and Luca. "That is really hostile. We weren't going fast enough to draft."

"I know, but they inquire all the same." Michel's shoulders drooped further. "And I can't allow you to be alone together, or they cry collusion. They might say that even with we three."

"Four." Christopher hadn't forgotten Paolo at his side. "They might argue that Luca's soigneur would say anything to protect his rider, but he would probably also say anything to discredit me, because he disapproves of journos getting too close to riders. So I think we can rely on him to tell the truth about this meeting."

Paolo glowered through his nod but said nothing.

"Even so, I can't let you stay. I'm sorry." Michel motioned him toward the door.

"Luca, I'm really sorry about Rolf." They'd have to drag him away before he'd leave without saying that. He offered open hands from the doorway, all Luca could accept, and got a brief bow of the head in response.

"I see you at hearing." The flick at the corner of his mouth wasn't even cousin to a smile.

Christopher let Michel guide him out, because what else could he do?

"Did you assist Luca Biondi in any way on the ascent of Mont Zoncolan?" a too-familiar man in a dark suit demanded. Again.

"No, I didn't," Christopher asserted for the third time. Why wouldn't they listen? Or would they keep asking until he told them what they wanted to hear? "I was there. He spoke to me. I spoke to him. He didn't touch me or my bike. I didn't touch him or his bike. We were going too slow for drafting to matter. I couldn't even turn around to see him because I would have fallen off. That's all."

What the crowds had done to keep them both moving wasn't part of this question, nor would Christopher bring it up. Neither had the officials, perhaps because they faced unwinding years of racing results if they declared a human-assisted start unacceptable.

"Enough, Friedrich." The voice of reason spoke from beside Luca's nemesis: a fourth man with an air of power and assurance and a much more finely tailored suit. "Please bring Signor Biondi and Signor Delage back in."

Luca slipped into the chair beside Christopher with scarcely an acknowledgement. He moved stiffly—the damages from being crushed by half the peloton must be catching up. He had to be frozen inside—the next few sentences could change his career. A disqualification would strip him of his stage wins in the Giro and send him on to his dreaded meat-cutting future. He clenched his hands together in his lap, making the tendons stand out. *I did my best, Luca. The truth has to be enough.*

"The FIC finds that Luca Biondi exceeded the winner's time by forty-three minutes, ten seconds. His time exceeded the cut-off by eight minutes, thirty-nine seconds, and he is therefore dropped from the race." The senior official didn't request any input from the suits flanking him, nor did he hesitate in making his pronouncement.

But he'd said "dropped," not "disqualified," and it was for the immutable fact of time. Christopher dared to breathe. Luca remained rigid—did he think that might yet come?

"The FIC regrets this—" A choking noise and a flinch from Friedrich said he regretted something else altogether: his superior quelled him with a glance. "We acknowledge your valor in achieving your stage wins and your overall standing as leader. All palmarès stand."

Luca softened: he bowed his head with a soft "*Grazie.*" His hands loosened across his thighs. Christopher dared not reach out to take one.

Friedrich squirmed and grumbled and his opinion apparently didn't mean a damned thing. Whatever his problem was, he couldn't touch Luca in any way. Probably shouldn't flip him the bird. Because of the next race.

The senior official continued. "We also acknowledge the loss of your teammate Rolf Knecht, and regret adding to your sorrow. We have reviewed all available video and doctors' statements, and find that his death was an accident of the road." He turned to the Antano-Clark directeur. "The FIC requests to know what your team intends to do for the remaining stages. The choice of finishing the race is yours."

What would the team do? Were they too demoralized by Rolf's death? Losing Stu had nearly pushed Christopher off the bike forever: what did the team think? Or Luca? He'd buried friends before, he'd said. Had the bike killed them? Yet he'd struggled up Mont Zoncolan and refused to quit.

Antano-Clark led the GC and team standings until today; would the directeur pull them for having no chance to maintain that? Or would he ask them to ride on?

"Our remaining seven riders have asked to finish the Giro. We thank you for making that possible." Michel spoke in a whisper.

"Team Antano-Clark will be given a ceremonial lap at the end of the twenty-first stage in Milan. We would honor our dead. Signor Biondi, if you wished to join the team for that lap, you will be permitted to ride."

Again Luca whispered, "Grazie."

He'd be there. Christopher could see him now, lined up with his friends and teammates, riding one hand or no hands, their arms linking them in a wide line across all the lanes. It would be a slow pace, a dirge, their eyes downcast as they pedaled, or looking out into a future when they'd have to ride beyond Rolf's death. Oh, yeah, Luca would be there. He was riding that lap right now.

LUCA HADN'T shooed him off, so Christopher went back upstairs with the other two. Michel embraced Luca with cheek kisses. "You go home, or somewhere that you can relax. Unplanned and unwanted vacation is yours for two weeks. You rejoin us in Milan." He left Luca at his door, calling to his team that they needed to be downstairs and on the bus in twenty minutes. "We travel to Conegliano for tomorrow's stage. *Muovetevi!*"

Luca met Christopher's eyes, one hand on the doorknob. Their bicycles stood in the hallway, spoked guardians to either side of Luca's door. "Thank you for—today. On the mountain, you gave me strength. You gave help *commissaires* couldn't see. I finished stage. That was important to me, not to quit."

Why did they have to be doing this in the hallway, with the bustle of packing coming through open doors? Men with suitcases, some the wiry young riders, others older and burdened with more equipment, poured out into the hallway. All of them stopped to embrace Luca with soft words. "You rest a while, and come to Milan." "Poor Rolf." "We need you. Rest. Heal." Others spoke words Christopher didn't understand.

They eyed him silently, taking in his sweaty, unzipped jersey and fixed-sole shoes. He carried the curse of the mountain on him, the effort, the tragedy. A few nodded to him; none spoke. Luca didn't explain him, but if they recognized a man they'd ridden with once, months ago and thousands of miles away, they said nothing. His press pass hung on a lanyard around his neck; maybe that was explanation enough.

Inside the room two men waited. Open suitcases, packed and ready to be zipped, lay on the beds. Paolo searched under the beds for escaped possessions, and another man sat in the one hard-backed chair. He rose, his arms out. "Luca."

"Damiano." Luca stepped into the Duclos-Wurth star's embrace, offering the cheek kisses Christopher still hadn't gotten used to. They broke apart.

Damiano spoke softly in Italian, but Luca answered in English. "I don't know. No plan yet."

That got Christopher a crusty look. "Your pet journo is allowed to know when you do have plan?"

"Not a pet, and this journo knows when to be quiet. We can talk."

"Hah!" came from under the bed. A guy whose butt stuck up in perfect kicking range shouldn't be snarking. Christopher estimated the distance.

"The kitchen at the villa is still full of all the food you didn't eat during Tour de Romandie. Use anything there: food, car, toothbrush…." Damiano produced a ring of keys. "You go there, it's quiet. High walls to keep out his *amici*." All journalists became enemies with a toss of Damiano's head—scorn, Italian-style, was awfully pointed. Christopher gritted his teeth.

"Keep him out too?" Luca didn't reach for the keys. "Christopher is a friend."

Damiano wrapped his fingers around the keys. Would he deny Luca refuge? "He's journo with big camera."

"Who put poison in your ear?" Luca demanded. "He saved me three times now."

Paolo had emerged from beneath the bed with a sock in his hand, but froze on his knees. What choice evils had he mentioned to Damiano? Whose side was he on? *Should have kicked him while he was such a tempting target.*

"I won't endanger your privacy, Signor." How had he become one of the paparazzi? "Or Luca's. If I'm even there." Because Christopher should be on the train to Conegliano too. What the hell was he going to do if Luca wanted him to come?

Unwrapping his hand, Damiano dangled the keys from one finger. "If you want him, okay. Maybe interviewing you is better than watching race."

Not everything was an interview, damn it! The words clogged in Christopher's throat—saying so begged the next question—why else would he be there? "Do you really think Luca should be alone right now?"

"He won't be alone." Paolo had risen to his feet. "I take care of him."

"Fine." Damiano pressed the keys into Luca's hand. "You choose who comes with you. Three bedrooms, lots of company." A horn sounded from the street in short bursts of impatience. He embraced Luca again, and Luca clung to him for a moment. "I have to go. See you in Milan." With a backward glance for Luca and a backward glare for Christopher, Damiano disappeared.

Paolo bustled between the two beds, zipping and tucking. "We need tickets to Como. I go get them, come back for you and baggage. We take night train, you eat, rest."

"I can't." Luca stopped Paolo in his tracks with the words. "I have to take Rolf's body home."

CHAPTER 25

"No!" If Paolo had knocked Luca down to keep him from the doorway, he couldn't have been clearer. "This task is not for you!"

"Then who?" Luca threw his hands up. "He was my friend. I can't ship him home to family like—like—like package of meat."

Christopher's stomach turned over. Rolf had existed in a turquoise and black vacuum for him, but not for the world. He had a mother and a father, maybe brothers and sisters, who had followed his career with pride. Grandparents, cousins. Everyone in a Belgian town who had watched their golden child grow up and bring honor and palmarès home. They'd be getting their hero back in a box.

Just as Stu's parents had. They'd be just as broken.

Luca shouldn't have to face that alone. Christopher's passport would get him into Belgium. "I'll—"

"No. No, Luca, you don't go. You need to rest, you need to heal." Paolo shook his head violently, a terrier in his opposition. "No two days on train with heartache, no rest, no exercise. More coming back. Very bad for you. I won't allow it!"

"Allow? Rolf was my friend, you don't allow or not allow!" Luca roared back, and that was the last word Christopher understood. The shaking fists, the raised voices, the in-his-face confrontation was pretty clear. Paolo might have been half a head shorter but he had a good twenty years' more experience in intimidation. Christopher didn't know whether to hide in a corner or sell tickets.

Paolo ended it with a whisper. "His family will chase you from their door."

The breath Luca had meant to turn into a shout whooshed out of him. What two hundred competitors, Mont Zoncolan, and the threat of disgrace hadn't done to him, Paolo's comment did. Luca slumped, defeated. "But… he should have escort to do him honor."

"I go. Luca, I go, tend him." Paolo reached up to wipe a tear from Luca's face, and one from his own. "I am still his soigneur, I take this last duty. Then I come back, tend you. You live, you need me more than Rolf, but I won't chase you all the way to Belgium with bowl of soup. Stubborn *asino*, you go to Damiano's villa. Feed yourself for four days, then I come before kitchen is empty."

"Longer than four days, Paolo." Luca nibbled his lip thoughtfully. "They need to hear the stories of this season, to learn from one who was there what his last days were like. All about King of the Mountain." Luca rummaged in one of the open suitcases, extracting two blue jerseys. "If they allow, Rolf should be buried in blue. Other jersey, maybe for Ghisallo."

"More than four days is too much for you to be alone, Luca."

"He won't be alone." Christopher didn't want to raise his voice, but getting a word in edgewise was a pretty dim prospect otherwise. "I'll go with him. Um, you. Luca, if you want, I'll come with you. You shouldn't be alone either."

"You would—?" Luca started.

"You? Because you find something more exciting than race, you have someone with exclusive story? Any journo can watch race, but only one has the *maglia rosa's* ear." Paolo's face had gone stroke-range red; his eyes bulged. "Of course you want to go with Luca: you want to write what he says."

"That's not why, damn it!" Throttling Paolo wouldn't get those words unsaid, and there had to be some other way to bring the suddenly damped spark back into Luca's eyes. "He's—" Oh fuck, there was no explaining to this opinionated little monster just what Luca was, or what Christopher wished he was. "He needs a friend, and I can be there." This wasn't Paolo's decision to make. But would Luca make it? "If you want, Luca, I'll come with you."

"You have race to write about." Luca spoke standing in one place—was that hope or despair that kept him still and bowed?

The race, right. *CycloWorld* wanted their coverage—they hadn't sent him to Italy for Luca's sake. At least, not for Luca off a bike. "I managed to cover Paris-Roubaix from Boulder, so I'll figure something out. The villa has good Internet, doesn't it?" He could still access the live streaming coverage in English, and he wouldn't have to be up at 4 a.m. to do it. "Maybe you'll translate some of the local television for me?"

"I could do that." Luca stood straighter. "If you come with me."

"Fine!" Paolo threw up his hands. "I go to Harelbeke, comfort family. You go to villa, do—whatever you do with this journo, I go home when they say go. Maybe I come to Milan, or maybe Harelbeke junior team needs soigneur."

The flood of angry Italian pouring out of Luca could have meant a lot of things, or what Christopher was snarling in English. "You want him to go to rest and stay away from Rolf's family, but you don't want him to do it with anyone but you." He broke off—Paolo had lost a friend and teammate too, one he'd cooked for, massaged, and looked after, and now they were all but saying Luca didn't need him. "That was unfair. I'm sorry."

Paolo had started screeching in Italian too, but the spew of incomprehensible words stopped—they both stared at him. "You're trying to be in two places at once and take care of everybody, and you've been hit as hard as Luca has. I shouldn't have yelled." Christopher offered open hands, wordless apology.

"Christopher is right. Our hearts aren't well." Luca took Paolo's upper arms and looked him in the face. "I need you. You make it possible for me to do what I do. And you're right, seeing me will hurt Rolf's family more. So in this, you act for all of us, for the team. For me. You do what I can't do." He stared down into his soigneur's eyes with an intensity that made Christopher feel like a voyeur again. "And I will need you in Milan. Please."

Paolo began to speak, but Luca shushed him. "English, Paolo. Christopher is with us."

"I will be in Milan. It seems we can't get away from Christopher." Paolo reached to hug Luca tightly for a moment, and lifted his face for the two brief kisses, right cheek, left.

They didn't actually kiss, when seen from the side, more pursing and sound than contact. Nothing like a real kiss. Was that part of Paolo's problem?

"I call from Harelbeke, tell you what happens." Paolo disentangled himself. "You remember to eat and sleep, *asino*." He zipped Rolf's suitcase with the same care he'd take to rip Christopher's intestines out. "And I see you in Milan, if not earlier."

"Paolo—" Luca stopped him with one foot out the door. "Tell them—tell them Rolf and I were friends again."

Oh hell, that just screamed complicated: why else would they turn Luca away at the door? What had gone wrong between them? His journalist's mind wanted to ask. But Luca would tell him, his friend, only if he wanted Christopher to know.

The door closed behind Paolo with a tinny click. Christopher dashed after him to drag their bikes out of the corridor. The crowd outside the hotel didn't look much thinner than it had earlier. Didn't the rest of them have a train to catch? Once the guards left the hotel's front door, their bikes would either disappear or betray Luca's location. The gearsets ticked softly until he parked them next to Rolf's bed.

They were alone. For the first time in two months Christopher was alone with Luca, and for the second time they stood with the shadow of a dead man in the room. Luca remained still enough to frighten Christopher, his head bowed and his face in shadow. Brown curls fell in a disheveled curtain around his face.

"Luca?" Christopher held out his arms, not daring to come close enough to embrace this breaking man.

"Christopher." Luca stepped into his offered comfort, wrapping his arms around Christopher's waist, burying his face into his shoulder. "So many bad things today." His whole body shook, tremors rather than sobs. "But you're here. Kept things from being worse."

He'd done what he could but… there wasn't a damned thing he could have done about the worst thing of all. "I'm so sorry about Rolf."

"So hard to believe he died. Any minute he comes through door and gives me shit for hugging you." Luca's brief shake of his head wiped tears into the overripe jersey Christopher had yet to shed after today's ordeal. "Tells me I could have King of the Mountain instead of weenie journo."

Huh? How the hell had they gotten to the dead speaking ill of the living? "Weenie"? "Have"? What? "I don't understand."

"Sorry, Christopher." Luca twisted away to stand an arm's length distant. He shook harder, and couldn't raise his eyes. "On one thing, I told only half."

Oh fuck. Two months of sharing teeny-tiny hotel rooms and most of their waking hours. How could Luca not respond to someone he could hide in plain sight? "Which half?" Christopher could barely get the words out.

"About boyfriends. Tried once, long ago, back in racing camp days. You asked if someone courts the butcher's son. I said yes." Luca raised his eyes now. "I didn't tell you yes was Rolf."

CHAPTER 26

ROLF. AND Luca. So much made sense now.

Rolf's blow-up in the bike store. His little jibes and jabs. Everything he'd done for Luca, even showing up at Stu's funeral, because Luca needed him.

The way Luca jumped at shadows in the beginning. How clearly he'd been hurt, devastated, in the past. But what of now? A chill north wind blew through Christopher's bones, sucking warmth and hope away with it. And he'd made some promises. Damn. Rolf. Rolf with Luca. Had to keep the promises.

If the past wasn't so past, he'd keep the promises anyway. But—now was now. He had to focus on the now, or he couldn't keep moving. Had to move. "I thought your yes now was to me. Or was that only yes in Colorado?" Luca had told him goodbye once.

"Rolf's yes was long time ago." Luca sagged in place. "His hope, still a little bit."

The north wind warmed enough for Christopher to move. "Uh, we have to talk about this. But not right now. I can't deal, and we have to get out of this hotel before the Army decides it's safe to stop guarding the door and we have a flood of journos in the hallway. You're packed, you have your bike, I need to clean up and get my stuff. And we need to eat. Which train do we take and when does it come?"

Luca pulled a train table out of the rickety nightstand between the two narrow beds. "Same train takes us to Como as to Conegliano. We have one and a half hours until last train."

Yeah, Luca could stand straighter now, but his reprieve on this Rolf thing would last exactly until they had enough privacy to talk, which might be in Como. Christopher peeked through the window, aware that he made a silhouette against the window for the observers below. They'd probably be on the last train too.

People walked around on trains. “Uh, Luca. Maybe we should stay in Lienz overnight and let everyone clear out for Conegliano.”

“Not here.”

No, not if it meant two of them in a single bed, because no way was Christopher sleeping on Rolf’s sheets. “My room is a single.”

“Let’s just go. You get your suitcase, meet me at train station. You have ticket, right?” Luca checked his wallet. “I get us food, ticket, we sleep on train.”

His own experience of that was pretty poor, but Luca had to be exhausted. “I’ll be at the train station in one hour and fifteen minutes at the most, with all my stuff. Try not to get mobbed, okay?” Damn, he’d just allowed Luca to dive into the shark tank.

“I ask nice *carabinieri* at door to go with me, no problem.” Luca snorted. “Perk of being infamous.”

“Whatever works.” Christopher closed the gap between them to pull Luca against his body. “I’ll be there, I promise.”

“You’re there every time I need you.” Luca hugged him, a tight, hard squeeze that lingered.

SLITHERING OUT the back door of the hotel and across three streets, Christopher thought fast. He needed to check in with Ron, and what he’d say to *CycloWorld*, he didn’t know. Ron might be okay with the sorts of interviews he didn’t want to press Luca for, and if not? He still had the return ticket to Denver.

He zipped up to his room, dreaming of the hot shower and clean clothes he’d wanted for the hearing and didn’t get. Through the door, out of the spandex, and—

“Hey, buddy. Took you long enough.” Bob lounged, feet outstretched, on Christopher’s bed.

“Jayzuz, Bob!” His jersey wasn’t much shield, so he used it as a weapon. Bob dodged the ripe clothing.

“That’s no way to greet the guy who saved you a copy of the official FIC statement.”

“Thanks.” Christopher already knew most of what was in there: he’d been at the hearings. “But how’d you get in?”

“Any door you can’t open with a credit card—” Bob mimed sliding a card through a door jamb. “—can probably be opened for cash.” He rubbed two fingers and a thumb together. “Your computer is unfortunately immune to bribery, although your password is not “Luca,” “Biondi,” “Luca Biondi,” or “*CycloWorld*” with any combination of caps or numbers for letters. I put it back under your dirty underwear.”

Actually, his password was b10nd1. Bob was having too much fun with him since his laptop remained in the hotel lockbox. Time for a stronger password anyway. "And you're lurking here why?" The clock was ticking—he wanted the explanation but he couldn't pause for it. Clean socks, last pair, clean underwear, last pair, hope the villa had a washer…

"To interview the journo who pulled Luca Biondi up Mont Zoncolan." Bob leaned back against the headboard.

"Hmm, that journo has an exclusive." No, he wouldn't share Luca's struggle nor his need with Bob, and he'd damned well ask Luca before sending in what he intended to write.

"Okay, then where is Luca Biondi going to spend the rest of the Giro?" Bob's words chased Christopher into the bathroom.

Blessing Dave's connections in getting en-suite facilities, Christopher stepped into the tub and twisted the taps. Bathrooms down the hall to share with everyone had been his most shocking discovery about inexpensive European hotels, and hand-held shower heads his favorite. "I can't hear you over the water!" He hosed himself down with the sprayer.

Bob stuck his head through the curtain. "Where is Luca spending the rest of the Giro?"

Christopher turned the sprayer on him. The blast of warm water knocked Bob backward. Nosy bastard. "Not with the team." He soaped fast and rinsed faster.

"Well, duh." Christopher could hear him moving around. "I'm sogging up your last towel for that."

The towels were a flat-weave, soft linen that soaked through with droplets. Christopher whipped open the shower curtain to see Bob wiping his face with a corner.

He looked up with a grin. His face changed abruptly. "What the hell happened to you?"

Christopher took a quick look at his arms and legs—had he scraped himself in the tunnels? Oh, those. He'd gotten used to the scars that streaked his skin. "I got hit into a barbwire fence a couple months ago."

"Ow. Sorry, man." Bob dangled the towel from his fingertips, just out of reach. "So where's Luca going? You can tell me."

"No, I can't, because I don't know." Well, not to pinpoint it on a map, or say what town they'd debark the train. He snatched the towel from Bob's hand and cut the water.

"Where are *you* spending the rest of the Giro?" Had Bob detected the evasion?

"*Cyclo World* expects reports on every stage, and that's what they're going to get." Christopher scrubbed at himself with the towel, stopping to wring it once. "The last train is in about an hour, and I plan to be on it."

"With Luca?" Bob fled the bathroom when Christopher grabbed the hand shower—there might be enough back-pressure left to squirt him. "Hey, I'm only trying to get the poop on the most interesting development of this stage." Bob peeked cautiously around the door frame.

"You and everyone else." If Bob was persistent, the rest would be too. He had to work something out with Luca about what he could say. "So be different. Look at the second most interesting thing. You know that sprinter who got dropped today?" Christopher pushed past Bob on the way to jeans and shoes.

"Yeah. He had some plans for making it through the mountains. He wants a big tour triumph." Bob guarded the door, lest Christopher and his information escape early, but Christopher was still shrugging into a T-shirt. "And he blew up instead."

"Get a picture of his bike from today and take a really good look at his front chainring. Do some math. He killed off his chances all by himself by thinking like a sprinter. He should have geared like a climber." Okay, backpack closed, laptop extracted from safe, wallet, passport…

"What about his chainring?"

"I can't do all your thinking for you." Christopher slung everything on his back and grabbed his bike. "Besides, I have a train to catch." He pushed past his captor. One hungry shark diverted, two hundred to go.

Luca and his rain-suited escorts waited on the platform. Christopher caught his eye but didn't approach. He'd get on the same car as Luca, and then join him, not lead the charge to his side. They'd have to stow their bikes in the same area: a casual meeting wouldn't look odd. Other journos taking the last train out noticed Luca, but his rainsuited guards kept them at bay. Could Christopher be as effective?

Once aboard, he noted where Luca went, and casually made his way down the aisle, one step ahead of two other men with press passes and hungry looks. He and his computer bag made an effective bottleneck—they grumbled from behind to hurry. "May I join you?"

Luca shoved over to the window seat. "Fine." Christopher took his time getting settled, long enough that the other two journos gave up and went back to their seats. They'd be back.

Before the train was underway, Luca produced sandwiches, thick with shaven ham and luscious but unidentifiable white cheese, a subtle reminder Lienz was in Austria and they wouldn't be in Italy again for an hour or two. "Good." And needed—so much had been crammed into this one day he felt he'd missed a dozen meals. Luca's color came back, bite by bite—he'd missed a month of food. The journos made surreptitious passes up and down the train car, hoping to catch

Luca when his mouth wasn't full, but he made his sandwich last, and then he produced *apfelstrudel.* Christopher licked flakes of pastry from his fingers. If anyone wanted to draw conclusions from them eating the same meal, they could assume Christopher was trying edible bribery.

Luca yawned so widely even Christopher could feel his jaw creak. "Can you sleep? I'll wake you when…" When they had to change trains.

"Good idea." Luca lay back, flopped into what didn't look like a comfortable position, and it didn't take long before he was buzzing softly. Christopher glared one of the journos away, daring him to risk broken bones for disturbing the sleeper. The train darkened, but Christopher was too wired to sleep. The light from his screen shouldn't bother his companion. He pulled out his laptop.

Before he could send in this piece, he'd need to clear some of the content with Luca, but he'd get started now. Bob would have a shit fit.

Start with pictures: he'd taken a number of shots at the start. Racers milled about, signing in to the race log and rejoining their teams. The *maglia rosa* had to be included—how could he leave the leader in the pink jersey out? Selecting a particularly good view of the Antano-Clark team, with Luca, of course, he cropped out the distractions. A K-Aero saddle wasn't a distraction—that poked up at Luca's side. Maybe Nick Leyburn would get the message.

Um, no. *He* needed to get the message. What had Luca said? Wait a month and get for free? Nope. He cropped off every bit of saddle but a tiny hump of unidentifiable black. Let the bastards wonder.

On to the text.

When I got up this morning ready to watch the eighth stage of one of the world's most important races, I only expected to watch. I had no idea I'd accidentally ride the Giro d'Italia…

His typing didn't disturb the sleeping train. Luca looked uncomfortable, although he moved with a little pressure here and a soft shove there. Now his neck no longer looked like a chiropractor's nightmare, and his head rested on Christopher's shoulder. No one could see; the couple across the aisle slept, one in the other's lap, and the seats came up high. Christopher pressed his cheek against Luca's head, a flurry of curls tickling his nose and lips. The familiar scent of Luca's hair called back memories of nights spent stretched out on a futon.

You're not really *expecting to have sex with him,* Stu whispered.

"You always were an ass when it came to my sex life," Christopher told him. This time he'd hold Luca through the grieving.

CHAPTER 27

EITHER LUCA was letting Christopher set the pace from the train station to the villa, or he was even more stiff and slow than he wanted to let on from sleeping more or less upright after getting banged up in the crash on top of a long, brutal ride. Still it was a long ten miles with too much uphill. "We could have taken a cab, don't you think?" If only for the luggage. Luca's suitcase had shoulder straps hiding in the back, so he was effectively toting a backpack twice the weight of Christopher's.

"With bicycles? We look like tourists." Luca accelerated to take point. Christopher shut up and pedaled. They left the water in the valley behind and headed into higher country.

He stretched the few remaining kinks out of his body once they reached the villa. Luca keyed in a code and unlocked the gates to let them in. The gates were the only breach he could see in the stone walls, eight feet tall and forbidding. Or maybe 2.5 meters and forbidding.

"Whoa. This is Damiano's?" Christopher tried to take in the two story stone house with the mottled, red tile roof that looked old as the hills it nestled into. Sharp hills, covered in green, towering over the narrow lake that looked glacier-gouged, blue, deep, and icy. The house melded into the landscape, as if it had formed itself to shelter men from the very bones of the land. Gardens, green and lush, and the shrubbery manicured to bareness to five feet above the ground, surrounded the house. An aqua jewel of a swimming pool twinkled in the sun, and beyond that, the lake sparkled.

"Beautiful and secure. Same house on other side of hill on big lake, another eight hundred thousand euro and no walls. But Lago di Pusiano is very pretty." Luca swung aboard his bike for the ride to the house. He disarmed the alarm system and touched another button to open the garage door, hidden at the side of the house. A bright red, five-door hatchback waited within. Christopher recognized it as a BMW 116i only by reading the nameplate, but that had to be one sweet vehicle. Maybe they'd have reason to take a car somewhere. Right now they could leave the bikes in the garage and wrestle the bags upstairs.

"In here." Luca led him into a spacious bedroom that might once have been two, bright and sunny and full of a king size bed made up with a blue and white swirled duvet. He dropped his own bag. "Unless you don't want to share…?"

"I want to share." How had they come to this careful asking of the questions that shouldn't be questions? "I remember needing to be wakened in the night, after Stu. I'll be here." *I might need to be wakened myself.*

Oh, I think I could give you a good kick in the butt. Christopher could feel the smile he'd thought buried months ago.

Shut up, Stu. He opened his arms to Luca, grateful to be touched, to be allowed to touch, even if only for comfort.

The kitchen was well-provisioned, as promised. Damiano's housekeeper had also stocked the fridge with fresh greens and fruit. Christopher heated up delicious frozen dishes in a microwave curiously modern against the plaster-and-stone walls.

"Why does everyone think they need to feed me?" Luca inquired around a forkful of cheese and spinach *malfatti.* "I'm man who starts with cow and big knife and ends with steak dinner."

"Maybe we like feeding you?" Christopher wanted to kiss whoever made the *malfatti* and the delicate cream, tomato, and basil sauce they floated in. If the tiny dumplings tasted this good after a trip through the freezer, they ought to be good for sainthood when fresh. Luca still only ate half of what Christopher put on his plate.

But that was the only jest Luca made. For days he was withdrawn, coming up to eat when Christopher prodded him, visiting the sauna and the hot tub that lurked under a portico in the back of the house when Christopher led him to it. He accepted a massage after two days, when the bruising had eased up, and wouldn't talk about anything. Christopher had obligations—he spent hours watching the race coverage and writing something that sounded enough like he was there that Ron didn't question him, other than to bemoan the lack of really good quotes from racers. Luca wouldn't watch the coverage with him, retreating to look out over the lake.

"Let's go for a short ride," Christopher urged him. The hills wouldn't be so tough without a backpack, and they'd get tougher for not being ridden.

But Luca only set his bike on the motorized roller-platform that tilted to give pretend hills and equally false descents. Damiano's state of the art equipment wasn't doing Luca the kind of good he needed. The rollers might be fine when the weather turned, but there was a beautiful countryside begging to be ridden, and Luca wouldn't venture past the villa's door.

Nights were equally quiet. Luca snuggled into the curve of Christopher's body and twined their fingers together. Maybe he slept and maybe he stared into the darkness, but he wasn't thrusting his butt backwards into Christopher's groin, and Christopher for damned sure wouldn't thrust forward where he'd never been welcome before and wasn't being invited now. Climbing Mont Zoncolan in his head, reliving limbs gone to granite and vision faded to blank, kept his lust contained. He hadn't been up for sex after his accident either, but he'd needed the comfort that was all Luca offered then. A tiny kiss on the bump of Luca's spine was just for comfort.

Paolo called after three days, and Luca didn't share the conversation, conducted in Italian and then taken out in the garden. Fucking complicated situation. Christopher hadn't forgotten for a minute that they'd left something important dangling. Paolo had gotten more words in the few minutes than Christopher had gotten since they'd arrived. He remained at the kitchen table with his laptop and notes spread out.

Okay, if Luca was in a talking mood, they could clear the air of this much. When he came back in, Christopher gave him a few minutes. Maybe he'd talk first. But he only poured a glass of mineral water from the two-liter green bottle in the fridge.

"How's Rolf's family doing?" Christopher finally asked.

"Their hearts are broken." Luca set the glass down on the marble counter. "It was good Paolo went to them. His stories are comfort." His smile carried a career's worth of sorrow. "He told them we were friends again. They hate me a little less now."

"Did they hate you because you and Rolf had some yes?" He could hate Rolf for that, for touching his Luca. For doing—whatever they'd done. Even ten years ago when they were skinny teenagers learning their sport.

"I don't think they ever knew. They never said." Luca rocked in place, a faint shadow of his whirlwind agitation. Because he wasn't upset or because he was too drained? "They think I sabotaged Rolf's bike before important junior race. That's enough for hate."

"Uh, yeah." Jumbled thoughts rolled through his head: one secret safe as Luca wanted, but an accusation of betrayal? "Did you?" Fuck all the secrets, he might as well ask.

"I wanted to. Would be easy. Raise the seat a centimeter, or drop it a centimeter, screw up power delivery through the legs. His brother found me touching Rolf's bike, still thinking, still planning, and deciding no. He shouted and I jerked my hands away. Looked guilty. And Rolf rode poorly, placed thirty-second. But not because of me." Luca clenched and unclenched his hands, rubbing his thumbs across his fingers. "But maybe because of me. I don't know. But I didn't change his bike."

Whoa. Too much. The honorable, humble Luca he thought he knew, coming *that* close to doing the unforgiveable? And Rolf.... None of this made sense. "Uh, Luca, why would you even think of doing something like that?"

Luca yanked his hair out of his face, though errant locks flew back in when he whirled away from Christopher. "Because he sabotaged me. Maybe not on purpose, but sabotage all the same. You read my palmarès back in Boulder. You said you knew I made national junior team. Made that team when I was eighteen. But tried first when I was seventeen." He spun, facing Christopher now, his eyes wild. "Failed by three places. I should have *won* that race, I could have started my career earlier, been top young rider two years earlier, could have been lieutenant for big name and maybe taken his place, could have... My whole life would have changed."

"But he sabotaged you. Oh man, I thought you'd been hurt bad by someone... This is about as bad as it gets." How could Rolf break his boyfriend's heart like that, even if he was only a teenaged dumbshit? If he weren't dead, Christopher would have to kick his ass from here to Harelbeke. Stupid shit had left such a lasting mark on Luca, but how? No wonder he went straight to goodbye when Christopher fucked up. He couldn't fix the past but maybe a hug would help now. He pushed his chair back enough to get up.

"Wasn't so bad when it was happening," Luca whispered toward the floor, the fire gone. "Was wonderful."

"Really? He was screwing over your chances?" Christopher leaped the rest of the way out of his chair. He ached to hit something. Rolf was out of reach and the walls were rock. "And it was wonderful?" What the fuck? How could this even be?

"Was wonderful," Luca repeated. "Then. Next day, not so wonderful. Couldn't ride fast enough. Couldn't stay on the saddle. I finished too far back to make team."

Eighty kilometers on bike tomorrow. It was always about eighty or a hundred kilometers on a bike, wasn't it? *I like, but...* "Well damn it all to hell!" Christopher burst out. "The one thing you never even consider doing, and you did it. With him." Damn it, damn it, damn it, he'd take his chances with his knuckles on the granite.

"We didn't plan for that. We... played. Touched... It happened, and, Christopher, I don't want to tell you details, but wonderful happened, and stop didn't. And he was sorry, as sorry as he could be about wonderful, but I lost that race and all the chances for that year." A tear dripped down Luca's cheek. Christopher couldn't lift his untrustworthy hand to wipe it—he still wanted to hit. But not Luca.

"So I wanted him to know what riding with wrong feeling in his body was like. A little, but enough to make the difference between fast and fast enough to win." Another tear dripped down. "But I didn't, because it's different to change a bike in secret. It was wrong, so I stopped, but his brother never believed I didn't do it, and Rolf only half-believed me."

And then all these years later…. "Did the directeur sportif know how awkward it was going to be to have you guys on the same team, and Rolf being your lieutenant?" Getting up to see your old lover every morning, never quite trusting, and maybe the attraction still being there… Shit. Christopher half-fell into his chair.

"Little awkward, but Christopher, we got over it. Mostly got over it a long time ago. We had success on different teams, couldn't change the past. Coming to Antano-Clark was great career move for us both. We really were friends again." Luca pulled out another chair to sit close enough to take one of Christopher's hands.

He wanted to jerk away, to hide his hand far out of reach, but he held still. Luca cradled Christopher's hand with both of his. Christopher tried to relax, but his fist stayed closed.

"And that's all we were. All I was. Those days were gone ten years ago. If I wanted him, he would have come back. Would have been easy. Easier than you. Rolf gave me shit about you, didn't like you. Was jealous of you." Luca rubbed his thumbs against Christopher's wrist. He softened under the pressure and let his fingers unclench. "No interest—he wasn't you. But he was a friend, and important in my life. And I rode away and left him to die." Luca raised Christopher's hand to press against his cheek. "Can't forgive myself for that."

Oh fuck. Maybe the past was the past, except it dragged into the present so damned much. Christopher turned his hand to cup Luca's cheek. "You didn't hear when Michel said what happened. He wasn't dying when you left."

Luca flung himself out of the chair, his eyes wide. "I don't understand."

Christopher scrubbed his face to buy enough time to explain. "He was down, but he was talking. He had bone sticking out of his shoulder, but if he'd stayed still he might have lived. Some big veins go under the collarbone." He rose. If he was standing he could make sure Luca saw what he meant. He drew two fingers along his own ridge of bone. "Michel said Rolf was talking while he was down, and he was just broken. But he tried to get up and then 'there was so much blood.' The sharp bone sawed through a big vein when he moved. And he bled out. I'm sorry, that's horrible, but it's not like you left a dying man. You left a man who should have lived."

"He… should have lived." Luca breathed the words. "But he didn't."

"No. He didn't." Christopher pulled Luca close enough to touch foreheads. "I'm sorry he didn't. But you didn't abandon a dying man." He massaged the back of Luca's neck and willed him to believe what fit the facts.

"You're sure?"Luca peered into Christopher's face, his eyes wide and blue as the lake outside.

"I'm not a doctor, but I know some anatomy, and it all fits. He must have been hurting, but you said he even made a joke." Men busy bleeding to death didn't crack funnies. "The butcher's son knows what happens when a big vein gets cut."

Luca slipped his hands around Christopher's waist. The heat of his body felt like hope: hope for healing, hope for the future, hope for something more than tears on his shoulder. "He said I should go, that I didn't ride off a cliff."

"Even if you had ridden off a cliff, he'd expect you to keep going." Christopher slipped fingers into Luca's hair, massaging the back of his head. Trying to chase away the pain. "You're as strong a man as Johan Bruyneel. And almost as crazy." Bruyneel would understand exactly why Luca completed Mont Zoncolan.

"Maybe." Luca pressed his face into the curve of Christopher's neck. "I finished the stage."

"It's a good kind of crazy." Rubbing his face into Luca's curls felt like another kind of hope. "You don't give up." *Don't give up on me. Don't give up on your career.* "Rolf would be kind of pissed if you didn't get back on your bike."

Christopher had an armful of nothing, and Luca stood three feet away, breathing fire. "The bike, the bike, it's always about the bike! Fuck the bike!" He swung his fists in the air—Christopher flinched in spite of the gap. "Everything in my life has been about the bike! School, travel, friends! What I eat, when I eat it. All about the bike! Who I can have sex with. How I can have sex. All about the fucking bike! Everything in my life is about the fucking bike, for years, since I was child. Enough! I hate the fucking bike!"

He turned and ran, through the glass door to the back garden where the pool glittered in the sun. Clothing fluttered in his wake—Luca was nude before he hit the water. Christopher chased after, ready to wrestle a madman to the surface, but Luca dove in smoothly, surging half the length of the pool in two strokes. His hair streamed behind him, straight and half down his back, his arms and legs tan, his body pale where his clothing stopped the sun, and mottled all over with the blue/green bruises from the crash. All the scars that traced his career rippled under the water, blurring him. He flipped and came back the other way, turning again when he ran out of pool. Back and forth, back and forth, like a lion in too small a cage.

But hey, Luca was outdoors under the cerulean sky. First time in days.

He swam hard for over an hour, his strokes smooth and efficient. Maybe he would make a good triathlete, if he wanted to change, but… one third of the events needed the bike. He came to a halt at last, his arms crossed on the lip of the pool, his hair dripping down, and the ends drifting in the slosh of the water.

He rested his head on his arms for a long time, and when he finally lifted it, Christopher decided towel service was in order. Luca accepted his hand to rise from the water, droplets shedding from his skin and hair.

Christopher pulled Luca's wet form against his own body, soaking his clothing into tissue and wrapping the big striped towel around him from the back. Luca settled against him, his heart rate nearly normal from resting in the water, but thumping hard enough to feel through two sets of ribs. Christopher rubbed terry-cloth over Luca's back and squeezed water from his hair, curling already once the weight of the moisture no longer pulled it down. "How many of those thin linen towels do you need to dry your hair?"

"One, if I twist it four times." He seemed content to stay, and Christopher would have remained with him until the sun went down.

The ends of Luca's hair were dry when he spoke again. "Why do you put up with me?"

Easy to answer, harder to answer without spooking him again. Telling half was still telling all. "Because I think I love you."

"Even after I yell and say goodbye?" The trembling in his frame might have been from the breeze pulling his heat through the wet towel.

"It's not a switch, Luca." Christopher tipped Luca's head back enough to brush a quick kiss across his lips. "I can't turn it off just like that."

"That goodbye was the most awful word I ever said."

"*Ciao* means hello or goodbye, doesn't it?" Christopher dared to ask. "Whichever you want it to mean at the time."

"Means 'hello' right now." Luca pressed more tightly against him. "*Ciao*, Christopher."

BLESSING DAMIANO and his housekeeper while foraging in the freezer, Christopher found more frozen dishes whose names he had to ask Luca. "More variety in Italian cooking than spaghetti and pizza, Christopher." Luca chose a pot of something he called *risotto alla pitocca* to heat. "It's better fresh."

If it was better fresh, Christopher might find himself whimpering on the floor. Who *knew* such things could be done with chicken and rice? Luca took seconds, instead of leaving all but three bites on his plate. He even spoke during dinner, of nothing important, but responses, even if they were only a few words, made an excellent change from his silence and half-hearted toying with food that didn't deserve such treatment. His shoulders drooped, but his kilometers in the pool accounted for it, and he started yawning even before Christopher stowed the leftovers in the fridge. Maybe Luca would want them as a midnight snack.

Christopher slid Luca into bed and followed even though he wasn't really tired. If Luca needed his shoulder for a pillow, his shoulder better be there.

Christopher woke feeling strangely alone. He patted for Luca and found only wrinkled sheets. A dim light shone from downstairs. He followed it to the source. Luca sat at the kitchen table, the laptop open.

A video clip from the Giro played. Cyclists heaved themselves up from a pile of men and machines to ride away in ones and twos. The fallen rose, until only turquoise and black riders remained on the ground. Luca twisted to sitting, pulling his leg from beneath his bike. Rolf stayed down but turned to talk—his lips moved but the sound didn't carry to the camera. The team car pulled up behind them to disgorge Michel and a mechanic, who ran to lift Luca to his feet and right his bike. Michel knelt at Rolf's side, running his hands over Rolf's torso, searching for damages. Rolf spoke—he might not have quipped about cliffs in English. Luca mounted, and with his assistant's pushing, started after the escaped peloton. The moto followed Luca. Of course. The leader.

The scene dissolved to an aerial shot. The helicopter zoomed in to Rolf, Michel, the mechanic, and two additional men who had arrived in a pink Giro car. The race doctor? They hovered around Rolf, staying on the clean pavement. A pool of red grew, flowing downhill, away from the man who lay unmoving under their efforts.

With one hand on Luca's shoulder, Christopher confiscated the mouse to minimize the window. "How many times have you played it?" He'd already seen this clip and didn't need to rewind to the beginning to see the black and tan dog dart out into the road.

"I have to be sure…"

Luca might watch a hundred times, but he wouldn't see more than this. "He talked to you as you left. Michel told you what happened. You didn't ride away from a dying man."

"Some of the press say I did."

"You were there. Michel was there. They weren't. And some of them might be trying to provoke you into responding." Maybe a shoulder massage would relax him into listening and not just hurting. "You haven't talked to the press officially."

"I can't."

Digging his thumbs into the rock-hard tension in Luca's shoulders, Christopher reminded him, "You already have. You talked to me. All you have to do is make it official and I could quote you."

"You said you didn't come here as journo."

"I didn't, but the whole racing world already knows me as someone who's interfered in your business enough to make you trust me. It makes sense you'd talk to me, after the FIC incident." He tried to work the tension out of Luca's back.

"You can talk some more, and I can leave out the parts that aren't anyone's business and put in the parts the world needs to know. Then your side is out there. You've probably said most of what I'd need to ask, anyway."

"Most. Not all." Luca felt like an oak plank under his hands.

"If it didn't happen this week, or it didn't happen with a bicycle, I don't need to include it. I'll look biased as hell if I leave some major item out, but, Luca, you were right when you said I was a sympathetic member of the press." He bent to nuzzle into brown curls. "You aren't going to get a better platform."

"Tell only half the story?" Luca turned enough to look into Christopher's eyes.

"Hmm." That wasn't how he'd describe it. "More like tell all the story, but without details. Depends on how widely known that sabotage issue is, and what exactly happened between you later."

"We didn't talk for two years and tried to blow each other off the road." Luca leaned his face into his hands, giving no sign that Christopher's massage was loosening a thing. "Everyone knew we were angry, but no sly hints about knowing why."

"Then I can describe that as 'a falling-out we both contributed to, and eventually got past.' See? That's not so bad." Much more benign than anything Bob would do with the information.

"All the story." Luca snorted. "And not all the story, at same time. I was glad to be on team with him, Christopher." Luca's shoulders relaxed just a bit. "He was strong rider, good climber. Even young. But no sense of timing, not on bike, not in life. Maybe I wasn't better. Maybe grabbing opportunities has to be good for the person you grab. Maybe I shouldn't have grabbed you."

"Don't *ever* say that!" Christopher shook Luca's shoulders one quick rebuke. "Maybe we're all messed up, but I wouldn't have missed one single minute, well, except the 'goodbye' part. I wouldn't be here as a writer if you hadn't grabbed me. There were opportunities, things you said, that I shouldn't have grabbed, and I'm trying to make up for it. I'm sorry I did things badly. I'm trying to do better."

Luca reached up to lay his hand over Christopher's. "I know. Any bad is lost in the shadow of all the good. Thank you. Maybe talking now to journo-you is more grabbing. For me, trying to save reputation." With a touch of the mouse, Luca expanded the browser and switched windows. "This says I knocked him down, left him, all on purpose. For old angers. Why would I do that to anyone? Why would I hurt my lieutenant? I need him. Team needs him."

"This writer needs to get attention. He's making things up. Luca, we'll put your own words out there, and ignore the slime. We'll call Michel. I'll ask him if I can quote what he said, and we'll get the truth out. Damiano probably has a video camera—we'll do an interview, post it. Your own words will be more important than this trash."

"Let's do it now. While I have the courage to talk."

Damiano had a decent video camera and a tripod, lurking in a cabinet below the TV. Christopher aimed it at two chairs sitting under the brightest lights in the midnight house. Luca joined him, hair combed, his turquoise jersey zipped to the neck. Christopher started the camera and darted to the second chair, butterflies the size of cormorants in his gut.

"This is Christopher Nye of *CycloWorld*, speaking with Luca Biondi of Team Antano-Clark. Signor Biondi wore the *maglia rosa* of the Giro's leader before the tragic accident that ended his hopes and deprived him of his friend and teammate Rolf Knecht. Signor Biondi has agreed to tell us about that final stage..."

His questions directed Luca to necessary points: their long rivalry, sharing hotel rooms on tour, the dog, the joke and its reference, and his grief. Luca talked to Christopher, not the camera, and wiped his eyes before he was done. So did Christopher.

"...I will miss him for the rest of my life." Luca bowed his head.

Christopher wouldn't press him for more, and besides, that would make a good slow dissolve. Not to mention that the interviewer was sniffling and waiting for the smartass voice in his head to say *Aww, do you miss me like that?* And yes, he did. Christopher jumped up to turn the camera off and find tissues for them both.

Luca wiped his eyes and stood to lean into Christopher's embrace. "He was a good man. We just weren't good for each other. Too young, wanted too many exact same things."

I'll never be more than a recreational companion on the road. But I am what you need out of the saddle. Even your life isn't spent entirely on a bike. "I'm pretty sure we won't have that problem. Come on back to bed, Luca."

MORNING CAME, and again Christopher woke to an empty bed. He found Luca in the back garden with a cup of coffee, watching the light play on the lake below. "This is so beautiful. How do we thank Damiano for letting us stay here?"

"We leave some good wine." Luca took a deep pull at his coffee cup and seemed surprised to have drained it.

"Okay. Want a refill while I'm getting mine?"

Luca handed over his cup.

While Christopher ambled around the kitchen, his eye fell on the BMW key fob hanging on its hook. Damiano had clearly said to use the car. They'd been cooped up in the house for the better part of a week. It was a rest day for the race, so he didn't have to spend hours in front of the screen trying to soak up what he was supposed to be watching live. Consoling himself that he'd be watching the bulk of the race on a screen in the press area if he were there didn't make it right, or even much better, but until he had a better solution for being in two places at once, it would have to do.

He wouldn't ride without Luca, and Luca hadn't wanted to ride. *You will know when it's time to ride again.* Yeah, he had, but his own time didn't have a lucrative contract attached, and more races yet in the season. Luca needed the days off, but he also needed to maintain his form if he was going to race well following the Giro. Coming to a second peak in time for the *Vuelta de España* was probably his goal, but an extended period of pretend-riding indoors wasn't going to keep him in top shape. Christopher wanted to ride, and Luca needed to ride. He wouldn't push Luca to anything, not sex, not cycling, but he'd for damned sure put the opportunity for both out there.

Luca got his coffee and a kiss, and Christopher went inside to consult maps.

He knew where he was going. Now for how to get there. The back seat of the sporty, compact liftback BMW folded down. More than enough room, good. Christopher hit the quick releases on their bikes' front wheels and tucked the pieces into the car. He tiptoed back into the house, peeking carefully for Luca. He was still sitting outside staring at the lake, or maybe at his past, and nothing moved but his hair in the breeze. Not a good sign. A still Luca was a brooding Luca, and if the catharsis from yesterday hadn't lasted, this plan Christopher was hatching might refresh it. Either way, they'd get out of the house.

Tugging his cycling shorts up over his butt, Christopher considered which clothing of Luca's to bring. What had Paolo left him? He was entitled to wear pink shorts to go with his *maglia rosa,* but for what Christopher had in mind, that might be like strolling into a grocery store in a tux. Team colors—better. Turquoise and black jersey and shorts, socks, good, cycling shoes, good. A tube of chamois cream. He'd better take that.

Christopher pulled jeans over his shorts and added his turquoise jersey to the pile he'd hide in the car. A polo shirt would be fine until Luca decided what he was going to do.

He parked clothing and shoes in the car and went in search of his target. "Had enough coffee?"

"Yes." Oh boy, Luca was back to monosyllables.

"Great. Go put your shoes on. We're going for a ride." He pulled Luca to standing.

"No, we aren't." Luca kept his eyes on the ground.

"Street shoes. We're taking the car." Christopher lifted Luca's chin enough for a nose-bump/almost kiss. "Damiano said we could use it."

"I don't know how to drive."

Argh. "I do. You've ridden with me. I won't crease the BMW's pretty red fenders." He swatted Luca's butt lightly. "Go put on your shoes."

At least he was getting that much cooperation. It would be seriously awkward to throw Luca over his shoulder and drag him to the garage.

They were out of the garage and halfway through the gate before his reluctant passenger noticed the cargo. "We have car full of bicycles."

"They wanted to go for a ride too." Christopher touched a button on a remote and the gates closed smoothly behind them. Lovely technology, and now Luca was well and truly stuck, since the car doors wouldn't open while they were in gear.

"Where are we going?" A decided edge colored Luca's voice.

"Just shut up and enjoy the scenery." Luca had probably been up and down their intended route half a dozen times, since the *Giro de Lombardia* used this road, but had he ever really been able to look around? "It's lovely." Did he remember what lay at the other end of this road?

"Hmmph." Luca pointedly stared out the passenger window, but calmed down and really studied the green-covered hills dotted with houses as elegant as the villa.

Strada Provenciale 41 took them up an unpopulated, tree-lined canyon, and they steadily gained elevation. If Luca were willing to ride, they'd scoff at taking a car the few miles they needed to go, but now.... Luca needed the choice.

Christopher parked at an overlook above the eastern leg of Lake Como, slender and blue in the valley below. If Luca were in a kissing mood, this would be a great spot to park and get frisky. Maybe not. A car shot by on the road below them. Some cyclists in a motley assortment of jerseys and hair tending to the gray went past going the other direction. Tourists. Getting all over. Jeez.

"The lake is pretty." Luca stared through the windshield. "But I was looking at a pretty lake before."

"Gorgeous," Christopher agreed. "But not why we came." He scanned the hilltops to their left. The topographical map suggested he should be able to see their destination from here. "We're going over there." He pointed to a white building with a gray tower one hill over. "And we stopped because you need to make a decision."

Luca said nothing.

"I know you know where we are. And I stopped because we need to decide how to get there. I can drive us the rest of the way." Christopher tried peeling Luca's hand away from the gearshift. He covered it with his own instead. "But I think that's disrespectful. We've both lost people we care about. It's right for us both to go there. We are cyclists, our dead were cyclists, and we should approach this shrine on two wheels."

Luca swallowed hard, staring at the church in the distance. "It would be very wrong for us to visit the place of our patron saint in a car."

"I won't make you go, but I need to go." Where'd this lump in his throat come from? He wasn't usually a praying man. Except when he needed to beg Whoever was running the universe to keep Luca safe.

"I promised to place Stu's name among cyclists. His nameplate is in my bag." Luca spoke slowly.

"Should we go back and get it?" No, please no. If they went back he wasn't sure he could get Luca in the car a second time.

"Need to get permission first. We come back, have ceremony." He stared past Christopher to the shrine. "But I need cycling shoes."

Christopher reached behind the passenger seat and set both pairs of fixed-sole shoes in Luca's lap. "Done."

"This isn't proper clothing." He plucked at the neck of his T-shirt.

Christopher reached again for the colorful pile of miracle fiber. Before Luca could find another objection, he produced the chamois cream. "We'll get our gloves and helmets when we get the bikes out."

"What about you?"

"One of those jerseys is mine." And clean—the villa did have a washer. He peeled his jeans down to reveal black spandex. "I think I brought everything."

Without a word, Luca unzipped his jeans. In a moment, he was again the splendid cyclist who had won or placed in nearly every event he'd ridden this spring. All except for the deepened sun-lines around his eyes and the tautness in his lips.

They reassembled their bikes and swung aboard for the last few kilometers to *il Santuario della Madonna del Ghisallo.*

CHAPTER 28

LUCA LET Christopher lead, staying on his wheel but not pushing. The road flattened enough to allow them to draft for a few meters at a time, but dipped and rose to "stand on pedals" steepness in between. Two kilometers of steady climbing had Christopher's legs talking to him. Luca made no comment, but in the last half kilometer he zipped around to take the lead. Christopher followed in his wake.

The square, white church stood on the highest hill on this side of the lake, its gray stone bell tower pointing to the heavens. Tourists roamed, snapping pictures and chatting.

They racked their bikes and clopped into a chapel scarcely larger than Christopher's apartment. Christopher gasped, but Luca must have been here before. He passed the walls pinned with race banners and tiled with plaques, each with a picture, name and dates, heading straight to a tiered table with candles, some burning. He lit one and knelt at the table, his hands clasped.

Maybe that was the way to pray here, though Christopher usually spoke more directly with God. He needed to be here, but what he needed was outside, where heaven was close enough to touch and blue enough for eternity. Inside, the history of his sport rested under the yellow arched ceiling, where bicycles lined the upper racks and crowded the floor at one end. The bikes were labeled with their names and races: Gianni Bugno's machine stood against Eddy Merckx's and Gino Bartali's. Jerseys, yellow, pink, blue, and polka dot, adorned the walls. Offerings of thanks, reminders of mortality, dedicated to la Madonna del Ghisallo to keep them all safe. The bicycle that carried Fabio Casartelli to his death in the 1995 Tour de France loomed overhead, its forks bent like knees. Rolf's blue King of the Mountain jersey belonged here with other mementos of the renowned, fallen and living. Stu's name belonged here, to be remembered.

An eternal flame burned in the center of the church—if Christopher stared into the flame maybe only a few tears would spill over.

Luca rose and joined him. "So much greatness here," he whispered.

Christopher nodded; another tear escaped. "And so much sorrow."

"We remember them." Luca rested a hand on the small of Christopher's back, guiding him out into the piazza. He dropped his hand but turned them to the bronze statue framed against the mountains across the lake. One weathered metal cyclist rode forever, his arm raised. For victory? To scream at the universe for his companion's sake? The other man had fallen, tangled in his bicycle, and would stay on the ground forever.

"They are us," Luca whispered. "We ride. We ride for them."

"We ride." Christopher struggled to read the words on the bronze border. "*Caddero sulla strada—*"

Luca spoke from memory. "*—inseguendo un sogno de Gloria. Che raggiunsero nella luce del sacrafìcio delle loro giovani esistenze.* They fell on the road, following a dream of glory. They reached the light in the sacrifice of their young lives."

Stu. Rolf. Maybe there was glory in going out doing what you loved best in all the world. But falling at all.... A Stu-shaped void opened in Christopher's heart.

"They are the *fuga bidone,* Christopher. They broke away. They're too far ahead to reel in," Luca whispered, his voice breaking into the wind that licked the mountain top. "We are the peloton."

"We'll see them again at the finish line." Pain that felt like hope lanced through him. *Luca.* He groped for Luca's hand.

Luca clasped back with crushing tightness. Christopher tipped his head, trying to find some angle that would keep the tears back but he hurt too much, and Luca's hand was all that anchored him. Luca's hair lifted in the breeze, fuzzily, and then clearly when the tears fell anyway, and his face was already wet.

"Christopher," he whispered. "Live forever. It would kill me to come here for you."

"Crazy man who thinks he'll ride Mont Crostis, what do you think it would do to me?" It was too much, too much, and he didn't know how they went from hurting each other to stave off the tears to holding each other and letting them fall. *Please, God, he's going to keep riding. Keep him safe.*

"I stay off Mont Crostis. But I can't stay off bike."

"I know. I'll learn to deal with the fear. Somehow." His voice cracked on the last word. He'd have to learn how to send Luca off to the wars on the road with a smile, to do nothing that would interfere with his confidence. Best start now. "And you will come home victorious and be rewarded for it."

"Come home," Luca repeated. "I like."

Their storm had shaken them to ignoring everything, everyone around them, but Christopher let go of Luca to muttered comments, some of which he understood.

"That's the Antano-Clark rider who lost a teammate."

"Who's the other guy?"

"Don't know. Friend of the dead guy, maybe?"

"Poor fellas."

The click of a camera interrupted someone who was probably saying the same thing in Swedish. Fucking tourist. Taking pictures of other people grieving. The photographer needed a swift kick in the nuts.

Luca dropped his hands and stepped back, taking one more look at the bronze. "I go talk to priest about Stu. And for Rolf. Team will come here after Giro, have ceremony for him."

"His family might want to come." They'd spend their own two days on the train, but they might think it time well spent, to see how Rolf's comrades honored him.

"I tell Michel. We bring them." Luca dragged the back of his hand across his face. "You want to look in the museum?" He nodded at the graceful, curved building sailing on the stone of the mountain beyond the chapel. "More bicycles, more history. Not the sad parts."

"I'll wait here."

Luca clattered away across the stone piazza. Christopher turned again to the statue. Did the fallen man collapse to the ground once his teammate rode away? Captured forever in his last moment of life, his face was full of pain.

Rolf had gone quickly. Had Stu? Or had he been aware for much too long? *Please let it have been fast for him.*

"Didn't expect to see you here."

Christopher turned slowly, lest his fist fly out and smash Bob the Goddam Barnacle in the face. "Aren't you supposed to be somewhere far, far away?"

"Not on a rest day. Trying to do some 'think outside the race' stories. You've been getting some readers with them. Haven't seen you around." Bob smirked at him. "Been getting cozy with the best story never to hit the airwaves? You looked friendly enough to be getting an exclusive."

Deep breath. Take another deep breath. And don't jerk that camera off his neck and throw it into the lake. "Do you not remember what happened? Can you not recognize grief?"

Bob shrugged. "Didn't think you knew Rolf Knecht that well."

"It's not just Rolf." Okay, keep a lid on the temper. Nothing quite like getting livid to make crying a thing of the past though. "You asked what happened to me when you got a good look at all my scars back in Lienz, remember?"

"Yeah, you said you got knocked into some barb wire." Okay, he looked like the brain was engaged.

"I wasn't the only one in that accident. My best buddy Stu got hit too. He didn't make it." Christopher pulled his phone out of his pocket and flicked the gallery to show Bob pictures from six months and a year earlier. He and Stu on the top of Flagstaff Mountain. He and Stu at the reservoir. Stu popping a wheelie, shit, like Rolf at the finish line. "We were tight. I miss him every day and when I see that—" Christopher looked toward the bronze cyclists. "—yeah, I'm gonna lose it. The Antano-Clark riders caught the car. Luca was there for Stu's death too, and then Rolf…" Damn it all, he did *not* want to cry again. Not in front of Bob.

"Rough. Sorry about your friend." Bob looked mildly concerned. Okay, Stu was a nobody to him. "So he's not talking, even to you?"

Thinkthinkthinkthinkthink. "He's said some things."

"But you haven't published."

And Bob had pictures. That smug, shit-eating grin meant he had to have pictures. "Not yet. Last edits, ya know?"

"Then looks like I have an exclusive." He patted the camera.

Christopher regretted every tip and deflection he'd fed the man. "You mean you'd really post a pic of a buddy with snot streaming down?"

"Might Photoshop that much out," Bob considered.

"Well at least use a pic of my good side." If Luca could fool some of the wiliest riders in the sport into believing he was exhausted when he still had a tire-burning sprint inside him, then Christopher could play vain. "And his, ya know?"

"Which is your good side?" Bob punched up the pictures in the window and showed Christopher. He flipped through a couple. Christopher flicked to a fourth. How many had the man taken?

"Any" was too many—Christopher pressed down the two buttons that would wipe the memory card entirely. "Oops."

Bob snatched the camera away, but too late. "What did you go and do that for?"

"Let the man grieve his dead, Bob." Christopher went for grim. "Don't make news on him with that."

"I'd fuc— I'd punch you if I hadn't downloaded all my pictures from the rest of the race." Bob poked buttons as if it might disgorge a picture after all. "You're the only journo who gets exclusives with the great Luca Biondi, is that it?"

"Depends on what it is." Had he just opened a huge can of ill-will? Riders who did that didn't get much help from the peloton. "Catch him after his next race, because he'll be news, win or lose, and I won't fight you for it."

"You'd do that?"

Once. "Yeah. That was kind of a dirty trick just now, but let him have some dignity, okay?" One more sop, to keep the thrown elbows down. "Did you ever figure out the sprinter's chainring?"

"Not yet." Bob glared. "There's a trick to it, isn't there?"

He wasn't stupid or malicious, he just wasn't an equipment geek and he was a journo. "His elliptical chainring was the equivalent of a forty-two tooth gear, and he was up against guys riding on thirty-fours and thirty-eights. He was working way too hard for the same distance on the grade. You can do the math for watts, right?"

"Oh hell, yeah." Bob looked up from his camera. "Okay, I might forgive you some day." He shot another picture of the statue. "I have to redo these. You want to pose?"

"Nope." Luca was on his way out of the chapel. "Gotta go."

He met Luca at the bike rack, "ready to go" being the world's biggest understatement. With drawn smiles they mounted and left the bronze riders behind.

The three kilometers back to the car went fast, less than two minutes. Christopher tried not to ride the brakes—he didn't want to hold Luca up. Every pebble and bump threatened to smear him across the road. The steady 7% grade needed all his attention and the brief 12% and 14% grades felt like elevator shafts. *Stay loose, move with the bike.* He nearly overshot the BMW.

"Good descent, Christopher." Luca stayed straddled on his bike. "Like a pro."

"Thanks." Maybe practice would make that less terrifying at speed. Christopher popped off his front wheel and laid both sections of bike in the car. "Want to hand me your frame?"

"No." Christopher spun around to see Luca's glorious smile, whipped by wisps of hair blowing into his face. "Feels good. I ride back to the villa."

"Oh, okay." *Yes!* "I guess that makes this the team car?" Christopher grinned back and swung into the driver's seat, fumbling for his street shoes. He'd follow Luca, just in case.

Luca didn't wait for Christopher to get back into the lane—he was off and peddling. With his back hunched into racing position, his legs pumping smoothly to get to speed on the hill, and the flutter of his hair, he was velocity itself.

He sailed down the pavement with Christopher in heart-pumping pursuit. Not too close, but not too far behind, swinging the BMW through the curves. How did the directeurs sportifs manage yelling on a radio, keeping track of their teams and the rest of the race, all while driving among two hundred unprotected riders on roads worse than this? He tried not to look at the speedometer. The needle fluttered well above sixty. *Kilometers, it's calibrated in kilometers. Please, God, keep him upright. If he goes down, don't let me hurt him.*

Luca leaned through the curves, pedaling intermittently, a turquoise and flesh missile on a downhill trajectory. The road sometimes took him out of sight. The BMW's accelerator was enemy and tool—Christopher maintained his pace behind, sweat pooling between his shoulder blades.

Luca flashed on, every line of him melded with his machine.

Sixteen kilometers of twisty road brought them back to the villa. Christopher staggered out of the car, wiping sweat off his temples.

Luca leaped from his bike, nearly dancing. "Wonderful ride! Perfect!" He flung his arms around Christopher, staggering him backward.

Christopher thought he could breathe again, but Luca smothered him in kisses, crushing closer than clothing to his body. He managed to get his arms up and around his beloved whirlwind, and found enough air to laugh. "Wonderful ride." Oh yes. Wonderful. Luca was back.

Back with joy, back with need. He was all over Christopher, pushing him into the house and yanking him to a stop to squeeze tight. Trying to keep up with his kisses wouldn't work—he'd meet Christopher's mouth fast for a flash of tongue and lip, to dart away for a taste of neck or shoulder.

What was he going to say? Slow down? Luca never slowed down unless something was wrong, and this wasn't wrong, this was days, weeks, of missing right. It had been so long since they'd done anything beyond the merest suggestion of kisses. "Take off your helmet," Christopher finally begged after one thump too many.

Luca unclipped his headgear and tossed it on the coffee table—he'd backed Christopher into the living room. "And everything else." He captured the zipper tab of Christopher's jersey in his teeth and tried pulling it down. He gave up and went back to hands to get Christopher stripped—that went faster, though Christopher might have been on his back on the couch before his jersey hit the floor.

Luca knelt beside him, touching everywhere, tasting everywhere, frantic. "I'm not going anywhere," slowed him down a fraction. Christopher finally got his arms around Luca and pulled him on top. Abandoning fast for thorough, Luca sealed his mouth to Christopher's, his tongue flicking, demanding, conquering. Anything Luca wanted, okay—Christopher opened under his onslaught, wrapping his arms around Luca's slender chest and demanding equality in a handful of muscular butt. Luca pushed against him, their cocks throbbing hard under their racing shorts.

Too long since they'd demanded anything from each other. "I don't want to come yet," Christopher gasped.

Luca slid to his knees on the floor, still in Christopher's embrace. "Pacing, yes." He changed tempo, his mouth quieter, his tongue slower, and Christopher matched him now, nibbles and licks, nose bumps and smiles. He could map the terrain of muscle under clothing; he'd find the sweet, familiar planes of Luca's body.

His hair tickled where it fell around his face on his path down Christopher's chest. His tongue tickled too—he found Christopher's nipples and the indent under his breastbone where his heart thudded so hard. Was it his own heart he felt slamming against his ribs, or was Luca's pounding hard enough to shake them both? His chest pulsed under Christopher's hand.

Oh Luca was back—this was his lover, more ardent then he'd ever been in Boulder, more demanding, more confident that Christopher would move with him, anticipating and matching him. Hell to the yes—he'd come across an ocean and slain dragons for Luca. This was his reward too.

Luca hooked his thumbs into Christopher's spandex waistband—his hips rose smoothly to let him pull the cycling shorts down far enough to expose what they both wanted. Harder than he ever remembered, Christopher waited for what Luca would do next, but only a few seconds. Swirling his thumb through the droplets of precum, Luca flashed him a blinding smile. He swooped down to met Christopher's lips again, and turned his attention south.

Oh, damn, Luca's mouth was hot. One breath to slipstream over Christopher's cock, and then nothing but lips, tongue, and palate.

Moaning wasn't enough, words were beyond him. He wouldn't last, not when he was getting what he'd missed so badly. Luca plunged down on his cock far enough to need to pull back in a hurry once, but he went on, going deep. He cupped strong fingers around Christopher's balls, rolling them with devastating gentleness. Trying to be equally gentle, Christopher threaded his fingers into Luca's hair, crushing the silky spirals but not tugging.

"Luca." He had to taste his lover's name. Then—"Luca! I'm gonna—" and he did, but Luca pushed down and stayed with him while he arched, incandescent and helpless. *Luca, oh….*

Coming up slowly brought sweet aftershocks—Luca took his time releasing Christopher's barely softening shaft, caressing him with tongue and fingers, parting with a kiss. Sliding his arms under Christopher's shoulders, he bent for a meeting of lips. A salt splash entered at the flick of his tongue—Christopher tasted himself in his lover's mouth. *It's mine, I gave it to him, he's sharing.* Luca swallowed the rest.

They had time for something slower now. Luca let Christopher set pace on the brushes of lip and tongue. "Now you." He slid a hand down the back of Luca's shorts, cupping one muscular buttock. "Take these off." He squeezed, arching his wrist out to make the spandex slip down. "Only these."

Luca rose and shed the bright shorts with the wet spot in front. His cock curved out from his body, proud, and no more still than Luca ever was—jumping with each beat of his heart. With a hand on the column of Luca's thigh, he brought Luca to kneeling over him. With one knee to either side of Christopher's head and his hands on the couch's arm, he moaned when Christopher engulfed his cock.

His skin slipped back away from the head under Christopher's tongue. Oh damn, his Luca, his lover, musky from riding, slick with driblets of his desire, and all for Christopher. *Yes, Luca…* It was all yes as he dove down Luca's length, meeting short thrusts that became longer.

Lifting his eyes upward showed him turquoise overhead, brilliant as the sky had been over them at Ghisallo. Glancing farther still, Luca smiled down on him, his ringlets dancing, framing his face. His sun-crinkles were smile-crinkles now, his eyes hooded and so damned full of what Christopher didn't think they'd ever find all the right words for, but who needed those useless things when all he had to do was look. He slipped a hand under Luca, coming up to grip one hard cheek. Even now he wouldn't slide a finger between those two firm buns.

He'd lick, and change Luca's face from desire to slackness, and his mumbled encouragement to wordless sounds. He cried out, filling Christopher's mouth with his come, pulsing for long seconds until he was drained. Salt and a faint bitterness, but so sweet for how long it had been since his last taste.

Luca lay down on top of him, his heated skin touching mostly spandex, his bare sections meeting up with Christopher's remaining clothes. They'd fix that soon, but for now he wanted to hold Luca and bask in what they'd done. He rubbed his cheek across the top of Luca's head, and smoothed away a few strands that threatened to tickle him into sneezing. With his arm curved around Christopher's chest, Luca stroked his thumb back and forth on Christopher's skin.

Dozy thoughts went all over. Christopher had wept today, and most of his tears were for Stu. Some were for Rolf. The two young men who had reached the light were worth mourning. There'd been some for Luca, who stood in his embrace, crying his own tears for his friend and perhaps more. Why for Luca? Was it more for his grief or for the different pain of having lost him? Now Luca was back, his own sorrow attenuated, and he was lying in Christopher's arms. Good place for him. Keep him there forever.

Some of Christopher's tears were for himself. For losing Stu. For losing Luca. That made sense. For losing dreams. But wasn't any dream he'd cherished of making a name for himself on a bicycle only that, a dream? His best rides were nothing compared to Luca's—they'd struggled up Zoncolan together, but Luca matched him there, exceeded him, even with a crash, and had already covered three times the distance and four other climbs. He'd never be in Luca's league, not if he'd started training at six and doped besides.

Except—Luca still rode with him. Luca lay with him and came to him for what he needed as much as winning. Words Luca had spoken at the quarry came back now. *You stop and look with me. You're better than the entire team in this important way.* A soft laugh escaped him, making Luca look up, his brow wrinkled. "I'm just figuring out that maybe I don't have to ride at your level for you to want to be with me."

Luca shook his head, rubbing his face against Christopher's shoulder. "You pulled me up the Zoncolan of my life. Help with officials, yes, but you let me be Luca who looks at fossils and weeps for friends. And sucks cock."

Christopher snorted so hard he nearly rolled Luca onto the floor—they had to flail to stay on the couch and Luca ended up sitting beside him. Wrapping his arm around Luca's waist to keep him there, Christopher blurted, "I don't want you sucking any cock but mine."

The sun came out above him. "Yours is the only one ever, since... since young."

Since Rolf. And thank you for not saying his name.

"*Frate*, remember?" Luca combed his fingers through Christopher's hair, pushing it back from his forehead.

"Not with me, you're not." Christopher squeezed a squeak out of Luca. "And any vows of celibacy I make don't apply to you."

"You make such a vow?" Luca's brows lifted.

"I'll keep any promise you need about that, but Luca—" Christopher sat up to enfold Luca. "I don't want anyone but you. Not since you got mad about a cop and the Tour de France. Or maybe when you explained that tortelloni looked like bellybuttons. Speaking of which...." He poked Luca's middle. "Yours doesn't. Look like a tortelloni." He poked again, and Luca doubled over laughing.

"Maybe if I had two of them." He poked Christopher's belly. "Yours does look like a tortellono."

"Just don't bite if you're hungry." Christopher jolted sideways. "Which I am. A mouthful of come is only part of a healthy breakfast."

"Then eat." Luca pulled Christopher to his feet for a hug and a dash to the kitchen.

The refrigerator yielded a bowl of something they hadn't finished two nights before and didn't bother putting on plates now. Christopher found the forks while Luca waited for the microwave to ping. His lower body had bruises going greenish, their outlines fading and blurred by the light brown stubble on his legs and groin.

"Don't think I've ever seen you with this much body hair." Christopher ran an appraising hand over Luca's butt and down his thigh. "You might give me the best rug burn of my life."

"Last time I shaved was in Lienz." Luca lifted a heavenly forkful to Christopher's lips. His voice dropped. "We eat and then I shave for you."

Forget sitting down and forget savoring the food—he'd get it inside and go turn on the water. Luca slowed him with sultry eyes and a suggestive nibble at the tidbit on his fork. "Uh, okay." Christopher couldn't take his eyes away, stabbing at the dish three times in his search for a morsel.

Dishes could wait, strewn clothing could wait, anything that stood between him and the bathroom could wait. He peeled Luca out of his jersey and dropped his own cycling shorts on the floor. The shower had both a wall-mounted head and a hand sprayer. Luca turned them both on.

Hands and soap and skin—Christopher rubbed Luca sudsy and used him for a giant washcloth. His groin was prickly with growth, but Christopher curved against Luca anyway, hard again and wanting. Luca slid his chest across Christopher's, never breaking their basil-flavored kisses. With the flat of his hands against Luca's back, Christopher spread lather over every cord and sheet of muscle. Hands on buttocks should be okay—he wouldn't venture farther toward the midline. Luca writhed in his embrace, and popped every bubble between them.

"You're going to shave for me?" Most of Luca was clean, all the parts Christopher dared reach for. His lover would have to take care of the rest. Their trust felt new and flexible—he wouldn't test it before he was sure it had set.

"Oh yes." Luca turned to lean back against Christopher and propped one foot on the tile, turning his leg white with suds. Long streaks of smooth skin appeared with each stroke of his razor, but Christopher only had one eye for that—Luca had his crack pressed right up against Christopher's cock. *Don't move, don't move, don't even hint, even if you're way above target and can't go in even by accident. Just hold him and enjoy.*

"Smooth enough?" Luca lifted a knee for approval. Christopher stroked his thigh. "Mmm. Nice." He muzzled a kiss onto Luca's face. So was the next leg, once Luca wielded his blade. He turned to drape his arms over Christopher's shoulders. "You like that?"

"Oh yeah." Wet swipes of tongue and sliding into Luca's mouth would reinforce his approval. "Let's go."

"Not done." Luca broke away to work up more lather on his groin and belly. Turned to Christopher, his cock jutted from the white foam that disappeared one swath at a time. Goodbye, treasure trail, but that was okay; Christopher knew the way. "You're being very careful, right?"

"Always." At least that was a safety razor he was guiding around the curves of his balls. And farther. Christopher held Luca's shoulders while he raised one leg and removed hair Christopher never expected to touch. Well, made sense not to chafe, even with chamois cream. Luca held Christopher's eyes. "Hand shower, please?"

He groped behind his back, snagging the hose and finding the head. "Want help?"

Luca smiled. "In a minute." Okay, after more soap. Luca might be the cleanest cyclist ever to bathe with a journo, but damn it all, he was also the biggest tease on the planet, rubbing his hand up and down back there. Christopher swallowed hard. "Check for missing spots."

Christopher let Luca guide his hand to his now-smooth nads, finding nothing to complain of. "Oh yeah, Luca. Oh you feel good."

So damn good—Luca was hard, his erection batting against Christopher's arm. "Check all the way back."

All the way? Uh, okay—Christopher slid his hand under Luca, stroking his taint, familiar and on the very boundary, and farther back. He skated past where he wanted to linger—Luca was breathing shallowly through his mouth, and there was a look around his eyes that—was that fear? Or want? Damn but this was daring—he wouldn't spook Luca into backing away. Christopher came forward to cradle Luca's balls. "Smooth everywhere." He'd calm Luca with kisses.

Luca clung, the razor falling to the bottom of the tub with a clatter. "I don't want stubble."

Better put both hands where he could see them. Taking Luca's shoulders, Christopher swept his lips across cheeks and nose. "You feel really good. Wonderful."

Luca relaxed, enough to play the hand shower over both of them. He rinsed in their crevices, lingering on his own. "I want wonderful."

"I'll do my bes—oh." *Oh.* He swallowed hard and didn't move when Luca played the water over him again. "Even if there's eighty kilometers on the bike tomorrow?"

Luca nodded, his smile gone. "Because it's eighty kilometers with you. If I don't go as fast as team, you don't think problem. If I need to stop, you stop. If we want to look at beautiful or interesting, you do that too." He stopped rinsing them and turned off the water. "I can do these things this week, with you, riding with you only, and I trust you."

Why did trust sound even more intimate than love? Christopher took the sprayer from Luca's unresisting hand. "I will make it wonderful for you." He folded them in a big terry towel, patting them dry and bringing Luca close. "And I won't do anything you don't want." He'd said that before, months ago, and Luca had relaxed more then than he did now.

"I want everything," Luca insisted, but his voice had a tremor, and his face was hidden in Christopher's neck, not tipped back for a kiss. The stiffness that had poked Christopher squashed against his thigh.

"We're going to go slow, and there's a lot of steps on the way to wonderful, and they're all nice." Christopher stopped rubbing to just hold Luca. He was dry, so he couldn't be cold, but… he was trembling too much for a horny man. "We'll do one at a time and we don't have to do it all today. Luca—" Damn it, he wasn't going to take Luca to bed if it was the equivalent of facing FIC officials. "I'm not going to just throw you down on the bed and jam my cock in."

"I didn't think that," Luca argued, but he softened against Christopher's body. "Maybe a little."

"I'll make it lots better than that." Christopher kissed him a promise, catching Luca's lower lip in his own. "Let's go to bed."

Luca still wobbled, but once among the pillows, he relaxed a little more.

"I won't surprise you with anything, okay?" Christopher lifted his head from an extended exploration of Luca's ear and neck. Luca nodded, and his smile was back—that was all Christopher needed to see. Luca writhed under his attentions, and was trying to give as well. Oh, this felt like old times.

Sprawling between Luca's legs, Christopher could scoot down slowly, licking all the way. He pressed his ear against Luca's chest for a time, listening to his heart. "About a hundred and twenty," he teased, but his own wasn't much lower.

The calmer Luca got, the harder he got, pressing against Christopher's belly. "We need lube, right?"

"Right." He hadn't got that far in his head—he'd planned to gentle Luca with things they'd already tried before. "We don't need it yet, but what do we have? Do I need to steal the olive oil out of the kitchen?"

"No, I have bottle." Luca corkscrewed a hand into the bedside table. "Thinking ahead."

"Okay." He'd need to grease the extra-virgin carefully. "Leave it there for now." He poked his tongue into Luca's navel. "Mmm, tasty." The chuckle from above said Luca appreciated the joke.

He was always good with head—Christopher went for oral soothing. Sliding that sweet curved cock into his mouth, he listened for the signs from above that Luca was with him here. Throaty moans went in time with his slow travel up and down Luca's shaft. Playing, not going for the finish line, would get Luca to melt into the mattress. But he had more territory to cover—sucking Luca's balls into his mouth one at a time made him appreciate his lover's efforts with the razor. He slurped and tickled until the mumblings from above became words he couldn't understand. Good. Because Luca's taint was next, and when he'd thoroughly licked that flat plane….

"Lift your legs for me," he asked, but he couldn't reach properly without folding Luca nearly in half, and that would undo the entire mood he'd been trying so hard to create. "Roll over on your knees. Just for kisses," brought him the beautiful sight of Luca's exposed hole, and if he was way too tight for "wonderful" yet, that wouldn't last. Christopher put his face down to lap.

Lavender from the soap lingered over the scent of Luca's skin. The little ridges of muscle jumped under Christopher's tongue. He'd do his best to reduce Luca to a pile of quivering pleasure and lick away every bit of tension that would stand between him and wonderful. "You doing good?" he asked, but the moans and thin whimpers were the only answer he got. He'd keep licking for a while.

Oh, man, yeah. Luca was letting him do this… If he thought too much about what he was trying to do, he'd come, and then… well, he'd keep doing this until he came back up again to do what Luca had asked for… He should be *really* relaxed by then.

And those beautiful buttocks—he wanted a bite of those glorious mounds, but nothing with teeth—nothing to spook a jittery lover. Christopher rose to his knees: he could see Luca's face profiled against the crisp white sheet, his eyes closed and his lips parted. "Gonna get you slick. You don't have to move."

"Can't move," Luca mumbled. "Don't want to."

Well, well, this once a still Luca was a blissed-out Luca. Christopher stroked his back and reached for the bottle. Some for him, some for Luca. He dripped and started to rub over the surface of Luca's hole. Luca's eyes flew open but he didn't leap sideways or even flinch. "In?"

"Kind of. Getting you slick inside." Christopher looked at his hands—he'd really gotten greasy, and he couldn't wipe his hands, and why did he want to? He needed more.

"One finger, Luca, okay?" No surprises, he'd promised. Luca whimpered when Christopher breached him, but it wasn't "stop" and it didn't sound like pain. He paused anyway, lost in the wonder of heat and grip. Luca had been inside him so many times, but this… first… oh. He pushed in deeper, his cock throbbing hard with the newness and the want. Brushing against Luca's buttock made Christopher moan. "Oh you feel good. Do you like this?" Because if he didn't, there'd be no pushing onward. Luca moaned and rocked against Christopher's hand.

Okay then…. Christopher rested his cheek against Luca's butt and gave him what they both wanted, more motion, and some swirls inside. Luca's gland lay under the pad of Christopher's finger—time to press the "wonderful" button. And reach around, or—under was better. With a hand around Luca's erection to pump in counterpoint to his finger, Christopher reveled in the "yes" coming out of his lover.

They'd always had to be quiet, but not here, where they were the only ones in the sprawling house on an acre of land behind high walls. Luca cried out words Christopher didn't understand, but his name, oh that he understood—he'd made Luca call his name, and it all sounded like "yes."

Until it sounded like "stop." Luca pulled away, twisting to face Christopher. "I don't want to come yet."

Oh. *Oh.* "But it felt good?" D'oh, coming, good, yeah, but… he had to ask.

"Wonderful." Luca pulled Christopher against his chest. "But if I come now, I—" He clenched his fist to demonstrate. "—for later." He pulled his mouth sideways, staring at his fist. "Better to stay relaxed."

"Yeah." Christopher cupped his hand over Luca's, stroking. "As long as you were enjoying what I was doing."

Luca let his hand uncurl. "Very much." His cock jutted over his thighs, bouncing its own agreement in heartbeat rhythm.

"Okay. We were good then, but my finger and my cock aren't the same." *Thank goodness, except for just now where size matters for him.* "If you're ready, we can try two."

Something flickered across Luca's face. Laying his cheek against Luca's, Christopher whispered, "I think I can make it twice as good as one."

"Okay." Luca lay on his back. The head of his cock rubbed against his belly.

More lube. Christopher slathered his hand. One finger, just to remind Luca how much he liked that, and he smiled when Christopher slipped inside. But two wasn't doing so well—he flinched, and he'd tightened beyond what Christopher would push past. "Sorry, Christopher."

"Don't worry about it. We're not in a hurry." Christopher drew tickly fingers up and down Luca's torso, anything to take his mind off his butt.

"Why can't I…?" Luca reached to his hole, and from the squinch of his eyes, he wasn't getting any farther than Christopher had, and seemed willing to hurt himself more in the process. "I want this."

"I know, but don't do that." Christopher pulled Luca's hand away, immobilizing both of them over Luca's head. He swooped down to kiss the frustration off Luca's face, which might require lips like Jagger's. "Roll over. We'll do something different for a while."

"But…"

"We have all the time we need."

If he massaged Luca, that ought to help…. Luca was used to being touched, although if Paolo had the same methods, there might be a cranky Italian greasespot on the floor next time they were all together. Christopher poured some oil over Luca's butt and worked his glutes, squeezing and parting as much as pushing down. Good, from Luca's deep groans, but maybe not the same good he'd mumbled about before. But yeah, if he could just keep Luca thinking about the good things instead of what wasn't working. Besides, this was kind of nice in its own right, and he wasn't going to die of an unsatisfied erection. At least, not until after dinner…

But it would be nice to get some contact. Luca was calmer, and slick, but more goop never hurt. Christopher applied a dollop to his cock, working the slickness around his shaft. Might take a while to come at that—just getting Luca to relax wasn't keeping him on the edge. "Gonna snuggle on you."

Luca twined his fingers into Christopher's, pulling them partly under his chest. "You're still hard."

"Getting harder." Christopher lay down with his cock in Luca's crack. Even this was more than Luca had ever been comfortable with. "Do you want a glass of wine or something?"

That got some serious consideration. "Maybe later, if…." Yeah, if he was going to push himself into accommodating body parts.

Plastered against Luca's back as he was, Christopher was just as happy not to get up to go to the kitchen. Oh, but Luca felt good, and the furrow of his ass was really slick. Christopher had to slide up a ways. And back.

"That's…" Luca lifted his butt to help with the sliding. "I like."

"I like too." Christopher wasn't sure how much liking it would take to turn it into coming: Luca was getting a little vigorous under there. Damn. He could reach for slightly sideways kisses which Luca matched, chuckling with his tongue straining around the corner of his mouth.

"Christopher—" Luca stuck with his hips on "up". "Try to go in."

Okay, but… "You were pretty tight."

"Just try." Luca spread his thighs farther. "Please."

This wasn't going to be much of a try if Luca didn't feel ready, no matter what he said. "You have to tell me if you need me to stop." Not that Christopher trusted the answer. Luca pushed himself past the agony point for something he wanted badly enough. He'd reached the top of the Mur de Huy ahead of the rest, and he'd finished Zoncolan.

"Try."

Christopher would try, but he'd stop faster if he thought it was necessary. *This is for him, not for me. He trusts me this much.* "Okay." But he slipped back and forth a few more times, just to lull Luca and then he pulled back far enough to find where he wanted to go. "Push down." Aaaannndddd … *In.* Oh, Lord. In. Christopher froze. "You okay?"

Luca breathed shallowly through his mouth, not answering, but pulled in more air after a few seconds. "Yes." His fingers tightened on Christopher's. "Okay."

He was feeling more okay, looser—Christopher pushed in slowly until he was sheathed as deeply as he could fit. Slow, he had to go so slow, or he'd shoot his load right this second into the unbelievable hot clasping around his cock. But Luca deserved his wonderful.

"Slow," he whispered into Luca's ear, but since when had Luca ever gone slow on anything? He'd have to set the pace.

If he could. Luca lifted against him and pulled away until Christopher was sure he'd fall out if he didn't follow Luca's lead.

He'd follow Luca—anywhere. Up a mountain or across an ocean. And Luca trusted him. Maybe even loved him. So following his pace meant trusting Luca, and thinking was slipping away. *He feels so good. Wonderful.*

"Christopher!" Luca's cry cut through his fog. Passion or pain? The clenching around his cock said passion, and yes, and everything went to bright lights and waves of pleasure pouring out of him and into his beloved Luca. *Oh Luca. You gave me wonderful too.*

A slight hiss told Christopher to pull out, they were finished, and he turned them to their sides, unwilling to let go in any other way. He twitched the sheet over them. "Did we get to wonderful?"

"Oh yes." Luca found his hand again and squeezed. "Most wonderful." He twisted as far as he could to catch Christopher's lips. He settled into the curve of Christopher's body. Christopher curled around him. Soft words Christopher didn't quite understand came from him, but "…*amore mio*" had to be….

"I love you too," he whispered into a faceful of brown curls.

CHAPTER 29

CHRISTOPHER WOKE first, torn between stroking Luca into awareness and more lovemaking or gazing down into his face. Luca's lashes lay flat against the delicate skin below his eyes, paler than the rest of his face. He'd been sleeping so badly Christopher wouldn't disturb him, even for a kiss, if he'd been loved into peaceful rest.

Christopher's grumbling belly would cause a less pleasant awakening. Breakfast for dinner after their afternoon nap sounded right. He slithered out of bed and had some prosciutto and veggies chopped for an omelet before he heard Luca moving around. Once the shower water stopped he poured the eggs into the pan. Luca, his hair damp and curling and his smile toothpaste bright, emerged to a ready meal that they took out to the patio overlooking the lake. Luca inhaled every scrap and eyed the emptiness of his plate.

Guess he should have cracked another egg. Christopher shoved a quarter of his omelet onto Luca's plate. One of them had been eating more or less properly this last week. He took his plate back to the kitchen and returned with another piece of buttered bread for each of them, plus the bowl of fresh strawberries.

They ate the berries from each other's fingers.

"Thank you, Christopher." Luca sighed against his shoulder. "I needed today. All of today. Ghisallo. Riding. And you."

"You have me forever." How else could he say it when Luca wouldn't say anything in a language he knew Christopher understood?

"Forever?" Luca lifted his eyes to Christopher's face. "If you keep me when I'm broken-down old cyclist who can't ride or even advertise pain pills. Might be soon as next year."

Christopher had to laugh. "Do you really think I'd care? I'd make you translate race broadcasts for me, and I'd kiss you whenever the spectators rang cowbells."

Luca smiled. "Some races, that could be many kisses."

"It'll be many kisses anyway." Christopher shifted to get both arms around Luca. And he'd say what Luca skirted. At least then he'd know. "I love you."

"I love you too." Luca met Christopher's lips. "I don't deserve you, but I love you."

Deserve? What did that have to do with anything? And since when was he such a prize? But...okay. There wasn't anything to say to that, but holding Luca under the wide Italian sky was all the answer either of them needed.

"I'm glad you're not brooding any more." Christopher rocked Luca slowly back and forth in one of the intervals where they'd come up for air.

"I needed to visit *il Santuario.* It cleared my mind." Luca rested his head on Christopher's shoulder. "Who was that you were talking to?

"Bob Rasmussen from *Gear Up.* Um, I had to do a little horse-trading. Do you mind talking to him first after your next race?" Better let Luca know what he'd promised.

"Ahead of you? Yes, I mind, but for you, I do it." Luca swatted Christopher's thigh lightly. "What sort of horse did he trade you?"

"I wiped all the pictures out of his camera. He'd taken several of us crying on each other, and that pissed me off. Horning in on a private moment. Even if it was kind of public. I told him not to make news out of your loss." Christopher finger-combed through Luca's curls. "But there may have been other people who took pictures, and I know some people there recognized you. I heard them talking. Luca, we may have a problem."

"Other people with pictures." Luca spoke slowly.

"Yeah. And some of them may end up on Facebook. Or in a magazine." Christopher could kick himself for not thinking things through. "And someone's likely to ignore all the tears and the grief and make a different kind of deal about it."

"That deal is true, but not why we were there." Luca wasn't letting go—miracle.

"Truth doesn't always matter." Should he let go or hold tighter? "It's possible someone will scream about how gay we are."

"Possible. Rolf is a fact. Facts help." Luca spoke slowly. "Did you ever talk in magazine about Stu? I never saw that."

"No. I didn't." Amy had to write her article without him, but had she finished and gotten into the print queue? "Someone at the magazine was writing about deaths on the road, and my editor wanted me to talk to her, but... I didn't."

"You talk about something so important only if you see big purpose. Not for keeping my secrets." Luca hugged him so tightly he squeaked. "Photographer with lens three times longer than my *cazzo* might be on other side of lake taking pictures of us right now."

"I hope not." Christopher shot a fearful look at the woods and houses across the water. "I'm sorry. I thought that going to the shrine would only be healing."

"It was. I needed to go. And—" The strength of Luca's words pulled Christopher's eyes back to his face. "—I needed to be there with you. You needed to be there. I like to think you needed to be there with me."

"I did. But—"

"No buts. Anything that happens, happens. Can't change it."

Where had this philosopher come from? "But—the peloton? What if—?" *What if all your worst fears came true?*

"New tactics. Anyone acts stupid, I do what I did in other races. Get so far ahead they can't catch me." Luca grinned. "They want to make big deal of me being *froscio*, they can lose to the *froscio.* They act professional, they only lose to fast, smart rider." He went serious. "Not saying we start kissing with tongue at finish line, Christopher. Still must be careful. But not living afraid every minute either."

"Wow." Stroking brown curls away from Luca's face, Christopher tried to wrap his heart around Luca's words. Could this be the same man who'd blown out of the sports expo in a haze of anger? "What made you change your mind?"

"Being without you." Luca pursed his lips a moment and broke his pose with a laugh. "Also, winning a lot."

Uh huh. Eighty kilometers on the bike for both of them tomorrow. And one more problem. "I will support you no matter what anyone says about pictures from today, but… it could be the way your parents find out from a newspaper. You didn't want that to happen."

"Still don't." Luca tucked his face into Christopher's neck in a way he hadn't hidden in, oh, a day now. "I… should tell them."

"Luca, they love you. You know them pretty well." But Christopher didn't know them at all, and anything he said would be wishful thinking, not based on knowledge. "And they know you. Do you really think it's a problem?"

"Yes." Luca burrowed more tightly. "Pictures and world are maybe. Parents are certain when I tell them."

"Certain isn't the same as a bad reaction." *Please let the elder Biondis be reasonable people.* "Do you really want them asking you about pictures in a paper? They might be fine about you but hurt you didn't trust them."

"Yes."

The silence lasted a long time. Christopher could hear the gears turning in Luca's head, and just waited him out.

"What happened when you told your parents? They know?"

"Oh boy, do they know." Choking on a laugh, Christopher struggled to get the words out. "That was the worst experience ever!"

Luca went rigid. Oh, fuck, wrong way to explain.

"I have never been so embarrassed in my life. Mom and Dad sat me down and tried to give me a safe sex talk. Dad sputtered and Mom handed me a box of condoms and said I'd probably need them for all my 'study sessions' with Josh McAllister." He snorted again. "It's a good thing you can't die from blushing or all three of us would have been on the floor. I was eighteen."

Luca drew back to stare into Christopher's face. "So you didn't tell them. They told you."

"Yeah. I think pretending it was a secret got old." He thought back to those days of "library time" and sneaking around. "My grades weren't very good, in spite of all the time we spent 'studying.' They got better once we could actually open the books. Then studying was studying and a date was a date."

"Did they like Josh?"

You mean 'Will they like me?' Or 'could my parents like you?' "Yes. Although they thought the multiple eyebrow piercings were a bit weird." He pulled Luca closer. "They will like you, because they trust my judgment, and you will be the first man I ever bring home and say, 'I'm keeping him.' They'll love you. Because I do." He stared into Luca's eyes, willing him to believe, and when acceptance softened the lines around his eyes and mouth, Christopher sealed his declaration with a kiss.

"I still have to tell them." Luca was halfway to the door when he turned. "Please be with me."

"Of course." He'd already taken three steps.

Luca chose to sit on the big brocade couch in the living room, but Christopher's whirlwind wouldn't be there long. Luca snuggled in between Christopher's thighs and leaned back into his embrace. "Hold tight." He clenched Christopher's wrist with his free hand.

Of course. And a kiss for luck. *Here we go.*

Luca stared at the phone the way he might have eyed the Mont Crostis road. And hit the button.

"Mammina?"

Of course he'd speak his native language to his mother; Christopher understood little, although the blurts and pauses told their own story. So did Luca, whose face brightened. When he jumped up to bounce around the room, it was happy bouncing, or relieved bouncing, about as Tiggerish as Christopher had ever seen, but it wasn't distressed pacing, not with the smiles and some soft laughter, and his outstretched hand. Christopher took hold, to be yanked to his feet and into a one armed embrace. Luca looked up into his face, still talking at a hundred kilometers per hour, until he stopped and squeezed more tightly.

"Papà?"

Now his words came slowly—Christopher hugged him tightly and could almost understand. "*…uomo buono… …journo… …amore… …sì… .*"

That had to be good—leaping past the bare fact to the worth of Luca's choice. Could he measure up to the expectations of the father with the biggest knife in the Veneto? Christopher hadn't imagined what failing there might entail—he held on to Luca for a shield.

"...Sì, Papà. Here." Luca held up the phone to Christopher's ear. "Talk to Mamma. She speaks some English. Papà doesn't."

Oh Lord. Forcing "Ciao, Señora Biondi," in garbled Spatalian past the lump in his throat used all of Christopher's breath.

"You call me 'Mamma', okay?"

Chapter 30

Where had he put the chalk? Christopher dug in the seat pack on his bike, where the white stick was pretending to be an Allen wrench. Should have put the stupid thing into Luca's day pack with their lunch.

At least they'd gotten to a good spot before the roads had been closed to traffic. A dawn ride to Como, followed by a train ride to avoid a route on a major highway, and another eight kilometers on their bikes put them in a prime viewing area outside Brescia, where today's stage, the nineteenth, would finish. They could have stayed in Brescia; Christopher's press pass entitled him to be at the finish line in prime viewing territory, and no one would tell Luca to leave. But there might not be much Luca to take home after the journos' feeding frenzy.

Home—he and Luca would be back at the villa tonight. They'd share his reservations in Milan, and then Luca would be bunking with the team again. They'd have to see how things worked with Christopher following the team from race to race. How long did it take to rehab from a broken pelvis? Dave Pauwels needed physical therapy long enough that Ron had already emailed travel information for the *Critérium du Dauphiné* and the Tour de France and reminded Christopher to change his plane ticket for some date far enough into the future that it wouldn't expire.

But just imagine Paolo's face if he came in with tea first thing in the morning and found them cuddled up....

Uh, no. Don't imagine that. Christopher would need Papà's butcher knife to keep Paolo at bay.

"Write big." Luca raced him to the road. "Two lines. Write big enough for helicopter to see." He measured out a meter with his hands.

Christopher duck-walked from letter to letter, stretching "Antano" across the lanes. "Here. You finish." Luca put a big flourish under his "Clark."

"Let's put Damiano's name too." Their host might not see the graffiti, but it was a small way to thank him.

"Good idea." Luca scrawled again about ten meters downhill from their first sign. "Hope my team remembers who to support in next race."

"They'll be glad to have you back." Christopher playfully punched Luca's arm. "Mind if I write about "tactics for a team without a leader"?

"You say, 'help ride tempo for Antano-Clark.' Fastest article ever." Luca grinned at him and lost the humor in thought. "Not sure who my new lieutenant will be. Laurent, maybe. He's good climber."

Luca was looking to the future. Good. He didn't brood in the night any longer, between Christopher's attempts to wear him out and his own peace of mind. He'd chased Christopher up and down the roads around Como, their speed depending less and less on what they'd done the night before. Yesterday they'd ridden the very steep road from Bellagio, on the shore of Lake Como, to the shrine on the mountaintop. Christopher'd sent Luca on ahead and finished his nine and a half kilometers of straight up a good hour and a half after Luca reached the summit. It was a hell of a lot harder a ride coming at Ghisallo from the other side. Christopher told himself he was doing his route research for the Giro de Lombardia in the fall. But Luca had waited for him, and together they'd mounted the small metal plaque etched with Stu's picture and had a moment of bowed heads before the bronze bicyclists. Their descent took less than fifteen minutes, and when they got back to the villa, Luca okayed Christopher's article about the crash and Rolf's death.

Tomorrow night Luca might lie awake thinking of Rolf and how only one of them would ride with the team for the end of the race in Milan, but last night he'd slept the sleep of the well-loved. That tactic might work again.

No news is good news. Most of a week had passed without any incriminating pictures popping up, though Christopher hadn't finished holding his breath. The best news was the calmness with which Luca's parents had greeted his dud of a bombshell. "You wait to say until you find nice young man," Mamma Biondi had said. "But we knew." Christopher kept finding Luca shaking his head over this.

His cell phone *queeped* from his pocket. "What are you doing for this stage?" Ron wanted to know.

"I'm hanging with a crowd and an interpreter." Christopher looked for his interpreter, who was emptying out the bread, sliced *bresaola*, and olives from his pack onto a red-checked picnic tablecloth next to whatever the cheerful woman with the tinfoil packets was unwrapping. "We're about eight kilometers from the finish line. I'll have a 'race-watching Italian style' piece plus stage results."

"Heard rumors you've been slacking."

Well, hell. He'd watched every minute of the stages, had Luca's expert commentary, and turned in at least one, sometimes two pieces a day. And— "You clearly haven't checked your email."

"I just got to the office, okay?" Tapping sounded in Christopher's ear. "Let's see what you have here…"

It had taken two days of work on top of the race coverage to get Luca's interview the way he wanted in print, and the video portion wasn't done yet. He'd sent it, because post production was beyond what he could do. "Just to keep *you* from slacking, I marked some spots in the interview that need race clips. Go chase down permissions. Most of the footage is network or from the streaming service I cited, but it needs to go where I've marked it." Christopher would extract some effort from that "slacker" comment—how many words and how many exclusives did Ron think one writer could produce? Maybe he was making it look too easy.

"You… How did you… Oh buddy," Ron sputtered, and read words Christopher knew—he'd written what Luca had spoken.

"'I met Rolf Knecht at racing camp, where smartass Belgian teenager had to admit Italian coach offered advice he couldn't get at home. He was tireless rider then, fierce competitor, and we would race whole field but only mattered to beat each other…' He talked to you about the crash… He hasn't talked to anyone…" Little mumbles into the silence while Ron finished reading were going to rack up the roaming charges. "I don't know how you got an exclusive like this, but I think we'll keep you."

Totally worth it.

"Just remember that all racing isn't Antano-Clark."

Hey! Christopher'd been very careful to be balanced, and had only mentioned the team once in the last week, to note that they'd remained in the middle of the team standings even without their stars. Standing in the middle of the road, he shot a selfie with a crowd and, oops, "Antano-Clark" in the background. But his blue, white, and black Garmin jersey ought to balance it out. Christopher sent the picture anyway.

"I didn't think it was." Just the part that mattered most.

"You're doing okay. I gotta finish this. Can I get it into…." Ron signed off, mumbling issues and layouts.

Luca had worried about being too recognizable in his own logo-plastered top, but with his hair braided into a tail, jeans, and sunglasses, he was pretty well disguised, even in Christopher's plain turquoise jersey. So far, none of the group around them had identified him. Guess he was highly out of context, being beside the road, not on it.

The advertising caravan came and went—the shower of promo provided Christopher a can of energy drink, and Luca had a new, logo-bedecked cap to hide under. But the riders…

Men in bright jerseys sailed up the light incline, through the gauntlet of screaming fans stretching out their hands to their idols. "Is it weird to watch that from here?"

"Yes. At least here are Army men to hold back the crowds." Luca shivered. "And no naked man with inflatable whale running next to me."

What? That visual… Oh Lord. Maybe he needed to do a piece on crazy fan behavior.

Luca yelled out for the riders as loudly as anyone around them, picking them out by name. "*Alè*, Berto! *Alè*, Damiano! *Alè,* Vincenzo!" Vincenzo wore pink. Just like the jerseys Luca won.

"Go, Antano-Clark!" Forget journalistic impartiality, Christopher screamed for the team he'd followed across the sea, who streamed by, turquoise mingled with the pinks and blues of the team they helped. "Go, Damiano! *Alè!* Uh — " He remembered what he was wearing. "*Alè,* Garmin!"

The leaders passed, chased closely by the peloton, strung out like beads on the road. Fewer than 130 riders remained. Motos buzzed through them; a team car passed with a soigneur hanging out the window trying to place a bandage on a rider's leg. The rider dripped, but he didn't stop. Luca looked away, as if the *gruppetto* at the very end of this parade mattered desperately. Christopher reached for Luca's shoulder to squeeze. He got a wistful smile, and then deafened when another group of riders came by.

The last riders passed, and the last press and official cars. The road would be officially opened to traffic shortly. Luca and Christopher lingered, listening to the finish on their fellow spectators' radios. Luca translated, finishing with "Vincenzo won. Late sprint. Damiano second, back four seconds. Back 1:24 overall." He shrugged. "A great stage tomorrow, he could still win. So could Berto—back 1:31."

A minute and a half could be nothing or an eternity. They got on their bikes before any of their companions questioned Luca's use of first names.

They had an hour or so to wait for the next train out. They'd probably spend it in race analysis or language lessons. *Quando parte il prossimo treno per Como?* Christopher rehearsed in his head, building on the lesson from this morning when their destination was Brescia. He kept it to himself when Luca's phone rang.

Luca's gaping mouth could be nothing except wordless "Holy shit OMG-WTFBBQ." He showed Christopher the screen with its caller ID.

"Don't just stand there: answer it!" Christopher hissed. Oh my God, about fucking time.

"*Ciao.*" Of course Luca wouldn't identify himself in a public place. He hit the speaker button and stood close to hold the phone close to both their ears.

"May I speak with Luca Biondi, please?" The accent was American. Was it…?

"*Sì?*"

"This is Nick Leyburn, from K-Aero Cycling." *Yes!* "I understand you prefer to ride on K-Aero saddles. I'm calling to find out if you're still happy with our product."

"I won several races this season on your saddle." Luca seemed to be picking each word with the same care he needed for a badly maintained cobblestone road.

"We're always glad to be associated with success, Mr. Biondi. We weren't sure if you were still riding K-Aero—the pictures from your last stage of the Giro didn't include enough of your bike to tell."

Hah! Got 'em! Christopher stifled a snort. Luca glanced sharply at Christopher. Hoo boy, he didn't need words to hear *you had something to do with this, didn't you?* He worked on "bland face." Could a squashed smile be mistaken for innocence?

"You can't rely on the journos to do advertising, no?" Luca's glower promised a frank discussion later.

"No." Nick sounded regretful. "We can't. We understand you'll be riding the finish in Milan. We'd like to make sure you have a new saddle for the ceremonial lap."

"My ride in Milan is to honor my dead teammate." Luca's voice took on a dangerous edge. "Not to advertise your saddle."

"Oh nonononononono!" Nick sounded shocked. *By the suggestion or for getting caught at it?* "More that you'd be comfortable, and in case your other saddle was damaged in the crash."

"I see." Luca's voice hadn't warmed one degree, Fahrenheit or Celsius. "For a moment that sounded like world's ugliest endorsement deal."

"I am so sorry," Nick burbled. "I've stated this badly. My condolences on your teammate. We would like to equip you with a saddle suitable to the solemn occasion in Milan. Also yes, we would love to have you endorse our product line. That is, if you haven't already committed to the competition?"

"I haven't signed contract." If Luca needed a post-racing career, he ought to be in politics. That was *smooth,* true, and a long way from *Jindo isn't talking to me anymore.*

"Hmm, they are taking their time…" Nick's words disappeared into the hubbub of the station. "In that case, we'd really, really prefer that you signed with us. We're capable of moving very fast with our contracts, and with our payments. Does one third at signing sound reasonable to you?"

"Maybe. One third of what?" Luca's words were confident, but his breathing was shallow.

Christopher held his breath. What would they pay, and what would they want for their money?

"We'd like a two year contract, and we'd pay twenty-five thousand euro."

Luca met Christopher's eyes over the phone and his teeth flashed. "For that, we talk. Email list of projected appearances, ads, and responsibilities to here—" He rattled off an address. "—I look over." A few pleasantries and he ended the call.

"Was that as good as—the other people—offered?" A loudspeaker blared, cutting off Christopher's words, but signaling time to load. They wheeled the bikes toward the open train car.

"Better already, maybe." Luca handed a bike up to Christopher. "Depends what they expect to get." He followed his bike into the train car and tested the lock. "You did something to make that phone call happen."

Busted. "I may have mailed them an article I cut out of *Cyclo World*."

Luca's head shake wasn't the same without his dance of curls, but the braid down his back waggled with his amusement. "Let's go home."

They found an open row near the front of the car, with the plush, high-backed seats Christopher had discovered were only in first class. Luca kept his cap and sunglasses on, his face bent to study race results on his phone while the train filled up. They spoke of the race, and Christopher was careful not to use his name.

The train pulled away from the platform, once again purring beneath Christopher's feet, before he dared to ask, "Is the villa the kind of home you want?"

"Damiano's been star a long time, has money for big house with high walls. I don't yet, but—" Luca chopped off, and started more slowly. "I don't need big house to be happy. Happiest place I ever lived was small apartment in Colorado."

"Me too." Christopher didn't reach for Luca. That would still have to wait until they were alone. He spoke quietly, not trusting to language barriers for their fellow travelers, but Luca would understand. "Lately I've been spoiled by a real mattress. Think you could stand that much change?"

"I can sleep on pavè if I sleep there with you."

Epilogue

Christopher shook the just-escaped-from-the-packaging wrinkles from the blue-striped duvet. The king-sized bed replaced the were-furniture he'd slept on since his student days, and was the prize in his newly-purchased condo overlooking Boulder Creek. He added pillows and one lone plushy, which was anything but a memento of childhood. The fuzzy dog marked Luca's first stage win and now lolled his felt tongue without drooling on the bedding. What could have been a huge pile of critters had gone to various children's hospitals, but Luca had broken with cycling tradition enough to gift Christopher with this keepsake. The clock flicked away another minute—Luca would be home soon.

Christopher had closed on the condo while Luca was on the one racing tour they couldn't share. Another set of keys waited on the dresser. A few boxes cluttered the floor, but most everything was unpacked. He'd put Luca's clothes in half the dresser drawers and hung his collection of yellow, pink, and red prize jerseys in the closet next to his one suit and button-down shirt. The cycling shoes on the closet floor outnumbered the dress shoes.

The old basement apartment on College Hill probably would have been okay for the two of them, since they only lived in Colorado a few months out of the year, except for security issues and the annoyance of bouncing bikes up and down stairs on the way in and out. Christopher had popped for a building with a ramp now that his permanent *Cyclo World* gig and a syndicated column paid the bills, plus some. Dave Pauwels sent a surprising amount of gossip from Provence. Retiring hadn't affected his connections.

They had more house-hunting to do in Padua. "I pick the price range here." Luca had finally laid down the law and refused to tell him the cost of the apartments they'd toured. "You make home for me where you understand, I make home for you here." They'd have a few days after Flanders Week to look some more.

Streaming coverage in the wee hours had to suffice for the last three weeks—*CycloWorld's* circulation may have doubled in the last year, but their travel budget still didn't extend to sending their journo to the Middle East, where Antano-Clark rode the Tour of Qatar and the Tour of Oman in what passed for a cold month. This year's racing season was starting out as triumphantly as last year's; Luca had more prize jerseys in his suitcase. The team would spend February in Boulder, and then head back to Belgium. Christopher would be in Europe for every race this year.

Were those footsteps? He pelted to the door to find his lover with a hand on the knob. "Come on in." Luca waited only until the latch clicked to fling himself into Christopher's arms, and that was three milliseconds too long.

His Luca—his warm, lithe, mercurial, champion, and above all, loving Luca—was home. "*Ciao*, Luca, *mio amore*."

About the Author

P.D. Singer lives in Colorado with her slightly bemused husband, two rowdy teenage boys, and thirty pounds of cats. She's a big believer in research, first-hand if possible, so the reader can be quite certain Pam has skied down a mountain face-first, been stepped on by rodeo horses, acquired a potato burn or two, and will never, ever, write a novel that includes sky-diving.

When not writing, playing her fiddle, or skiing, she can be found with a book in hand. If you can't find her, check in the rubble. Her house may collapse from the weight of the printed page.

Follow the adventures at PDSinger.com or contact Pam at PD.Singer@live.com.

Other Rocky Ridge Books

From P.D. Singer:

Donal *agus* Jimmy
O'Carolan's Seduction
On Call: Afternoon
On Call: Dancing
On Call: Crossroads
Training Cats
On Call: Omnibus

From Eden Winters:

Collusion
The Match Before Christmas
Fanning the Flames
The Prodigal
Summer Boys

www.ingramcontent.com/pod-product-compliance
Lightning Source LLC
LaVergne TN
LVHW091047080826
845145LV00002B/659
* 9 7 8 1 6 2 6 2 2 0 0 6 5 *